I0662494

Changed Through Blood

Courtney Maxwell

Blue Mustang Press
Boston, Massachusetts

© 2008 by Courtney Maxwell.
All rights reserved. No part of this book may be reproduced in any form without written permission from the publishers, except by a reviewer who may quote brief passages in a review to be printed in a newspaper or magazine.

First printing

ISBN 978-0-9759737-7-6
PUBLISHED BY BLUE MUSTANG PRESS
www.BlueMustangPress.com
Boston, Massachusetts

Printed in the United States of America

To My Family and Friends:

"The best part of life is when your family becomes your friends, and your friends become your family."

~ Danica Whitfield ~

One

M y heart, once whole, now lies in more pieces than I care to count. Over the years, I have waited for someone to pick up those pieces and mend them. Instead, the pieces are further broken into something that used to resemble my life. This cycle is what has made me lock away the pieces. Now, no one can harm my fragile heart. And so, I welcome you to *my* world: filled with darkness and cold, solitude and isolation.

For years I wandered the earth, wishing to feel anything other than the inner anguish that housed itself deep within my soul. Unloved, I searched for meaning in my life, wondering if it really was worth it all. But it seemed that the more I searched, the more I longed for death to embrace me. Everywhere I traveled, there was love and happiness all around me: something that I seemed unable to possess.

I was not always like this. I have loved and been loved, more than once I might add. However, it all ended in the same way: heartache and loneliness. It soon became a trend in my life, and no matter what I did; I seemed unable to control it. But one night, I came upon someone just like me. Someone who had also shut out the rest of the world and seemed to lack the ability to hold onto love and companionship. He turned out to be the greatest love of my life. Yet he was also the bringer of my death…and my entrance into a new world.

His name was Ayden. Now, it may seem typical to say that he was gorgeous, just like most movies and books depict the main male character, but it's true. Ayden was just plain gorgeous. Standing at a decent height of five foot ten, with a thin but muscular body frame he was more than pleasant to the eye. I will always remember his vibrant hazel eyes with a tint of auburn. But his smile, on that first encounter, I cannot recall. The one thing I do remember most clearly about that day was the way our eyes met.

****

It was just after sunset. He was sitting at a table outside a small café in Giza, Egypt. I was walking along the road, opposite the café, working my way towards the Great Pyramid. As I walked, something drew the attention of my eyes towards that café. He was the first one I spotted, looking directly at me, clothed in all black although he must have been sweltering in the heat of the day. Right away, I felt that there was something about him, something mysterious; I felt the need to investigate that feeling. Instead of continuing towards the Pyramid, I changed direction and headed towards him. As I approached, I could see the immediate change in his disposition. His mood seemed to lighten and then I began to notice more things about his physique. His complexion was far too pale, especially for the type of climate we were in. His skin had not been reddened by the hot Egyptian sun. Sunscreen perhaps? Yet at the same time, his face barely had any defining qualities: no lines, wrinkles or scars. I briefly thought on how these features seemed odd for a normal person but it quickly left my mind once I caught his eyes again. There was that feeling again, something mysterious emanating from his very being. And when he looked deep into my eyes and finally spoke softly, it took my breath away:

"The Sight of her makes me well! When she opens her eyes, my body is young;

Her speaking makes me strong..."

"...Embracing her expels my malady." I softly finished the poem, which I had read so many times before.

"I see you have read the many poems of Ancient Egypt before coming to this great city," he calmly stated. "That one is my favorite. It speaks of the ability for a woman to cure a man's ailments."

"Indeed I have. Egypt has become a passion of mine…oh, forgive me for being rude; I must seem strange reciting poetry with a complete stranger. My name is Calista." I extended my hand in greeting.

"Calista…" his voice lingered on my name just long enough for me to pick up an Irish accent, which I seemed to have missed when he first spoke. "It's nice to meet you. My name is Ayden." He stood and returned my gesture by shaking my hand.

His grip was firm, but it felt like he was holding back his true strength. I was also rather surprised to feel his hand was cold as ice. He noticed my surprise and quickly informed me that he had just had an iced drink shortly before I had come over to speak to him. He invited me to sit with him and have a drink. I graciously accepted, in hopes to further investigate my curiosity about him, and ordered lemonade.

As we waited for our drinks, I took my chances in looking him over. He couldn't have been more than twenty-eight years of age. His hair was strawberry blonde, and long, though not as long as mine. He wore it shoulder length and obviously took brilliant care of it because it shined like a diamond. His jaw line was well defined. His lips, full and nearly perfect, were a faint rose color. My eyes worked their way down his body, marveling at his muscular arms, while the rest of his body seemed averagely fit. He was dressed well, wearing a designer black trench coat, black slacks and a black button-up shirt. Then I thought about his eyes once more and went to look into them for a third time. In doing this, I suddenly realized that he was examining me as well!

So perhaps this is a good time to jump back for a second and describe myself. My height is not one of my best features, standing at a petite five foot two, which sometimes diminishes the fact that I am twenty-five years old. My own hair is dark brown, but it has lightened over the years thanks to the sun. Its full length extends to my waist, most of the time worn in a braid. My eyes are hazel in color, as are Ayden's, though mine do not contain the tint of auburn that gives his their brilliance. My lips are a deeper pink than his, and my skin nicely tanned which made Ayden look like a ghost compared to me. But enough about me! Back to Ayden.

7

The waiter arrived with our drinks and I quickly began to drink my lemonade, not realizing how thirsty I was. It could have been perhaps that I was a little nervous around this strange man, but I wasn't about to let my guard down just because he was gorgeous. Plus, the male species was not a topic that I really wanted to think about or get involved with anymore (or so I thought). I had left all that behind back in the U.S.

I was about to break the silence when Ayden beat me to it. "So where are you from?" he asked, his accent even more noticeable than before.

"I'm not really sure how to answer that," I replied. "Five years ago, I left my apartment in Las Vegas, Nevada and began traveling the world. Ever since, I've never gone back, so I don't think I can really call it home anymore."

"Why did you leave? If you don't mind me asking."

"It's kind of a touchy subject, but let's just say that there had been enough of pain and suffering on my part and I wanted to get away from it." My voice drifted off as I spoke the last few words.

Ayden quickly replied by saying, "Hmm…well, I won't pry into your life if you don't want me to, but I think I know how you feel. I myself have been through much pain in my life and one day, decided that I had had enough as well."

"Is that why you're here in Egypt?" I asked.

He pondered the question for a moment or two. "Well, yes and no. I am a traveler, same as you. But I am sort of here on…business as well."

I nodded in response to his statement. I didn't feel like I had a right to dig my way into his life either since we had just met. But of course, that statement only increased my curiosity about him. I wanted to spend some more time with him, if he would let me.

A silence fell over us and I stared down at my empty glass. I glanced in his direction and finally noticed that he had never touched his coffee the whole time we had been there. "That's odd," I thought to myself. But I just shrugged it off and proceeded to watch the people walking through the busy streets. There are very few cars ever seen in this part of Egypt: mainly people walking or on horseback. At the corner a short ways down the street was a vendor selling fresh fruit, and the thought of a juicy strawberry in my mouth suddenly made me hungry. I wished I had bought something when we had ordered drinks but maybe I'd just grab something at that stand on my way to the Pyramid. The Pyramid! I was hoping to get there while tours were still going on so that I wouldn't have to deal with strange guards later in the night, although it's never stopped me before.

I was about to turn to Ayden and explain where I was headed but he beat me to the chase.

"You want to be on your way to the Pyramid, yes?"

I was a bit startled. "Y-yes…how did you know that is where I was headed?"

"Didn't you mention it when we first met? I was sure that you did."

"Hmm…I can't really remember…perhaps I did." I was lying through my teeth. I clearly remember not mentioning the Pyramid at all. Confusion swept over me. How could he possibly have known where I was going? Did he read my mind? But that's not possible…is it?

"You look confused," he quickly stated. "Perhaps we should part ways…I have some things I need to get done before the night is over."

"Sorry…you just startled me is all. I'm fine though. I should probably get going as well."

Ayden finally stood, allowing me to see his full height. "Well, enjoy the Pyramid. It is quite exquisite. Perhaps we shall meet again." He extended his hand to say farewell.

I hesitantly accepted, but made sure to give him a firm grip so as not to make him suspicious of my curiosity. Giving me a half-smile, he dropped some money on the table, turned and walked in the direction I had originally come from. I watched him leave until his figure was lost in the darkness of an alleyway, and then looked at the table. The coffee mug was still there, filled to the brim. I took a moment to let everything that had happened sink in and then paid my share.

The Pyramid was just as Ayden had said: exquisite. Standing at more than four hundred feet tall, it was one of the most beautiful architectural structures I had ever seen. Even a poet would not be able to describe such beauty as I saw standing at its base. It was just before ten o'clock, so the daily tours hadn't finished yet, lucky for them. I was sure they wouldn't have wanted to deal with a break-in if it had been later. I paid the guard at the north entrance and made my way through to the main chamber. There were several corridors to choose from, but I wanted to see the King's chamber, located at the heart of the pyramid. A tour sign with an arrow pointing down the middle passageway directed me towards my destination.

I took my time walking down the corridor, soaking in all the splendors of ancient times. Hieroglyphics on the walls depicted people together living peacefully and worshipping their gods. After several turns (and dead ends) I was able to find the entrance to the King's tomb. I slowly walked towards the doorway, my right arm outstretched and letting my fingers graze the wall, somehow wishing all the knowledge it contained could be absorbed through my fingertips. The King's chamber was more beautiful than books had described it to be. With the walls and the sarcophagus being made of orange red Egyptian clay and stone along with beautiful etchings carved into every inch of the room. Located in the very center of the room was King Khufu's sarcophagus. I walked up to it, facing the door which I had come through and placed my hands upon the lid. Closing my eyes, I thought to myself that there is an ancient ruler buried here…this is what is important in life…these moments. These precious moments where time stops and peace hovers over your soul. I was so content in my state of mind that I didn't even realize another person had entered the room. It wasn't until he was standing right next to me that I opened my eyes. I almost screamed and nearly fell over where I stood. To my astonishment, it was Ayden who was standing beside me!

"Hello again," he said with a strange gleam in his eyes.

"H-hello," I stammered, trying to steady myself. He stared at me for a moment and then began to walk around the room.

"So…what do you think?"

"I think…this is the most beautiful thing I have ever seen," I replied, starting to feel calm again.

"I was hoping you'd think so." He gave me that half-smile I had seen earlier that evening. He turned and came towards me, actually causing me to back myself up against the nearest wall.

"You suddenly seem frightened. Is everything all right?" He still had that half-smile, which was making me uneasy.

"It's just that you startled me and it's a bit strange seeing you twice so quickly in one night. Did you follow me here?"

He lost the smile and bowed his head. "Actually…I did. I apologize. You had just interested me when we met earlier and I was hoping to speak with you again. And also to perhaps persuade you to join me for a long walk tomorrow night…to learn more about each other…man…you know, I don't normally do this…a long time ago I swore off women…but there was just something about you…" He couldn't seem to finish his thoughts.

At first I was inclined to say no right away, but that feeling about him was still lingering inside me so I couldn't help but accept his rather enticing offer. We agreed to meet in front of the café where we first met, at eight o'clock the next evening. With that accomplished, he flashed me his signature smile and left the tomb. As soon as I was sure he was gone, I took a deep breath and sunk to the floor with my back against the wall. I had been so afraid but at the same time utterly attracted to him. Why on earth did I accept to meet him?! This was not like me at all. I should have gone with my instincts and said no. I had sworn to stay away from men a long time ago. But perhaps this was a chance for me to figure out what it was about him that was so captivating. I went back to my hotel room that night and had a strange dream.

I was back in the Pyramid, walking down one of the long narrow hallways. Ayden was right behind me, watching my every move. I stopped and turned to say something to him but before I could speak, he vanished. Blood began to drip from the walls. I panicked and tried to run, but blood was surrounding me at a rapid pace. I couldn't escape. The blood continued to pour and it swallowed me completely.

Two

Just as my head was about to be submerged in the hallway full of blood, I awoke from my dream in a hot sweat. Immediately I realized I was in the safety of my room, but I felt that the dream was supposed to mean something. The blood…was something bad going to happen to either me or Ayden? Was it a warning not to meet with him? Or a warning not to return to the Pyramid? I couldn't be sure, but I decided that I would still meet with Ayden regardless. If he acted strangely again, then I would break ties and go to South America, as I had planned to after exploring Egypt. Reluctantly, I lay back down and tried to sleep the rest of the early morning hours.

I woke up at nine o'clock, surprisingly feeling refreshed and energetic. I walked to the balcony windows and drew back the curtains. The sun was high in the sky, shining bright, and the streets were buzzing with people. I took a deep breath of the morning air and then went to take a shower. I was disappointed to find that there was not much hot water, so my shower was quick. Rummaging through my clothes I was able to find a nice outfit for the day, which would also suffice for my evening with Ayden. Dark blue jeans, a black tank top with a white blouse, left unbuttoned. Although I thought it would be a nice change to wear my hair long, I had no choice but to braid it due to the heat. It stopped my hair from frizzing in such hot climates. Maybe I would unbraid it before meeting with Ayden when the night cooled things down.

Finally, feeling satisfied with my appearance, I headed out into the city. I decided it would be a marvelous day to visit the Sphinx and adjacent pyramid of Khafre. As I walked, I realized that I was near the café where I had first met Ayden. I slowed my pace a little as I passed it. I glanced up, with a little part of me hoping to spot him, but he wasn't there. Just an elderly couple having tea.

The walk through the city was a wonderful sight, with all the kiosk owners bargaining with their customers and children playing stickball in the alleyways. After about a half hour of walking, I arrived at the kiosk where horses and camels could be rented. One needed such transportation in order to make it to the pyramids. If anyone had ever tried walking through the desert to see the pyramids, they probably would have never made it there or back alive. During the afternoon hours, when the sun is at its peak, the temperature could be anywhere around one hundred degrees or higher. Yet at night, the temperature can drop to levels where one could freeze if not kept warm enough.

I had ridden a horse to the Great Pyramid the night before, so I thought it would be interesting to try out a camel. I paid the man two hundred and eighty Egyptian pounds, which I felt was rather high being equivalent to fifty American dollars. But from the slight amount of Egyptian that I could understand, he informed me that it cost much more to rent a camel than a horse. I didn't feel like arguing with the man, so I went on my way.

Interestingly enough, I wasn't venturing out into the desert on my own, although I had done so many times before. There was a young couple traveling into the desert as well, explaining to me that they were on their honeymoon. Of course, my luck, I get stuck traveling with newlyweds. As much as I found their lovey-dovey air to be rather annoying, I did my best to put on a happy face and enjoy the journey. The girl felt the need to keep conversation along the trip. She was quite the talker. A real chatter-box. One of those types of girls who talks a lot when she's nervous. She began by introducing herself and her husband as Juliette and Corbin. I could tell from her accent that she was French. The husband was harder to place. Well, once she started, it soon became clear that she intended on telling me her entire life story. When she finally came up for air, she asked if I was in Egypt for any particular reason. This gave me an opportunity to try and cut the conversation short. I gladly took the chance, but decided to have a little fun while I was at it.

"I'm a tomb raider," I stated nonchalantly.

The couple looked at each other and then back at me. "Umm…I'm sorry but, what exactly does that mean?" Corbin asked.

"I travel the world, seeking ancient tombs and secret rooms within temples, to find precious treasures." I had to hold back a smile.

This time, Juliette spoke up, "But…is that even legal?"

"Well, I suppose it depends on whose perspective you are looking at. Most archeologists would claim it's illegal, because tomb raiders 'steal' items of great value, which don't belong to us. But there are others who see it as…how does that saying go? 'Finders keepers'?" I gave a little laugh at this, enjoying my fabrication.

I think my story did the trick because the couple fell silent for the remainder of the trip. I did, however, notice them stealing glances at me and whispering secrets to each other. I smiled to myself as I thought about the possible things they were saying to one another. They were probably trying to figure out if I was going to be a danger to them.

The tomb raider story was my usual for naïves like Juliette and Corbin. Since I no longer became close with anyone that I met, I figured it wouldn't hurt to enjoy my time and make up a story or two. It had happened once and then became a habit whenever I met new people along the way due to the fact that I happened to enjoy it. I was never to see them again and I figured it would give them a little bit of excitement to talk about when they returned home.

After about an hour's travel, we finally arrived at the Sphinx. From a distance, it was a wonderful sight, but up close, it was even better. It was phenomenal. I tied off my camel's reins to a post near the entrance and then made my way in, not waiting for the newlyweds. I wanted to experience this in solitude.

The first room was gigantic with cathedral ceilings. Hieroglyphics and murals covered every wall. One mural in particular caught my eye, off to my right. The pictures showed a mummification procession, followed by burial, and lastly there was reincarnation. It was extremely interesting and I wondered if I would find a mummification room somewhere in the depths of the temple. Although I knew I had the entire day to explore, I was eager to reach the heart of the temple. That was always where I felt the most energy emanating from the tomb. I turned towards the left end of the room and headed towards an open doorway.

I hadn't taken more than three steps inside the corridor when déjà vu suddenly hit me. This hallway...it seemed way too familiar. Then it all came together: the corridor from my dream. This was it! I couldn't believe my eyes; the hieroglyphics, the length of the hallway, the height of the ceiling, it was all as it had been in my dream. I didn't know what to do. My heart began to pound; my vision began to blur. Images of blood seeping from the walls flashed through my mind. Reaching for a wall, I fell to the ground and everything turned to black..

I awoke with a start, not knowing where I was. At first I thought I was in a hospital, but then realized I was still on the floor of the pyramid hallway. Looking around me, I immediately recognized the newlywed couple I had traveled in with as well as one of the guards from the main entrance.

"Are you alright?!" Juliette asked, looking extremely concerned.

I sat up slowly. "Yes...I...I think so." A sharp pain shot through my forehead causing me to falter.

Corbin caught my arm. "What happened? You took off ahead of us and when we made it down this hallway, we just saw you lying there on the floor."

"I'm guessing I fainted...it must just be the combination of heat and dust in here."

The guard handed me an ice pack. "You've got quite a bump there. Make sure to ice up and get back to your hotel to rest as soon as you can."

Quietly I thanked him for the ice and made an attempt to stand. Corbin took my left arm. Juliette was to my right. She offered her assistance but I used the wall to steady myself instead of accepting her hand.

"I'm fine, really." I gave them both reassuring looks.

"Some tomb raider you are," Juliette said jokingly. "Fainting five minutes after entering the place." She gave me a playful smile.

"Ha-Ha, very funny," I sarcastically shot back.

After a few attempts, I was able to convince them I could stand fine without help. Juliette and Corbin seemed insistent on accompanying me for the rest of our time in the pyramid but I politely declined.

"I'm just going to head back to the city. I have to meet with someone. Thank you for your help and enjoy the rest of your time here." I gave them a quick smile and headed towards the exit.

Once outside, the cool evening air was refreshing, but the hallway still haunted my mind. I hoped that it wouldn't interfere with my meeting Ayden later that night. I figured it was best to just head back to the city and grab a bite to eat and then focus on unraveling the mysteries of Ayden.

By the time I got back into the city, I had about an hour before I was supposed to meet Ayden. I figured it would be easiest for me to get some dinner at the café and just wait there for him. The menu at the café turned out to be quite good. I started out with an appetizer of *Feteer Meshaltet*, which is an Egyptian pastry served with a creamy cheese. For the main course, I chose roasted duck, which turned out to be absolutely delicious.

I was just finishing up my meal when I noticed Ayden walking towards me. He was gently wiping his lips with a dark colored cloth. Apparently he had just finished eating as well. He slipped the cloth into his coat pocket and stood directly across from where I was sitting. I quickly swallowed my last bite and invited him to sit down with me. He seemed reluctant to accept but sat down anyways.

"Hello again, Calista. Enjoy your meal?" The question was asked in an almost sinister manner.

"Why, yes I did, thank you. The duck here is fabulous. I take it you have already eaten?"

He quietly laughed at this. "Indeed I have. Perhaps more than I should have."

I found his tone to be a bit odd. My facial expression must have reflected my thought for he quickly changed the subject. "Well, shall we journey out into the night?"

"Sure," I replied. "And where are we headed?"

"It's a surprise. But I think you'll enjoy it." Again, there was something strange about the way he spoke his words.

I pulled a few bills out of my wallet, tossed them on the table and stood up. Ayden quickly stood as well and gestured for me to walk ahead. I gave a small nod and walked passed him and into the street. He followed closely, just near enough for me to smell his cologne. Smelled familiar…almost like Tommy Hilfiger, but I couldn't be sure.

"It's Freedom, by Tommy Hilfiger." He must have sensed I had caught wind of his cologne.

"Oh, sorry," I looked at the ground, blushing. "I just caught the scent in the breeze. Reminded me of someone I once knew."

"Ah, I see," he said. "Friend? Boyfriend?"

"Umm…*ex*-boyfriend actually. But I'd prefer not to talk about it." I quickened my pace a little.

He caught up to me and asked, "But how are we to get to know each other better if we don't talk about our pasts?" He certainly sounded sincere.

"I suppose you're right…but it's just hard to talk about something you've left behind…something that you've tried to block out, you know?" I looked up at him, searching for an answer in his eyes.

He smiled gently, "I think I know how you feel more than you would believe. We have similar pasts, you and I. There is a greater connection here than either of us would suspect."

His words comforted me a bit, so I gave in with a smile. We walked together through the market square, exchanging stories about our lives. It was nice to finally learn new things about this mysterious man. He was born in Northern Ireland. He lived there for a few years and then he moved to California with his parents. He earned his masters degree in Archaeology and History of Ancient Civilizations at UC Berkeley. Since then, he has spent most of his life traveling around the world, studying ancient structures.

He soon changed subjects, anxious to know more about my life back in the U.S. I was hoping to hear about why he felt we were so similar, but I decided to humor him.

Three

I was born and raised in Las Vegas. At the age of fifteen, my parents informed me that they were getting a divorce. I was able to choose which parent to live with, so I chose my mom. Throughout my high school career, I was continually rebellious and always getting into trouble. My mom finally got fed up with me when I was almost seventeen, and made me move in with my father. Things were better at first, but my rebellious streak continued. As soon as I hit the age of eighteen, my dad told me I had to move out and learn to live on my own. I wasn't upset or angry with them at all. It wasn't like my parents didn't love me, I was just too much to handle. So, that day, I packed up my stuff and headed out into the "real world."

Ever since then, I've never looked back. I have never regretted anything I have done, or haven't done for that matter. I didn't need my parents; I was perfectly content on my own.

Since I no longer had the financial support of my parents, it was time to look for income. My first job wasn't really anything special. I tried getting work at all the big casinos, but the Aladdin Resort and Casino was the only place that would hire me. They started me out small, training me as a bartender and waitress. I worked at that for about a year and was then trained to become a dealer.

Ayden must have noticed me staring off into space because he gently laid his hand on my shoulder. "Are you alright?" he asked.

His touch quickly brought me back to attention. "What? Oh yes, I'm fine, sorry. It's just all coming back to me now. I haven't ever talked to anyone about this."

He tilted his head to one side. "Well, perhaps this is a good time to start. Get it all out, you know? I'm sure you've kept it bottled up inside for far too long."

I let out a sigh, "Yes, perhaps it is time…" And so, I continued my story.

Working at the casino, everything ran pretty smoothly. I had become a regular dealer at the blackjack tables and I knew just about every other dealer that worked there. Then one night, when I was working the late shift, 11pm to 4am, this attractive, young guy approached my table. I had noticed him several times before around the casino. Now that wasn't an uncommon thing at a casino. A lot of guys would travel to Vegas and only attend the tables that had female dealers. Not really sure what the appeal was, considering we were trained to basically act like brick walls when dealing with customers, but whatever kept them betting was what mattered here.

He was tall, six foot two, with bright blue eyes and dark brown hair. He had one of those smiles…you know, the kind girls just swoon over. Well, he sat down directly across from me and flashed *that* smile.

Extending his hand out to me he said, "Hey there, name's Shane."

I politely shook his hand and then pointed to my nametag, "Calista."

I began to do the usual routine, asking for his bet and then dealing the cards. He went along with it, betting the minimum of twenty-five, but continued to try and make conversation.

"So…how long have you been working here?"

Without looking up I asked, "How long did it take you to come talk to me?"

He seemed to enjoy my retort, so he went with it. "Well, you know, you're pretty intimidating standing behind that table looking all tough. I had to come up with the perfect approach so that you wouldn't try and kick my ass. Hit me." He tapped the table for an additional card.

I kind of gave a half smile and gave him another card. Twenty. I checked my cards, I only had ten but I was confident.

"What do you say we make this bet a little interesting?" he shifted in his seat, "How about, if I win, you have to have dinner with me tomorrow night. But if you win…"

"If I win," I interrupted, "you have to promise to stop stalking me." He hesitated but then nodded in agreement.

I flipped my second card, "Dealer shows ten. Dealer hits." I turned my third card: Twenty-one. This time, I looked him dead in the eyes and smiled. "Sorry, dealer wins." I scooped his bet and then placed the cards in the shuffler.

"Damn, looks like I'm not allowed to come by anymore, huh?" He looked genuinely disappointed.

I felt kind of bad and had to admit to myself that it would be nice to get to know this guy. "Alright," I said, "I get a half hour break at one, if you want, we can get a drink at The Blue Note. I always go there for my break."

His mood immediately lightened. "I'll be there!" With that settled, he took off with a little wave and, of course, a smile.

At 1 am, I switched out with a new dealer and headed to The Blue Spot for my break. I grabbed my usual table in the back left corner. Tonight was a good night to be in the jazz club. B.B. King was in town and agreed to play a few shows over the weekend.

My usual waiter, Marc, came over with my drink: a Shirley Temple, "As always, a Shirley Temple, on the house."

"Thanks Marc." I patted his arm and he went on his way.

Not five minutes later, I spotted Shane near the front searching for me. I stood up and started waving to get his attention. He finally saw me and made his way over. As we both sat down, I called Marc over to take Shane's order.

"What'll ya have?"

Shane looked in my direction, "You first beautiful."

I blushed, not sure how to respond to his statement. "I'm all set, Marc." I lifted my drink to show I wasn't in need of a second yet.

Shane ordered a beer and then placed all his attention on me. "So for real, how long have you been working here?"

"About two years, I started right out of high school. My parents sort of kicked me out." I could've slapped myself. Why on earth did I open up so quickly?! I was not one to do things like that and I hadn't even had any alcohol, not that I was of age to do so anyways.

"Man, that stinks. I'm in college right now at the University of Nevada right here in Las Vegas."

"Oh cool," I said. "What year are you?"

"Senior, trying to figure out if I want to continue onto the masters program or not." He took a sip of his drink.

"Well, I am sure it will come to you," trying to be helpful. "Maybe you just need to research it more and see if that's what interests you."

He looked directly into my eyes, "Honestly, what interests me most right now…is you."

I almost fell out of my chair. I didn't know what to say to him! No guy had ever said anything like that to me before. I was sure he would notice my blushing so I felt I had to take a breather.

"Umm…will excuse me for a second? I need to run to the ladies' room."

I stood to escape to the restroom but he stood up at the same time so I bumped directly into him. He caught me in his arms and just kissed me. My whole body melted in his arms. I couldn't believe what was happening.

Our lips released and we looked into each other's eyes. I completely forgot about the bathroom and sat back down. He expressed his feelings for me and told me he wanted to continue to see me. Only if I'd allow it of course. I immediately agreed.

That was the night that our relationship officially began. Ever since then, one night a week and every weekend night, Shane would come to the casino and meet with me during my break. It turned into the perfect romance. He'd surprise me with flowers, plan romantic candlelit dinners, write me notes on napkins and drop them at my table. I'd help him with his schoolwork if I could and would sometimes surprise him at his apartment. It was almost too good to be true.

Our relationship continued like this for a year. On my twenty-first birthday, something happened that I would have never expected:

Shane proposed! Of course I accepted and I thought that things couldn't get any better than that moment. Well, little was I to know that I was right—things were only going to take a turn for the worst. Not two months later, I had planned a surprised visit to Shane's apartment and ended up walking in on him having sex with another girl. I stopped dead in my tracks, at first not knowing what to do. Then I did the only thing I could, I took the engagement ring off my finger, threw it at him and told him I never wanted to see him again. I left his apartment that day and decided I had to get away…from everything. I gave my two weeks notice at work and started to pack some necessities for my journey. I had already planned to become a wanderer of the world and knew I couldn't afford to drag around too much baggage with me.

Shane continually tried to call me and visit me at work. I got rid of my cell phone and asked my superiors to make him leave if he ever showed up at the casino. I don't understand why he even tried; he had to have known that I wouldn't see him. As much as it hurt me, it was the inspiration I needed to get out and explore the rest of the world. A few days later, I jumped on a plane to London. Since then, I swore I would never open my heart like that again and never looked back….

By the time I had finished telling my story, Ayden and I had ended up in front of the eastern cemetery next to the Pyramid of Khufu. We decided to sit on the stonewall surrounding the cemetery.

"So, what about you?" I asked him, playfully pushing his shoulder. "What makes you so similar to me?"

He laughed at this. "Well, I too have had my share of heartache."

"Well, time for you to spill it since I already shared my story." I was eager to hear what he had to say.

He hesitated, but then began to speak quietly. "Well, I was not engaged like you had been, but I loved a woman very deeply. She was my best friend and she betrayed me."

I laid my hand on his. "Oh, I am sorry…I hate to ask but…how did she betray you?"

He finally looked at me. "She took something from me that I can never get back."

"What was it?"

His eyes flashed in the light of the moon. "…My life…."

"What do you mean 'your life'?" I asked him, clearly not understanding what he meant.

He stood up and started to pace in front of me. The question had clearly troubled him, but I wanted to know what he meant. Plus, he was the one that brought it up; he had to have known that I would ask him to elaborate. If he didn't want me to know then he never should have mentioned it.

Ayden suddenly stopped and turned towards me. "Calista, I think it would be best if you headed back to your hotel now." His eyes looked almost red in the moonlight.

"What? But why?" I was utterly confused. What was happening here?

He began to pace again, "You just need to go. I can't explain why right now. But please…just go…before…" his voice trailed off.

"Before what?"

He quickly faced me and grabbed me roughly by the shoulders, "JUST GO!" He released me once he saw how scared I had become.

I had no choice but to do what he asked. I wasn't usually one to follow orders but I was starting to let my guard down with this guy and didn't want to anger him. I left him there without looking back and made it back to my hotel within thirty minutes. It was nearly two in the morning so I figured it was best to just end the night and get some sleep. Perhaps I could find Ayden tomorrow and try to get him to talk about what happened. Lying in bed, I began to think about the better parts of the night. It was nice to finally have someone that I could talk and relate to, but I still couldn't figure out why he had snapped. Was it something I did? Was it my asking about the girl who "took his life"? Similar thoughts continued to drift through my head as I began to drift off to sleep. Finally, sleep overtook my body and I was not to wake until late the next morning.

I was woken with a start by a loud knock on the door. Quickly, I threw on a robe over my shorts and tank. I ran to the door and checked the peephole; just house keeping. I cracked the door open just enough to speak with the woman. "Sorry ma'am, could you please come back in about an hour?" She merely nodded and was on her way to the next room. I shut the door and leaned up against it. What time was it? Looking to the clock on the nightstand, I saw it was nearly eleven o'clock. Eleven o'clock! I couldn't believe I slept that late. I had meant to get up earlier so I could hopefully find Ayden and talk to him about what happened.

After showering and dressing in under twenty minutes, I headed downstairs to the hotel lounge for a quick breakfast. There wasn't much to eat, mainly bagels and muffins with OJ, water or coffee. I was never a fan of orange juice and was definitely not drinking coffee, so I decided on a muffin and water. I didn't even bother staying in the lounge. I immediately headed out into the city to search for Ayden.

Of course, the first place I checked was the café. Much to my dismay, he was not there. I walked around the entire marketplace but was still unable to find him. Then I decided to start asking people if they had seen him. Most people I asked just shook their heads and continued walking. Those who actually stopped to listen to my description of Ayden were not much help either.

Finally, after a few hours, I got lucky. A young boy nodded excitedly when I described Ayden to him.

"Do you know where he is?" I asked anxiously.

The boy looked down in sadness. "I sorry, but no. He not tell me where. Only gives me coins for delivering letters."

"Letters? What letters?"

"I not read them!" he yelled in anger, as if I had just accused him of stealing.

"I'm sorry." I gently patted his head. "Did you see on the envelope where they were being sent? Or to whom he was sending them?"

He looked up at me with a smile, nodding quickly. "Yes! Letters sent to a lady. She had weird name. I couldn't read it. But place was Greece."

"Greece, interesting…alright, last question," I said. "Was there another address? The address of where he is staying here in Egypt?"

He quickly shook his head. "Nope. And he never give me letters from sleeping place. Always on street corner." He turned and pointed. It was the corner right before the café where Ayden and I had met.

I thanked the boy, patted his head again and gave him a couple of coins. He responded by flashing me a big smile and then ran off with his newly acquired treasure.

The thought of Greece was enticing, but I knew Ayden hadn't left the city yet. I was determined to find him, so I continued my search. However, after questioning a few more people, I decided it was time to quit for the day. No one knew the person I was describing. I wasn't getting anywhere. Plus, it was starting to get dark and I needed to eat.

Although I considered it, I did not eat at the café again. I didn't want Ayden showing up and having to deal with an awkward moment between us in the middle of a crowd. So, I chose a small bistro about four blocks away that looked inviting. I took my time eating as well. I figured that it would give me some more time to think about what to say to Ayden when I finally found him.

After about an hour at the restaurant, I paid the bill and headed back to the hotel. It was already dark but it didn't deter my plans of scouring the city. Though, perhaps a long shower would perk me up a bit before I returned to my search. As I reached my door, I considered checking the Pyramids. I had met up with him at the pyramid of Khufu that first day and we also ended up near there the night after. It couldn't hurt to check; maybe he went back there in hopes that I would also be there. Who knows? But I decided it was the best place to at least start looking.

I placed the key in the lock, turned it and opened the door. Walking in, I glanced up and saw Ayden sitting in a chair in front of the balcony! Startled, I gasped and dropped my keys on the floor.

"Oh my god, Ayden! How did you get in here?" I exclaimed.

His expression was somber. "Hello Calista," he spoke slowly. "I heard you were searching for me. I felt I should come to you directly and explain my actions. Please…close the door and come sit." He gestured to the chair in front of him.

I quickly placed the "Do Not Disturb" sign on the doorknob, shut the door and locked it. Then I hesitatingly made my way to the empty chair and sat down.

"Ayden...where have you been? I have been anxious to speak with you. Last night was extremely confusing and I...."

He immediately motioned for me to be quiet, "That's why I am here. Please...allow me to talk without interruption. You need to hear my full story."

I nodded slowly, clasping my hands together in front of me. I stared at him, wondering if I was going to be prepared for the story he was about to tell.

"Calista...I am not who you may think I am. Well, I think the more appropriate thing for me to say is that; I am not *what* you think I am. Calista...I am not human...I am...a...a vampire...I have been for nearly one thousand years now."

He stopped at this part, probably to see how I had reacted to his words. I was in utter shock. At first I thought he was joking, but by the look on his face, I knew he was telling me the truth. I had no words for what he told me. I could only stare, wide-eyed and, to be honest, I felt a bit terrified. If he had plans to harm me for any reason, I would not have been able to evade him. My feet felt like they were cemented to the floor.

Seeing that I had nothing to say to him just yet, and he had not wanted me to interrupt, he continued, "I can tell you are quite shocked at this, but my intentions last night were completely noble. I wanted you to leave so I wouldn't harm you...You see, when I said that you and I were more similar than you'd think, I meant it. I continually get in the same situation as you: I meet someone, come to find that I care about her, but then it all ends badly. And by badly, I don't mean that she breaks up with me or vice versa. By badly I mean that...she usually ends up dead...because of my need...my need for...blood."

The second he said the word; my dream came flooding back to me. That's what the blood on the walls must have meant...vampire. It now became clear to me that my dream was a warning that Ayden was a vampire.

Ayden's voice quickly interrupted my thoughts, "I know that all this may frighten you, and I am sorry, but I felt that I should tell you

in person. I…" he bowed his head, "…I didn't want to hurt you…I…"
He lifted his head and looked into my eyes, "…I have come to care
about you, Calista. That's why I had to come here to speak with you
and tell you the truth. I didn't want you to end up like all those other
girls." He paused for several moments, searching my eyes for
something. Though for what, I wasn't sure. He pleaded,
"Please…say something."

At first I didn't know what to say. I was ready to bolt out of there.
But his words seemed genuine, so I pulled myself together and told him
what I thought about the situation. "Ayden…this really is a huge
shock, and my first thought was of finding a way to just getting the fuck
out of here, but I have to admit that I care about you too. That's why
I was looking for you today. But now I don't know what to do about
this. I mean, I obviously can't be with you because of…what you
are…and since you have warned me of the consequences of what
happens when you care for someone…" I was sure I was in for it after
that, but Ayden remained where he was. I think he was anxious to hear
what else I had to say, so I continued. "Ayden…I really think that we
should just say goodbye right now and go our separate ways.
Honestly…I…" I almost couldn't get it out, but it was the truth, "I
don't feel safe with you right now."

Immediately I could see the pain in his eyes. This was really hard
for the both of us and we both knew it. But it had to be done, for both
our sakes.

Before I could speak again, Ayden stood and looked into my eyes
one last time. I attempted to stand but he just shook his head. Without
another word, he turned, walked out onto the balcony, and jumped
down to the street below. The moment he jumped, I ran to the balcony
railing. I looked over the edge, but he was not lying on the ground in
a pool of blood as I had half-expected. But then I remembered…a
vampire. He was most likely capable of doing anything he wanted, so
his jump no longer came as much of a surprised to me. Since I couldn't
see him, I figured he had gone off to sulk in solitude and decide what
his next plan of action would be. Me, I planned on leaving for South
America as soon as possible. I went inside, locked the balcony doors,
double checked the lock on the main door and reluctantly tried to sleep.

Four

It was quarter to six in the morning when I woke up. I felt rather groggy considering I had only gotten about four hours of sleep that night, but it didn't matter. I had to leave as soon as I could. I jumped out of bed and ran to shower. Lucky for me, there was hot water. Ten minutes later I was packing my bag when there came a knock on the door. I froze, wondering if it would be Ayden or not.

"Who is it?" I called.

There was hesitation, but then a small voice came from behind the door, "Hi lady. I bring you letter from Mister Ayden. He tell me is very important that you get it right away." It was the young boy I had met yesterday afternoon during my search of the city.

I walked to the door and let the boy in. He scampered to the bed and hopped onto it, holding out the letter. I took the letter from him cautiously, examining every part of it looking for anything suspicious.

"It's ok lady. We not poison it or anything."

I gave the boy a little smirk and then tossed him a coin. "I'll give you three more of those if you wait for me to write back to him and deliver it for me."

He smiled big and nodded excitedly. I walked to the table in the corner, near the balcony and opened the letter.

My Dearest Calista,

I know that you plan on leaving the city before sunset, and I understand why. I truly do. And I am sure that you will not be surprised to hear that I plan on leaving the city as well, soon after sundown. I cannot express to you enough my deepest apologies for not telling you what I was from the beginning.

Honestly, when I first saw you, I thought you would make an excellent companion…to join me in my dark eternity. But when I thought more on it, I realized that it was not fair to bring you into such a world as the one I live in. As much as I care for you, I will not submit you to the horrors I have seen and experienced. And so, it is with great sadness that I bid you farewell. But I do wish you great happiness, for I know you deserve it. I wish I could have been a part of your life but it is apparently not our destiny.

Please know that I will not follow you or try to find you, wherever you may go. Your life is your own and I wish you to live it to the fullest. I also ask of you not to search for me. If you were ever to find me, I am not sure what the consequences of that would be. Do your best to forget about me.

With All My Heart,

Ayden

I gently ran my fingertip across his name, picturing his face in my mind. How I longed to speak with him about his letter but at the same time, the thought of what he was created a nervous knot in my stomach! There was no choice for me other than to say my goodbyes and leave. I folded the letter and snatched up a piece of paper and pen from the bedside table to write my own letter:

Dear Ayden,

In all honesty, I am not really sure what to say. After all that you told me, I am at a loss for words. I do care about you as well but I am scared for my own safety now fully knowing what you are…I wish I could see you one last time but I know it's not a good idea. Perhaps you are right, this is not our destiny. I am going to continue with my travel, as planned. However, I am not sure if I will be able to put you out of my mind, but if this is what you want, then I shall do my best to obey your wishes. I appreciate your respect in agreeing not to follow me. It's best for both of us. But please, do take care of yourself.

Yours Affectionately,

Calista

I folded the letter and sealed it in an envelope. As I gave it to the boy, I handed him three more coins, as promised.

"Alright, now make sure he gets this right away, ok? But I have to go now. Thanks kiddo." I patted the kid's shoulder.

"Yes, yes. Very important…Thank you, thank you," he said holding up the coins so that they glinted in the light. "I go now and wait for sunset. He never meet me when sun in sky."

With that, the boy hopped off the bed and ran out the door, letter in hand. As soon as he was out of sight, I finished packing my things and headed towards the elevator.

In the lobby, I told the concierge I wanted to check out of my room. I fumbled for my wallet but the concierge held up his hand in protest.

"No need my lady, a young gentleman has already paid for your stay."

I wasn't sure how to react but then it hit me. "Ayden…" I whispered.

"I beg your pardon, Miss?"

"Oh, umm…nothing. Thank you, sir." I placed my key on the counter and walked out the front doors.

Once outside, my first thought was of hailing a cab but then remembered that I was in Egypt and the closest thing to a cab was a horse. Also, the airport in Giza wasn't too far from the hotel, so I decided to travel on foot instead.

It was eight-thirty when I finally reached the Embada Airport. Thank goodness the wind wasn't bad this morning. Sand storms can delay flights for hours. I certainly wouldn't have been thrilled with that considering I really didn't want to be around here anymore come nightfall.

I knew exactly where to go since I had arrived at this airport when I flew in from England. I strolled through the revolving doors and made my way to the ticket counter. Slapping my passport on the counter, I asked the clerk for the first plane to South America. The clerk tapped away at the computer, checking for the flight I had requested.

"Ah yes, there is a flight leaving for Brazil in forty-five minutes. Would you like to travel first class or coach?"

"Coach is fine." I pulled out my wallet. Lucky for me, flights out of Egypt were cheap. I tossed two hundred Egyptian pounds on the counter and waited for my ticket. The clerk typed quickly, printed my ticket and I was on my way.

Being a small airport, I didn't have to walk far. The gate was only about thirty yards to my right. I sauntered over to Gate Three and plopped down in a chair near the window. I thought the best way to make the time pass would be to read while I waited, so I pulled my book out of my bag. I was only about ten pages into it when the announcer said it was time to board the flight to Brazil. I shoved the book back in my bag and headed toward the gate.

The plane was small but cozy. There were already five people aboard. There was an old man with a young boy who must have been his grandson. The young boy was talking quickly in Egyptian so I couldn't really understand what he was saying. I caught the words "afraid" and "too high." Must have been the boy's first time flying. In the middle were the three remaining passengers: teenagers. They must have been either studying abroad for a semester or on some sort of vacation from school. I ignored their awkward stares and made my way towards the back. I was happy to see that it was vacant. I placed my bag in the overhead compartment and then sat myself next to the window. I fastened my seatbelt and leaned my head back against the seat. Closing my eyes, I began to think about Ayden. I was asleep before the plane was even off the ground.

The plane jolted as it hit the runway, jerking me from sleep. I looked out the window and smiled at the beautiful view. There were bright green trees and gorgeously colored flowers everywhere. I had reached a paradise that was thought to only be found in books.

Trying to shove my way off the plane was never a pleasant experience, so I waited until everyone else had deplaned before I even grabbed my bag. The Rio de Janeiro airport was quite a sight. Just like the scenery outside, the airport lobby was filled with flowers and lush greens. The air smelled like springtime after a fresh rainfall. I took a deep breath and walked out into the wilderness of Brazil.

The nearest hotel was too far to walk so I looked around for some transportation. Lucky for me, cars were popular so I hailed a cab. It took about a half hour to reach the Golden Tulip Ipanema Plaza. Located right on the beach, it would be a wonderful change from the dust and heat of Egypt. I strolled into the lobby and took a look at my new surroundings. A large fountain sat in the center of the lobby. There were, of course, palm trees and bright blooming flowers everywhere one turned. The concierge's desk was to my left. As I approached the desk, the young lady working there smiled and welcomed me to the hotel. I gave her a quick smile and explained to her that I was planning on staying in Rio de Janeiro for a while and would like one of the best rooms they had. She immediately became excited.

"Oh Miss! We have the best suites around! Please, which floor would you like to be placed on? Would you prefer a view of the ocean? Each ocean view room has a balcony. And all of our suites have Jacuzzis…"

I quickly interrupted her, "Please ma'am. I know all about your facilities. I have done my research. I would just like a room. One high up, if possible, and facing the ocean. And I would also really appreciate not being disturbed either, please."

She nodded and began to input some data into the computer, "Of course, Miss. Let's see…we have a vacant room on the fifteenth floor, room 1515."

"That'd be perfect, thank you." I tossed my credit card on the counter.

She picked up the card and began to process the rest of my information into the database. This didn't take long. The only thing she needed me to do was sign a check-in list and receipt. As soon as this was done, she handed me my room key and I took the nearest elevator up to the fifteenth floor.

The room was better than I had imagined. There was a king sized bed, covered in white satin sheets and plush down pillows. A small living room was located towards the back, right area of the room, overlooking the beach. A pair of glass doors opened up onto the balcony. I dropped my bag and walked to the balcony. It was way better than the one I had had at the hotel in Egypt. After a few minutes of fresh air and the gorgeous view, I ventured back inside and began to unpack my things. Considering that I never carried much with me, this only took about ten minutes. Having accomplished that, I sat down in the living room and began to plan out the next few days.

It was absolutely necessary that I visit the ancient ruins of Machu Picchu in Peru. They were of great interest to me and I wanted to get the full experience of it. That would require a full day, if not more, to visit in its entirety. A call down to the concierge would probably be the best way to guarantee me a charter plane to Peru. I decided to take care of that before doing anything else.

"Hello, this is Calista Logan in room 1515. I was wondering if you would be able to book me a charter plane to Peru for tomorrow morning. Yes, six am would be perfect. Thank you."

Now that that was taken care of, I could spend the rest of the day relaxing. I decided to explore the hotel and see what there was to do. Since I was already so high up, I figured why not start with the roof? The roof was deserted, and to my surprise there was a pool. Not something you see at every hotel. It was a bit windy, but the view was gorgeous. I took a quick walk around the edge of the roof and then decided to head back downstairs. The rest of the hotel was just as beautiful. Everything was spotless and shining. All the flowers were fresh and in full bloom. And every staff member that I made eye contact with was extremely friendly.

The main floor of the hotel had a pool as well. There was also a fitness center and several elegant ballrooms. I decided to keep the fitness center in mind for something to do later. Exercising had always been a good way for me to clear my head. Plus, it wouldn't hurt to keep myself in shape while I traveled.

Once satisfied with my tour of the place, I was beginning to feel fatigued. My body was definitely feeling the jetlag and perhaps it was best to just give in and take a quick rest. I didn't have anything else to do for the rest of the day anyways. I didn't even bother changing or setting an alarm once I got into my room. I just plopped down and sank into the comfort of the bed. I was asleep in no time and another strange dream came to haunt my sleep.

It was dark and windy. I was standing out on the hotel balcony, wearing a silky black dress. The wind whipped my hair fiercely around my face. I looked down at the ocean and my breath caught as I saw that the water was red! Red as blood. Suddenly, a weird feeling came over me. It felt as if someone was watching me. I turned, and there he was standing in the doorway...Ayden. But he wasn't alone. I couldn't make out the face, but from the silhouette I could tell it was a woman who stood beside him. He took a step towards me. The moon lit up his face, but the look on his face was not of happiness. His eyes sparkled red, and his mouth was parted, just enough to show a hint of his fangs. The minute I looked at his face, I knew what he meant to do. I backed myself up against the railing of the balcony. He took another step, and then looked back at the woman in the doorway. She gave him a firm nod of her head, almost as if to say, "It must be done." He turned toward me again and took yet another step. I held out my arm, begging him to stay back. Ayden only shook his head and continued towards me. A tear rolled down my cheek as I turned toward the ocean. I looked back at Ayden once last time, mouthed the words "I'm sorry", and then leapt off the balcony. I closed my eyes as I fell, waiting for the impact.

Just before I hit the ground, I woke with a start. I looked around to make sure I was still in my hotel room. The balcony doors were open but I wasn't too concerned about it. I was just pleased to see that I was safely in my room. I was a bit disappointed to see that it was dark outside already. I must have been asleep for quite some time. I got off the bed and went to the bathroom to wash my face.

As much as I didn't really want to, I started to remember details about the dream. It had been worse than the one I had in Egypt. Far worse. The blood was a factor of both dreams, but it was starting to make sense now. Blood was Ayden's only source of nourishment. But the woman in the doorway—who was she? Perhaps she was the woman with the strange name that the little Egyptian boy had mentioned. Or maybe it was the woman that Ayden said had betrayed her. She seemed important but I didn't think there was any way that I could find out what her presence in my dream meant. But the most disturbing part of the dream was the look in Ayden's eyes. They were the same color red they had been when he told me what he was. Could it be possible that he cried tears tinted with blood that night? But the red in his eyes during my dream were certainly not bloody tears.

I found a pad of paper in the living room and decided to write down every bit of the dream that I could remember. As long as it was written down somewhere, I could always go over it later if I thought of something new that might help understand it better. I placed the written dream in the bottom drawer of the dresser, underneath some clothes. I took a quick shower, changed into something comfortable and then headed downstairs to the lounge. I needed some time to sit and reflect on everything that has happened since I had first arrived in Egypt.

On my way out of the elevator, a good-looking young man with very short brown hair bumped into me.

"Oh, I'm terribly sorry. My fault," he politely apologized.

"It's ok, don't worry about it." I gave a shrug of my shoulders and continued walking.

I looked back at the elevator, and as the doors began to close, I noticed the guy was staring at me and he had an eerie grin on his face. I stared back at him. He gave me a quick wave just before the doors closed. That was odd, I thought to myself. I didn't let it bother me though, so I just shrugged it off and went into the lounge. I grabbed a table way in the back of the room. The dark, isolated tables away from all the people were always my favorite. The waiter came and took my order: vodka rocks. I couldn't drink beer or mixed drinks anymore. Hard liquor was the only thing that satisfied my taste these days. I certainly felt I needed it after what I had been through the past few days.

The face of the young man I had run into lingered in my mind for just a moment, but then Ayden's face took its place. How could he expect me to not think about him? He was too beautiful and mysterious to forget so easily. I almost considered heading back to Egypt but then I remembered his letter. He had said he was planning on leaving Egypt soon after me. Also, I had to think about my trip to Machu Picchu. I couldn't leave the country without checking out the ancient ruins; I just wouldn't feel satisfied.

By the time I had finished my drink, I stuck with my decision to visit the ruins the next day. However, once my visit was complete, I would pack my bags and go on a search for Ayden. I know that he had told me not to, but he and I were connected somehow. I could feel it. I had to find him and speak with him again.

The waiter came by to ask if I needed a refill but I just shook my head and handed him some cash. He accepted with a small nod and took off in the direction of the bar. I got up and headed back to my room to go back to sleep. I wanted to be well rested for my adventure tomorrow.

As soon as I got off the elevator, I saw the same young man that I had seen earlier. He was at the other end of the hall, just starting at me. I wasn't sure what to do, so I just gave him a quick wave like he had done to me earlier and headed in the other direction towards my room. I opened the door and got in as quickly as I could. I locked the door as soon as it was shut and checked the peephole to make sure he hadn't followed me. He wasn't standing outside the door, so I supposed he was either still at the end of the hall or maybe he decided to leave. That's when I noticed an envelope on the floor. Puzzled, I picked it up. It had my name written on it in beautiful calligraphy on parchment, not regular paper. It looked almost as if it had been written back in medieval times and somehow made its way to the twentieth century. Cautiously, I opened the envelope and pulled out the letter. At first I thought it was from Ayden but then I realized it was not his handwriting. I almost dropped the letter in complete shock when I started to read it.

Calista Logan,

We know of your encounters with our dear Ayden. We know that he has informed you as to what he is. We are certain that you are aware that there are others like him. However, this should not be of concern or interest to you, for it will only bring you much trouble.

We have also become aware of your plans to search for Ayden. It is highly recommended that you do not follow through with such plans. If you do, unpleasant consequences could be headed in your direction. We do not usually deal in threats but we must take whatever means necessary to protect those who belong with us. Please do not engage with matters that you do not understand. And do not cross those whom you know nothing about. Nothing good can come from what you seek.

Yours Respectfully,

The Ancients

The Ancients? Who were they supposed to be? And how did they know that I was going to try and find Ayden? I had decided upon it not ten minutes ago. But did they really think that I was going to cease my plans of searching for Ayden because of some stupid letter? Well, they could just forget about it because I was going to go out and find him whether they liked it or not.

I crumpled the letter and threw it on the table. The letter did not frighten me, as I am sure they were hoping it would. It only sparked my interest even more. It did make me wonder though, how they actually figured out my plans. Maybe they really *could* read minds. I had suspected it of Ayden that first day we met, but it didn't seem possible. People just can't do that. Although, I had to remember, these people are not human.

This meant that one of them had either followed or tracked me here. Then I remembered the young man in the hall. I quickly ran to the door and checked the peephole again: no one. I slowly unlocked the door and peeked my head out into the hallway. He was no longer at the end of the hall, but I was certain he was one of them. No wonder he had been staring at me. But how on earth did they know who I was? Had Ayden described me to them? There was just so much to think about. However, it would have to wait until tomorrow. I had to prepare for my trip and get some sleep. Tomorrow's plane ride could be spent thinking about things and deciding on what else needed to be done before beginning my search. I undressed quickly and climbed under the covers. Surprisingly, it didn't take long for sleep to come, however, it didn't stop the dream from coming.

Five

I *was standing in front of a large mansion. There was a ring of fire surrounding it, where a moat would normally be. The two large stone doors in front of me looked to be my only way in. As I approached, I thought of how I could possibly open such heavy looking doors by myself, but then they suddenly opened on their own. I entered cautiously. For some reason, many things inside did not have much detail to them. The furniture and walls looked blurry and plain. The only sharply defined object in the entire foyer was the stairway. It was made of white marble speckled with black. I could barely see the top stair when I looked up. I could see though, that right after the stairs ended, there was a light emanating from somewhere close to the stairs. Now filled with curiosity, I began to head towards the faint light. The light became brighter with each step I took. As soon as I reached the top, the light became almost blinding. I could see someone standing in the doorway, but I couldn't make out exactly whom it was. The person was reaching out for me. I extended my arm and tried to move towards the light but my feet wouldn't move. It felt as if someone was holding me back. The more I tried to go towards the light, the more darkness began to fall over me. Finally, the light was only a beam in the doorway. The unknown person was no longer there and I was left alone. I felt cold inside. But suddenly, I was no longer on the stairs, but outside in a courtyard. Flames began to spurt up from the ground all around me. There was no way for me to escape. I looked up towards the sky and I could see something. It looked like a bird at first, but once it dropped nearer, the shape became more defined. Before*

*I could even move, it was Ayden who dropped down beside me.
I couldn't speak, but I didn't have to. He quickly scooped me up
and away we flew, away from the fire and the darkness. I felt safe
in his arms. Sadly, the feeling didn't last too long because the
mysterious woman from my previous dream appeared before us.
A dark veil covered her face. She held out her hand in protest,
stopping Ayden from advancing any further. He went to speak
but she put up her other hand to prevent his words. When she did
this, a strong wind began to blow against us. Ayden tried to fly
against it but he just wasn't strong enough. She pushed hard and
a violent gust forced Ayden to release his grip on me. I fell from
his arms far too fast for him to catch me. I was hurled through the
air. I tried to look for Ayden, hoping he would save me, but he was
nowhere to be seen. My body fell faster and faster towards the
ground.*

I sprang out of bed to the sound of the phone ringing. I almost
forgot that I had arranged for a wake up call so I wouldn't miss my
flight.

I answered it quickly, "Hello?"

"Hello Miss Logan, this is your wake up call. It's 5:00am." The
voice was friendly and inviting.

"Thank you very much," I replied.

"Would you like breakfast sent up?"

My stomach rumbled at the mention of food. "Oh yes, please.
Pancakes and bacon would be great. Along with some fresh grape
juice, if it's not too much trouble."

"No trouble at all, Miss. Your meal will arrive shortly. Have a
nice day."

"Thanks, you too." I placed the phone back in its cradle.

I quickly ran to the dresser and pulled out the paper that contained
my dream from the previous night. On the remaining blank pages, I
recorded my most recent dream. This one puzzled me even more than
the last. The fact that this mysterious woman has shown up in two of
my dreams now intrigued me. She must have a role in all of this

somehow. And she obviously has a connection to Ayden. If I couldn't find him on my own, perhaps I could get to him through her. The only problem was that her face remained undefined in my dreams; so locating her would also be a difficult task.

There was a knock on the door. It must be room service. I strolled to the door and opened it. A young lady rolled a cart through the door.

"Where would you like it, Miss?"

"Oh, the table would be fine, thank you."

She rolled the cart to the table and placed all the items onto it. Once finished, I handed her a couple of bills as a tip.

"When you are finished, you may place the dishes on the cart and leave it outside your door. Someone will be by to pick it up later." She bowed her head in thanks and then quietly left the room.

I sat down and ate breakfast rather quickly. I was anxious to get out to the ruins. I shoveled two pancakes into my mouth, inhaled the bacon and then downed a full glass of juice. I took a quick minute to brush my teeth and wash my face, but then I was out the door in a flash. I grabbed the elevator down to the lobby and went straight to the concierge's desk. The same young woman who had checked me in the day before was there.

She smiled as I approached. "Good morning Miss Logan. There is a taxi outside ready to take you to the airport."

I was impressed. "Wow, thanks." I'd never gotten the type of royal treatment I was receiving at this place but I wasn't about to complain. I gave her a quick nod and headed out the front doors.

The young lady was right; the taxi was right out front, ready to go. I opened the door, threw my knapsack in the backseat and hopped in. The driver flashed me a smile in the rearview mirror and took off immediately.

The airport wasn't far, only about six miles. It wasn't a major airport either, just a small one for charters such as the one I had booked for the day. The taxi dropped me off right next to the charter. I got out, thanked the driver and handed him what I owed for the ride. As soon as he drove off, the stewardess came off the plane to greet me.

"Good morning, Miss Logan. Would you like me to take your bag?"

"Sure," I replied, holding out my bag. "How long is the flight expected to be?"

She took my bag and answered, "Today's flight should take about six hours, Miss. Please, feel free to board the plane. The pilot will be ready to take off whenever you are."

I thanked her and then headed towards the plane. The stewardess followed close behind. The charter was actually much nicer than the plane I had taken into Rio de Janeiro. The seats were leather and there was much more leg room. The first seat looked comfy enough so I plopped into it. There really wasn't a need to sit at the back since I had the whole place to myself. The stewardess came up beside me and placed my bag in the overhead compartment. She then proceeded to the cockpit to tell the pilot we were ready to go.

It wasn't long before she returned. "Would you like anything before we take off?"

I politely declined her offer, "No thank you. I'm fine."

The stewardess nodded and then made her way to the back of the plane to be seated as well. The pilot came on the loud speaker and gave a quick read off of the weather and estimated flight time. As I was buckling my seatbelt, I noticed that there were several books in the pouch in front of my seat. I pulled a couple out and read the synopsis of each to decided which one I felt like reading. The first book was called *Cell* by Stephen King. It was about a strange force that was scrambling the brains of cell phone users. Sounded like a typical Stephen King book, full of mysterious happenings. Since I had read just about all of his previous works, I set it aside for the time being. I found the second book to be quite intriguing. It was called *Gone* by Lisa Gardner and was about a former F.B.I. agent searching for the kidnapper of his ex-wife. I placed the Stephen King book back in the seat pocket and started to read the Lisa Gardner book instead.

I got about halfway through the book before the plane landed. The pilot came over the PA system again and gave the current weather conditions for Machu Picchu and said we would be landing in about five minutes. I dog-eared the page I was on and placed the book on the seat next to me. I planned on finishing it on the ride back to Rio de Janeiro.

The landing was nice and smooth, unlike the flight from Egypt. The stewardess came to the front of the plane to get my bag for me. She asked if I would prefer that the plane stayed put and waited for my return. I told her that it wasn't necessary; I wasn't planning on leaving until later that evening. She gave a nod, handed me my bag and asked if it would be alright if they returned at 9:00pm. I gave a small smile and a nod, then exited the plane.

I was able to find a horse rental nearby the landing area. The man who gave me the horse was very nice. He spoke to me in English but his wife refused to do so. I was able to pick up on their conversation. They were speaking in Portuguese and she was trying to get him to charge me more for a full day's rental. He was explaining to her that he would feel guilty trying to rip off an American who didn't know the area that well. I just stood there smiling, pretending that I couldn't understand them. Finally, the wife gave up and the man only charged me thirty dollars instead of the seventy his wife was shooting for. I thanked him several times and promised him that I would take good care of the horse. He just smiled and waved as I headed out towards the ruins.

Apparently my horse didn't want to travel any faster than a walking pace, so the journey to the ruins was much longer than I had expected. It didn't bother me all that much though because the scenic views were more than perfect. The surrounding jungle was magnificent. Nothing but greens, blues, pinks, yellows and reds. The other great thing about South America, besides the scenery, was that animals were free to roam wherever they pleased. No one tried to fence them in. I watched pythons slither through the tree branches as I rode past dense parts of the jungle. Monkeys were everywhere, calling loudly to each other. The males were swinging from tree to tree, chasing after their female consorts. It was amusing to watch.

It took me nearly forty-five minutes to get to the outskirts of the ruins. The ancient Incan ruins sit inside of Machu Picchu, which is five square miles of intricate stonework. Every area of the ruins is linked together by three thousand steps.

I hopped off my horse and took a moment to marvel at the beauty of the Incan fortress. From where I stood, I could see every section of the city slightly detailed by crumbling stonewalls and long staircases. It looked like it was about an hour or so to reach the heart of the city but I wanted to explore each and every crevice. This was almost as exquisite as the pyramids in Egypt had been. If only Ayden were here to share this moment with me....

I shook my head to shake Ayden from my thoughts. As much as I wanted to think about him and my plans to find him, it would have to wait. Being at the Incan ruins was *my* time and I wanted to enjoy every second of it. I grabbed the reins and started to lead the horse down the hill towards the city. I figured I would give the poor animal a break for a little while.

The terrain was rough all the way down, plus I had to guide the horse slowly so it wouldn't break a leg, so it took about twenty minutes just to get to the first wall. Finding an opening, I led the horse into the city and quickly located a post to tie him to. Interestingly enough, there was a pile of hay nearby, so I grabbed a bunch and placed it near the horse in case he got hungry. Of course, as most horses do, he went straight for it. That wouldn't last him the whole day so I grabbed some more, gave him a pat on the neck before heading into the city.

I took my time examining each piece of every building, wall, and step as I ventured through the ruins. It probably would have seemed boring to the average person, but it was things like this that brought out my inner most fascinations. As I walked through the city, I was happy to see many artifacts lying around and surprisingly intact. I was tempted to take something as a souvenir, but I couldn't bring myself to do it. I would be disturbing a peace that had existed for so many years before I had even come here. The mere fact that everything was still here after so many centuries made me feel certain contentment, so I continued on without touching anything.

When I was pretty sure I had reached the very center of the city, I checked the time. It was 2:00pm, which meant it had taken me two hours to make it this far instead of the one hour I had originally guessed. Though, I figured I still had plenty of time to make it to the other end and back before the sun had fully set. I looked around for a good walking stick before I continued. As much as I loved long treks like this one, my knees would usually begin to ache after a few hours. Having a walking stick or some type of support usually eased the pain a little bit.

Lucky enough for me, there was a decent tree branch leaning up against one of the nearby buildings. I grabbed it, relieved it of small protrusions and then headed west. Hopefully I could make it to the opposite side of the city and then back to my starting point before the plane was scheduled to return. Just to be safe, I decided to pick up the pace.

Around 4:45pm, I came to a high stonewall. It had to have been at least twelve feet tall, if not more.

"This must be the edge of the city," I whispered.

I was satisfied with myself that I was able to make this journey entirely on my own. I placed my right hand on the wall, closed my eyes and whispered a Celtic blessing:

> *Grace of the love of the skies be thine, Grace of the love of the stars be thine, Grace of the love of the moon be thine, Grace of the love of the sun be thine, Grace of the love and the crown of heaven be thine.*
> *Blessed Be.*

I opened my eyes and looked up towards the sky with a smile. But then my smile began to fade once I saw how low the sun was. I checked my watch and then looked towards the east. I had to get moving quickly if I hoped to make it back in time. I was starting to wish that I had brought the horse with me and then my timing would have been better planned. It almost seemed a waste to have rented it and not brought it through the city but I didn't want it to get injured along the way and not be able to make it back in time. Nevertheless, I had to head back as quickly as I could without the extra help.

I started out on the same path that I had come on, or so I thought. Looking around, some parts of the city looked extremely unfamiliar to me. I had only been walking for about twenty minutes, how could I possibly have gotten lost already? I gave the area another look around and then checked the position of the sun. It was setting directly behind me, which meant I was facing east. East was where I wanted to go, so I decided to just keep going. As long as I was headed in the right direction, I'd make it back to the landing area at some point.

The more I walked and the darker the sky became, the more I started to worry. I shouldn't have because I knew I was headed in the right direction; I continually checked my compass just to be sure. Still, my surroundings continued to look unfamiliar to me. I still wasn't sure how I could be lost but for some reason, I chose to ignore it. By this time, my knees were starting to ache quite a bit. They weren't too bad yet but I knew they would get worse within the next hour. There would be a point where I would have to sit down and rest, but I wasn't sure I wanted to do that in the middle of this place in the dark. I thought it wouldn't be a bad time to start a slight jog, just to pick up the pace. I ran for as long as I could without becoming too exhausted and then slowed to a walk and checked the time. It was 6:15 pm, which meant I was either in the center of the city or very close to it. That was at least a good sign for the time being. Only about another two hours maximum and I'd be out of the city.

After another hour and a half or walking, it was rather dark but the moon was high in the sky. Luckily, I had remembered to pack a flashlight. I stopped and sat down on a nearby step to get the flashlight and also quickly rest up my knees. As I searched my bag, I looked up towards the east to see if I could see my horse yet. Interestingly enough, there he was, grazing at the top of the hill. But to my surprise, there was a figure standing next to him. I was immediately alarmed. Very few people knew I was here and my plane wasn't scheduled to be back for another hour. My hand finally found the flashlight and I pulled it out, still staring at the figure on the hill. I wasn't really sure what to do. I was curious to see who it was, but I was also a bit frightened. I had no idea who this person was or what he or she wanted. At first I thought it might be the horse rental guy, checking up on the horse but how would he have known I would leave it at the edge of the city?

45

About five to ten minutes passed before either of us moved. I watched as the figure turned and slowly walked away from my horse. The person didn't walk towards the landing area located up the hill to the left. Instead, the figure walked to the right, which as far as I knew, was nothing but jungle. I carefully watched the person disappear into the darkness before I decided to start towards my horse. This was extremely puzzling, yet intriguing.

I finally stood and started to make my way towards the hill where my horse awaited me. I was thankful for the flashlight, for if I had forgotten it, I surely would have twisted my ankle or something on all the rocks jutting out from the ground. Luckily it only took me another twenty-five minutes to make it up the hill. At my approach, the horse lifted his head in greeting. I gave him a quick pat on the nose and then noticed a blank white envelope poking out of the saddlebag. I pulled it out, looking around to see if the mysterious figure was waiting at the edge of the jungle, but there was no one around. I decided to wait on reading it until I had better lighting on the plane. I placed it in my knapsack and then untied the horse. I mounted as quickly as I could and then urged him to trot up the hill. Lucky for me, he obeyed this time.

The nice man who had rented me the horse was waiting for me. He smiled big once I rode up and dismounted.

I handed him the reins, "Thank you very much, sir."

Taking the reins he asked, "Did you enjoy your journey, my dear?"

"Oh yes, it was better than I had imagined."

"Very good, very good," he said, turning to take the horse to the corral.

"Thanks again, sir," I called as I started to walk towards the landing area. The old man just waved and kept walking.

The plane was already at the landing area when I got there. The stewardess was waiting by the stairs. She immediately smiled as I approached.

"Good evening, Miss Logan. The pilot says we are all set to go. Would you like me to take your bag?"

"Um, yes," I replied, "but I need to get something out of it first, if you don't mind."

She nodded, "Of course, Miss Logan, whatever you need."

I carefully removed the envelope and then handed her the bag. "Thank you."

The stewardess took it and then gestured for me to board ahead of her. "After you, Miss Logan."

I nodded, smiled briefly, and then boarded the plane. I sat in the same seat as before and noticed the book was still on the adjacent seat. The book would have to wait, this strange letter was much more important. I buckled my seatbelt and waved to the stewardess to let her know I was all set for takeoff. She briefly disappeared into the cockpit, but then soon returned and took her seat at the back of the plane. The pilot's voice came on over the PA system, but I tuned him out. Instead, I opened the envelope and began to read.

Calista Logan,

First of all, we would like to say that we hope you enjoyed your time visiting the Incan ruins of Machu Picchu. They have always been a beautiful sight. We are ones that cherish such things and are glad to see you have similar feelings regarding precious items.

However, we are disappointed to learn that we must, yet again, discourage you of your plans. We felt that we were perfectly clear on what would be the consequences of your actions, but still you choose to ignore us. That would be very unwise. We are beginning to fear that it will take more than just words to cease your search. Violence has never been our preferred way of dealing with such issues, but they are not uncommon to us. We hope that it does not have to come to that. For the last time, we implore you not to go through with your plans on finding Ayden. It is in your best interest to take heed of our words.

Kind Regards,
The Ancients

I carefully folded the letter and placed it back in the envelope. At first, I wasn't really sure how to react to it. I couldn't understand how they knew I still planned on trying to find Ayden. I hadn't even started yet! That strange man from the hotel had not been around me since last night. There hadn't been any other suspicious people following me either. It was all so hard to comprehend.

The letter probably should have discouraged me, as was intended, but it only made me more determined to find Ayden. I tossed the letter on the seat next to me and picked up the book. Thankfully, I was able to enjoy the book's ending before the flight was over.

Six

The plane landed in Rio de Janeiro around three in the morning. The stewardess was nice enough to call a cab company for me so that it would be waiting when we arrived. I told her I really appreciated it even though she didn't have to go out of her way like that. She only smiled back and nodded her head. I shook her hand and then made my way off the plane.

Surely enough, the taxi was waiting nearby, ready to go. I hopped in the back and the slid down on the seat. I was so exhausted from my trip and couldn't wait to climb into bed. I hadn't even realized I had dozed off until we arrived at the hotel. The taxi came to an abrupt halt in front of the hotel. I snapped to attention, paid the driver and got out. The taxi quickly sped off and I walked slowly into the hotel. The concierge was wide-awake and chipper when she saw me. She gave me a huge smile in greeting but I just waved at her quickly as I walked by. I didn't have the energy to deal with her extreme perkiness. I pressed the elevator button to go up. It only took about thirty seconds for the car to come down but it felt like forever. I just wanted to get into my room and crash for the night. The doors opened, so I got in and pressed the button for the fifteenth floor. The dull hum of the elevator was not helping with the fact that I was already exhausted. I tried my best to keep my eyes open. The elevator came to a stop. I got out and headed to my room. My eyes were so heavy; it took me a few extra seconds to actually get the key in the door. Once I got the door opened, I stepped inside and then made sure to lock it. I dropped my bag in the hall next to the bathroom and then headed straight for the bed. I didn't bother getting undressed or pulling the covers over myself; lying down was plenty. The moment my head hit the pillow, I was in one of the deepest sleeps I had had in weeks.

I awoke that morning to the sun shining through the windows and the sound of the ocean crashing against the shore. I felt well rested and ready to begin my search for Ayden. The most recent letter from "The Ancients" didn't even cross my mind. I wasn't planning on leaving until later that evening since I wasn't even sure where I was going to start. First thing to do was take a long hot shower, have a full breakfast and then do some research. I gave room service a quick call before showering to order food and inquire about gaining access to a laptop. The man on the other end of the phone was glad to take my order and he said he would call the front desk himself to get me a laptop. I was extremely appreciative of his efforts. He only replied, "As you wish, ma'am," and then hung up.

The hot water felt great falling over my face and body. It was heaven compared to the very limited amount of hot water I had had back in Egypt. I took full advantage of it and stayed in the shower until the water began to cool.

Stepping out of the shower, I heard a knock on the door. I quickly dried off and grabbed the robe hanging on the back of the bathroom door. I tossed it on and then opened the door. It was room service with my breakfast as well as the laptop I had asked for.

"Good morning, Miss Logan," the young man said. "Breakfast is served, along with the laptop you requested."

"Oh thank you very much. I really appreciate this." I handed him forty-three Brazilian Reais.

His eyes widened. "Oh Miss Logan, this is far too much."

I held up my hand in protest. "No. Please take it, you have been a great help and I feel you deserve something in return."

He blushed a little and then slowly took the money from my hand. I assured him that I was all set with everything and he left with a hurried bow. I sat down at the table and started to eat. The food selection was marvelous. I had asked for a combo meal and it looked like I had ordered a full buffet! There were delicious looking pastries, some cereal, biscuits, and fresh fruit. I knew I couldn't possibly finish it all by myself but I made sure to sample a little bit of everything.

After I had stuffed myself to the brim, I set up the laptop on the table nearest to the balcony. I wanted to sit out on the balcony, but the power cord wouldn't reach, so sitting near the open doors would have to suffice. Luckily the hotel had Internet access as well. I clicked on the browser and watched the home site load. I quickly typed in the address for the Google search engine. Before actually starting a search though, I took out a piece of paper and pen. I needed to really think about the possible places Ayden could be. The first place I wrote down was Greece. I remembered the young boy from Egypt telling me that he had seen Greece written on the letters Ayden had asked him to deliver. It was a possibility, but I didn't want it to be my only option. It was unlikely that he had gone to a single country and stayed there after leaving Egypt. He had said so himself that he was a traveler, like me. He could be anywhere right now.

It was then that I remembered Ayden's accent. Ayden has an Irish accent! Plus he had told me he was born there. It was quite possible that he had gone back to his homeland. I wrote Ireland on the paper and underlined it twice; it seemed promising. Other memories from our time together began to come back to me. Ayden had also told me that he had moved to California with his parents and earned his degree there. The United States immediately became another option; I wrote it down as well.

I leaned back in the chair and looked over the paper; only three options so far. I wasn't really sure if that was enough. However, I didn't really want to waste any more time than I had to, so I decided I would go for Ireland first. I typed Ireland into the search box and click OK. Within seconds I was bombarded with thousands and thousands of websites regarding Ireland. Looked like I was going to have to refine my search. I couldn't recall the town where Ayden was born, but I did remember it was located in Northern Ireland. I tried searching for that instead, and of course, I was again swamped with websites. However, the very first link was called "Discover Northern Ireland." I decided to click on it and see what it had to offer. The website was perfect. It had maps, transportation sites and all sorts of tourist information. I checked out the map first. Ireland itself wasn't all that large, and Northern Ireland was only a small part of the entire island. So it looked like my search wouldn't be too difficult.

Next, I clicked on the "Travel & Transportation" tab to figure out how to actually get there. There were three major airports I could fly into: Belfast International Airport, Belfast City Airport, or City of Derry Airport. I decided to go with the International airport since it was most likely the only airport that received flights from other continents. With that settled, the next step was to actually book the flight.

I was partial to Orbitz.com, so I clicked my way to the site and started typing in the details of my flight. I always made my tickets one-way because I never knew how long I was going to be in one place. The earliest flight I could get was for 5:00pm and it was already noon. I booked it quick and then shut down the computer.

I only had a few hours before I had to leave for the airport, and there were a few things I needed to take care of first. I made sure to call the front desk first and return the laptop. They told me not to worry about it and just leave it in my room; they would take care of it when I checked out. While I had the concierge on the phone, I asked if there were any shops nearby where I could buy a notebook, pens and any other supplies I might need. She explained that there was a gift shop right across the street, that was the best place she could think of. I thanked her, hung up the phone, grabbed my wallet and headed downstairs.

The shop was called *O Pouco Loja*, which in Portuguese means *The Little Shop*. Not very original, but it was still cute. I stepped in and took a quick survey of the place. It was a little dusty, but quaint. The shop owner looked excited to have a visitor. I gave him a smile and proceeded to look for a durable notebook. At the very back of the room was a shelf of notebooks and journals. I picked out one that felt sturdy and had plenty of pages. I also grabbed a small packet of pens, then headed to the front of the store. The man tried to get me to buy some silly souvenirs but I politely declined his persistence. Almost sadly, he rang up my items. I paid and thanked him; he followed me with a smile as I exited the store.

Once I got back to my room, I pulled out the papers that contained my recent dreams. I wanted to copy them into my newly purchased notebook. The notebook was going to serve as a type of journal to record what happened during my search for Ayden. The dreams had to be of some significance and they were obviously tied to my search for Ayden, so they would be my first entries.

By the time I had finished writing out the dreams, along with some personal thoughts on what certain parts of each dream meant, it was time for me to check out and head to the airport. I ripped up the loose papers and tossed them in the garbage. Then I made a quick call down to the front desk to have a taxi arranged to take me to the airport. The concierge was glad to do so, brimming with her usual enthusiasm. I hung up the phone and performed a last check around the room to make sure I hadn't forgotten anything.

I was sure I was set to go. I had grabbed my bag and was adjusting the straps when I noticed something shining in the sun out on the balcony. I hadn't even thought to check out there because I had only gone onto it once or twice during my stay. As I walked closer to the railing, I realized that the object was a necklace. It was nicely laid out on the small table near the front right corner of the balcony. I took a quick observation of the surrounding balconies before picking up the necklace. There was no way anyone could have jumped from one of the adjacent balconies to mine; they were too far apart from each other. And it was completely impossible to have climbed up from the beach; my room was fifteen floors up! I placed my bag on the floor and picked up the necklace to examine it. My heart skipped a beat once I saw the pendant hanging from the chain. It was a silver scarab, finely etched with blue stone for the legs and eyes. I immediately knew that it was a gift from Ayden. My heart began to race from the thought that he had been so near to me and I hadn't even known it. But why would he have done something like this and not even talked to me? And what happened to his promise not to follow me? Even so, the necklace was beautiful and not something I was willing to toss away.

Silently, I thanked him for the gift and placed the pendant around my neck. It hung perfectly against my chest, lingering about a half inch above my breasts. Then, I took one last look out at the ocean and grabbed my bag so I could leave.

The concierge seemed sad to see me go, but I fibbed to her and said I would return someday just so she wouldn't start crying. I hadn't even been there that long and she was all emotional as if I were her best friend or something. Nevertheless, she checked me out of my room and said her goodbyes. I smiled and waved as I left, but the minute I was out the door, she was out of my mind. I didn't have time for sorrowful goodbyes. I had things to do and places to go.

Seven

As before, a taxi was patiently waiting for me. I hopped in and told the driver to take me to the airport as quickly as possible. He merely nodded and stepped on the gas with quite a bit of force. The burst of speed was a bit startling. I wasn't expecting him to take me that literally. I strapped myself in and spent the entire ride watching everything pass by as the taxi sped along, gently playing with the pendant around my neck. Ayden never once left my thoughts.

We arrived at the airport sooner than I had anticipated, but it was fine. I paid the driver and then watched him speed away. I was anxious to get to Ireland, so I went through the check in process right away. Unfortunately I was stopped for a random bag check by security.

"Excuse me, Miss. You've been selected for a random search." The officer was at least polite about it.

"Sure thing, Officer," I replied. "It won't take long will it?"

He smirked. "Not unless you've got something that doesn't belong on a plane."

I chuckled a little, holding out my bag. "I'm pretty sure I don't but knock yourself out."

He took my bag and brought it to a small folding table, motioning for me to follow. Setting down the bag he started to ask the routine questions. "Are you carrying any sharp objects such as a knife or nail file? And could you please remove your shoes?"

"Nope, no sharp objects, Officer." I quickly removed my shoes.

"Alright," he started to rummage through my bag. "Are you carrying any illegal substances?" Another officer had picked up my shoes and was scanning them with some type of device that I wasn't familiar with.

I had to hold back a laugh, "Nope."

After another minute, the officer looked satisfied. He closed up my bag and handed it back to me. "Here you are, Miss. There doesn't seem to be anything in your bag that would pose a threat. You can put your shoes back on now and head to your gate."

I grabbed my bag and then put on my shoes. I thanked the young officer and headed to gate number twelve. There was still another hour and a half till the plane left, so I decided to grab a quick bite to eat. Of course, there was a McDonald's near my gate, as there is in just about every other airport. One can never go anywhere without seeing at least one McDonald's. As much as I didn't want to stuff myself with greasy fast food, the McDonald's was the only place that looked appetizing enough.

With a chocolate milkshake and cheeseburger in my hand, I dropped into the seat closest to the gate entrance. Hopefully I could be first on the plane to grab a rear seat. I took my time eating so as to hopefully help time pass by a little faster. I just wanted to be on that plane.

Right after I had tossed out my garbage, a voice came over the PA system and announced that the plane to Ireland was going to start boarding. I jumped out of my seat and practically ran to the door to be first in line. The ticket clerk ripped off the end of my ticket and handed me the stub. I quietly thanked her and then boarded the plane. Taking my usual seat at the back, I tossed my bag in the overhead compartment and plopped down next to the window. Lucky for me, the plane turned out to be one of the luxury types and each seat had a miniature video screen embedded in the seat directly in front of you. As soon as everyone had boarded, the stewardesses were going through the usual steps of securing the plane and explaining the emergency procedures. I had sat through that routine way too many times and chose to ignore it.

Ten minutes later, we were finally on the runway, ready for takeoff. I waited patiently as the plane charged the runway and made its way into the air. Not two minutes later, the stewardesses were offering headphones for movies, along with beverages and snacks. I gladly accepted a pair of headphones and a bottled water. The choice of movies to be played during the flight was between some French film and the American film *Red Eye*. It was almost fitting since the movie took place on a plane. I decided on that one over the foreign film. I enjoyed my share of foreign films every now and then but this wasn't one of those times. I was looking more for something to just help the time pass.

The movie helped a little bit, but it only took up about two of the eight hours. I decided perhaps it was time to start writing in that journal I had bought. I sifted through my bag until I found it and then sat back down and began to write:

April 15ʰ. My journey starts on the plane to Ireland. Well, it actually started the moment I decided to search for Ayden; that was in Rio de Janeiro. Certain things are coming together now, the more that I pursue this. But there are still so many unanswered questions. Who are these so-called "Ancients"? Why are they so insistent upon my staying away from Ayden? And why threaten me? Do they really think that it will keep me from finding him? I'm not one to scare so easily. It doesn't really matter because I plan to continue this, no matter what happens. I know now that the man I saw in the hotel and the figure near my horse that night were "Ancients." Was it the same guy? I'm not sure. If not, then they must be servants or work for those people in some way. Of course it is obvious that the Ancients are vampires like Ayden. It would also explain how easily they were able to follow me. But who knows what kind of powers they may possess? Ayden was able to read my mind, I know that now. They must be able to do the same. But by the indication of the name these people choose to go by, it's possible that they know much more than Ayden does.

As I write this, I wear a scarab pendant around my neck. I found it on the balcony of my hotel room only moments before I left for the Brazilian airport. It is no doubt from Ayden. I met him in Egypt and the scarab is an important aspect of Egyptian culture. He surely knew that I would recognize it and know it was from him. A gift...a sweet gesture from him but why did he not visit me in person? Why be so secretive? And why break the promise he had written in his letter about not following me? It's possible that the Ancients are watching him and if he was seen with me, there could have been consequences to that. If these Ancients are adamant about me staying away from him, they must be urging him to stay away from me as well.

This trip to Ireland is my first stop in searching for Ayden. When we first met, he told me that he was born in Northern Ireland but he and his family moved to California after a few years. I am not sure how true that story is but he most certainly originally from Ireland—his accent proves it. It's understandable if he fabricated a story to make him sound more human, for he obviously doesn't want to let others know what he is. But I would like to hear his true story and how he came to be a vampire. I take it from the way he reacted to my questions that night by the cemetery, the woman he spoke about must have been the one who made him a vampire. She "took his life." It's the only explanation that would make sense at this point. But that is all I know of her. No name or description. Hopefully, when I find him, I can learn more of her and of his own past. For now, all I can do is stay on course and hope for the best. I am prepared for whatever I may encounter on this journey. But I hope that the Ancients now know that I am serious about my quest and I hope they don't try to stop me. I will not be stopped....

I put down the pen and rotated my wrist. My watch told me that I had been writing for nearly an hour. No wonder my wrist was sore. There was a slight ache in my right shoulder as well; must have been from writing so much. I tried my best to massage out the knot. I looked to my left and noticed a good-looking guy sitting across the aisle. He was looking at me. For a moment I thought I recognized him but then thought better of it. I raised an eyebrow and gave a short wave. He smiled and waved back, then proceeded to move to the aisle seat.

He leaned over the arm of the chair, "Hi there."

"Hi," I replied. "Do I know you?"

He laughed. "No, I don't think so. I had noticed that you were writing. You were writing for a long time. Anything interesting? Are you a novelist or something?"

I looked down at the notebook. "No, no, just my thoughts."

"Oh, cool. I thought you were maybe writing a book or an award winning magazine article. We were very focused," he chuckled a little.

I let out a small nervous laugh. "Oh no, I am not sure if I would be able to do something like that. I'm not very creative."

"Hey, you never know. Some people have hidden talents that they never knew were there. And then one day, poof! It just pops out."

"Are you speaking from experience?"

Again, he laughed. "I suppose, maybe. But then again, I'm not all that creative either. Oh, I'm sorry! I must seem rude. My name is Trent. Trent Murdock." He extended his hand across the aisle.

I politely accepted his hand. "Calista Logan."

"Well, it's nice to meet you Calista. What takes you to Ireland?"

I looked back down at the notebook. "I'm...looking for someone. Someone I miss...a friend."

"I'm looking for someone too," he replied. "Well, more like people...looking for several people."

"Really? Friends? Family?"

"Not exactly. It's just business."

I nodded, not wanting to pry anymore. I changed the subject. "So, have you ever been to Ireland before?"

He nodded enthusiastically. "Oh yeah, I have been there a few times before. It's a beautiful place. Glad to be going back again. What about you?"

"Oh no, I have never been there before. But my friend's family is there so I was hoping that they could help me find him."

"Him, huh?" he asked raising his eyebrows. "Boyfriend? Ex-boyfriend?"

I looked up at him with wide eyes. "Oh no! Nothing like that. He's actually a guy I met during a recent trip and I didn't get to know him as well as I would have liked. I know that sounds bad, I promise I am not a stalker or anything, but he was…really great."

"Oh well, that's understandable. When you find someone like that, you definitely want to know more about them and see if anything becomes of it, right?"

"Well, one can hope." I said the words quietly as Ayden's face floated through my mind.

He tilted his head to one side. "You don't seem too confident about that statement."

I began to twirl the pen in my hand. "Well, I'm sure I am not the only one in the world who has experienced heartache. It's almost as if I am betraying my own heart for having feelings for this guy after I had sworn to never open my heart again."

He reached out and touched my hand. "You can't close off your heart forever. Everyone needs to love and be loved at some point during his or her life. Sometimes it just takes some time because you need to heal. But you shouldn't cut that lifeline too quickly."

I glanced at his hand on mine. A gentle touch, almost like Ayden's. He must have noticed me looking because he quickly withdrew. "Oh, sorry…" He looked at the floor.

"Oh no, don't worry about it. It's fine." A silence fell between us for a few moments.

Finally, Trent spoke up, "Well, I'll let you get back to your writing. I have some things I need to work on as well. It was really nice talking to you. Perhaps we can meet up again in Ireland? I could give you the grand tour." He winked as he made the suggestion.

I was a bit surprised. Was he asking me out? "I don't know, Trent…I…."

He didn't even let me finish. "Please? I promise I'll be good," he said smiling. "Maybe I could help you find this guy of yours."

I was still skeptical. He seemed nice but I had just met him. "I am not really sure...I'd have to think about it."

"No problem! How about I give you my cell number and you can give me a call if you change your mind?"

"Ok, that's fine," I said. He quickly wrote his number on a piece of paper and handed it to me.

"Well, hopefully I'll hear from you later. I'll let you get back to your stuff. If I don't talk to you later, enjoy your time in Ireland. And good luck finding that guy."

"Thanks, good luck to you too." I shoved the paper in my pocket and then went back to my notebook. I had my suspicions about this guy, so I made a quick note of it in my journal. I didn't have anything more to write about Ayden so I put the notebook aside. I spent the rest of the flight looking out the window and watching the clouds float by.

Eight

According to my watch, the plane landed in Belfast International Airport around midnight but I hadn't changed it yet to account for the different time zone. I checked with the flight attendant before leaving the plane. She told me it was actually 6 am. I thanked her and quickly changed my watch.

As I got off the plane I remembered Trent. I hadn't even noticed when he had left the plane and thankfully he wasn't waiting for me outside the gate. It was better off that way. There was something about him that didn't sit right with me. Plus, I could have sworn that I had seen him somewhere before. He looked rather familiar. There wasn't much that could be done about him now so I decided to just ignore it and go find a hotel.

I located the help desk and asked how I would go about getting a cab to get to a hotel nearby. The man at the desk said I didn't have to bother calling a cab. He explained that just about every taxi in the city waited outside in hopes to get business from all the incoming passengers. I thanked him and then headed outside.

Just as the man had said, there were cabs everywhere. I didn't even have to hail one; so many drivers were holding open their doors and waving for people to pick their cab over another. I gave one driver a quick wave to let him know I accepted. Once I got close he offered to take my bag but I told him it wasn't necessary. I slid into the back seat and he shut the door behind me.

After a few minutes, he situated himself in the front seat and asked, "Where'd ya like to go, Miss?"

"Wherever the nearest hotel is please."

He became excited. "Aye miss! The Park Avenue Hotel is the closest one to *this* airport. Best around!"

I nodded to let him know that was fine and then sunk down into the seat. I was excited about being in Ireland for the first time, but I couldn't ignore the butterflies in my stomach. When I got to the hotel I'd have to sit down and figure out what exactly it was that I was going to say when I finally found Ayden. There was just so much to think about.

I didn't bother chatting up the concierge this time. He didn't seem to be in a good mood and I wasn't in that great of a mood either. He checked me into a standard room, which was fine with me this time, and then shoved the key into my hand. I muttered a thank you to him and made my way to my room.

The room was nice, not the "best around" as the cab driver had said, but it was still pleasant enough. There weren't any balconies at this hotel, but that actually made me feel better rather than disappointed. I dropped my bag on the bed and went to the window to check my view. It was actually pretty decent. The hotel was located very close to the center of the city. I made a mental note to make sure to check it out at some point during my trip. It looked like a pretty cool place to explore.

I turned away from the window and walked over to the bed. I decided it was time to relax and really think about what my next plan of action would be. Lying down, I propped myself up on my elbow and pulled out my notebook. I hadn't planned on writing any more but after rereading my notes, I realized I had more thoughts on the current situation:

After meeting Trent Murdock and thinking about everything that has happened so far, I realize that there is more I have to plan now. Much more than I had originally thought. First, there's Trent. Who is he? He seemed like a nice guy but there were certain things about him that aroused suspicion. Why had he been watching me on the plane? I am certain that we had never met before, yet he

63

seemed familiar. Perhaps I had seen him somewhere before. I'd have to think on that some more. Also, he said that he was searching for a group of people. It wasn't friends or family...and he said it was some sort of "business"...it didn't sound like real business in the whole office building sense...enemies maybe? Or maybe he really is here for plain old business. I can't be sure. As suspicious as he was, I can't help but be curious as to what he is up to. I know he can't have any connection with Ayden, or myself, but there's just something about him. Why did he pick me to talk to? There were plenty of other girls on the plane.

Second problem is what exactly am I going to say or do when I finally find Ayden? I wanted to say, "if I find him" but I want to try and stay optimistic. Another thing to think about is if I'll even be able to find him. I can't ignore the fact that these Ancients have threatened my life not once, but twice. I may want to look into buying some sort of weapon to protect myself. Knife? Gun? I think I would prefer the knife. I'll check out the local shops and see what I can find.

Back to Ayden...will he be angry with me for following him? He had explicitly asked me not to in the letter he wrote me in Egypt. But then again, he was the one that came to Brazil and left me the pendant. It had to have been him. I could always use that against him if he chose to argue about it. And what am I to tell him? That I tried to find him because I find him interesting and mysterious? That sounds pretty lame. And he knows that I have feelings for him, but what about what we both vowed about love and relationships? We were both betrayed and had closed off our hearts. Yet it seems like each of us has become a safe place for the other. He is the first person I have opened myself up to ever since that day I found Shane with that girl. And it seems as if I am the first person he has opened up to as well.

I guess the first thing I will do tomorrow is explore the city. See if anyone has seen or heard of Ayden. If I have no luck there, I'll go to the next major city. I guess I will continue that until I have been all over Ireland. If I can't find him, I'll go to the next destination on the list I made back in Brazil. I am certain now that Greece will be my next stop if Ayden isn't here.

I closed the notebook and slid it into the bedside table drawer. As early as it was, I decided to call it a day and rest up for tomorrow. But first I thought it'd be nice to take a hot bath. I went into the bathroom and turned on the water. The bathroom wasn't huge but it was still spacious enough. I rummaged around the place to look for some bath essentials. Sadly, I was unable to find any candles. Probably a fire hazard issue. I was, however, able to find some bath oils and bubbles. Lavender and Jasmine; good combination of scents. I poured a little of each bottle into the tub and then went into the other room to grab a pair of lounge shorts and a t-shirt for bed. When I got back to the bathroom, it was filled with steam, just the way I liked it. Then I remembered that I wanted some music as well so I quickly ran back to the bedroom to get my Discman. I chose a CD of Latino songs to listen to. Finally ready for my bath, I turned off the water, got undressed and eased myself into the hot water. It felt great, immediately relaxing pretty much every muscle in my body. I put on my headphones and pressed the play button. The sound of a Spanish guitar quickly flooded my ears. I leaned back in the tub and closed my eyes. Tonight would probably be the most relaxed night I would have for a while. Finding Ayden was going to be stressful.

A loud pounding on the door snapped me back to reality. I had no idea how long I had been sitting in the tub. It's possible that I had even fallen asleep! Not all that safe of a thing to do but I shrugged off the though. I threw off the headphones and grabbed the nearest towel.

"I'm coming!" I yelled. Who on earth could it be?

I ran to the door and undid the lock. Swinging open the door, I was amazed at whom I saw: Trent.

"Trent!" I jumped back a little in surprise. "What are you doing here? How did you know I was here?"

"Well, it's good to see you too, Calista." He leaned up against the doorframe.

"You didn't answer my question," I said holding my towel up with one hand and placing my other hand on my hip.

He looked me up and down, obviously glad to see me in nothing but a towel. "Did I interrupt something?"

I rolled my eyes. "Yes, as a matter of fact, you did. I was taking a bath before bed. Now I'll ask again, what are you doing here?"

"Oh yeah, sorry," he stood up straight, "I have to admit…I kind of followed you here. I didn't get a chance to say goodbye on the plane and I wanted to ask you about the idea I had suggested. Want a tour of this place?" He gave me a wink, which seemed to be becoming a habit when he was around me.

My hand dropped from my hip. "Look Trent, I know you mean well but I can handle things on my own. Plus, it's more fun for me to explore unknown territory without someone telling me what and where everything is…no offense."

He looked disappointed but persisted. "You don't know what you're missing, kid. I promise it'll be fun." A mischievous smile formed on his face.

I placed my free hand on the door, getting ready to close it. "Like I said, Trent, I know you mean well and all but I'll be just fine on my own. I prefer it that way, actually. Now if you don't mind, I am going to go get ready for bed."

I tried shutting the door but he stopped me. "But it's so early, wouldn't you like to go get a drink or something and talk some more?"

"Trent, please remove your hand from my door. I have a lot to do tomorrow and would like to be well rested in order to do it. So, I'd appreciate it if you would just head back to wherever your hotel is." I tried to shut the door again.

He just wouldn't give up. "Oh, didn't I tell you? I am staying here too. Two floors down. Room 235."

I couldn't believe it. "Are you serious? You're staying here? You really did follow me…and it's starting to creep me out, so could you please go before I decide to punch you?"

He laughed and held both his hands up in the air jokingly. "Ok, ok. Sorry. Wouldn't want you to kick my ass or anything. Well, like I said, if you change your mind…about anything…Room 235." He winked and left with a wave.

I quickly shut the door and locked both the chain lock and the deadbolt. This encounter was definitely notebook worthy. I went back to the bathroom to get dressed and clean up. After that, I double-checked the locks, just to make sure and then went to write. I pulled the notebook out of the drawer and brought it to the small table near the window. I sat down and began to write about what had just happened:

Night of April 15th. I just had the strangest encounter with that guy Trent. He came to my hotel room! And oddly enough, he is staying in this same hotel. He must have asked for my room number at the front desk. Bothers me a bit that the concierge gave it to him without my permission, but I can't really do anything about it now. But just now speaking with him, I am noticing even more weird things about him. I'm not sure if it means anything or not, but he continually winks at me. It could be nothing. He could just be a sleazy pervert. But I also feel like he is hiding something. And it certainly must have something to do with the people he is looking for.

But back to what happened…he came to my room and I had been in the bath. I was wearing only a towel when speaking to him, and as it does for most guys, it was the main part of his focus. The way he was eying me was rather unnerving. The part that gave me the most discomfort was the way he stopped me from closing the door on him. He was so persistent in trying to spend more time with me. What could he possibly learn from talking to me? I have no desire to give him any knowledge of my personal life. The only thing he knows is that I am searching for someone as well, but I made sure not to mention any names or specific locations. I'll have to figure out a way to lose this guy. Tomorrow will be a test. I'll have to make sure that he doesn't follow me to/through the city. If he does, then I'll have to find a way to lose him. If only Ayden were here to help me...he'd get rid of this guy in a heartbeat....

Closing the notebook, my thoughts drifted to Ayden. I actually missed him. This was a different feeling for me than it had been with Shane. When I had first met Shane, I was attracted, yes, but my love for him had grown over time. Whatever this was with Ayden was almost immediate. But I don't think I can call it love. Actually, I am not sure if I even *want* to call it that. Not after what both Ayden and I have been through during our lives. I'd just have to wait and see what happens when I see him again. For now, all I can do is get some rest and then begin the search in the morning. I lay down and closed my eyes. It took me a while to fall asleep though, for my recent encounter with Trent continued to race through my mind.

Nine

I woke up the next morning, soon after sunrise. I went to the window and drew back the curtains. It was a beautiful morning. There was a slight mist hovering above the streets, but it made the city look all the more enticing to explore. And to think that Ayden could be down there, somewhere, perhaps waiting for me to find him. The thought tossed me into a rush. I just had to get out there and start looking.

My shower was perfect in temperature, which tempted me to linger, but I didn't want to waste any more time. I was clean and dressed in under ten minutes. I did a quick run through of what I needed and where I was going to go first. My bag had the usual provisions: water, a couple fruit bars, paper and pens, a map, compass and of course my cell phone. It was basically for emergency purposes only. I pretty much never gave out my number. I didn't even give it to Ayden. I now realize that I should have, it probably would have made my search a lot easier.

The last thing put into my bag was the notebook. I figured it would be a good thing to have in case anything interesting happened. I wanted to record everything and anything that was connected to my finding Ayden.

I was all set to go but I was feeling hungry. I didn't want to wander around Ireland with an empty stomach. I usually didn't have a problem skipping meals but the hunger would often distract me and I'd lose concentration. However, I was concerned about seeing Trent again. It was quite possible that he'd be waiting for me somewhere considering how he randomly showed up at my door last night. I decided it was best to head into the city first and then grab something to eat there. That way, I'd have a better chance of avoiding him.

The concierge informed me that the nearest taxi company was more than ten miles away and it would be quite a wait considering the morning traffic. He recommended taking the local bus. A bus came to the hotel every ten minutes and went straight into the city. I thanked him and went outside to wait for it.

The bus was actually pretty decent. Not grungy or unkempt like you'd see in some American metropolitan cities. It cost me one and a half Euros to ride the bus but that wasn't really that much. I would rather pay that than the twenty or more Euros it probably would have cost me to take a cab. It wasn't too crowded either, probably because it was so early in the morning.

The ride into the city wasn't too long. Maybe about twenty minutes tops. I got off at the first stop just inside the city. I was surprised to find a lot of the shops already open. I checked my watch: 8:15 am. Well, I guess some places open at 7:00 so maybe it wasn't that big of a surprise. The time wasn't bad though; at least I had a good start on the day. First thing first though, I had to get something to eat. I took a quick survey of the surrounding buildings and spotted a small café on the corner. It looked cozy enough, so I thought why not?

I didn't spend more than thirty minutes for breakfast. I had a large area to cover before dark. I know it may have seemed pointless to search for Ayden during the daytime, since I now know he can't be out in the sun, but it didn't matter to me. People would still remember him if he had been around at night on a regular basis. Before leaving the café, I made sure to ask the wait staff if they remembered anyone who had Ayden's description. The men weren't very helpful, they said a few different guys with his description came through. Most of the women said similar things. But then I got a lead from one of the older women. I asked her if she wouldn't mind taking a quick break to answer a few questions. She said she would be glad to help.

"So, you remember meeting this guy that I described to you?" I asked anxiously.

"Oh yes, I remember him. He came here every night for about two weeks solid. This was only about a month ago. I personally waited on him every time he came in. What a gentleman he was." She smiled at the thought.

"Did you ever hear anything from him about where he was staying? Or perhaps anything about where he was planning on going after leaving here?"

"No, my dear, I'm sorry. He didn't speak to anyone all that much. Spent most of his time sitting in a corner." She took off her glasses. It looked as if she was trying to concentrate on something more specific about him. "And he would always order coffee or tea, but I don't recall him ever actually drinking it. Each time I cleared his table after he left, the mug was still full…strange…."

I nodded at this; he had done the same when I first met him in Egypt. "Was there anything else at all that you remember? Something distinct that would lead me somewhere else?"

She wrinkled her brow. "Why yes! Now that you mention it, I think he chose the back corner of the restaurant so he could have some privacy and isolation. He would sit back there and write letters, or he would draw for hours."

"Draw?" Something new that I hadn't known about him. "Did you ever see what he was drawing?"

"Oh, well he was usually pretty good at keeping it away from prying eyes. But I did catch a glimpse once." She paused.

"And?" Urging her to continue.

"Oh yes, sorry my dear. I drifted for a moment. I remember what it was. It was a charcoal drawing of a young woman. She was quite beautiful…" she looked at me and studied my face. Then a huge smile appeared on her face. "Why, it was a picture of *you*, darling! Oh, you must have snagged his dear heart."

I was astonished. A drawing of me? I had trouble finding something else to say to the old woman. I looked at the floor, "Well…I…umm, thank you for your help, ma'am."

She smiled, put her glasses back on and then placed a hand on my shoulder. "You better go after that boy, sweetie. He sure had his heart set on you, I mean, with a drawing like that! No boy draws a pretty girl with such detail as he did without some degree of love in his heart."

I blushed a little and then thanked her again for her help. I left the café not sure how to feel about what the woman had told me. I had to find a quiet place to sit and write. However, as anxious as I was to write, I took my time walking through the town square. I wanted to experience the city life of Ireland. I wanted to feel what Ayden felt when he walked through the streets buzzing with people.

The deeper into the city I went, the more the buildings started to dissipate. Eventually, I came to a park. There was bright green grass everywhere with countless trees and a few picnic tables. There was also a small pond with a few ducks swimming in it. I chose a table near the pond as my writing spot for the afternoon. I took a few moments to watch the ducks play around in the water and then took out my notebook. I began to write about what the elderly woman had told me, and my personal thoughts on the matter:

April 16th. I just had my first breakthrough in finding Ayden. I spoke with an older woman who works at a café towards the outer limits of the city. She said that a man fitting Ayden's description had come in every night for about two weeks. She said that was about a month ago. So he must have been here before going to Egypt since we were there not more than a week and a half ago. Also, the woman said that Ayden would sit at the back corner and write letters and/or draw. I was unaware that he was an artist. I'll have to ask him about it when I speak with him. I am also curious to see these drawings of his...because the woman said that one drawing she caught a glimpse of looked like me! How is that even possible when she claims he was there over a month ago and I hadn't met him until less than two weeks ago?! Is there a chance that he noticed me somewhere else during my traveling and I caught his eye? I can't be sure. Who knows if the drawing the waitress saw was truly me. It could have been a girl who just happens to look like me. I am not really even sure how I feel about the drawing. I suppose I am excited, but at the same time saddened. Why would he think about me that much to sketch me, yet not even attempt to contact me? And now that I am actively looking for him, he probably knows I'm here. So why doesn't he just come to me? He has to know...if the Ancients know, then so must he.

The Ancients also probably know that I have yet again ignored their threats. Something will surely happen soon. But what, I have no idea. Maybe they'll send one of their helpers after me, like the figure I saw at the ruins in Peru. The person most certainly works for them, if he/she is not already one of them. And this all brings me back to Trent. I was lucky not to have to deal with him this morning, but his presence still irks me. Could he possibly be working for the Ancients? He might even be a vampire...the only times I saw him were at night: both on the plane and at my room that same night. I may have to investigate that as well. If I can't find him at some point in the day while I am here, then my suspicions will be close enough to true. I doubt I would be able to get him to take a message to the Ancients for me...they probably sent him here to kill me or something before I got too close enough to Ayden. But at the same time, I wonder if they would order someone to kill me. Would Ayden try to stop them from doing such a thing? I would love to hope that he would, but (as the Ancients have informed me) "he belongs with them." I am going to take another walk through the city, maybe question a few more people. Mostly at places where I think Ayden would have gone: antique bookshops, other cafés, local inns, etc. Hopefully I will be able to get all that done before nightfall. I don't really feel like running into any vampires tonight....

Before I even realized it, the sun had begun to set. It was already late afternoon, which meant I had better start heading back to the hotel. Unfortunately my continuing search would have to wait until tomorrow. I packed up my bag quickly, but decided to take one last look at the ducks in the pond. After a few minutes, I snatched up my bag and headed back toward the city. As I walked, I contemplated grabbing a quick dinner before catching the bus. Not soon after the thought had crossed my mind, my stomach was in total agreement. Maybe there would be a small restaurant I could stop at on my way to the bus stop.

The walk into town seemed to take much longer than the walk out to the park. It didn't help that my stomach started to growl even louder; extreme hunger was kicking in. That dinner stop was going to occur whether I wanted it to or not. I was skeptical about sticking around town at night but then again, I was quite sure I could take care of myself. I don't know what I was getting all worked up about. Vampires or no vampires, whoever happened to cross my path wouldn't deter my quest.

I finally came to a fancy looking restaurant about a half-mile away from the bus stop. It looked like a pleasant place so I decided to check it out. The outside of the building was a perfect disguise for the inside. I had even been fooled. Outside, I thought I was heading into an elegant, expensive restaurant. However, once I stepped inside, I realized I had walked into a typical Irish sports bar. Tricky people, these Irish. I just laughed to myself and went to find a small table near the back.

A waitress came over and took my order. I didn't realize how hungry I actually was until I looked at the menu. But I knew what I wanted as soon as I spotted it: double cheeseburger, well done with fries and pickles, a side order of chicken wings, a large soda and a beer.

The waitress raised an eyebrow and looked me up and down. "Ya sure you can eat all that, honey?"

"Oh yeah, trust me," I said, "I'm starving."

"If you say so honey," she replied. "Ya order will be out soon. I'll be right back with your drinks."

I thanked her as she turned to go to the bar. She must not have believed me after I told her how hungry I was because I could see her leaning over the bar, talking to the bartender. He looked in my direction and smiled. I gave him a little wave to humor them and then turned away. There was a TV located on the wall about three tables in front of me. A soccer game was being shown, I wasn't sure what teams were playing but I wasn't all that interested in it anyways. The waitress returned with my drinks. I thanked her again and took a large gulp of the soda. It was nice to finally have something to quiet my stomach.

I spent the next fifteen minutes staring at the television, even though I wasn't actually paying attention to the game. I was actually thinking about Ayden. It wasn't until the waitress placed my food on the table that I snapped back to reality.

"Are you alright?" she asked politely.

"Oh yeah, I'm fine," I said. "I was just thinking."

"Alrighty dear, here's your order. Give a holler if you need anything else," she said with a smirk and then left to tend to other tables.

I couldn't stand the hunger anymore so I dug right into the burger. When I had gotten through half of it, I suddenly had this strange feeling that someone was watching me. I shivered all over because the thought of someone watching me eat drove me crazy. I put down the burger and quickly surveyed the rest of the bar. As my eyes moved over the opposite end of the bar, a young man caught my eye. I was so startled to see him looking at me that I almost fell off my chair. Before I could move or do anything, a couple guys walked into my line of sight. But the moment they moved, the man was gone. At first I thought that maybe my mind was just playing tricks on me but I was certain I had seen him sitting there. We made eye contact! He was definitely looking straight at me. I took another quick look around the rest of the place, but I couldn't see him anywhere. I decided to not let it bother me too much for now and finished up my meal.

I checked my watch before paying the bill. It was getting late and the busses would only be running for a few more hours. Plus, I still had another half-mile to walk to the bus stop. I dropped my money on the table, grabbed my bag and headed outside.

It was much darker than I had expected. Time zone differences always messed me up the first day or two that I was in a new country, but I would usually get used to it quickly. I was still adjusting since it was my first day in Ireland, so I tried to ignore it and walked briskly towards the bus stop. It didn't take me long to get there, but the bus hadn't arrived yet. That was fine though, I didn't mind waiting. Several people were already there waiting and more continued to show up as the time passed.

The bus finally arrived after about fifteen minutes. As I boarded the bus, I paid the small fair and then searched for a place to sit. There were several open seats but, as always, I preferred sitting at the back. I looked towards the back and was shocked by what I saw. There he was…the guy from the bar I had seen staring at me. He was dressed in dark clothes, as Ayden had always been. He even had similar features as Ayden, except his hair was much shorter and more blonde than Ayden's. I was immediately certain that this young man was a vampire. Probably like one of the guys I had seen in South America: a messenger boy of some sort.

I decided it would not be a good idea to sit back there near him, so I found the nearest seat to where I was standing. How badly I had wanted to pull out my notebook and write about him, write out his physical description but I just couldn't. If he saw me start writing, I was sure he would make the connection that I was writing about him and attempt to take the notebook from me. No, writing was best saved for the isolation and privacy of my hotel room.

Ten

The ride back to the hotel felt like an eternity. Knowing that that man was sitting back there, staring me down, just made time slow down to a crawl. I tried my best to clear my thoughts, figuring that he must capable of reading them. I didn't want him to know that I was a little frightened. I wouldn't give the Ancients the satisfaction they were looking for. But I couldn't help but think of Ayden. Was he nearby? Or had he traveled to some far off place, making it even harder for me to find him? I could only hope that he would help me in some small way. Perhaps give me clues as to where he was. But as time passed, I was becoming more and more certain that if he wasn't in Ireland, Greece was where he would be.

The bus finally arrived at the hotel. I stood up, ready to get off as quickly as possible. I wanted to look back and see what the guy was going to do, but I didn't want to show him any signs of fear. I kept my eyes to the front and got off the bus as calmly as I could. I didn't even look back as the bus drove away. The hotel was right in front of me and I would be safe inside in less than thirty seconds.

I walked quickly through the hotel doors and bee-lined it to the stairs. I ran up the entire four flights and made it safely into my room. I locked the door; double checked the locks and then leaned up against the door, letting out a sigh of relief. However, looking down I noticed an envelope on the floor next to my left foot. I slid my body down the length of the door and sat on the floor. Reluctantly, I picked up the envelope and opened it. Much to my surprise, it wasn't a letter from the Ancients! It was actually a note from the concierge. He said that I had received a phone call while I was out. It had been a young man calling but he didn't leave his name. Apparently the guy said I would know who he was. My heart skipped a beat. It had to be Ayden! I jumped up without reading the rest of the note and ran to the phone.

I pressed the number for the front desk. "Hello? Hello? This is Calista Logan in room 441. I received your note about the young man calling for me. Did he have an Irish accent?"

The man on the end of the line was slow in his answer, "Hmmm…let me think. Well, I think…yes he did, now that I recall it."

Excitement ran through me like an electrical charge, "Did he mention anything about where he was or what it was that he wanted? Were there any noises in the background that you could here to figure out where he was?"

"Slow down, Miss!" the concierge was overwhelmed. "One question at a time. First, he did not say his name. He merely said that you would know who he was just by me telling you he called."

I quickly replied, "Yes, I certainly know who it was now that you confirmed his accent."

"Alright. Next, he did not tell me his whereabouts. He did sound rather urgent to talk to you, but didn't say so. Also, I didn't take the time to listen to the background noises…not my job, Miss."

"Oh of course, I'm sorry. I was just a little over-excited about him calling. Was there anything else he said? Anything at all?"

"Not that I recall."

"Well, thank you very much for your help, sir."

"My pleasure, Miss," he politely replied. "Have a good night."

"Thank you, you too." I hung up the phone.

It was then that I looked back at the note from the concierge and realized there was more to it. Apparently Trent had come looking for me and asked the concierge if he had known where I was. The concierge was nice enough not to give out any information. He obviously wasn't the same person who gave my room number to Trent yesterday. He explained that it was his job to maintain the privacy of all his patrons. I'd have to thank him again for that later. It was time for me to write about yet another vampire encounter. Before doing so, I checked the door locks again and made sure that the windows were tightly locked as well. Satisfied that everything was secure, I pulled out my notebook:

April 16th. Things are continuing to look promising in my search for Ayden; however things are starting to become a bit more frightening. Trent apparently came looking for me today. Good thing I left early this morning. The concierge was nice enough not to tell him where I had gone. He didn't even seem to mention that I had gotten on the bus. Lucky for me.

The most exciting thing that happened was that Ayden tried to call me. If only I had given him my cell phone number, this would have been easier. He called here at the hotel while I was out. The concierge confirmed it by telling me that he did have an Irish accent when he spoke with him. Sadly, he didn't leave any other message other than the fact that he had called. The concierge also told me that Ayden had sounded urgent in trying to reach me but wouldn't say why. I am wondering if he was calling to warn me about his fellow vampires. It's quite possible since these Ancients are so determined in getting me to stop looking for Ayden that they feel the need to threaten me and have their people follow me around.

Speaking of that...I was followed back to the hotel tonight. It was one of the vampires, I know it. He was dressed in the same way I had always seen Ayden dressed: black slacks, a dark colored shirt with a long black overcoat. This man even had similar physical features as Ayden. The main difference was that this guy's hair was much shorter than Ayden's and it was much more blonde. I couldn't see the color of his eyes but I wasn't really concerned with that at the time. I didn't want to get too close to him. Who knows what he could be capable of doing. He could have somehow manipulated me into going somewhere with him or something crazy like that. I just can't allow that to happen, not while Ayden is still out there somewhere.

I didn't have much else to write except for those few paragraphs. But the more I thought about the man from the bus, the more I wondered why he hadn't tried talking to me or send me another warning. Why didn't he try to do anything at all? These people seemed so adamant on me staying away from Ayden, but they didn't seem to be putting a very strong effort into stopping me, except for writing threatening letters and showing up wherever I went. I had just turned on the water to fill up a bath when there was a knock on my door. I wasn't really sure who it could be, but I had a bad feeling it was going to be the one person I didn't want to see. I played it safe and checked the peephole before opening the door. Low and behold, it was Trent. What did this guy want? He was starting to show up when I wasn't really in the mood to deal with him. I opened the door and stood firmly in the doorway so he couldn't push his way in.

"Hi Trent…can I help you?" I gave him a quick look over. There were some gray marks across his cheek, neck and forearms. It kind of looked like chalk or something similar.

"Hey there Calista! I just back from being out in the city. Were you there today? It's pretty great huh?"

"Yes, I did go there today. Got some things done." I wrinkled my nose and pointed to his neck. "Um…what's that on your neck? Is that chalk? Ash? There's some more on your face and arms. Your pants are nearly covered in it! What on earth were you doing?"

He immediately became alarmed, his eyes darting from side to side. "Ash? Really?" he replied, furiously rubbing at the spots I had pointed out. "Wow…interesting. I wonder where that came from…" He slapped his pants a few times and dust flew in all directions.

His reaction alone gave me suspicions. "Were you cleaning out a chimney or something? That's the only place I can think of where you'd get ash all over you."

He completely ignored my question. "Think I could use your sink real quick to wash this stuff off?" He took a step to come into the room.

I quickly put my hand on the doorframe, blocking the rest of the doorway. "Sorry, I don't think that's a good idea. Besides, I just started a bath. I want to be alone for the night."

"Oh, yeah…sure thing, Calista. Well, if you want to afterwards, I'd be up for having a few drinks downstairs. Feel free to come by my room if you're interested."

"Ok Trent, thanks for the invite. Talk to you later." With that, I closed the door and locked it quick.

Even with the door shut he continued to try and talk to me. "Well, ok then! Sorry I bothered you! Maybe I'll see you later!"

"Yeah, maybe Trent," I called through the door. "Bye bye now!"

I took a look through the peephole to see if he had left yet. He stood there for a few seconds, looking at the door, still rubbing at the ashen spots on his arms. Finally, but reluctantly, he turned away and walked down the hall.

I went into the bathroom and poured some oils into the water. As I waited for the rest of the tub to fill, I got undressed. As I took off my clothes, I for some reason began to think about Ayden. Not just thinking about *him*, but thinking about what his body might look like naked. I remembered my last time with him. His arms were so muscular. I would in no way be surprised if the rest of his body was the same. He had a slender build but that didn't mean he didn't take care of those abs. The thought of him having a washboard stomach just made me melt inside. I almost felt ashamed thinking about him that way. I turned off the water and stepped into the tub. Visions of Ayden being in there with me started to fill my mind. Blushing, I sank down into the water and tried to get comfortable. As much as I wouldn't have minded naked thoughts of Ayden to flood my mind, I forced them out. I'd save those thoughts for another day when vampires weren't stalking me and creepy guys covered in ashes weren't showing up at my door.

After about forty-five minutes of sitting in the tub, I decided it was time to do some more research. As much as I wanted to continue physically searching Ireland, I was beginning to get a strong feeling that Ayden wasn't here. My instincts were still telling me Greece was the place to go next. I called down to the front desk to see if they had a computer I could use to gain access to the Internet. The concierge said that there was only one laptop and it was currently being used by another guest. I asked him if he didn't mind telling me who was using it. I thought he was going to give me the same excuse he had given Trent when he was looking for me but he was quick to answer. Interestingly enough, Trent was the one using the computer. I rolled my eyes and thanked the concierge for his help.

Hanging up the phone, I was feeling really disappointed about the laptop. I was not really in the mood to go beg Trent for a quick use of the computer. But I was too set on getting to Greece as soon as I could so I decided to give it a try. I got dressed and then headed downstairs to room 235.

Trent was more than happy to see me when I came knocking on his door. "Calista! Came by to go get a drink with me?"

"Actually, no Trent…I came by because I need to use the hotel laptop. I was told you were using it."

A smile came across his face. "Oh, I see. What do you need it for, if you don't mind me asking?"

"Well, Trent, if you want the truth, I am planning on leaving tomorrow so I need it to book my plane tickets. So, can I use it please?"

His smile faded. "Yeah, sure thing," he stepped aside, inviting me into his room. "Welcome to my room. I'm sure it's very similar to yours."

I stepped inside and looked around. "Yeah I guess, except my bathroom is on the right, not the left."

He shut the door and looked towards the bathroom. "Really? Interesting." He walked past me and into the main part of the room.

I quickly followed him. "So…what are you using the laptop for, if you don't mind me asking?"

He smiled again. "So now you're interested in what I do?"

"Hey, you asked me first. I was only asking what you were using it for. You don't have to tell me if you don't want to," I quietly snapped at him.

"Hey hey," he put his hands up in protest, "no need to get feisty. I was just playing with you. I'm using it for some research on the people I am looking for. It's amazing the stuff you can find on the Internet."

I nodded in agreement. "Yes, it can be quite helpful. And I remember you mentioning looking for these people you mentioned. But you never told me exactly who it was you were looking for." I was anxious to try to get some information out of him.

He walked over to the table where the laptop was and quickly clicked out of the window he had open on the desktop. "It's not really important who they are. You needn't worry about that."

I wrinkled my brow in frustration; that wasn't the answer I wanted and it was a strange answer at that. "Well, I am willing to listen if you ever feel like talking about it. Just to let you know."

He turned to me and smiled. "Why thanks, Calista. Good to know there are still some decent people in the world. Anyways, here's the laptop. Do you want to use it here or take it back to your room?"

"Oh, I can use it here, if that's ok with you. It won't take me very long."

"It's no problem whatsoever. Take your time. I'll just sit here and watch some TV while I wait." He plopped himself down on the bed and turned on the TV.

I sat down at the table and opened up the browser. I immediately went to Orbitz.com. I was eager to check the browser history to see what Trent had been looking at, but I resisted since he was so close by. He would probably notice and then ask me to leave.

It only took me five minutes to book my flight but I was a little disappointed because I wasn't able to get an early morning one. My plane was scheduled to leave at 4:25pm. I was about to take a quick look at Trent to see what he was up when he got up and headed to the bathroom. Perfect! It was my chance to see what he had been looking at before I came by his room. The second the door snapped shut; I opened up the browser history. When I looked at the names of all the websites he had gone to, I could have fainted right then and there. Every single one had something to do with vampires. There had to be at least twenty to thirty different sites listed.

Before I could close up the window, Trent emerged from the bathroom. He must have known that I was going to look at the history the second he was out of sight.

He walked up to the table and stood across from me. "Well, I take it you looked at the search history to see what I have been researching?"

I nodded. "I'm sorry Trent...I was curious. You've been making it sound so mysterious, how could I not look?"

He shrugged. "Oh well, I am sure you were suspicious already and you would have eventually found out about it anyways. It's usually easy to keep my job a secret but when I run into people that are suspicious of everyone, like yourself, then it gets more difficult."

"So...what is it that you do?"

"Well, to put it bluntly...I hunt down and kill vampires. I'm known as a slayer."

I nearly fainted. "Vampires?" I grabbed onto the table to keep myself from falling out of the chair. But I kept my cool and played with it.

He quickly reached out a hand to help me regain my balance but then drew himself back. "Yes, vampires. They do exist. I have been tracking this one guy for a long time now but he continues to slip through my grasp. And to be honest, I think you've been contacted by a vampire...if not more than one." He glared down at me.

I went straight into defense mode. "What?! What are you talking about? I've never believed in them so how would I know if I came into contact with one or not?"

He pulled out the chair in front of him and sat down. "I followed you today. I saw the man dressed all in black staring at you from across the bar. I watched him follow you onto the bus. I was unable to catch him though. He's much smarter than the others, which tells me he's older. Most of the vampires I kill are newly made. They haven't had the time to adjust to their powers so they become careless and are easier to find and exterminate."

I accidentally let out a small laugh, and received a glare in return. "I'm sorry. This just all sounds really silly to me. Vampires are only known in stories and legends. It's never been proven that they truly exist."

He laughed at this. "You only *think* that it hasn't been proven.

Many people know about them, it's just been kept a secret. The ones who know don't want the world to know about vampires. It would cause worldwide havoc and maybe even cause the vampires to all come out of hiding and try to take over. But the vampires also don't want us humans to know about them. We are their main source of food. If we were to know about them, it may cause us all to do what I do…hunt them down and kill them."

"But how do you know who is a vampire and who is human? Don't they look like regular people?" I asked.

"Of course they look like us. You just have to know what to look for. They have certain mannerisms that are unlike ours. It's hard to see unless you are specifically looking for it. I've been trained to do so."

My eyes widened. "Wait…trained? People are recruited for this sort of thing?"

"No no, most of us are slayers because we *choose* to be. There are the occasional recruits every now and then but that's really rare. Those that choose, come looking for us and we allow ourselves to be found and that new person in turn, becomes a member of our team. Most slayers that you'll ever talk to will tell you that they decided to become one because they ran into a vampire at one point in their life. And a large percentage of the time, the vampire had killed someone the slayer knew and/or loved."

I looked up at Trent. "So, is that your story?"

He turned his head to look out the window, "I ran into a vampire once. But he didn't kill someone I knew. He fed on me." He looked back at me and pointed to two small, circular scars where his neck meets his shoulder.

I leaned forward to get a better look. "You've got to be kidding me."

"Does it look like I'm kidding?!" he yelled, pointed at his neck. He was starting to get angry and I didn't really want to be around for it.

I stood up, ready to leave. "Look, I didn't mean to make you angry. This is all just very hard to believe."

He stood up as well. "I know, I'm sorry. I didn't mean to yell at you. It's just a touchy subject with me. Please, sit down."

I slowly sat down again and watched him sit as well. "So, how exactly were you able to escape whoever it was that bit you?"

"I didn't escape. I was completely helpless and the bastard left me for dead in an alleyway." He looked down at the floor as if ashamed by it. "I was lucky, however…a slayer had been tracking him and saved my life. It was just too bad that he killed the vampire *after* he had fed on me. I would have loved to track that asshole down and kill him myself! But, the slayer who saved me became my mentor and I have been doing this ever since that day…fifteen years…."

"I don't want to sound naïve or anything but…I thought vampires couldn't be killed."

Trent laughed loudly. "Of course they can be killed! What do you think I've been doing for half of my life? Sunlight works great but it's hard to capture them so close to sunrise. Capturing them alone is hard enough; they have multiple times more strength than the average human. Silver is the next best thing. I prefer silver bullets but I have become good with bow and arrow, using silver arrowheads. Guns are usually too loud unless you use a silencer. Forget crosses…they usually don't do shit. Garlic is a good way to startle them, it works just like pepper spray would to a human, but besides that it's pretty much useless."

I leaned back in the chair. "Wow…I never knew any of this."

He propped his feet up on the table. "Yeah, not many people do. The books and movies are full of alterations and fabrications."

"You know, I am actually surprised you are even telling me any of this. Don't you slayers have some kind of agreement of confidentiality? Everything within your group stays within your group type of thing?" I raised one eyebrow as I awaited his answer.

His eyes widened with a bit of alarm. "Well, naturally it's not common practice to share this sort of information with common folk but since I have come across evidence that leads me to believe you already have been or perhaps will come into contact with a vampire, I feel you should know this stuff. It's important to protect yourself against those blood-suckers."

A silence fell over us and all I could think about was getting out of there so I could find some way to warn Ayden. I wasn't going to let this guy kill him. "Trent…it's been interesting but I really ought to go pack…my plane leaves tomorrow afternoon and I need to be well rested for the flight."

Trent quickly dropped his feet to the floor. "Wait, are you sure you have to go? Sure you don't want to get some drinks downstairs and chat some more? I could give you some pointers on how to escape if you find a vampire tailing you!"

"I'm positive Trent…I really need to get some rest, it's been a long day." I stood to leave and Trent followed suit.

"Well, if you have to go, you have to go. But remember what I said…I really think you've been contacted even though you may not know it." He quickly walked over to the nightstand, grabbed something and then handed it to me. "Here's my card in case you run into some unsavory people…if you get my drift. They could very well be vampires."

I hesitated but then decided I better take the card to be nice. "Ok…thanks…" I slipped it into my pocket.

"So anyways…where are you going tomorrow?"

I started to walk towards the door. "Somewhere else…I found out my friend isn't here."

"Oh that's too bad…hope you find him."

I opened the door. "Thanks." I left, closing the door behind me.

I didn't waste any time getting back up to my room. I had much to write about and I was starting to have trouble handling all that Trent had told me. Once I was in my room and had the door locked, I sank the floor and let the tears flow. This couldn't possibly be happening. I had just spent time with a man who was searching for the same man I was…but the problem was that this man wanted to kill my Ayden! The worst part was that I really had no way in stopping him. I couldn't tell any authorities about Trent and what he does; they'd lock me up in a nuthouse. And now that I know he carries around weapons to kill vampires, I couldn't physically stop him alone. I hadn't even bought myself a knife like I had originally planned. Also, finding Ayden was hard enough as it is…how was I to warn him?

I let myself cry it out for about ten minutes and then finally gained composure. I had to write everything down that Trent had told me before I forgot about it. Wiping my eyes, I stood up and went straight to writing in my notebook:

Night of April 16th. Everything has just gone into a violent downward spiral. Trent Murdock has just informed me that he is a vampire slayer...apparently he has been doing this for the past fifteen years. The reason this all came out is because I went to his hotel room to see if he wouldn't mind me using the hotel laptop quickly. I checked his search history (because I'm nosy like that) and every website listed was about vampires in some way. My suspicions about him were justified although he's not a vampire or vampire messenger like I had originally thought...but I never thought we would be connected through a vampire...The worst part of it all is that I have no way of contacting Ayden to warn him, nor am I able to stop Trent on my own. He basically told me that he carries around guns with silver bullets and a bow and arrow with silver arrowheads. Plus, I'd sound like a lunatic if I went to the police! I guess the best thing I can do is follow my instincts that are telling me to go to Greece.

That's why I went to Trent's room: to book my flight to Greece. After today's events, there's just something inside that tells me Ayden is not here in Ireland. The old woman at the café said he had only been here for two weeks a month ago and Ayden had called me. Why would be call me if he was actually here? Wouldn't he come see me in person?

The little boy from Egypt had said the letters Ayden sent out were going to Greece. Perhaps I should have gone there in the first place. If I had, maybe I wouldn't have run into Trent and gotten into this mess. I was lucky that Trent believed my playing stupid. And I wasn't about to tell him that I had had several encounters with different vampires, let alone that I had actually talked to one or even worse yet that I have feelings for one! He probably would have never let me go. So now all I can do is go to Greece and hope that I find Ayden. There is so much that needs to be talked about....

I closed the notebook and let out a yawn. I had to get some sleep; packing could wait till the morning. Of course, I checked the door and window locks one last time. Satisfied, I quickly washed my face and brushed my teeth. Then I changed clothes and climbed into bed. It took quite some time before I fell asleep, but that was only because feelings of worry continued to fill me until I felt like I was going to burst.

Eleven

The morning couldn't have come sooner, but I was more than relieved. Even though there was still six hours to go before my flight left, I planned on going to the airport as soon as possible. And hopefully I would be lucky enough not to run into Trent on my way out. I didn't want to have another awkward conversation with him.

Since I had plenty of time to get ready to leave, I took full advantage of it. The hot shower was a blessing; spending a good forty-five minutes in there was practically heaven. It gave me some time to think out a plan if I did happen to see Trent downstairs. And that's when it hit me: I didn't clear the browser history on the computer before I left! He could easily go back and check my flight plan to see where I was going. He did ask me while I was there, but I wasn't planning on telling him. If I had said Greece, he surely would have made plans to follow me. But it was quite possible that he already planned to follow me there. Maybe he didn't buy my act as easily as I thought he had. He probably played me right back so that I would think he was off my case. Looked like from here on out, I would have to keep an eye out for him and make sure I didn't lead him straight to Ayden. That could be exactly what Trent was hoping I would do.

As I dried off and dressed, I continued to think of what I would say to Trent if I saw him. If he were trying to play me, he wouldn't mention Greece at all. Probably in hopes that I wouldn't suspect him of following me there. However, maybe there was a way I could either lose him or trick him into thinking I was headed somewhere else. Well, a combination of the two could possibly work. I was heading to the airport super early. That would give me plenty of time to walk around the place and even hang around the wrong departure gate to make him think I was taking a different flight. It might just work. And as long as the place was crowded, I could easily slip away and be out of his sight before he even realized it. Yes…it had to work.

I finished dressing and packed up all my belongings. I wanted to make a run into town first so that I could buy a few provisions. Then I would go straight to the airport from there. I picked up my bag, did a quick double check of the place to make sure I had everything and then headed out the door. I decided to take the stairs down to the lobby. Trent seemed like an elevator guy, so the stairs seemed a better way to avoid running into him.

Once in the lobby, I went straight for the front desk. No time to waste in checking out, I had to get going. The concierge tried to throw me some pitch to get me to stay there longer. I told him I couldn't because of a family emergency. He immediately gave his condolences and checked me out of my room. I thanked him and went outside to wait for the bus. So far, so good; no sign of Trent.

Just as the bus was pulling up to the curb, there he was: Trent coming through the front doors. I almost panicked. But I kept my cool and got on the bus as quickly as I could. I made my way to the back and watched the front, waiting for Trent to board. Interestingly enough, he didn't get on the bus. I looked out the window and saw him getting into a taxi. He was carrying two bags. That told me he had checked out as well and things were not looking good for me. I couldn't help but suspect that he was heading to the airport. No matter, he could try all he wanted; I still wouldn't let him get to Ayden. I'd stake my life on it.

The ride into town was longer than the day before. Too much traffic. The city itself was more crowded than the day before as well. There were dozens of people everywhere I looked. I had to push through a large crowd in order to get into the store. I tried to make my visit in the store as short as possible. I grabbed the essentials I needed for the trip and anything else I felt was necessary. I paid and went outside to wait for the next bus that would drop me at the airport. Sadly, I was informed that it was behind schedule due to the traffic. I'd have to wait twenty-five minutes instead of the usual ten. Good thing I carried around a crossword book with me to pass the time. I pulled it out of my bag and started on a new puzzle. Thankfully it worked and the time went by so quick, the bus had arrived almost before I realized. Another twenty minutes and I'd be at the airport. I could only hope that Trent was not waiting for me.

The airport wasn't as busy as I had expected it to be. It gave me both an advantage and disadvantage. Less crowding meant I would be able to spot Trent more easily however; it would make it harder for me to lose him if I needed to. I walked quickly to the nearest ticket kiosk so I could print out my ticket. Right as I pressed the print button, there was a tap on my shoulder. Every muscle in my body tensed. It was Trent...I just knew it. I slowly turned to face him.

He had the biggest grin on his face. "Hey Calista! Fancy seeing you here!"

I gave him a confused look. "Umm...actually, not really considering the fact that you knew I was leaving today. What exactly are you doing here?"

"Oh, I'm heading out too," he quickly replied, "but don't worry! I'm not stalking you, I promise." He gave me one of the infamous Trent Murdock winks.

I knew he was lying. "Oh really? One can only hope...where is it that you're headed to?"

Though, to my surprise, he whipped out his plane tickets and showed them to me. "I'm off to Russia, pretty lady."

"Russia? That's an interesting place to be going to...wouldn't be my first pick for a vacation, or let alone a place for vampires to hang out."

He looked around in alarm. "Careful what you say in public! You never know who's listening."

My expression was full of confusion again. "But Trent...it's daytime." I turned to take my printed ticket as I said this.

He relaxed a little. "Yes, I know. But still, who knows if they have people working for them. They are powerful beings. We have come across instances where a few humans have become almost like pets and do anything their master tells them. It's quite sad actually." He took another look around the immediate area.

I couldn't help but laugh. "I'd like to doubt that, Trent. But I suppose you never know. So, what's in Russia?"

"Special, mandatory meeting. Some important issues need to be discussed. You never told me where you were headed, Calista."

"Well, it's not where you're going, I can tell you that," I replied with a smile.

"Oh come on, Calista! Not even a hint! I told you flat out where I am headed. Even told you what I was going there for!" It sounded like he was starting to get a little frustrated with me.

"Well, I suppose that would only be fair. I'll tell you where I'm going, but that's all. And you'll just have to accept it or I won't tell you at all! Understand?" I was putting my foot down; no more prying from him.

"Alright, fair enough," he backed away from me a little. "You're entitled to your privacy, just like everyone else."

Holding up my ticket I said, "I'm going to Greece. OK? And my plane leaves within a couple hours so I need to go check in and get something to eat before boarding. You should probably think of doing the same."

He nodded. "Yep, yep, I'll be sure to do it. Perhaps we could grab a bite to eat together. Which gate is yours?" He never seemed to give up.

I took a quick glance at my ticket. "Gate 13. You?"

He also checked his ticket and then a frown appeared. "Bummer. Looks like I am at the opposite end: Gate 2. Guess we'll have to rain check it, huh?"

"Yeah, sure Trent. Another day." I pulled my passport out of my bag and turned to head towards the security check-in. "See ya, Trent. Have a nice flight."

I thought he would follow, but I didn't hear his footsteps. "Oh I'm sure you will, Calista…enjoy your flight as well," he called.

I didn't look back to see if he was planning on following or not. It didn't matter anymore now that I knew he was headed to a completely different country than me. I took in a deep breath of relief as I dropped my bag on the conveyor belt at the security checkpoint.

Luckily I wasn't selected for a random check like I had been at the last airport. Who knows if those checks are even random. I am sure they pick people with strange names because they'd never suspect Miss Susie Homemaker to be a terrorist. I mean, I know that Calista isn't an average everyday name, but my last name isn't all that different from the next guy's. Oh well, I guess there's not really much one can do about it.

I grabbed my usual airport meal before heading to the gate: double cheeseburger and a chocolate shake. I took the seat nearest to the door so I could be one of the first to board the plane. I had another hour to wait, so the food and my crossword book kept me occupied until then. I got through three puzzles before the plane arrived. A young girl had sat next to me and even tried to help. I thought the puzzles would be difficult for her but she managed to figure out a couple of the answers. I began to talk with her as we stood waiting to board the plane.

"So you're headed to Greece, huh? Are you traveling with your parents?" I politely asked.

She looked over her left shoulder and I followed her gaze. "That's my mom," she pointed to a woman not too far from where we were standing. "We are going to Greece to see my dad."

"Well that sounds exciting," I replied. "Is he there for his job or something?"

"His job is in Greece," she said softly, "he lives there. We are just going to visit. We don't live with him…Mom and Dad don't love each other anymore." She looked at the floor and dragged her feet as we walked towards the door.

"I'm sorry to hear that, sweetie. But you should be happy that you are getting to see him. Have you ever been to Greece before?" I asked, trying to cheer her up a little.

She looked up at me with a smile. "Oh yes! We have visited Daddy loads of times. I love it there. I wish I could live there with him. It's so nice."

"That's good to hear. I've never been there before. This will be my first visit. I'm going to visit a friend of mine."

"Don't worry, lady. You'll like it so much that you'll never want to leave! I never want to leave when I go there. I think the reason Mom always comes on the trip with me is because she is afraid I won't come home. But she tells me that she comes because I'm not allowed to fly alone until I get older." She glanced in the direction of her mother.

"Well, it's good to know that your mom cares about you that much, you know? But I am sure if you show her that she can trust you, she'll let you go on your own someday."

The girl smiled up at me and nodded in agreement. "I will certainly show her! Dad already knows how responsible I am, but Mom just needs to catch up I guess." She giggled.

At this point, it was our turn to board the plane. The clerk took our tickets and let us pass through.

The young girl gently poked at my elbow and asked, "Can I sit with you?"

"Actually, I wouldn't mind that at all. Sometimes it's nice to have a flying buddy."

She smiled with glee. "Where will we sit? My mom always makes me sit in the front but I don't like it."

I laughed a little. "Well, I rather like sitting in the back of the plane. I just feel more comfortable back there. Sitting at the front makes me feel like everyone is staring at me from behind."

"I have always wanted to sit back there but Mom never lets me!" She nearly took off in a sprint, tugging on my arm. "Let's go before everyone else takes the seats!"

"Whoa, whoa!" I gently pulled her back. "No need to run kiddo, there'll be plenty of room for us, ok?"

She frowned slightly, but then nodded. "Oh yeah! My mom will probably yell at me for sitting with someone I don't know." She held out her hand to shake. "My name is Aspen. What's yours?"

"Aspen huh? Mine's Calista." I politely shook her hand. "How'd you get that name? It's very pretty."

"Thanks! So is yours. My parents named me after the Aspen Tree." She leaned close and whispered, "They were Hippies."

I couldn't help but laugh. "I see."

"What about you?" she asked. "What does your name mean?"

"It means 'most beautiful' but I am not really sure why my parents chose that one."

We found two seats next to each other in the very last row. Aspen grabbed the window seat. She said she loved watching the clouds pass by while in the air. It made her feel like she was flying. I didn't really have a preference on seating so I didn't mind.

Once I was settled in my seat, I took a quick survey of the cabin. I was just making sure that Trent had told me the truth and wasn't on the plane with me. There was no one there that even resembled him so I relaxed. I leaned back in my chair and closed my eyes. Aspen asked if I was going to sleep during the ride. I told her that I was kind of tired and I might sleep at first, but I would be sure to wake up before we landed. I think she wanted to talk to me some more, but I was a bit too tired to listen. However, she was really good and was able to keep herself entertained while I slept. I handed her my crossword book in case she got bored later before I woke up.

Twelve

I woke up about an hour before we were scheduled to land in Greece. I asked Aspen what she had done during the time I was asleep. She explained that she had a brought a book with her and read most of that. She had tried working on a crossword puzzle but some of the clues were a little too difficult so she gave up. Apparently, she had also crept passed me to visit her mother up towards the front. I asked how her visit up front was. Apparently her mom wasn't too happy about Aspen sitting in the back with me, but Aspen turned the situation into a chance for her to show her mom she was trustworthy and responsible. I congratulated her on her quick thinking.

For the rest of the flight, I just listened to Aspen talk about her father and how much she wanted to live in Greece with him. As much as I liked the kid, my mind was on other things since we were so close to Greece. I had to start figuring out where I was going to go first in my search for Ayden. If I couldn't find Ayden first, perhaps I could find the woman he was sending letters to. She had to know where to find him. However, how much help she would actually be to me was hard to determine. What if she was a vampire too? I hadn't even thought about it. It was possible that Ayden may have a human confidant but she could just as well be a vampire. Then it hit me: she could very well be one of the Ancients! It was more than a possibility. The young Egyptian boy said he had sent out several letters to this woman in Greece. If Ayden trusted enough in her to send her so many letters, she had to be like him. It was probably well discouraged by the Ancients to have close relations with humans: too dangerous; their existence could be too easily unveiled.

Our plane finally landed at Athens International Airport. Aspen was upset that we had to part ways.

"But can't my mom and I stay with you, Calista? I could be your tour guide!" Her mother was gently tugging on her hand, urging her to leave.

I patted her on the head. "I'm sorry kiddo. I have things I must do on my own. And I'm sure you and your mom are eager to go see your dad."

Her eyes watered as she looked up at me. "But Calista…"

I shook my head. "No Aspen, I'm sorry. But please don't be sad. Things will be ok. Make sure that you behave and show your mom what a responsible young lady you are."

The frown finally left her face and she nodded. "Will I ever see you again?" she asked. Her voice was full of hope.

"I honestly don't know, Aspen." I felt awful saying it, but it was the truth. "You never know, but keep your eyes open while you're here. Maybe we'll bump into each other at some point."

She smiled and then came to hug me. Her hug caught me off guard and I nearly fell over. Once she let go, Aspen gave her mother the signal that it was OK to leave. Her mother looked relieved. I watched Aspen wave as her mother pulled her off the plane. I waved back, but then my mind immediately switched into thoughts of Ayden.

Stepping outside was both nerve-racking and exhilarating. This could turn out to be a place of a wonderful reunion or a complete disaster. My first order of business every time I would go somewhere was to go to the nearest hotel to rent a room. However, a hotel was far from my thoughts at that moment. I wanted to start looking for Ayden immediately. It was mainly because it was almost dark, which meant he would hopefully be out and about soon and I should have an easier time finding him.

The only thing I could think of to do first was to go around and ask people if they had seen Ayden. Also, it would help to see if I could find out about the mysterious woman Ayden had been writing to while in Egypt. Most people I asked said they might have seen Ayden around but weren't really sure. I had a hard time trying to explain the woman I was also searching for, mainly because I had no name or description of her.

I was about to give up my search for the night when I stumbled upon an old bookshop. I decided to take a quick look inside. The owner seemed excited to have a visitor in his store. Even though I was expecting to be disappointed, I figured I would give it a try and ask the owner about Ayden.

"Excuse me sir, I don't want to be a bother but I was wondering if you could help me with something. I am looking for someone."

"Yes yes, who might you be looking for young lady?" He seemed very anxious to talk with me.

"Well, I am looking for a young man. He's about five foot ten with hazel eyes, strawberry blonde hair. He looks pretty young, probably between 25 and 30 years old. Have you seen him?"

The old man was more than enthusiastic. "Oh yes! My dear boy, Ayden. He is one of my best customers!"

He knew him by name! I felt like dropping to the floor from the wave of sudden relief I felt. I grabbed the nearest wall to steady myself. "Oh thank god," I whispered to myself. "I think I've finally found him."

The old man quickly grabbed a chair for me so I could sit. "Please Miss, sit down. You look slightly ill. Can I get you anything? Water?"

"No, no, thank you, I'm alright. Is there anything more you can tell me about Ayden?" I asked, trying to catch my breath. My heart was racing.

He pulled up a chair and sat across from me. "Why yes dear, he comes in here at least once a week. He always buys several books each time he comes in. He's been very polite in letting me know which weeks when he won't be able to make it in."

"Ah, yes," I replied. "Those must be the times when he travels."

"That's right," he continued, "and each time he returns, he brings me a souvenir from his journey. I now have a wonderful collection of trinkets upstairs. It's wonderful of him to do such a nice thing since he knows I have never been outside of the country."

I nodded and smiled. "Yes, he is very sweet like that."

The man wrinkled his brow, "I am curious, Miss...how is it that you know Mr. Ayden? I have not seen you in these parts before."

"I met him in Egypt. We had a wonderful time getting to know each other but he never left me a phone number or address to reach him at. I only remember him mentioning Greece so I decided to come find him myself."

The left corner of his mouth crept up. "Smart girl."

"Thank you sir, but I have another question for you."

"Of course my dear, what is it?"

I hesitated, but then decided to ask anyways. "Have you by any chance ever seen Ayden with another woman? I am sorry I have no name or description, I only know *of* her."

He frowned just slightly. "Yes, I am sorry to inform you that I have seen him with another woman before. He brought her here one night, but that was the only time I have ever seen her."

I was both disappointed yet intrigued. "What did she look like? Did you happen to catch her name?"

He leaned back and laughed a little. "Yes, yes, one question at a time my dear. She is quite a beautiful lady. Probably no more than thirty-five. Her hair was black and curly, very long. And her name…I'll never forget that name. Ayden only said it once, but once was enough…Sabine. It's probably one of the most beautiful names I have ever heard."

I bowed my head at his description of her. If she was as beautiful as this man said, vampire or not, how was I to compete with that? "Yes, that is a beautiful name."

He leaned forward and rested his hands on his knees. "There was one thing that struck me as odd with her though."

My interested was sparked at this. "Really? What was it?"

He squinted his eyes as if he was remembering the image of her. "It was her clothing. She was wearing a red velvet dress. Beautiful yes, but it was extremely old fashioned. Certainly not of this day and age attire. It looked like she had just come straight out of Medieval Times! Although, she looked quite natural in it, people don't dress like that anymore."

"That's rather odd, but interesting," I replied.

"Yes…yes it is. Oh! And did I mention the mansion?"

My eyes opened wide with excitement. "Mansion? What mansion?"

"Oh, I must not have mentioned it. I thought I did. My mind is getting too old and sometimes I think I have said something when I have really only thought about it. Yes, mansion. There is a large mansion located just a few miles out of town. I would assume that that is where Ayden resides. Every time he leaves my store, he *always* walks in that direction. If he were to be anywhere, it would probably be there. Since he obviously has the means to travel so often, continues to buy from me *and* bring me souvenirs, I assume someone of his stature would live in a mansion like that. It just seems to fit."

This was better than I ever could have imagined. Not only did this nice man confirm Ayden and personally know him, he knew where Ayden lived! I thanked him many times and even purchased one of his books as a token of my appreciation. He was very pleased and told me I was welcome back any time. He also wished me luck and hoped that everything turned out all right when I spoke with Ayden. I thanked him again and again and then headed outside. The man followed me out so he could point me in the direction of the mansion.

"You really can't miss it, my dear. It's straight on this road, just a couple miles over the border. It's completely isolated. But be careful, it's dark now and the crime rate in this town has increased quite a bit over the years. Would you like me to find you an escort?"

"Don't worry, I'll be fine. I can take care of myself. But thank you again for all your help. I can't even tell you how much I appreciate all this."

We shook hands and then I started walking in the direction the old man indicated. With every step I took, I could feel my heart beating faster. I could only hope that Ayden truly did live at this mansion. But then I thought of the man's description of Sabine. I may finally meet the to woman whom Ayden has put all of his confidence. However, I am not sure what I will do. I don't really want to steal Ayden away from her, but I doubt that the Ancients would let him and I continue our relations.

Luckily I didn't run into any malevolent characters but the walk was long and tiring. I stopped to rest only once and I took the time to write in my notebook. I figured it was a better time than any because who knows when I would get a chance to write down everything I had come to learn since I left Ireland. I wrote down all the new suspicions I had of Trent and how he ended up going to Russia the same day I left for Greece. Also, I wrote out the entire conversation I had with the bookshop owner. I wanted to have his every word written down about Ayden. And I especially wanted the description of Sabine. Although I was nervous about meeting her, I was intrigued. I just hoped that she wasn't some girlfriend of Ayden's.

Once I was finished writing, I wrote Sabine underneath the last paragraph and circled it. I had a feeling that she was going to be important and would play a huge role once I figured out my plans with Ayden. I closed up the notebook, placed it back in my bag and started walking again.

It took another twenty minutes or so before I came upon the mansion the old man had told me about. My heart skipped a beat as I stepped up to the iron gates. The thought of Ayden being just on the other side of the wall was exhilarating. I thought about scaling the gates but they were far too high. As I was about to press the intercom button, the gates suddenly began to open. I lingered just outside the gates for a moment, taking a quick look around the courtyard before entering. There didn't seem to be anyone waiting there, so I stepped in and headed towards the front door. The iron gates barely made a sound as they gently closed behind me. My eyes stayed fixed on the front of the mansion.

The house itself was beautifully old fashioned. Large white columns spread across the entire front of the large porch. The windows on all three floors were at least ten feet wide each. All curtains were drawn but the inside lights peaked out through the sides of the fabric.

Cautiously, I stepped up each stair of the porch. I looked for a doorbell but there was only a large doorknocker in the middle of each of the doors. The knocker's shape was that of a viper, startling yet at the same time fitting for the creatures that presumably resided inside the house. Slowly, I reached for the knocker. To my surprise, the door opened before my hand could grasp the knocker and a young woman stood in front of me.

"Hello Miss Logan," she declared. "You are expected."

Should I have been surprised? I was unsure how to react. "I am?" I quietly asked. "Are you sure?"

Her blank expression never changed. "Yes. Please, step inside. I'll let the lady of the house know you have arrived." She stepped to the side, allowing me to pass.

I thanked her and stepped inside. She quietly closed the door behind me and then asked that I wait there for just a moment. I nodded and chose to take a seat on the bench to my left.

The waiting felt like an eternity, but then the young woman returned. She beckoned me to follow her into another room. As I followed, I soaked in the beauty of the house. It was furnished with antiques from so many different eras. Everything I saw was shining brightly. I was in complete awe of the place and had so far only been twenty feet inside the front door.

The young woman suddenly stopped short and I nearly ran into her. She held out her hand towards our right. I looked in the direction she was gesturing and my eyes were greeted with even more brilliance. A gigantic curving marble staircase took up half of the room we were in. I started to walk towards it when I noticed figures were descending from the right hand side. As they moved down each step, I watched as a woman led the way, followed by two younger looking men. Once they stepped into the light, I knew who they were. The woman looked exactly as the bookkeeper had described her. Long, curly black tendrils fell to her waist and she wore a flowing, renaissance styled dress. The young man following her on her right side I recognized immediately. He was the good-looking brunette I had run into while I was at the hotel in Brazil. When I looked at the man following her left side, I was startled to find that I recognized him as well. He was the young blonde who had followed me to my hotel while I was in Ireland. I finally began to notice the butterflies fluttering around in my stomach as the trio made their way down the stairs.

The woman didn't speak a word until she was standing not three feet in front of me. Her blazing green eyes stared hard into mine.

"Calista Logan…welcome to our home." She kept her hands clasped gracefully in front of her. "Shall we proceed into the den? Ayden will be joining us shortly."

I could only nod and wait for her to lead the way. The two men followed behind me as we made out way to the den. It was twice the size of the foyer. Lush couches lined the room. There were several velvet chairs surrounding the large fireplace. She took a seat on the largest couch located at the back of the room. The two men seated themselves on both sides of her. I wasn't sure where I was to sit, but she then gestured to a chair diagonally to her left. I sat, placing my bag on the floor next to me and then folded my hands carefully in my lap.

"Calista, my name is Sabine. I am head of this household. These gentlemen are my…assistants," she looked at each of them with a small smile, "but they are nearly as old as I."

I wasn't sure if I was allowed to speak or not, but I took my chances. "Sabine…um, may I call you Sabine?" She nodded in response so I continued. "I know I probably shouldn't have come…but I must speak with Ayden."

Sabine smiled. "Yes…my darling Ayden…" Then she turned to the blonde man on her left, "Caelum, would you please go upstairs and ask Ayden and Selene to join us?"

Caelum nodded, got up and walked in the direction of the stairs. I watched him disappear into the other room and then looked back at Sabine. I wanted to speak with her more but I felt I should wait for Ayden. I took the time to fully look over both Sabine and the other young man still with us, his name still unknown to me. Both of them seemed completely calm. I, on the other hand, was a nervous wreck but I did my best not to show it.

Five minutes passed by and we heard footsteps coming towards the room. I straightened in my chair, anxiously waiting to at last see Ayden. Caelum was the first to enter the room and he made his way back to his place next to Sabine. Ayden walked into the room next. I leapt from my chair and ran to his arms. He graciously accepted me; however he seemed extremely alarmed to see me there. I was certain he had been told of my arrival, but apparently that was not the case.

I wanted to talk with him immediately but then I noticed a young blonde woman standing behind him. She was staring at us with what seemed to be an angry look on her face. Sabine cleared her throat and the woman's expression dropped. She walked around us to take a seat nearer to the other three.

Ayden hugged me gently and then lifted my face so he could look into my eyes. "Calista…what on earth are you doing here? As happy as I am to see you, I thought my letter was clear."

My gaze wanted to drop to the floor but I couldn't stop looking at him. "I know Ayden…I'm so sorry. But I just had to see you and talk with you."

He looked over my shoulder in the direction of Sabine and the others. "That may have to wait, my dear. There is much to discuss with them first. Let us go sit with them."

I took a deep breath. "Alright…" A shiver ran through my body.

"Calista, look at me." He grabbed my hand. "I promise I will not let any harm come to you. I have known them my whole life…they are gentle people. I promise."

I gave his hand a squeeze and nodded. "I trust you, Ayden."

He smiled and then led me over to the chairs facing the four of them. The blonde woman, again, looked somewhat angry that Ayden was sitting with me and not her. I tried my best to shrug it off. Ayden and I sat down together, but I wouldn't let go of his hand. I needed to hang on to him, it made me feel safer, calmer.

It wasn't long before Sabine began to speak. "Ayden, my darling, I must first apologize for not telling you that your friend was coming here tonight. I knew she was near the moment she had arrived into town. It was only a matter of time before she made her way to our home. The only reason I did not tell you was because I didn't want you to run off and perhaps send her away. I wanted a chance to speak with her."

He quickly replied, "I know, Sabine, but I just didn't want any harm to come to her. And I didn't want to anger any of you because I know what your rules say about humans…"

Caelum jumped into the conversation, "But Ayden, you do know that those rules are set in place for *everyone's* protection, not just our own. They are meant for you as well. You can't just think that the rules don't apply…!"

Sabine quietly silenced him with a wave of her hand. "That's enough, Caelum. This is meant to be a calm, civilized conversation." She then addressed Ayden again, "Caelum is right though. The rules are for all of our protection."

"I know Sabine," Ayden said quietly. "I don't want to place blame on Calista, but she was so captivating…I wanted to get to know her…" He bowed his head as if he was ashamed of what he had done.

"Ayden, we all know that you always do things with the best intentions, so I think that we are done with that part of the discussion. I would now like to speak with Calista, as long as it is alright with the both of you." Her eyes shifted between the two of us.

Ayden nodded in agreement and then looked at me. "Yes, I am very interested in speaking with all of you," I stated.

Sabine smiled, "Yes, I thought you would be. This is a very rare occasion. It's not often that we have humans chasing us in order to just talk with us and want to know us on a personal level. Most humans wish to exterminate us, which is part of the reason we have certain rules set in place. Would you like to start or would you prefer that we ask questions first?"

"Oh, I have many questions to ask but I don't want to bombard you. Please feel free to go first." I was starting to feel a little more comfortable even though the other woman was still glaring at me.

"Well, perhaps introductions are best to be done first. As I explained before, I am Sabine." She turned slightly to her left and gestured towards the other woman, "This here is Selene and this is Caelum." He was the blonde one to her left. She then turned towards the other young man, the brunette, and said, "Last but not least, this is Tristan. If Ayden has not informed you already, the three of us are the Ancients…" gesturing to herself and the two men, "the ones who wrote the letters."

I was a little surprised at this bit of information. "Ancients? But you all look so young! None of you could possibly be older than twenty-seven or twenty-eight years old!"

All of them laughed and Tristan was the one who spoke up, "We may look that way, but we are all quite old...thousands of years older than you are, my dear. Perhaps Ayden didn't tell you that we vampires don't age as humans do."

I looked at Ayden quickly and then back at the Ancients. "No, he didn't tell me that. But I guess I could have easily figured that out from all the movies and books that are out there."

This time it was Selene who spoke out. "Ha! The movies and books aren't exactly one hundred percent true, girlie." She crossed her arms and swung one leg across the arm of her chair as she spoke.

Sabine gave Selene a scolding look and then turned back to speak to me, "Yes, the books and movies don't really serve us justice, young one. There is so much that the outside world does not know about our true lives. Some of the basics are true, but there is certainly so much more...But on another note, I am very interested in hearing why you have gone through so much trouble to defy our...instructions...and try to find our Ayden."

I started to wring my hands in my lap. "Well, when I first spotted Ayden in Egypt, there was just something about him that sparked my interest. There was something mysterious about him that I was anxious to figure out. Once we started to talk and get to know more about each other, I began to have feelings for him. And I was of course, physically attracted to him as well..."

My last statement made Ayden blush. It was easy to notice because of his pale complexion.

Sabine smiled at Ayden's reaction and then said, "Well Calista...I don't want to frighten you, but the others and I must discuss what exactly we plan on...doing with you."

Ayden immediately stood and placed himself in front of me as a defense. "Sabine! I forbid you from bringing any harm to her! I simply won't allow it. You must let her live, or I shall forever leave this house!"

Tristan and Caelum stood as well. It looked like they were ready to fight in case Ayden chose to take action against Sabine. However, Sabine was quick to reseat them. Selene sat there with a look on her face that looked like she was enjoying the moment.

"Ayden," Sabine spoke lovingly, "that was not what I was referring to. I just think this is a matter that needs to be discussed seriously. You may take the time to speak with Calista in private."

I gently touched Ayden's arm and he relaxed a bit. He took his seat next to me and apologized for acting rashly. At this time, Sabine had risen from the couch and the other three followed her lead. She said we were welcome to talk wherever we wished while they spoke in Sabine's private office. Ayden and I nodded; he said we would just remain where we were. Sabine gave a small nod and then led the others out of the room, politely closing the doors behind them.

The moment the doors clicked shut, Ayden took me into his arms. I could have stayed in those arms forever. His gentle embrace made me feel so secure, as if nothing in the world could ever touch me.

"Ayden, I am so sorry for causing so much trouble. I just…I care about you! I want to be with you."

I could tell my words alarmed him. "No Calista! I can't do that…I won't. I would certainly give up eternity to be with you, but I will not subject you to my world…it's not as exotic as it may seem."

"That's not what I am asking of you, Ayden. I just want to be with you. Is there anyway they would allow such a thing? I want to stay. But if they say I have to leave, well, I won't leave here without you."

Ayden reached out his hand and caressed my face. "Calista…you have such a big heart. I pity the men who have let you slip through their fingers. But I fear that I may be added to that list…I am almost certain that Sabine and the others would not allow it."

I stood up and started to pace the room. I was furious. "But why, Ayden! These people need to start living in the modern world. People don't chase around vampires with crosses and stuff anymore…" My own thought was interrupted by a flashback of my conversation with Trent.

Ayden must have noticed the look of concern on my face. "What is it, Calista? Is something wrong?"

I walked over and knelt in front of him, placing my hands atop his. "Actually, I take that back…Ayden…there is something I have to tell you."

He quickly grabbed my hands, deeply worried. "Please Calista, what is it?"

I took a deep breath, "Alright…here goes…I…I met someone during my quest to find you."

He almost didn't let me finish. "Then why did you come here?" he exclaimed, practically throwing me off his lap.

"I didn't mean it in that context! I met someone who I think is looking for you…he's a…vampire slayer…"

Ayden stood up in a panic. "Calista! How could this be? Did he follow you here? Did you give him any information? This is terrible!"

I bowed my head in shame. "I am so sorry. I have spoken with him and he has told me all about what he does. He was convinced that I had come into contact with a vampire but I'm pretty sure I convinced him otherwise. I know for a fact that he didn't follow me here. He was at the airport but I saw his tickets, he was headed to Russia."

Now it was Ayden who began to pace across the room. "This could potentially turn into a very bad situation, my dear. What was his name?"

"I know Ayden, but I felt that I had to warn you about him."

He stopped and smiled. "And I thank you for that, darling. But do you remember his name?"

"Oh yes, it's hard to forget a name like his. It was Trent. Trent Murdock."

Ayden looked at me with a strange look in his eyes. "You're certain that is his name?" I nodded. "This is worse than I thought," he whispered. "I have to inform the others about this."

I jumped up from my chair. "Ayden! Are you sure that's a good idea? I mean…what if they get mad at me for speaking with him? That could give them reason to…to…."

He held up his hand in protest. "Please don't even mention that, Calista. You know that I would never let them hurt you in any way."

I looked at the floor and dragged the toe of my shoe across it. "I know Ayden…I just don't want to give them any reason to try and separate us."

Ayden took me into his arms again. "I know my darling. I won't let that happen. I'd give anything to keep you with me."

"Oh really?" It was Selene. "That's very interesting to hear, Ayden…very interesting indeed. However, the reason I came in was not to eavesdrop but because Sabine asked me to come get you. We've finished our discussion and would like to share with you the final decision." She scowled at us both before spinning on her heal to head back and join the others.

Ayden called out after her that we would be there in a minute. We weren't completely sure that she even heard him but it didn't seem to matter. He assured me that Sabine would be fine if we took our time.

After a few minutes, "Are you ready?" he asked me. "Please don't be afraid. They are truly good people. I have known them for so long; they are like family to me. If something or someone is important to me, then it is important to them as well."

I could only nod and hold onto his hand. He led the way and brought me to Sabine's office upstairs. Ayden politely knocked on the door before entering. Sabine and the others were patiently waiting. Sabine was seated behind a large mahogany desk. Both men were seated on each side of her while Selene chose to stand in the corner and glare at us. Sabine gestured for us to sit in the chairs facing them.

I thought Sabine would start the conversation but Ayden was the first to speak. "Sabine, I would like to speak first if it's alright with you. I have something to say that you must know."

"Yes Ayden, as you wish."

He looked at me quickly and then said, "My Ancients, Selene…Calista has been contacted by a slayer."

They wouldn't even let him finish. Caelum almost leapt out of his chair in a fury. "This is outrageous!"

Tristan spoke up as well. "Ayden, this is completely unacceptable!"

Unfortunately, Selene wanted a say in the conversation as well. "Ayden! How could you allow this to happen? Allowing a human to enter our house when she has most likely been followed here!"

Selene must have crossed the line with that statement because Sabine finally took it upon herself to silence everyone. "That's enough! I will not have such bitterness within my house. This is meant to be a civilized conversation." Caelum finally reseated himself. "Now, if we are all prepared to talk calmly, I would like to hear from both Ayden and Calista about this slayer. Unfortunately, I hate to say that I had a feeling this may happen."

"Well Sabine, if you wouldn't mind, I'd like Calista to tell you. She only said that she had spoken to him but I am sure she has more to tell than just that."

Sabine nodded and then all eyes were on me. "Ok well...um...I met him on my flight to Ireland. He seemed like a nice person at first but then I started to run into him way too often. He would show up at my hotel room and ask me strange questions. One night he showed up and had ash all over him. I asked what it was but he ignored my question and would change the subject to see if I would leave it alone."

Ayden jumped in quickly, "I hate to interrupt your story but I am not sure if you realized this but the ash is what becomes of a vampire when a slayer...does his work..."

"Oh god...I'm sorry..."

"No please, continue." He rested his hand on my arm.

"Ok well...one night I needed to use the hotel laptop but he was using it. So I went to his room and he allowed me to use it in order to book my tickets to Greece. But then he cornered me and said he believed I had come into contact with a vampire. I played it off as if I didn't know what he was talking about. I am pretty sure that he bought it because he didn't persist anymore but then he just spilled the beans about what he did. At that time, I became worried about Ayden and felt I had to warn him about this man. He kept saying how he was looking for someone and for some reason it felt almost like he was looking for Ayden."

"And what was the name of this man you speak of, young lady?" Tristan asked politely.

"It was Trent. Trent Murdock."

"Oh great...Murdock! Now we've got that guy to worry about," Selene exclaimed.

Ayden quickly came to my defense. "Selene, please. Calista has assured me that she was not followed here. I completely trust her."

"Even so," Sabine stepped in, "I think it would be best if Calista stayed here with us until we can sort out this slayer problem. Ayden, please show her to one of the spare bedrooms."

Thirteen

I tried to protest against it but Sabine insisted I stay. Selene, on the other hand, looked extremely angry at Sabine's request. I couldn't really understand why Selene was the only one there that seemed to dislike me. Yeah, the guys looked at me skeptically but Selene's look burned a hole right through me. But there would be time to figure that all out later. For the moment, Sabine was concerned about my comfort and everyone's safety. I tried to assure her again that Trent had not followed me there. Tristan and Caelum felt the need to inform me that slayers were trained to be very clever and tricky. It wouldn't surprise them if he had used his going to Russia as a decoy to get me to think I was safe.

"Slayers are well taken care of. They are given whatever means needed in order to track down their prey," Caelum explained. "He could easily have booked a second passage from Russia to here without you even knowing."

"Stop getting everyone all worried!" Ayden said as he got up from his chair. "Like Sabine said, let's just allow Calista to get settled first and then we can go from there."

Ayden scooped up my bag and led me down the hall to one of the many guest rooms in the house. He explained that I would stay there while he and the others kept to the basement during daylight hours. Apparently they had a huge, stone vault built in the basement for them to sleep safely. It was nearly indestructible, impossible for even a large group of humans to enter, and it blocked out all forms of light.

"Ayden…" I began, "what if what Tristan and Caelum said is true?"

He looked a little confused. "What do you mean?"

"Well, what if Trent did trick me by making me believe he was going to Russia when in fact he followed me here…it's possible that I have put all of your lives in danger…if anything happened to you…I don't know what I would do."

Ayden held my face in his hands. "Calista, if Trent Murdock were to ever come near here, Sabine would be able to sense it immediately, just like she did with you. And that would give us plenty of time to lock down the house, or even leave if we needed to. If anyone should be worried about someone, it is I who should be concerned about your protection. I will do whatever it takes to make sure you are safe at all times."

It looked like he wanted to kiss me at that moment, but he resisted. I would have loved to kiss him as well but the thought of his thirst for blood frightened me just the slightest bit. It never really occurred to me until I wondered what it would be like to kiss a guy who had fangs. An awkward moment of silence hung in the air. Just as I was about to try and bring up a new topic of discussion, Selene appeared in the doorway.

"Ayden, I sure hope you weren't planning on draining the young one."

Ayden's expression was one of pure shock. "Selene! Do not speak like that in front of her! It's rather unnecessary. How could you say such a thing?"

"Ok, ok…sorry. Anyways, the reason I'm here is because Sabine wanted me to let you know that it was time to…eat…and Sabine arranged for a cook to come stay with us and prepare meals for Calista. So, whenever you're ready, we can head out and she can go down to the dining room." With that said, she left the room.

Ayden stood and turned to me. "Well, like she said, you can go downstairs and get something to eat if you would like. I am not really sure how you feel about what I need to go out and do right now but it's necessary for our survival…"

"I understand…I admit, it's a little disturbing but there's not much that I do about it, so I'll just have to get used to it."

"The thing is, I don't know if I want you to get used to it."

I wasn't sure what he meant by that but by turning his back to me made it clear that he didn't want to continue the conversation. I stood and allowed him to lead the way downstairs to the dining room. A cook was waiting there, ready for instructions. Ayden made certain that the cook would do whatever I asked of him before kissing my forehead and then leaving to be with the others.

The cook didn't say a word the entire time he made my meal. It felt a bit strange sitting in such a huge place in silence. But it wasn't long before Ayden and the Ancients returned from their little outing. I wanted to go spend time with Ayden but he told me to take my time and finish eating. We would have plenty of time to talk afterwards.

Despite his request, I rushed through my meal and then started wandering through the house, trying to find Ayden. I came upon a large living room warmed by a roaring fire. I was hoping it would be Ayden or perhaps even Sabine whom I would find, but I was met with disappointment. Selene was the one sitting by the fire.

"Hello Calista...enjoy your meal?" She never took her eyes off the book she was reading.

"Yes I did...thank you..." I cleared my throat. "Would you happen to know where I could find Ayden?"

This was a good enough question to make her put the book down. "You're looking for Ayden, huh? Well, I'm not sure if I really want to tell you where he is."

I frowned and gave her a hard look. "Why not?"

She stood and started to walk towards me. "Those letters you received from us...I wrote them, with Sabine's approval of course. But I meant it when I said that Ayden belonged to us. What I wish I could have written is that he belongs to *me*."

She was starting to come a little too close for my liking, so I took a few steps away from her. "What are you talking about? People do not belong to other people unless you're talking about slavery. But that was ages ago and besides the point. You can't just make a claim like that unless it goes both ways. Ayden is his own person and he can do whatever he wants. And he has never told me that be belongs to anyone so I think you've been mistaken."

"Oh you think so, huh? Well, I'm going to let you know right now that I am not going to let some human take him away from me. I made him what he is so that he would stay with *me*, not chase after some weak human. So I would advise staying away from him, girlie." There was a flare in her eyes as she said this.

I didn't know what to do. I was angry yet frightened at the same time. There weren't any more words that needed to be said so I left the room quietly. I could feel her stare burning a hole in my back.

How could she say something like that? Ayden did not *belong* to her, let alone anyone. But her words just made me want to pursue him even more. If it was competition that she wanted, then she'd get it. I continued to search the house until I was able to find Ayden. However, I was uncertain as to whether or not I should tell him what had happened between Selene and I.

Ayden was in the library located at the very back end of the house. The library itself was the size of a small barn. The selection of books was rather appealing. Something was pulling at me and making me want to sit there and read till I couldn't read anymore. But I decided it was best to talk to Ayden and see if I could get him to open up about Selene.

"Hey Ayden, what are you reading?"

"Oh Calista, there you are. Did you enjoy your dinner?"

I smiled and took a seat next to him. "Yes I did, you are all being far too kind to me. But thank you, I really appreciate it. So what are you reading?" I pointed to the book in his hands.

He looked down at it. "Oh this! This is a very old book. Sabine has had it her entire life. She was one of the first that we know of. She told us once that there are many who are far older than she, but she has no knowledge of their whereabouts. It's possible that either slayers have killed them off or they are in a deep slumber. Sometimes some of us feel the need to sleep for many years. Could be as short as a year or as long as a couple decades. It could be for various reasons: to get away from things, to lay low after becoming too well known, or to just get some plain old rest. But who knows who else is out there? The very first of our kind could very well be sleeping right now."

This vampire history was sounded pretty intriguing. I felt myself yearning to know more. "So, do you know how it all started? I mean, how far back does your history go?"

"That's the thing, we aren't really sure. I mean we know that it goes very far back in time, but we don't know exactly *how* far. Sabine is over five thousand years old, so it could be anywhere from that time to thousands of years before she was even born."

"Wow, this is pretty interesting," I said. "How old are the others?"

Placing the book on the table, he leaned back in his chair. "Let's see...well, like I said Sabine is over five thousand years old. Selene is around four thousand. Caelum is as well. Tristan is only about thirty five hundred years old. Even though he's the youngest of them, he is still just as wise."

I wasn't sure how he would react to my asking about Selene but I couldn't resist. "If you don't mind my asking...when did you meet Selene? When did everything happen?"

He was certainly a bit shocked at my question. "How did you know it was her?"

I bit my lower lip. "She told me..."

I was certain he was going to become angry, but he stayed calm. "Well, I guess I figured you were going to find out sooner or later." He stood and began to pace the room. "Yes, it was Selene who made me a vampire. I was a foolish young man when I met her. I fell in love with her instantly and she took full advantage of it. It only took her four days to decide to make me her companion."

"Do you ever wish you were still human?" I asked.

He pondered the question for a moment or two. "Well...yes and no. Sometimes I do...like when I am with you..." He looked at me with sad eyes. "It's amazing how much humans take advantage of...I sometimes regret my human life because I lived it foolishly."

I tried changing the subject. "Have you ever turned someone before?"

This question alarmed him. "Absolutely not! And I never will. I don't think this is a topic we should be discussing. I already told you that I do not want this type of life for you. It's not as enchanting as it may seem through a human's eye." He sat down again, crossing his arms in disgust.

I folded my hands in my lap and lowered my eyes. "I'm sorry Ayden…but the temptation is there and it's hard not to even think about it when my feelings for you grow stronger every moment we are together."

After a few moments of silence, Ayden stood up and took my hands. "You look tired, my dear. Wouldn't you like to sleep? I am sure all your traveling has exhausted you."

He was right. "Yes, I am rather tired. So much jet lag. What am I to do during the daytime when you are all sleeping? I wouldn't want to leave the house without you."

Ayden smiled. "I wouldn't worry about that now, Calista. You could always come here to the library. Or feel free to explore the house…minus the cellar of course…but everything else is free reign. I would prefer you not leaving the house during the day either. You never know who is watching. But for now, get some rest and I will see you tomorrow evening. I won't be awake for too much longer either. It's only a few hours till dawn."

We left the library together and Ayden guided me upstairs to my room. He also showed me where the bathroom and toiletries were so I could make myself at home. I thanked him and we hugged before he headed downstairs. I watched him walk down the hall, but I couldn't help but notice Selene standing at the top of the stairs, waiting for him. I wondered how long she had been standing there and if she had overheard our conversation earlier. As much as it pained me to watch the two of them walk away together, I thought it would be best to get some sleep and deal with it tomorrow.

Not at all surprisingly, I slept for most of the afternoon. The traveling had finally caught up with me. I was pleased though because it meant I had less time to have to waste until Ayden woke. I took my time showering and then went downstairs to see if the chef was around for breakfast. He was and was nice enough to make me a brunch of pancakes, fruit and juice.

Once I was finished eating I decided to explore the house, as Ayden had suggested. I walked around the second floor first, checking out all the beautifully decorated rooms. There were countless bedrooms but also several offices. I recognized one of them as Sabine's office from the previous night. However, it wasn't long before I found myself back downstairs in the library. I was curious about the hundreds of books upon the shelves. Perhaps I could use this free time I had to read up on vampires and learn everything that I could. They were such mysterious creatures. The lives they led *were* enchanting; it didn't matter if Ayden disagreed.

I hadn't even realized that it was evening until Selene walked into the library. "Well well, reading up on your vampire knowledge, are you?"

"Hello Selene," I said as politely as I could. "Is Ayden up yet?"

"Sadly for you, no. I am usually the first one up; I like to get an early start on the night. Ayden probably won't be up for another half hour, maybe." She crossed the room and took a seat in the corner across from me.

"Selene, may I ask you a question?"

"I suppose." She stretched herself out in the chair.

I put down the book I was reading, "Well, I was just curious as to why it is you dislike me so much. Ever since I got here I have gotten nothing but dirty looks and snide comments from you. And then there was the whole fiasco about Ayden belonging to you. What's the problem?"

She sat up and leaned forward, her elbows on her knees. "You want to know what the problem is? You. You are the problem because I don't like the fact that Ayden cares so much for you. I made him a vampire for myself. He's mine. Mine! Understand? And I already told you before that I will not allow you to steal him away from me. But if he truly cares that much about you and you won't listen to me…well then, I can just make things all the more miserable for the both of you."

I sat up in alarm. "What do you mean?"

Selene stood and came towards me. "I overheard your little conversation last night. Ayden is one hundred percent determined to make sure that you never cross over into our world." Now she was towering over me, but I had nowhere to go. "And I know that it would be simply horrible for him if something like that were to happen. Which is why I have decided to do it for him."

I tried to stand but Selene pushed me back into the chair. "What are you talking about? Let me go, I am going to go speak with him about this."

"I don't think so, girlie. Since you care so much about each other, and *you* seem so interested in our kind, I'll just give you the full experience of it."

My initial alarm turned into full-fledged panic. I tried to push the chair out behind me so I could make a run for the door but she was too quick and too strong. No matter how much I struggled, I couldn't escape her grip. My chair was kicked away from us. I tried to scream, but Selene covered my mouth.

"Oh don't worry, Calista, you're definitely going to feel this and it's going to hurt more than any pain you've felt before."

That was when Selene bit down on my neck. The pain was excruciating. I continued to kick and tried screaming again but it was no use. Several seconds later, the pain began to subside. I began to lose feeling in my body. My vision was starting to get hazy. A feeling of lightheadedness came over me. I was sure I would faint any second.

I had almost lost consciousness when Selene dropped me to the floor. My body hit the ground hard but I barely felt it. I couldn't see what was going on around me. Everything I heard sounded distant and muffled.

Selene dropped to her knees and leaned down to whisper in my ear. "I could most certainly leave you here and you'd be dead within the hour. However, I won't do that…Ayden most certainly won't stick around if you're dead. So, instead I am going to turn you into one of us…don't worry, it won't take long, just a few minutes."

She rose and grabbed a letter opener off of the desk near the door. First thing she did was prick her finger with it. She turned my head and let the blood drops land on my neck where she had bitten me. She explained that the vampire blood was so powerful that the body healed almost instantly when infused with it. I barely heard the remainder of her words as she continued talking; I was too weak to pay much attention. My mind just kept telling me that I was going to die.

Selene lifted my body and propped it against the table leg. She tilted my head back and said all I had to do was just let the blood flow down my throat; don't resist it. I couldn't tell where it was coming from but the warm liquid filled my mouth and throat. I wanted to cough it up but had no strength to do so.

I must have lost consciousness at some point. I woke up in a bed on the second floor. There was shouting coming from down the hall. I sat up and took a look around the room. For some reason everything looked a little bit different. The colors of the wallpaper and curtains looked more vibrant than I remembered them. I could taste a sweetness in the air. Something was definitely different but I couldn't quite put my finger on it.

Before anything else, I had to go find out what everyone was shouting about. I slipped off the bed and started to walk in the direction of the voices. I could have sworn they were just down the hall but I ended up finding everyone downstairs in the living room. I was a bit shocked at the fact that I was able to hear them from so far away.

All conversations stopped as soon as I was spotted in the doorway. Ayden looked at me with tears in his eyes.

"Ayden...what's the matter?" I started. "I heard shouting. But something's different. I can't believe this...I was able to hear you all from upstairs. I really thought that you were only a couple doors down from my room..." I stopped trying to explain once Ayden walked over to me. "Ayden...what's wrong? Why are you so upset?"

He placed his hands on my shoulders. "You don't remember what happened to you?" I shook my head.

Ayden turned to look at Selene. "How could you do this, Selene? You knew that I didn't want this for her!"

As soon as he said the words, I knew. It all came flooding back to me. The library...Selene...pain...she had bitten me and turned me into a vampire without even thinking twice. She had known exactly what she was doing. She made me a vampire because she knew Ayden would never have done it. He had been purely against it and she defied him.

He let me go and walked towards her, his rage growing stronger. "Selene, this is the second time you have betrayed me! Give me one good reason why I shouldn't kill you right now…"

Sabine's patience had been tested before but she couldn't stand the current scene any longer. "ENOUGH!" she shouted. "This is going to stop right this minute. No death shall ever occur in this house. Ayden, you will contain yourself and please tend to Calista…as much as it may upset you…there is much that you now must teach her."

Ayden nodded and came over to me. "Selene…what you've done is unacceptable. You did it without the consent of anyone in this house, and you did it when Ayden had explicitly forbade you against it. I am afraid I have no choice but you banish you from this house…."

"Banish?" Selene exclaimed. "You can't do that! I am a part of the eldership here. How can you cast me out?"

"Selene, you have left me with no other choice. Your ego and pride have gotten the best of you and you have caused disaster in my household. You have until tomorrow night to remove yourself from this house. I suggest you make whatever arrangements necessary for the removal of your belongings. You may contact us if absolutely necessary but I do not want to see you here again within the next century."

Selene's anger was starting to rise. "I can't even believe you would do something like this! Cast me out of my own home? Over something as trivial as this?"

Caelum stepped in. "This is not a trivial issue, Selene. You severely broke the rules. Sabine is right, you let your ego get the best of you and now you must suffer the consequences of your actions."

"I can't believe this!" Selene was outraged.

Sabine asked if Ayden would take me to the lounge and fill me in on the details. He nodded and we silently left the room. Ayden kept his arm around my shoulders. He still seemed pretty upset about everything.

We walked into the lounge and sat on one of the couches. Ayden hugged me tight and apologized over and over again.

"Ayden, it's really ok…I know you are upset and you didn't want this but I guess it's not so bad. Now we can be together and you won't have to worry about hurting me. I guess it just kind of sucks that it happened the way it did.…"

I felt my neck where Selene had bitten me. There wasn't physically anything there but the memory of the pain still lingered.

"Of course I am glad to have you with me, Calista. Things are just different than we had both expected. There is so much that you have to learn now. About being discrete with your identity and controlling your strength and…" He stopped, obviously not wanting to continue.

"And what, Ayden?" I touched his hand.

He looked into my eyes. "And hunting…you have to learn how to hunt and dispose of your victims."

"Oh…how is that possible without getting caught by someone?"

"That's what you will learn, my dear: To hunt and kill discretely. You shouldn't ever do it in public, but we have done it occasionally. Best places are dark alleyways, empty parks, hotel rooms, etc. Solitary places where no one will see you."

I held his hand firmly. "And you'll teach me all this, won't you?"

He nodded. "Yes, myself and the Ancients will help. They know far more than I do, so they may even be of better help. But don't worry…I'll never leave you."

Selene left the next night. If she was still in a rage from the previous night's conversations, she didn't show it. I thought she would try to get every last moment of time possible with Ayden, but surprisingly she kept to herself. And when she did finally leave, not a single goodbye was spoken to anyone; not even Ayden. No one knew if we were ever to see or hear from her again.

Fourteen

I trained for weeks on end with Ayden and the Ancients. There was far more that I was meant to learn than I'd imagined. The first thing I learned about was our incredible strength. But it was something that had to be controlled or it could bring unwanted attention. At first I found it a little difficult to get a handle on. Whenever I held or threw something, I thought I was doing it with my normal strength, as it had been when I was human. However, each time, the object would crush in my grip or be thrown further than I planned. Ayden tried to explain that it was a psychological thing that I would have to overcome and learn to control.

"Don't get frustrated with it, my darling. It will come with time." His hands rested on my shoulders, hoping to pass along some assurance. "Just think you are dealing with a baby. You must be gentle with everything you handle."

I placed my hands on his hips. "I'm trying but it's just so aggravating when I can't do something as simple as this!"

He couldn't help but laugh. "It's not as simple as you think. Perhaps that is the problem. I'd take some time to think through it before you physically try it again. Just remember what I told you— think about babies. You wouldn't handle them as you normally would an adult. Just think about it."

I nodded and turned away from him. I needed to take a walk to think about things. Ayden offered to accompany me, but I declined. I needed some time of solitude.

Even though I was not trained to the full potential the Ancients believed I had, I was now allowed to wander on my own. I was also allowed to hunt on my own. That was the very first thing taught to me, for it is probably the most important aspect a vampire must know. Unfortunately, blood was a vampire's only source of nourishment. I wasn't hungry though, as I walked along the streets of Greece. Furthering my vampire education was the only thing occupying my mind.

I was soon to find that I should have been more alert of my whereabouts. I had to have been walking for nearly an hour when I realized that I had wandered farther than I was supposed to. The street names and buildings were unrecognizable to me. And not soon after I realized I was lost, something in the air changed. I could sense it, but I wasn't entirely sure what it was. I looked all around but I couldn't see anything out of the ordinary. I thought it was probably time for me to head back in the direction I had come, just in case the Ancients started to worry.

As I walked, I tried to ignore that strange feeling I had, but it just wouldn't go away. I was actually starting to feel like someone was watching me. Ayden had warned me that if that ever happened, never go directly back to the house. I didn't want to lead anyone to where we lived, for it could result in unwanted carnage.

Whoever it was that was following me I felt I'd be able to handle them if they decided to attack. Now that I was a vampire, even a man three times my size was no match for me. But then a thought crossed my mind: what if it was a slayer? I wasn't one hundred percent sure that I would be able to take on a slayer. They knew more about us than any other human. And the worst part of all was that they knew how to kill us. I had to somehow keep my guard up without seeming paranoid.

I walked as quickly as I could without drawing attention to myself. The best place for me to go until it was safe would be within a crowd. At this time of night, the only places crowded enough were the bars. Lucky for me, there were three bars in a row on the first street I turned onto. I quickly ducked into the closest one.

The place wasn't ridiculously crowded, but it would suffice. I made my way to an open table in the very back of the bar. It was somewhat secluded but I still had a decent view to see everyone that walked in and out of the front entrance. No more than two minutes after I had sat down, two men in dark clothing entered the bar. They both looked around the bar; it looked like they were searching for someone. Most likely me by the way they were dressed. They looked too out of place with their dark trench coats and sunglasses to be searching for friends.

For a split second, I thought for sure one of them had spotted me. I looked quickly for the nearest exit. Restrooms and a kitchen area to my left, and there it was, the good old neon sign of freedom. I checked back on the two men to see if I had a chance to sneak out. The guy on the left leaned over and whispered in the ear of the other. Even with my new powers, I was unable to hear them over the roar of the crowded bar. To my surprise, the second man nodded and then they left.

I was more confused than relieved as they left the bar. Was it possible that they really didn't see me? Or was it some kind of a trick to try and get me to go outside? I couldn't be sure. I decided it was probably better to be safe than sorry, so I waited. I knew that Ayden would come looking for me if I wasn't home within the next hour. He was always worrying about me.

After about thirty minutes, waiting for Ayden had become almost agonizing. I hadn't been hungry earlier but now the thirst was building. It was still pretty crowded, but I still wasn't sure I should go outside yet. The thought of possibly draining one of the many drunken humans in the room was becoming tempting. However, I wasn't sure my skills were developed well enough to be able to feed in public. Ayden had said that they didn't usually do that sort of thing. Too easy to get caught. He had nearly mastered it and the Ancients had no trouble with it at all. But I definitely wasn't up to par yet.

I was about to get up to take a peak outside when Caelum walked through the door. I was a bit surprised to see him. I had been expecting Ayden. He spotted me immediately at the back of the room and came over to me.

"Calista, my dear, where have you been? Ayden and the rest of us have been worried." He held out his hand for me to leave with him.

I stood and linked elbows with him. "I'm sorry Caelum, I've been here for a few hours…I think I was being followed earlier…"

A strong sense of alarm filled Caelum's face. "Are you certain? Did you see them? We must get you home immediately, but we must also be cautious. When we get outside, make sure you scan the area, but do it as discretely as you can. There's no need to make us look panicked and paranoid. It will only aid them in their pursuit. Try and stay calm."

I nodded in agreement while trying not to laugh. Caelum was worried about me panicking when he was the one asking so many questions. Nevertheless, we slipped out the back exit. Once outside, I did as he had said: took a quick scan of the surrounding area as we walked down the alleyway. I couldn't see anything suspicious and there was not even an inkling of that strange feeling I'd had earlier. Caelum whispered in my ear that everything looked all right and that we should head back to the mansion as soon as possible. He thought it would be best to take a longer way home, just in case we were followed. The longer route would allow us to determine if we had a tail and then lose them if need be.

We had soon come to a park and Caelum felt it safe enough to start questioning me about my being followed.

"Now tell me all that happened, Calista."

I gripped his arm a little tighter. "Are you sure we should be talking about this out in the open like this? What if they are listening?"

He placed his hand over mine and gave it a consoling squeeze. "Don't worry my dear, they do not have the supernatural hearing that we have been given. They are mere humans who happen to know some of our secrets. But if you would feel more comfortable waiting until we arrived home, that's perfectly fine."

"Yes, I would actually prefer to wait. Plus it would be easier for me to tell everyone at once instead of repeating my story."

"Ah, good point." He patted my hand. "Well, let us at least enjoy the walk while we can."

The walk home was quite pleasant. I had always enjoyed the nighttime but never really appreciated it in all its splendor. With each step, I examined our surroundings. The leaves on the trees were a dark green. I was able to capture, with great detail, the veins of each leaf. The flowers along the sidewalks were in full bloom. All the pinks, purples and yellows seemed more vibrant than I had remembered such colors to ever be. It was almost as if each part of nature had its own life and energy surrounding it. I had noticed such things before but I made a mental note to speak with Ayden about it later. It just amazed me that I was unable to remember such brilliance in any of my memories as a human.

Twenty minutes later we were finally at the front gates of the mansion. Caelum punched in the security code and the gates opened. We waited and made sure that the gates were locked and the security system armed before heading inside.

The moment I walked in the door, Ayden rushed to my side. "Calista! We have been worried sick! Where have you been all this time?"

I hugged him gently. "You were all worried sick? Or just you?" A small smirk inched in at the corner of my mouth. Ayden was not please by my comment. "We *all* were."

I held his hands and looked straight into his eyes so he knew I was serious. "I'm fine Ayden, really."

Caelum rested his hand on Ayden's shoulder. "Ayden, be calm. As you can see she is perfectly unharmed. I made sure to get her home safely. She was in a bar about five blocks away. She played it smart and didn't come home because she felt it unsafe to do so."

Caelum's words only made Ayden more distraught. "Unsafe? What do you mean? What happened?"

I took Ayden's face in my hands and looked into his eyes. "Will you please calm down my darling? Everything's fine. I think we should all go sit down so I can tell you what happened. Ok?"

Ayden barely nodded, but he did give in and led the way to Sabine's office. She and Tristan were there, working on something in which I had yet to be included. Caelum said I would soon be taught about all of the businesses and such that the Ancients conducted. But that was information that could certainly wait until another time. For now, discussing my most recent adventure was of the utmost importance.

Sabine and Tristan were patiently waiting behind her office desk. I was almost surprised not to see Selene there, but then remembered that she had already been gone for several weeks. Most of the time, not seeing her was a relief. But other times, I wondered how Ayden felt about her absence. After all, she was the one who had made him a vampire. There had to be some sort of personal connection between them. Perhaps that was why I sometimes wondered about her. She was also the one who had turned me…maybe we also had a connection that I just wasn't feeling yet.

Ayden and I took a seat across from Sabine. Caelum took his usual place next to her. Ayden suddenly grasped my hand. I looked over at him.

"Are you alright? What's up?"

He gave my hand a quick squeeze. "I just wanted to let you know that you don't have to hold anything back. This is for the benefit and safety of everyone in this house. So don't spare any details."

I couldn't help but smile. "I know, Ayden. I'm quite certain you've told me this at least once before. Every little detail will be told, I promise."

My words must have comforted him because he leaned back in his chair and seemed to relax a bit. He didn't release my hand, however, but I was more than content having him hold onto me like that.

"Alright Calista," Caelum said, "now that we are all here, please feel free to tell us all what happened."

"Alright," I started. I took a deep breath before speaking again. "I had gone out walking because I had a lot on my mind. I was trying to think through all you have taught me and how I can better my skills. It was probably about an hour maybe before I realized that I was lost. Nothing really looked all that familiar."

"Yes," Caelum interrupted. "I found her in one of the bars a few blocks away. You know the street just off of the main dirt road? That's where she was. Not as lost as she had thought but…"

Sabine placed her hand on his knee. "Thank you Caelum, but I am sure Calista can fill us in on all the details." She looked back at me. "Please continue dear."

I cleared my throat. "Ok…so it was then that I had this strange feeling. I couldn't quite pinpoint what it was but then it started to feel like someone was watching me. I immediately remembered Ayden's words that I should not go back to the mansion if I felt I was in danger or being followed. As much as I wanted to head back, I remembered Ayden saying it was best to go to the nearest crowded area. I knew the only place crowded enough at this time of night would be the bars. I ducked into the first one I came to and sat in the back. A few minutes later, two men wearing dark clothes and sunglasses came in. They seemed to be looking for someone—probably me. I was sure they had seen me but then one whispered to the other and they left."

Now it was Tristan who chimed in. "Do you remember what they looked like? Specifics about their appearance?"

To most humans it would be a difficult question, but I had lately been able to remember tiny specifics about many things. "Well, I was certainly unable to see their eyes because they were both wearing sunglasses. Both had on three-piece suits with trench coats, one dark blue, and the other black. Both had short hair, one light red, and the other either black or dark brown." It was all I could remember.

"Were there any details about them that stood out dramatically?" Caelum asked. "Tattoos or piercings? Birth marks?"

I shook my head. "Not that I can remember. That's really all I can think of about them. They looked like pretty ordinary humans, except for the suits and glasses. I don't know of any men that go around bars in business suits that late at night, let alone sunglasses."

The three men turned their attention to Sabine. She seemed to be deep in thought. I decided not to say anything; I didn't want to be the one to interrupt her thought process.

Tristan gently placed his hand on her shoulder and she snapped back to reality. "Sabine? Do you have any thoughts?"

She patted Tristan's hand and then looked at me. "I admit, I had sensed the presence of slayers before you left the house earlier this evening. As much as it may have put you into danger, I wanted to test your abilities. Congratulations, you did quite well my dear."

I thought Ayden was going to fall over in his chair. "A test! She could have been killed, Sabine!"

"I wouldn't have let it happen, Ayden. Caelum was keeping watch over her. That's why he was able to find her so easily. No need to fret over it."

"So there are slayers here then?" I asked with curiosity.

"I'm afraid so my dears. Which means I would advise against leaving the mansion for the rest of the night." Sabine rose from her chair. "Now, if you'll excuse me, I have a few phone calls to make."

We all stood as well and began to file out of her office, one by one.

"Oh Ayden," Sabine called out.

"Yes Sabine?" He stood in the doorway before I could exit the room.

"Would you please make sure that you get something to eat for Calista? I can see that she hasn't fed tonight. There are reserves downstairs."

"Of course." Ayden slightly bowed his head and then led me out of the room.

I was quite intrigued that Sabine had known I hadn't fed yet. I had meant to while I was out, once my thirst had finally risen. But it wasn't really an option for me while being followed by would-be killers.

The reserves Sabine had spoken about were located down in the vault. My first night as a vampire, Sabine had made sure that I had a place to sleep in the vault with them. Ever since that night, I had been accepted as a permanent member of the household. It felt really nice to finally belong somewhere, but at the same time I was skeptical, mostly because of my past experiences. As much as I wanted to resist, I accepted it for what it was and tried my best to enjoy it. Ayden brought the most contentment into each night that passed.

There were bottles and bottles of blood reserves down in the vault. They were cleverly disguised as wine bottles, just in case anyone other than ourselves happened to make their way in there. It was nearly impossible, but the boys were always the ones who felt it better to be safe than sorry.

I was far thirstier than I had originally thought. Before I knew it, I had drunk an entire bottle on my own. At first I felt bad; I hadn't thought to ask if it was all right to do so. Ayden hugged me gently and explained how they replenished the reserves whenever it got below a certain number of bottles. Apparently there were times when they have had to stay cooped up in the vault for a few days and the reserves were their only source of food.

Now that my thirst was finally satisfied, I was starting to get drowsy. Ayden said that drowsiness was sometimes a side affect when gorging oneself on too much blood at one time. But it was also getting close to dawn. Sleep was definitely appealing at that moment. I decided to give into it. Ayden was more than helpful in helping me to my corner of the vault. I was still a little weary about sleeping in a coffin but the Ancients assured me that I would get used to it eventually. As Ayden lay me down, I was starting to dislike the look of my coffin more and more. Just because I had to sleep in it, didn't mean it had to look so dreary and dismal. I decided I would spend the next night giving it some life so that it would look like something other than a death box.

Ayden must have read my thoughts, for he started laughing. "Is it really all that bad, Calista?"

I let out a big yawn. "It is for me, Ayden. It's still rather unnerving. Every time I lay here, I feel like death is going to come and swallow me up. I think if I dressed it up and it looked cheery, then maybe I'd feel better about it."

He caressed my cheek and then kissed my forehead. "Whatever makes you happy my love."

I gave his hand a squeeze before he closed the lid. It didn't take long for me to fall asleep. The blood had done its work and my body would be content until the sun was set again.

Fifteen

The next night I awoke feeling completely refreshed. I was continually amazed by the affect of blood to our bodies. It was like nothing I had ever experienced as a human. At times it was like alcohol, making us drunk if we drank too much. Other times it was merely like water, quenching a small thirst. But whenever I woke, my body felt re-energized and powerful, almost as if I had drunk some sort of revitalizing elixir.

As usual, I was the last to rise. Ayden said it was common for "newborns" to sleep a bit longer than the elders. He used to hate it when he first became a vampire because he felt that he was missing so much those first few hours after sunset. But now, he says, it doesn't bother him all that much because he knows he has lifetimes to experience the world. A few hours missed in the early evening doesn't hurt every now and then.

I made my way upstairs to see what everyone else was up to. I figured Sabine would be in her office getting work done. I thought it best not to bother her for the time being. Ayden was most likely in the library so I headed that way first.

When I stepped into the library, I thought my heart was going to stop dead. There was Selene, standing by the window. I didn't know whether to scream for the others and run out of there or strangle her. Before I could even move, she turned around.

Surprisingly, there was no expression of malice on her face. "Hello Calista."

"Selene…" I spoke her name quietly. "What on earth are you doing here? Sabine banished you from the house. If the other Ancients find you here, you're going to be in a lot of trouble."

She held up her hand as if you stop my words from touching her. "Please Calista, I know all this. I am sure Sabine has already detected my presence. I know I am not welcome here but I come due to a recent tragedy that effects us all."

I looked back out into the hall to see if anyone was coming. "Something has happened? Maybe I should go get someone?" I was looking for a quick escape in case she decided to attack.

She turned to look out the window again. "I would advise on getting someone other than Ayden. He tends to overreact sometimes."

I didn't bother staying to talk with her much longer. I figured Sabine would be the best person to speak with, as much as I didn't want to disturb her. If I happened to run into either Tristan or Caelum, they would most likely have me go to Sabine anyways. Even though they were Ancients as well, they almost always conferred with Sabine before taking any action.

Tristan and Caelum seemed to be out or just hiding in a room somewhere. I had trouble figuring out if they were around or not. I was able to tell that Ayden wasn't in the house though. Sensing his presence was one of the very few things I had been able to master that past couple weeks. I briskly walked to Sabine's office. The door was closed. I was about to knock when she asked that I enter.

I opened the door slowly. "Hi Sabine…I'm sorry to disturb you but…"

"Yes, I know," she spoke without looking up, "Selene is waiting for us in the library."

"So you *did* know she was here."

She finished signing a couple papers and then looked at me. "Of course my dear, it's one of my gifts. I know you have begun to develop your own sense. Mine has been strengthened over many centuries."

"Of course…well, Selene is downstairs. She said that she is here on account of some tragedy…."

"Tragedy?" she asked, "That doesn't sound good at all. We need everyone here though, before she gives us such news…would you mind going downstairs to ask her to wait a few moments while I gather the boys?"

"Of course, Sabine." I gave a quick wave and ducked out of the room.

Selene was in the same spot as when I had left her. And as before, she didn't turn around when I stepped into the room. I slid myself up against the wall just beside the doors. Ayden had gotten me into the habit of not seating myself until the Ancients were seated first. Even though Selene had been banished, she was still a member of the Ancients.

Not one word was exchanged between Selene and I as we waited for the others. I felt like saying something to try and console her, for there seemed to be a sadness hanging over her. However, I was unable to read her mind. I think I had tried reading her mind once before, when she was still living in the house, but I was always unsuccessful. I made a mental note to ask Ayden about it, because I was starting to be able to read his.

About two minutes later the Ancients came into the room. Tristan and Caelum must have been somewhere in the house since it didn't take them that long to join us. Ayden, however, was not among them.

"I thought you wanted everyone here for this…" I bolded stated without thinking.

Sabine smiled at me. "Yes my dear, Ayden is on his way but there is no need to wait for him. We will begin and then fill him in when he arrives."

The three of them took a seat at one end of the long table located in the middle of the room. Sabine gestured for me to take a seat in the chair next to Caelum. I did as she asked and then watched Selene seat herself at the opposite end of the table.

Several moments passed before anyone spoke. As I had hoped, Sabine spoke first. However, I wasn't really sure that I wanted to hear what Selene had to say just yet.

"I know that something is troubling you and that you have come here for help. Although I am not pleased that you have so quickly disobeyed my sentence of banishment, please tell us why, exactly, you are here." Sabine leaned back, folding her arms and tossing one leg over the other, her skirt ruffling as she shifted into a comfortable position. It was probably the first time I had ever seen her do something that didn't look completely proper.

Selene softly cleared her throat. "My fellow Ancients, I come here bearing some sad news, but I also come seeking aid. I am actually surprised that the news has not already traveled here before me..." She hesitated.

"Go on, Selene," Tristan encouraged her.

"I know that it will be no surprise to you to hear that I witnessed a vampire slaying recently. It has happened to us all at one point or another. However, the slaying I unfortunately had to watch was that of our dear Cousin Vidor..."

Gasps came from everyone but me, having never heard of or seen this cousin.

Selene held her hand up to her forehead, making her story even more dramatic. "I know, I know. It's terrible. But I was unable to help him. He was attacked by more than one slayer. If I had tried to save him, I surely would have been killed as well."

"Selene," Sabine began, "I know that this is a terrible loss to us all, but being attacked by more than one slayer is not uncommon. It's been done before. It is not really that something that would make one defy such a sentence as banishment. You could have just sent word through other means."

Selene smiled as she nodded her head. "Yes, I knew you would try to use that against me. But I would hope you know me well enough to know that I wouldn't have gone against strict orders unless it was of the utmost importance; something that was a threat to the vampire race."

"Well if it's of such great importance, as you say, then you should get on with it and tell us." Caelum seemed annoyed with her very presence.

Selene squinted her eyes in his direction but then continued her tale, "Just because I said Vidor was attacked by more than one slayer, that doesn't mean there were just two or three. When I said he was attacked by more than one, I should have said several. I just didn't want to frighten you with the actual number I saw. Vidor was slain…by at least fifteen slayers…yes!" Selene practically leapt from her chair and began to pace the floor. She was obviously working the story to make it more dramatic. I wondered if Sabine was buying it or not. "I know that this is absolutely unheard of, but that is how many I saw. They were quick, silent, and they of course have developed new technological weaponry."

I found myself to be intrigued by her last few words. Perhaps that sneaky Trent Murdock had been a part of it. I thought about saying something but decided not to chime in. Sabine would most likely give me a chance to talk later, if I wanted.

Caelum didn't seem to be impressed with her story. I thought he would be the one to say something, but it was Tristan who asked the questions. "What can you tell us about them? What would cause them to increase their numbers like that?"

"I am not sure," Selene replied, "but something had to have triggered it. It looks like they are upping everything just to try and take us all out as soon as possible. This gang of slayers worked like a machine when they tracked down Vidor. It was amazing that they didn't detect me."

Sabine held up her hand for attention. "Please, could we have possibly believed that the humans would never evolve to such an extent in their search for us? It was bound to come around eventually. We just tried to ignore it. Well, it looks like now that time has come for us to up our stakes as well and take a stand."

Caelum looked worried. "Sabine, you're not talking about a full-fledged war against the humans, are you?"

Sabine's eyes widened. "Oh, no! Absolutely not. I just think we need to increase our security and keep out a better watch for anything suspicious. My advice is just…don't be careless…."

"Vidor was never careless though, Sabine. You know that. How could this have happened?" Tristan was starting to look like he could go into panic mode any second.

Selene took her seat and answered his question before Sabine could, "Why do you think the slayers felt the need to use fifteen of their members? Because they knew Vidor was powerful and much easier to take down with numbers. I don't think *any* vampire could have survived a team of fifteen."

We had been talking for a little over a half hour when we heard the front door shut. Ayden was finally home. Everyone waited, silently, as we listened to his footsteps coming towards us down the hall. He must have sensed something was up the moment he walked in the door. And based on the look on his face, I don't think he was prepared to see Selene sitting there. Sabine asked him to take a seat next to Tristan. He did so, the whole time staring hard at Selene.

"Ayden, dear…Selene is here right now because she has been witness to the slaughter of our Cousin Vidor." Sabine's eyes watered just the slightest bit. "Selene said there were at least fifteen of them…and so I feel that it is time to take defensive steps and increase our protection as much as possible."

At first Ayden didn't know what to say. He still seemed confused and angry from seeing Selene, but then he addressed the Ancients. He made sure not to make eye contact with Selene. It seemed as though he didn't consider her to be part of the Ancients circle anymore. "My Ancients…I would like to help in any way possible. What can we do to stop the slayers?"

"I am not sure if we have the option of full out stopping them, but a strong defense should suffice." Tristan looked to Sabine for approval. "We shouldn't have to leave the mansion, right?"

"Of course not!" Caelum exclaimed. "This house is one of the safest places we have ever lived. Although we usually move every thirty years so the humans don't get suspicious, we have never had any major security problems with any of our homes."

"True…" Sabine began, "but a plan for evacuation must be considered…for emergency purposes only of course. If things are escalating as Selene has described, then we must take all necessary precautions."

Now it was Ayden's turn to speak, and his tone was completely unexpected. "Well, that's it though!" He stood and began pacing across the room. "You are talking about all this just based on what she has said. How are we to know that she is telling the truth?"

Selene jumped up from her chair. "Are you calling me a liar?"

He turned and faced her. "Maybe I am. I'm not sure that we can trust you...not with all that has gone on lately. You've already betrayed me twice, who's to say you won't do it again?"

He had crossed the line with that statement. Selene came flying across the room at him. She grabbed his throat and pinned him up against the wall. "How dare you! I gave you a better life *and* a companion. What more could you ask for? You don't deserve such gifts. Perhaps I should have left you to die that night!"

"That's enough! This is not just about you, Ayden," Sabine cried. "There will be no more of that in this house! Both of you control yourselves, now! You both should know better...plus, you're not setting a very good example for young Calista...."

Selene slowly released Ayden. He rubbed his neck as he took his seat again. Selene returned to her own chair as well. All I could do was sit there in amazement. I could now tell that Ayden was never going to forgive her.

Sabine took over the conversation and quickly changed the subject. "Well, it's still early. Ayden, I know you have already fed but perhaps you'll take Calista out. I don't want anyone venturing out alone anymore. The boys and I will most likely head out shortly."

Ayden nodded and got up to whisk me out into the night. I took his hand and we headed towards the doors. I was hoping Selene wouldn't follow.

"Selene," Sabine addressed her firmly, "I think it would be in your best interest to stay here. There is still much that needs to be discussed and I would rather you not cause those two any more grief tonight."

Ayden didn't even look back as we exited the room. I could almost feel his anger seeping through his skin. It was like a fire was burning inside him and the heat was trying hard to escaping.

We barely spoke a word to each other as we prepared to leave. The nights were becoming brisk with each passing day, so Ayden insisted I bundle up. Lately, Ayden had also been trying to get me to wear elegant gowns; similar to the ones Sabine commonly wore. I had humored him several times, but I was still partial to my usual outfits of jeans and tank tops. I wasn't really into the whole idea of Ayden trying to dress me up. I enjoy a nice dress every now and then but I'm not all that much of a girly-girl. However, the gowns were quite gorgeous so I didn't mind wearing them every now and then.

Our silence continued until we walked into town. I couldn't take it anymore so I decided to question Ayden about it.

"Ayden…will you please tell me what's wrong? I know that Selene upset you but…"

"Calista…" he stopped and faced me, "I know you may feel some lingering sense of emotion for her since she *is* the one who made you, but my love for her has faded. Like I said…she has betrayed me twice; once with me and once with you…and I can't stand her lies anymore. And Sabine is not helping things by allowing Selene to come back to the house."

I grabbed his hands. "But Sabine is such a gentle heart, Ayden. I think she sees the better part in all of us and wants to give Selene a chance to redeem herself."

My words frustrated him. He let go of me and started walking again. "It's not that simple, Calista. You can't just forgive something like that. Over the years I have been with her, she has broken more rules than I can count. And because she is an Ancient herself, she gets away with it. If anyone of lesser stature did the same things she has, he or she would have surely gotten a worse punishment than banishment."

"Do you mean…death?" I asked almost fearfully.

"Oh no, no, no! Well, I mean, I have never heard of it happening before and I am sure that the Ancients aren't the type to use such a harsh punishment. But you never know…."

I didn't know what else to say so I changed the subject. "So where are we off to, my dear? A bar? A club? I wouldn't mind finding a good club. I am kind of in the mood for dancing."

He gave me one of his sweet smiles and crooked his elbow for me to hold onto. "Whatever your little heart desires, my love."

We were able to find a cozy little dance club not too far into town. Tristan was the one who taught me that dance clubs were the easiest places to practice feeding out in the open when the time came for me to learn. I figured it would be a good idea to start practicing, but I really was in the mood to dance.

Even though Ayden and I usually stayed close together, we split up once inside the club. It was actually harder to hunt with someone of the opposite sex. People would think you're a couple so they tend to keep their distance.

I decided to do something different for the night and chose a seat right at the edge of the dance floor. Apparently it was a good spot because I caught someone's eye real quick. To my surprise, it was a beautiful young woman. Now, this was a first for me. I had never been into girls before, but when it came down to blood, gender didn't really matter all that much. I glanced quickly in Ayden's direction to see if he was watching. He was, and he had a huge smile on his face. Noticing I had attracted a female obviously excited him. Apparently being vampire didn't suppress those male hormones and fantasies too well.

The young lady asked if I wanted to dance with her. I flashed a sexy smile and took off my coat as I stood. We wrapped arms around each other's waists and slid out onto the dance floor. She was a terrific dancer; actually better than most guys I had danced with in the past.

She tried yelling a question at me about getting my name and number. I was able to hear her perfectly but I pretended the music was too loud. She waved it off and pulled me towards her. Her hips trusted up against mine. At first I was a little uncomfortable but then I let myself get into it. I didn't care what anyone thought. I was a vampire now. I could do whatever I wanted. I threw my arms around her neck and tossed my hair back. The girl laughed and wrapped her arms tighter around my waist.

As we continued to grind on the dance floor, I could feel Ayden's eyes running over me. I knew he was enjoying it, probably just as much as the rest of the men in the club. For some reason, being so close to this girl was making me think about how Ayden and I still hadn't had sex yet. The more I thought about it, the more I wanted him. I thought that maybe I could use this girl as a way to get Ayden to take me to bed. Just because blood gave us pure pleasure didn't mean we had to forget all other pleasures. I was not about to give up sex for all eternity!

The music seemed to grow louder and strobe lights were flashing all around us. I quickly glanced where Ayden was sitting. He was still there, watching us like a little boy in a candy store. I slowly licked my lips with the tip of my tongue, gave him a wink, then turned and kissed the girl I was dancing with. I think I caught her off guard but she was quick to kiss me back. Cheers roared through the club. Just about every guy's fantasy has just been fulfilled.

It wasn't as good as kissing Ayden had been but it wasn't all that bad. We pulled away from each other as the song came to an end and another began. I asked her if she wanted to grab a drink. She nodded in agreement. I grabbed my coat and we head towards the back of the club. Lucky for me, there was a secluded table in a dark corner. We sat down and ordered drinks. She asked for a double. I kept mine light even though I wasn't even going to drink it.

We didn't really talk until the drinks came. Once she got through half her drink, there was no stopping her. She began to talk all about her life, the way we danced, her family, and anything else she could think of. I just smiled and nodded for most of it. I wasn't really sure what to say. But I was also rather hungry and wanted her blood. I gave a quick scan around us to see if anyone in particular was watching. Only Ayden was keeping on eye on us. I was sure he wanted to see some more action but he also wanted to make sure no one became suspicious when I started feeding.

Everything looked all right so I took the chance and kissed the girl again. I had stopped her mid-sentence but she didn't seem to mind. Her kiss in return was hard and passionate. Our lips broke and I made my way to her neck. I gently kissed and licked her neck, feeling her body rise up against mine. Her neck was obviously her weak spot, coincidently so was mine. She melted right into my arms and as she let out a soft moan, I sank my teeth in.

Her body became rigid for just a moment but then she went limp again. Tristan and Ayden had taught me how to transition from the kissing to the sucking blood to make it feel like the same pleasure.

Apparently I had done it well since she didn't resist me. I drank until I had had enough but not enough to kill her. She would just seem drunk when she found the energy to move. I released her and gently leaned her back against her chair. It was then that I noticed Ayden to be standing next to me.

He leaned down and whispered in my ear. "Well done, my gorgeous. You've successfully fed in public without anyone detecting you."

I licked my lips and kissed his cheek. "Thank you. Would you care to sit?"

"No thank you, I think it would be best for us to head back home now."

"You've fed already?" I asked.

"Yes, as a matter of fact I have. See the woman in the corner by the door?" He pointed in the direction.

"Ah, yes. I see her." She was probably in her mid-thirties. She looked drunk, leaning heavily up against a wall.

He held out his hand for me to take. I took it and then left some money on the table to pay for the drinks. We linked arms and exited the club. I felt completely relaxed, mostly from the blood, but also partially from being complimented by Ayden.

I wanted to take my time walking back to the mansion, but Ayden insisted on picking up the pace.

"Ayden, why are we walking so fast? Why can't we enjoy the night?"

He stopped and pulled me to him. "Because, you sexy vampire, I want you in my bed."

I was surprised at first but then smiled because my plan had worked. "Why Ayden! What brought this on?" I asked the question even though I knew exactly what had provoked him. I just wanted to hear him say it.

He pushed his hips hard against mine. "Oh Calista…watching you dance with that other girl…and then when you kissed her…I almost ran to the dance floor…I would have taken you right then and there!"

"Ayden!" I was practically speechless. "I…I was hoping this side of you was hidden in there somewhere. I've wanted you ever since my first night here."

"Well, you're not the only one. I've come to find that the sex drive is heightened once transformed from human to vampire."

His words only made me want him more. I grabbed his hand and started tugging him towards the house. We were only ten minutes away, but we could make it there in five if we hurried.

Ayden wouldn't even let me walk the rest of the way once we made it to the front gates. He carried me all the way inside and up to his bedroom. He gently laid me on the bed and then made sure the doors were locked.

I was a little nervous even though it wasn't truly my first time. But it felt almost as if it was my first time all over again. I was in a new body and new state of mind. However, I was confident that Ayden knew what he was doing.

I had hoped that things would start out slow and sensuous, but before we had even left the club, our hormones were raging. We tore at each other's clothes until we were completely nude. He took a moment to savor the moment, looking me up and down.

I pulled him close to me and whispered, "Take me now…."

He didn't hesitate. I was tossed on my back and he brought himself on top of me. He slowly slid himself inside me. It felt ten times better than I had remembered it as a human.

He smiled and said, "Everything is *always* better as a vampire."

He began to thrust a little harder. I wrapped my legs around his waist and locked my ankles, causing him to go even deeper. The squeeze of my legs made him moan softly. I curled my fingers around his neck and looked into his eyes. His eyes looked more vibrant than I had ever seen them.

Over and over again, he pushed hard against me. Whenever he pulled away, I would just pull him right back to me. I didn't want it to end. Everything just felt so good.

After a few more minutes, I climaxed, letting out a soft moan. I knew he wasn't finished yet so I kept pulling him to me. But the next thing I knew, he was lifting me and flipping me onto my stomach. He wrapped his arm around my waist and pulled me tightly to him. I held onto his arms and let him take me. I could feel the pleasure building again. Ayden's stomach was tightening as he thrusted harder. He was getting ready to come and it made me become all the more closer to that point as well.

Right as he orgasmed, he bit into my shoulder and began to suck some of my blood. I was shocked at first but then it felt like the pleasure in my body doubled. I moaned loudly, practically screaming from the ecstasy of it.

He held me tight for another moment and then let go. I dropped to the bed on my stomach and closed my eyes. I wanted to turn over so I could look at him but I was so exhausted. I thought about the wounds on my shoulder, but it didn't matter because they had already healed. Ayden lay down beside me and stroked my back.

I opened my eyes and tried to speak with what breath I had left. "I...have never felt...anything like that before...in my entire life."

He smiled. "Of course you haven't. Our senses are extremely heightened as vampires. The pleasure is just that much greater. Plus, we also receive pleasure through blood, which makes everything absolutely amazing."

"You're telling me!"

He laughed and then pulled the covers up over us. It was still early in the night but the sex had exhausted me. Ayden said that we probably wouldn't sleep long but he would have one of the maids wake us if we weren't up in an hour. I must have passed out soon after he left to find a maid because I don't remember him coming back to bed.

Sixteen

It felt like several hours had passed. I was forced from sleep by Sabine who was shaking my shoulders drastically.

"Calista, my dear. You must wake up!"

I opened my eyes and tried to get her to stop shaking me. "What is it, Sabine?"

She held onto my arms and looked me right in the eyes. "Get dressed…we must leave…now."

"What do you mean, leave now? What's going on?" I grabbed the robe that was hanging on the bedpost and slipped into it. "Where is Ayden?"

"Ayden's alright. He is helping the others seal up the house as best they can. The slayers are attacking." Her eyes darted towards the windows.

I collected my clothes and dressed quickly. "What can we do? Should we help them?"

"There isn't time, dear. We must gather the others and get out of here as discretely as possible. There is an escape passage near the vault."

I had so many questions to ask but there just wasn't time for anything at all. Sabine grabbed my hand firmly and led me through the hallways. Selene and Tristan were waiting for us at the vault entrance.

"Where are Ayden and Caelum?" Sabine questioned them.

Selene merely shrugged but Tristan was good enough to answer. "I remember seeing them near the rear entrance. I think they were trying to help the help staff escape. Selene and I had been working on the front. Perhaps they are still there."

I quickly volunteered. "I'll go get them!"

Sabine seemed unsure. "I'm not sure that's wise…Tristan…"

"Please!" I interrupted her.

A loud noise came from the front of the house. Sabine looked worried. "Go quickly!" She gave me a gentle push.

I ran toward the back of the house, calling out for Ayden and Caelum. There was banging coming from all sides of the house. It was difficult to tell how many slayers were trying to get in. It sounded like hundreds. I continued to yell for the guys. No answer was coming, which was starting to worry me. Luckily, I finally found them near the library. A large set of doors was adjacent to the library doors and the boys were trying to board them up. I jumped in to help them.

"Calista!" Ayden practically yelled in my ear. "What are you doing here? You should be with Sabine."

"I was," I said, pushing up against the doors. "But I volunteered to come find you two. Sabine says we need to leave right away. They are waiting for us at the vault."

Caelum pounded a few more nails into the doors. "There! That should hold long enough for us to get a head start. Let's go before we run out of time."

The three of us ran all the way back to the vault. Sabine and the others were still there. The moment we were spotted, Tristan and Selene pushed open a secret door next to the main door of the vault. We all ducked through the door and the two of them closed it behind us.

Even though it was pitch dark inside, I could tell that we were just inside a small room. There didn't seem to be any other doors besides the one we had come through.

"I thought you said we were leaving, Sabine." I tried not to sound irritated.

"We are, dear. Just be patient." She scanned the wall furthest from the door with her hand. I heard her press something. The moment she pushed it, the floor began to shake a little.

"What is going on?" I had to admit, I was a bit scared.

Ayden put his arm around me. "Don't worry, it's going to be alright. It's sort of like an elevator. This is actually going to take us up to the highest point of the house. There we should be able to hide out until the slayers are convinced we're not here."

I wrinkled my brow in confusion. "I don't understand…why are we staying in the house? We could get caught!"

"That's why we have the distraction," Caelum chimed in.

"What's the distraction?" I asked.

Selene rolled her eyes. "It's actually kind of stupid but it does work. There are several emergency call buttons located throughout the house. If anyone of us were to push one, it would send out a signal to our nearest of kin. Then they create a distraction to lead the slayers away from the mansion."

"That is pretty good I guess. But they already know where we live…wouldn't they come back?"

"That's an excellent question, Calista," Caelum said. "Which is why, once they all leave, we must pack up our belongings and make arrangements to move as soon as possible."

By this time, the elevator had stopped. A small doorway opened to reveal a room just large enough for all of us to squeeze into. We piled in and closed the elevator door.

"But where will we move to? I don't understand…" The thought of leaving my new home wasn't very comforting after I had already settled in.

Sabine stepped in to explain it. "Well my dear, we will move to another one of our houses. We own countless mansions across the globe. We'll move somewhere else and then if this house is safe again, one of our kin may move in. It's a constant cycle. We've lived here in this house for quite some time now but moving is always expected."

Right then we heard a loud noise from below. The slayers had finally broken through our barriers. They were inside. Sabine and the others listened carefully to make sure that we were not detected. I tried to listen as well but it was too difficult for me. The voices and thoughts were too jumbled for me to make clear. Ayden wrapped his arm around my shoulder and pulled me close to him. I rested against him, my head on his chest so I could listen to his heart. Since I wasn't able to hear the slayers' thoughts as they could, I knew any change in Ayden's heartbeat would tell me what was going on.

Surprisingly, the slayers started to dissipate within an hour's time. Even when the Ancients were sure that the very last one had left the house, they insisted we wait longer. And so we did: another hour. Sabine finally gave the OK that we could make our way back to the main floor. We left the small hideout and rode the elevator back downstairs.

Caelum was the first to check if the coast was clear. He poked his head out: nothing. One by one we stepped out of the small room. Everyone had left, but they had left our home in ruins. Literally every object in the house was strewn across rooms and hallways. Vases and statues were shattered into pieces. The slayers had searched everywhere for us along with any information they felt could be useful to them.

Sabine took a look around. "Well…at least we are all safe and sound. But I feel we must explore the house to see what has been taken."

The other three Ancients nodded in agreement. Selene headed towards the library. Caelum, Tristan and Sabine all left to check the offices upstairs. Ayden and I were left to check the remainder of the house. I would have been glad to check the rooms on my own, but I wasn't entirely sure what to look for. Ayden had me follow him through the house, letting me know whenever he believed something was missing.

"Should I make a list, Ayden?"

"No, that's not necessary. The two of us together should be able to remember what we find to be missing. So far, it only looks like minor paperwork has been taken. Things like receipts and a couple of letters from friends, but I don't think anything too important has ever been spoken in such letters. We know better than to divulge secrets within correspondence. It's too easily intercepted."

"Should we go see how the others are doing?" I asked.

He didn't answer. He just turned towards the stairs. I quickly followed. The first place we stopped was Sabine's office. She didn't even look up as we walked into the room. She was seated behind her desk, staring out the window.

Ayden approached her desk cautiously. "Sabine? Is everything all right?"

Sabine turned around in her chair to face us. "Ayden…I'm afraid it is time for us to move yet again…Calista, could you please go get the others?"

I turned and darted out of the room. Tristan and Caelum were in their own offices just down the hall. I ran to each room, quickly telling them we were all meeting in Sabine's office. Then I ran as quickly as I could downstairs to find Selene. She was in the library shuffling through the disaster on the floor and table.

"Selene, Sabine would like us all to be up in her office…she said…she said we have to move."

She looked at me, for the first time, with a little bit of sadness in her eyes. "Alright…let's go."

We walked briskly upstairs to join the others. Once in Sabine's office, everyone took a seat and waited for Sabine to tell us what she planned to do.

"My dears," she started, "after sifting through all this rubble, I have come to find that it will certainly no longer be safe for us to live here. We must move. The slayers have taken many personal letters, receipts, faxes and phone numbers. It won't be long before they start trying to track down our close friends."

"Should we warn the others?" Tristan asked.

"Warn the others? Are you kidding? Do you even realize how many vampires there are in the world?" Selene's tone was firm but a bit harsh.

"We can't just let them be tracked down and slaughtered, Selene!" Tristan yelled back at her.

"That's enough you two," Sabine interrupted. "There is no need for you to fight at the moment. Now, as much as I would like to 'warn' the others, I don't think it is safe to do so. We will probably be continually watched while still in Greece. It is best to take care of ourselves first and find a new haven."

I couldn't help but ask. "But…where will we go?"

Ayden was the one to answer. "Don't worry, honey. You heard Sabine earlier. We own plenty of homes around the world. There is certainly an empty one somewhere. We just need to check the records as to which one is the safest for us right now."

"Lucky for us, the slayers have been unable to access our records regarding our living arrangements. Those records are securely located off the property, only accessible to us vampires. I will have Caelum take care of it before sunrise. Once our new destination is determined, we shall arrange for our remaining belongings to be shipped there during the day. Then we shall travel the following night."

Caelum stood. "Let me go search through the records now. The sooner we can arrange to leave, the better."

"I agree," Sabine stated. "The rest of us should probably pack things up and clean while Caelum is out."

"Good idea," Ayden said as he stood up. "I think I'll go take care of Calista's and my bedrooms. Calista, feel free to help the others with whatever they may need and I'll come back soon to help finish things up." He turned and left the room.

The uneasiness that had been hanging between Selene and I suddenly became quite noticeable. Sabine obviously picked up on it because she asked me to help pack up what was left of her office. I followed Sabine out of the room. I could feel Selene's cold eyes staring hard at me, but I wouldn't glance in her direction.

Sadly, there was not much left of Sabine's office to even pack. There were several books, some computer disks, CDs and some miscellaneous papers strewn about the room. The desk drawers were practically empty. The slayers had taken just about everything, which were mainly letters and business documents.

Sabine picked up an empty cardboard box, placed it on the desk and began to fill it with papers. "I know you feel a distinct malice for her right now, Calista. But it shall pass with time."

"Oh, I don't hate her, Sabine. I really don't. There's just…"

She held up one hand to stop me, but continued to pack the box with her other hand. "Don't bother trying to explain it dear. It's too difficult. But you will understand what I mean when the time comes. Just be patient and the feeling will fade."

I didn't know what to say to her. I wanted to explain what it was that I felt towards Selene, but Sabine seemed to not want to discuss it further. I decided it was best to just take her advice and wait things out. Hopefully things between Selene and I would smooth over as Sabine had indicated.

I started to survey the room to see where I could start packing. I wasn't really sure where to start because I didn't want to disrupt anything that Sabine may have not wanted me to touch.

As usual, Sabine knew what I was thinking. "I wouldn't worry about disrupting anything, my dear. The slayers took care of that...but you could probably start by packing up all the books if you'd like."

I did as she suggested and found an empty crate to place the books in. As I packed, I started to wonder about the slayers. Sabine would know the answers to my questions. "Sabine...why not report this incident to the local police? Surely they can do something about it. I mean, those people broke into your house and stole things."

She stopped packing for just a moment to look at me. "Unfortunately my dear, they have connections with the police. There's not a country, state or province that I have not found such a connection."

"But I don't understand...why not pretend to be human like you always tell us we have to do? I'm sure the police could be just as easily fooled as other humans."

Sabine laughed softly and continued to pack. "Of course they can, but it wouldn't help. The slayers can get any police report they want. If we reported the break-in, the slayers would use it to their advantage. They'd know the report was ours because they now have this address. It would only help them track us down and destroy us."

I stopped packing for a moment and took a seat. "That's another thing I don't really understand, Sabine. How is it that we can move from one house to the next, and other vampires do it as well, when slayers find out where we live sometimes?"

Sabine wrinkled her brow. "I'm not sure I understand what you're asking."

"Well, like this house for instance. The slayers here know we live here. What if, after we move out, another set of vampires moves in? Who's to say that the slayers won't come here and destroy *them*?"

"Ah, now I see what you're saying. Well, the answer to that is that another vampire won't set foot into this house for several decades. We make sure that the house remains either empty or occupied by humans once our residence has been discovered. After many years, the house is then checked for safety. If it's secure enough, then whoever wants to can move in." She looked at me to see if I understood her answer. "But do keep in mind that they do so at their own risk with the knowledge that this residence has been previously breached."

"Well, I guess that makes sense. But wouldn't the slayers keep the address to this house on file? Letting later generations of slayers know that this house has been marked as a vampire residence?" I was starting to find that I had more questions about the slayers then I had originally thought.

"Well, that's where my genius young men come into play: Tristan and Caelum." A large smile came across her face. "Tristan and Caelum are wonderful when it comes to technology. Both continue to study it over the years and they make sure to keep up with the times. If a new technology is developed, they are the first to try it out and dissect it. Whatever the slayers use, the boys have it as well. Tristan loves to hack into their system and delete files whenever he gets the chance."

I couldn't help but smile. I could just picture Tristan sitting at a computer and laughing as he deleted file after file on the slayers' network. He may be thirty-five hundred years old but he still had the heart of a teenager.

I couldn't think of anything else to ask, so I continued packing up Sabine's books. I was able to fill two boxes for her. Sabine only filled one very small box with papers and CDs she felt important enough not to leave behind along with some personal effects she couldn't bear to part with. We gathered the boxes and carried them down into the main foyer of the house. Several boxes were already packed and stacked near the front doors. Tristan and the others were obviously packing much quicker than Sabine and I.

Sabine placed her hand on my shoulder after I had set down the two boxes of books. "Why don't you go help Ayden with the bedrooms? I'm going to go see how the others are doing and then make the necessary calls to have our things shipped out. Let Ayden know that I'd like everyone to finish things up as quickly as possible. Once you're done, please head down to the vault."

I nodded and turned to go upstairs. "Oh, Calista!" Sabine called after me.

I stopped and turned to look at her. "Yes, Sabine?"

"If you are truly that troubled by your feelings towards Selene, I would suggest talking to Ayden while you're up there. I'm sure he can give you a bit more insight than I can considering his…experience with the matter."

"Thank you…perhaps I will speak with him about it. We'll be down shortly." I turned and ran up the stairs to find Ayden.

When I finally found him, he was in Tristan's bedroom. Both Selene and Sabine's rooms had already been packed.

"There you are!" I said, hugging him tight. "Sabine sent me up to help you. What can I do?"

He smiled and kissed my cheek. "How about you go take care of our room? I thought it would be better for you to do that instead of these rooms that you're unfamiliar with."

"Sure thing. Oh yeah, and Sabine wanted me to tell you that as soon as we are done up here, she wants us to go down to the vault. And she'd like us to get it done as soon as possible."

"Ok, that's no problem. There are already boxes and a few suitcases in our room. If you need any more, there should be plenty of duffel bags in the closet."

"Ok," I said, starting to head out. Then I remembered what Sabine had told me. "Oh, Ayden…?"

"Yes? What is it, love?" His responses were always so sincere and full of worry. It made my feelings for him grow stronger.

"Ayden, I was just wondering…well…when Selene…when Selene…"

"Made me." He finished for me.

"Yes…when she made you. Did you feel anything? Well, what I mean is, were you angry with her?" I blushed and looked at the floor as I said those final words.

"Oh my darling," he said as he came to me and hugged me close, "there's no reason for you to feel ashamed of such a thing. I know that you are feeling some animosity towards Selene right now, but it will pass. I felt that way when she first made me too because it was against my will. But as time passed, I came to love her because she is my maker, and she is also my family now. Just give it some time." He stroked my hair gently.

"I'm sorry Ayden. I tried to explain it to Sabine, but she suggested I speak with you about it."

"And it was a good suggestion. Sabine is very wise and it's usually a good idea to listen to what she has to say."

"Oh I don't doubt that! I guess I just needed to tell someone about it and since she is one of the Ancients, I figured she would be the best candidate."

"Of course. But don't you worry. Things will get better. I promise. Now go ahead and pack up our room. I'll meet you downstairs in a few minutes." He gave my hands a quick squeeze and went back to packing.

I watched him for a moment, marveling at his perfect body. Every time I looked at the exquisite details of his body, I couldn't help but want him even more. But I shook the thoughts from my mind and ran off to our room to pack up.

As Ayden had said, there were several boxes piled near the bed as well as two large suitcases. I started with the suitcases first: one for Ayden's clothes and one for mine. Now that I was able to accomplish tasks ten times more quickly than humans, I took full advantage of it, packing both suitcases in five minutes flat. There really wasn't much else in the room to pack up. A few books and trinkets that I thought Ayden would maybe want to keep, but other than that the room was pretty much done. I wrapped up the breakable items in bubble wrap and placed them gently into a shoebox. The books easily fit into the remaining room of the suitcases.

After double-checking the room, I grabbed the suitcases and shoebox and brought them downstairs. There were twice as many boxes now as when I was there not a half hour before. The others were nowhere to be seen, however. I figured they were either still packing or were already down at the vault. I dropped the suitcases next to the pile of boxes and placed the shoebox on top of them. As

I started to walk in the direction of the vault, I noticed my eyes were feeling a bit heavy. Sleep was definitely on its way, which meant it was getting to be near dawn. With the thought in mind, I walked a bit quicker to the vault.

When I made it to the bottom of the stairs, Ayden was there alone, waiting for me. He immediately stood once he saw it was just me. "There you are, Calista! I was about ready to come upstairs to get you. Everything all packed?"

"Yep!" I sat down on the steps and yawned. "Is there anything else that needs to be done?"

He came over and sat next to me. "There are just a few more things, but you don't need to worry about that. The others will take care of the rest. You can climb into bed if you'd like. I know you're tired. Dawn is approaching."

"Well, alright…I can help some more tomorrow night if there's anything left to do." I stood and started towards my coffin.

"I wouldn't concern yourself with that. Tomorrow night, by the time you wake, we'll already have the moving trucks packed and ready to go. All you'll have to do is get into the car with me and we'll be off."

"Do you know where we're going yet?" I asked, pulling off my pants and shirt and slipping into a silky black nightgown.

Ayden watched me with hungry eyes as I dressed. "Yes, Caelum has been checking the system for quite some time but luckily he was able to find something. He said there's an available house in the States."

I almost tripped over my coffin when he said it. "The States? As in the United States?" I asked with a wavering voice.

"Well, yes…the United States. Is something wrong?" He wrinkled his brow in confusion and concern.

"Ayden…I'm originally *from* the United States…don't you remember?"

"Oh yeah! Oh…Calista, are you alright with going back there?"

"Well…where exactly in the States are we going?" I was dreading the answer.

"Hmm, come to think of it, Caelum didn't tell me. Let me go ask him." He stood to leave.

"No!" I started towards him. "Please don't. I'd rather not know until tomorrow. That way I can sleep a little more peacefully. Just let me know tomorrow when we get up, ok? I'm going to sleep now; the sun will be rising soon."

"That's a good idea." He came over and hugged me tight. "Get some rest. We'll talk tomorrow. And don't worry, ok? Everything will turn out fine." He gave me a quick kiss and then went upstairs to finish up whatever was left to pack.

I climbed into my coffin and pulled the lid over me. I couldn't help but lie there and try to listen to the voices and thoughts of the Ancients above me. I was sure that Sabine would soon detect my prying and block her thoughts, but I couldn't stop thinking about the fact that we were going to where I was born. What if we were moving to a place near where I used to live? My parents had stopped talking to me not long after they kicked me out, so they weren't really what I was worried about. I was thinking more about the people I became friends with at the casinos. And suddenly, thoughts of Shane entered my mind. Was he still in Las Vegas? I didn't know if I would really be able to handle seeing him again…if it actually came to that.

I thought that my racing mind would keep me awake but I found that the power of the sun was overwhelming and it quickly put me to sleep. Luckily I was able to sleep all through the day without any interrupting dreams.

Seventeen

Ayden woke me the next night. "Rise and shine, beautiful. There's no hurry, but we're going to leave as soon as you're dressed."

I sat up and kissed him gently. I looked around and noticed everyone's coffins were still in place. "Aren't we taking these with us?" I asked.

Ayden took my hand and helped me up. "Nope. We never take them. It's too much of a hassle and the humans find it odd when we travel with coffins. Brings up too many suspicions. So, it soon became customary for each house to leave their coffins in the vault. If there aren't enough for all of us at the new house, then we'll just buy however many we need."

It made sense. I grabbed my clothes and went up to the bathroom to take a quick shower. The others were very patient with me and waited as I showered and dressed. It didn't take me too long, so we were ready to go within fifteen minutes. There was black limousine parked out front to take us to the airport.

Once I heard the word airport, I suddenly became worried. I grasped Ayden's hand. "Ayden! Why are we flying?"

"It's quicker than by boat. You've never had a problem with flying before, what's wrong?"

"But…what if there's sunlight while we're in the sky? What if it's daytime when we get there? We could all die!" I was a little amazed at how worried I was. I had never gotten that worked up about something in my entire life.

Tristan was quick to answer my concerns. "Calista, it's really alright. Please calm down. We'll all be fine. We always plan things out so that we won't have to travel during the day or to a place that is currently in its daylight hours. Everything is carefully planned. No worries."

His words comforted me some but I wouldn't be fully convinced until we actually traveled and made it to our new destination safely. Caelum let the driver know that we were ready to go and the limo took off towards the nearest airport. The drive there wasn't too long, maybe forty-five minutes. Our plane didn't leave for another hour though. We waited at the gate for our flight to be called for boarding.

I couldn't help but look around while we waited. My most recent memories of an airport involved Trent Murdock. I kept wondering if he was still on his mission to follow me and track down the vampires that he believed had contacted me. I also wondered if he knew of my transformation yet. It actually wouldn't be surprising if he did. The slayers had to certainly keep in touch and inform each other of newly made vampire sightings.

Luckily we boarded the plane quickly, and out of pure habit I took a seat at the very back of the plane. Ayden followed me but the others sat near the front.

Ayden sat down next to me and whispered in my ear, "Sabine is curious about why you sit all the way back here."

I laughed a little. "Sorry. Whenever I traveled when I was still human, I would always sit at the very back of the plane. Just a habit I got into. I guess I just wanted to be as far away from people as possible. I'm sure you remember that I wasn't much of a people person."

"Yes, I do remember. But that's changed now, don't you think? I think you have opened up a lot more since you've been with us." He soothingly rubbed my shoulder.

"Yes, I agree. Should we go sit with the others then? I feel bad now."

"Oh don't worry about it, honey. They don't mind. Sabine was just curious because you bee-lined it to the back."

Ayden spent the entire trip holding my hand. Now that we were able to be together for all time, he wouldn't let me out of his sight. He was a sweetheart though, always looking out for me. I loved having him always near me and feeling his undying affection, but there were occasions when I wanted some time to myself. Ayden was gracious enough to give it to me, but Sabine was certain that I wasn't strong enough to be completely on my own yet. After that one night I was followed by the two mysterious men, Caelum had also followed me. Turned out that Sabine had always sent someone along to watch me whenever I took off wandering. It was a little unnerving but I supposed I would get used to it.

After a few hours flying over the ocean, I realized that Ayden never told me exactly where it was that we were going. "Ayden!"

I must have startled him, because he jumped a little in his seat. "What's wrong?" he asked, grasping both my hands.

"I'm sorry, I didn't mean for that to sound so alarming. But I just remembered that you never told me where we were going. Remember I asked you to tell me later so that I could sleep?"

"Oh yes! I do remember, I am sorry for not telling you earlier. Caelum told me that we are headed to Nevada."

My heart almost stopped. "I beg your pardon?"

"Nevada," he said again.

"Ayden…that's where I used to live…don't you remember? Las Vegas, Nevada."

"Of course I remember, Calista. I didn't think you would have such a big problem with us going there. I actually thought you might be excited about seeing your homeland again. Plus, it's the only possible place for us to go right now." He put his arm around me. "Are you going to be alright?"

"I…I think so…I just wish I had more time to prepare for this…I haven't been back there in years…" My thoughts trailed off and started to wander towards the image of Shane in bed with another woman. Ever since that day, I have had trouble purging the scene from my memory.

Ayden must have noticed my eyes watering up. "Calista, what is it? Please tell me what I can do for you to make this transition easier."

"I'm just nervous. What if I run into him…?" For some reason I couldn't look Ayden straight in the eye when I talked about Shane.

He placed his hand under my chin. A single tear rolled down my cheek as he gently lifted my face towards his. "Who, Calista?"

I finally found the courage to look him in the eye. "Shane…"

His expression immediately became bland. I could tell he wasn't fond of Shane because of what I had told him. "Oh…" he said, his eyes drifting away from mine.

I didn't know what else to say to him. From the way I reacted to us traveling to Nevada, I think Ayden could tell that deep down there was a part of me that maybe still loved Shane. Perhaps I even wanted to see him again. That decision would be one I would have to make soon. As much as Ayden may not like it, he'd have to let me do this one on my own.

We spent the remainder of the flight in silence. From time to time I would look in his direction, to see if he wanted to talk. But each time, he would be staring off in the opposite direction. I thought about trying to read his thoughts, but I didn't want to intrude and I wasn't even sure I could do it accurately yet. I was still learning.

The plane landed at the Las Vegas airport around 10pm. It felt like my heart was pounding in my ears. The moment we stepped off the plane, I started to scan the minds of those around me. Bad idea. Millions of voices came flooding into my ears. I was almost knocked over by the force of it.

Ayden caught me before anyone else noticed. "Are you alright?"

"Yes, yes I'm fine."

"What happened?"

I held his hand and gave it a squeeze. "I was trying to scan people's thoughts, like you've been teaching me. But I think I just opened my mind too wide and it all came flooding in. I am still having trouble just pinpointing a particular string of thoughts from a single person."

He squeezed back and kissed my cheek. "Don't worry, my love. It will come with time. Just be patient and keep concentrating. You'll get the hang of it soon enough."

Tristan and Selene had called ahead and got us a limousine. It was already waiting for us outside. We piled in and the limo took off.

Our new home was located on the outskirts of Las Vegas. I felt a little bit better because I used to live right in the heart of the city. Being out in the desert was certainly far enough away to allow me a little bit of comfort.

The mansion was about the same size, if not bigger, than the mansion in Greece. The siding was made entirely of bricks and there were large marble columns across the front. Of course, there was an iron gate surrounding the property. They made sure to always have a large fence as the first line of defense. The house itself was equipped with an alarm system so the house was safer than most of that size. The Greece mansion also had a security system but the slayers had somehow bypassed it. Tristan said he had checked into the system for this house and it was far more advanced than the one back in Greece. He also planned to continually check it for breaches and flaws.

The limo pulled up to the front of the house. The movers had already been here and placed all our things inside. One by one, we climbed out of the car and made out way into the house. I was a little surprised to find that the house was completely furnished already.

"But we didn't ship any of our furniture here," I said out loud to myself.

Ayden put his arm around my waist. "It's because we always leave it there. It's a hassle to have to ship all that heavy stuff from country to country. All of our houses are always furnished. If we need anything, we can buy it here. If you haven't figured it out yet, we try to make everything we do as simple as possible."

It made perfect sense so I didn't carry any further into the conversation. I allowed Ayden to lead me upstairs to show me our room. Even though I shouldn't have been, I was surprised to find that most of the rooms were somewhat similar to the ones in Greece. Another way of making things simple, I supposed. Ayden must have read my thoughts again because he let me know that I was always at liberty to decorate parts of the house however I saw fit. This excited me a bit because I had been anxious to do something other than learning everything there is to know about being a vampire.

I plopped myself down on the bed and watched Ayden as he began to unpack his bags.

"So, what's our first plan of action in this new place?" I was anxious to explore a little before calling it a night. And I wasn't really up for any unpacking.

"Well, what would you like to do? We can do anything you want."

I checked the clock. We still had quite a few hours of darkness left. "Are you hungry? We could go into the city to eat and then call it a night if you'd like. We'll have plenty of time tomorrow to check out the surrounding towns."

He closed the dresser drawer and tossed the empty duffel towards the closet. "Yes, I am a bit hungry. That sounds like a good idea."

I slipped my hand into the crook of his elbow and we headed downstairs. Tristan and Caelum were in the foyer figuring out which boxes went where.

"Where's Sabine?" Ayden asked.

"I think she took a couple of boxes to her office and may even be talking with Selene," Caelum answered.

"Well, I really don't want to interrupt if the two of them are talking. Just let her know that Calista and I are going into the city for something to eat. We'll be back soon."

Instead of going out the front, Ayden took me through a side door that exited next to the garage. There was a bright green Kawasaki motorcycle sitting in the driveway.

"Where did this come from?" I asked.

Ayden walked over to it and pulled two helmets off the back. "I had it sent here before we arrived. I wanted it to be a surprise. Do you like it?"

I walked closer to it, giving it a good look over. "I've actually never been on a motorcycle before," I answered.

"Well, we'll just have to change that then! Here." He held out the smaller of the two helmets. "Hop on. We'll take a quick ride up and down the driveway. And then I might as well show you how to drive it. It'll be good for you to know."

163

I put the helmet on a little reluctantly. I had seen hundreds of these while living in Las Vegas, but I wasn't sure how I felt about actually riding on one. They seemed kind of dangerous. There was always a story on the news about someone losing control or getting into a horrible accident. But I didn't want to disappoint Ayden, so I climbed on the back. Ayden climbed onto the front and kicked up the kickstand. I wrapped my arms tightly around his waist. He started it up, revved the engine and within a matter of seconds we were halfway to the street. He slowed once we got to the gate and then turned back towards the house. Another fifteen seconds and we were back where we started.

He stopped and killed the engine. "Now that wasn't so bad, was it?"

I had to admit, it was rather exhilarating. "It was kind of fun actually. Now I am not sure about learning how to drive it though. Seems complicated. What if I crash into something?"

"Oh, you'll learn quickly. It's really quite simple. You turn this handle for the gas and the other handle is the clutch, to change gears. These grips here are for the brakes. Make sure you use both or just the rear brake. If you squeeze just the front one, you'll go flying over the handlebars. Want to give it a try? It's almost like driving a standard car, only with little turn handles instead of a stick shift."

"Well, I do know how to drive one of those. Maybe it won't be so bad. Will you ride on the back incase I have any trouble?"

"Of course, but first we'll real start out slow and I'll come along side you." He got off the bike and let me scoot up to the front.

Ayden explained to me step by step what I had to do to get the bike started in first gear. I made sure to do exactly what he told me. I gave it a little gas and the bike shot forward. I immediately put on the brake and stopped short. Ayden laughed a little but I tried not to take it to heart.

"Don't worry, Calista. You'll get the hang of it in no time." He tried to reassure me.

I tried it again, this time things went more smoothly. It only took me about ten minutes to get comfortable. Soon enough, I was driving up and down the driveway as if I had been riding a motorcycle for years. Ayden looked so proud.

"Well," he said, "now that you have that all figured out. Why don't we get going?"

"Yes, let's. I'm rather hungry."

Ayden had me scoot to the back again so he could drive us into the city.

Eighteen

D riving through the city brought back so many memories. I couldn't help but wonder what Shane might be up to. He had been my first love, so thoughts of him were always with me even though I tried to dispose of them.

The lights of the casinos and shops were absolutely brilliant. More vibrant than I had remembered them to be. Ayden had been right: It actually made me happy to be back in my hometown. I wanted to go see if my friends at the casino still worked there. However, Ayden might not approve of it. I'd have to check with him first. That could wait though; my thirst was starting to build.

Ayden chose one of the many parking garages located just off the Strip. I hopped off first and waited for Ayden to settle the bike. As I waited, I did the usual check to make sure we weren't in any danger. The garage itself was rather dark and creepy looking, but I couldn't sense any threat to us.

Ayden took my hand and led me out of the garage. We walked over to the Strip and looked for a good place to find our prey.

"Where do you think we should go, my dearest?" His eyes looked more gorgeous than ever with the casino lights shining in them.

"Well, there are quite a few restaurants on this street. Also a number of clubs." I looked down each end of the street, trying to make a decision. "Well…how would you feel about going to a strip club? It'd be something fun and different."

The left side of his mouth turned up in a mischievous grin. "That sounds rather exciting. And I am a bit turned on by the fact that you suggested that…Let's give it a try."

With that decided, we turned left and went into the first strip club we came to. Being in Vegas, it didn't take us long to find one.

When we walked in, we immediately went our separate ways. It was far too difficult to hunt when everyone thought you were a couple. I did what my old habits told me to do and headed for one of the empty back corners of the club. The moment I sat down, a young dancer came over to me. She must have been no more than seventeen years old. She was obviously new, because most strippers were not trained to go straight for the females unless beckoned.

She wore a black leather thong with matching bra and silver tassels hanging from her nipples. Instead of sexy high-heeled sandals, as I had expected, she wore knee-high vinyl boots. She must have been going for the dominatrix look.

The girl stood in front of me with her legs spread wide open. "Can I get you anything?" she asked in a sultry voice.

I gave her body a thorough check. There was not a flaw on her. I could smell her blood: young and fresh. As much as I wanted her, she was far too young to kill. I would never be able to take a life so young.

I glanced around the room, looking for someone a bit older and spotted a hot middle-aged man in the corner opposite mine. "Actually, there is something you can do for me."

The girl walked up closer and put her right foot on the chair, right between my legs. "Anything."

I gently ran my hand up her leg and then pointed across the room to the man I had spotted. "See that man over there?" I asked.

She turned her head ever so gracefully to see where I was pointing. "The guy who has Shayna dancing in front of him?" Her question couldn't have sounded more innocent.

"Shayna, huh? Well, she's not the one I am interested in. I want that man, over here, with us." I spoke the words to her in the most seductive way possible.

She turned her head back towards me and licked her lips. "That sounds like a sexy idea." She bent over, placing one hand on my knee and the other on my shoulder. She had bent almost in half, making sure that her breasts were nearly touching my face. "Don't go anywhere…I'll be right back."

The young girl turned and walked in the direction of where the man was sitting. I watched as she pulled the girl named Shayna aside and explained the situation. Shayna looked reluctant but she gave in and left. Then the girl leaned over the man and whispered into his ear. A smile formed across his face and she took his hand to lead him over to me.

As they approached, I placed my left leg up on the chair next to me. The man's smile seemed to grow as he began to notice how young I looked. "Please," I said to him, gesturing to the chair my foot was on. "Take a seat, babe."

He let go of the young girl's hand and quickly came over to the chair. I lifted my leg and let him sit, but then placed it on his thigh once he was settled. He was certainly enjoying things already.

"Now, I am sure you are wondering why I asked this beautiful young lady to bring you over here." I gestured for the girl to come sit in my lap. She did as I asked. "I was hoping that the three of us could have a little fun."

The young girl pushed her hair back and pressed herself up against me. "I'm up for it."

Of course she was, she was a stripper. She'd probably do just about anything to make a few bucks.

"Oh man…" the man started, "this is like every guy's fantasy, let alone my own! Of course I'm up for it!" He looked about ready to burst with joy.

I stroked the girl's cheek. "Is there a private room we could retreat to?" I asked.

"Of course. There are plenty over there." She pointed to our right. "If one is not available, I'll be sure to clean it out." She stood to check the rooms.

I gave her a gentle pat on the ass. "That's a good girl," I said.

She ran off to check the rooms. I think she was actually excited about this. Probably her first time entertaining two people at once.

Meanwhile, the man was staring at my legs; I could tell he wanted to put his hands all over me. I was willing to allow it, as soon as we were in one of the private rooms. Part of it was because I didn't really want

Ayden to see another man groping me, but part of it was because I needed the privacy in order to feed. I had it all planned perfectly so that no one would get suspicious.

Moments later the young girl came running back. She let us know that the third room on the right was open and we could go into it now. The man and I stood and he placed his arms around the young girl's waist and mine. We walked into the room and closed the curtains. There were plush pillows and soft blankets all over the place. I turned and gently pushed the man so that he sat himself down into a pile of pillows.

"Well, what I would really like to do is have a little fun with her," I said pointed to the girl, "and have you watch us." The man nodded in excitement. "And then, I'd like to come have some fun with you."

"I am not opposed to any of that!" he almost shouted. "Please start whenever you are ready." I smiled and turned to the girl. She was still standing next to me. I grabbed her waist and pulled her to me. She wrapped her arms around my neck and allowed me to kiss her. I kissed her long and hard. I could hear the man rustling around in the pillows. He was obviously having some excitement going on in his pants.

I released the girl and ran my fingers down the front of her body. "Dance for me," I whispered.

She immediately complied and started out what must have been her routine for the night. She used my body as her dancing pole and grinded her hips up against my leg. I ran my hands all over her body, gently caressing her curves. We were facing the man and letting him watch every movement. The girl came around in front of me and I turned her around so her back was up against my stomach. I pulled her close and gently squeezed her breasts. The man almost jumped off the floor. I motioned for him to wait his turn. I then ran my hands down the girl's sides and barely brushed her sex as my hands returned to her hips. The girl gently moaned in my arms. I placed one hand on the inside of her thigh and the other on her stomach. I held her so that we could turn our backs to the man. I knew he would want to move with us to watch, but I motioned for him to stay where he was. Once I was sure he couldn't see anything, as gently as I could, I sank my teeth into the girl's neck. She moaned a little louder. I'm sure it made the man think I was fingering her. I drank for about fifteen seconds and then sliced my tongue to place blood on the wounds so they would heal quickly. The young girl had become limp in my arms. I gently lifted her and laid her down in the pillows.

"As you can see," I said to the man, "I've completely exhausted her."

He got on his knees and made his way towards me. "I certainly hope you plan on doing that to me."

"Oh yes. That was my plan." I stood and walked over to him. I spread my legs wide in front of him. "What would you like to touch?" I asked.

He looked me up and down quickly and then answered with the one word I knew he would give me. "Everything."

I merely smiled and knelt down on the floor with him. He placed his hands on my hips and looked at me, waiting for my signal that it was ok to touch. I gave him a single nod and then, almost as if he couldn't control himself, he began to run his hands all over my body. Of course, his hands would linger on my thighs, breasts, and ass. I allowed it to last for a few minutes and then I leaned over and began to kiss his neck. The movement of his hands slowed as he gave into my kisses. When his hands finally stopped on my ass, I took my chance and bit into his neck. At first he almost resisted against me but then gave into the drowsiness that quickly came over him. I drank my fill and gently released his body to the floor. I healed his wounds the same as I had the girl's, only this man would not wake up the way she would later.

I left some money for the girl on the small table near the room entrance as I left. I wasn't sure where Ayden was at the moment but I was sure he was fine. I decided to wait for him near the club entrance.

Luckily, I only had to wait about five minutes. He walked up to me and we linked arms as we left the club.

Once outside Ayden noticed it was starting to get late. "It's only a few more hours till dawn, my love. It's best we head back to the mansion."

"Yes, let's go. I am starting to feel tired already." I leaned up against him as we walked.

When we got to the parking garage, I noticed that it was completely void of all humans, even though it had been that way when we first arrived. However, I still thought it was a bit strange; there were plenty of cars parked around us. I was sure that people would be heading home by now but then again, we *were* in Las Vegas.

The motorcycle was exactly where we had left it, thankfully untouched. Ayden was about to hand my helmet to me when I noticed his body go rigid. He was alarmed, I could tell just by the look in his eyes. I tried to pick up what he was sensing and I was able to find it quickly. We were not alone. I looked all around us but I couldn't see anyone. It had to be a slayer though; otherwise Ayden wouldn't have that look in his eyes.

"Ayden…" I whispered to him, "I know what you're alarmed about…what should we do?" I was actually a little scared.

"Don't be frightened, my dear," he said. "Come to me, we'll be out of here in no time."

Ayden held out his arms to me. I took one step towards him and then heard a strange noise. It was almost a humming sound. Not a second later, a silver arrow was sitting in Ayden's chest.

He stared down at the arrow and then looked back up at me. "Run Calista…" was all he could say to me.

"No Ayden! I won't leave you!" Tears formed in the corners of my eyes.

I watched in horror as he pulled the arrow from his chest. "It's too late, Calista! You need to get out of here before they kill you too!"

"But…Ayden…" Another arrow pierced Ayden's beautiful body before I could get another word out.

He fell to the ground. I ran to his side. Again, he pulled out the arrow and tossed it aside. I could tell he was becoming weak. The silver was too powerful. If the arrows had pierced his heart, he would have been reduced to ash already.

I held Ayden in my arms and looked around for the shooter. I was still unable to physically see them but I knew someone was there.

"Ayden, we need to get you back to the mansion," I said. "Sabine will know what to do."

He reached up and caressed my face. "You never know when to give up, do you? It's too late for me…you must save yourself. I can't bear the thought of the slayers getting you too. Please just go!"

I didn't want to leave him, but at some level, I knew he was right. If I was captured or killed, the house would be devastated and I would have let him down.

Again I heard the humming sound in the air. Ayden pushed me out of the way and I watched as a third arrow sank deep into his heart. He screamed in agony and his body began to turn to ash. Tears rolled down my cheeks. There was nothing I could do to save him. Ayden mouthed the words "I love you" right before his body completely smoldered. I sat there and cried. It almost didn't matter to me that I could be killed right then and there. The slayer was still nearby, watching my every move.

Suddenly, behind me came a familiar voice. "Calista? Is that you?"

I knew that voice. But I couldn't quite picture the face. As much as I didn't want to look, I knew I had to see who it was who had killed my love. I picked myself up off the ground and turned towards Ayden's murderer. And there he was…the person I had been trying to evade for the past year: Trent Murdock. The moment I recognized him, a rage began to build up inside me.

"Trent…you?" I didn't know what else to say to him.

"Calista, what you are doing here? Why were you with that vampire? You're lucky I killed him." As always, he didn't answer my question.

I could sense he was unarmed now, so I felt confident to approach him. My rage was strong now. "Trent, are you really that stupid?" I said as I walked towards him.

He took a step back as I came closer. "What are you talking about, Calista? I just saved your life."

I couldn't help but laugh. "Wow, I can't believe you are really that naïve. That vampire was my lover. I *am* a vampire!" I showed him my fangs and lunged forward. He was somehow able to jump out of the way so that I just barely missed him. I turned to face him. "You better pray that I don't kill you tonight. You have killed the one person I have been able to open my heart to since becoming what I am. I will destroy you!"

My anger was almost too much for me to handle. I lunged at him again but this time, he hit me once I was close enough. I hit the ground but jumped up quickly. His strength was noticeable, but he was still only a human. I was about to attack him again when he turned and started to run in the other direction. I wanted to go after him but it could have been a trap. If I ran after him, it was possible that I would meet several more slayers and I wouldn't be able to take on more than three.

Sadly, I watched my love's killer get away. My anger was starting to subside and sorrow took its place. I looked at the pile of ash on the ground next to the motorcycle. That used to be my Ayden. I thought about trying to salvage the ash, to bring him home. But a breeze had already swept through and taken away most of him. Sabine and the others would just have to mourn his memory.

I gathered up the arrows to show to the Ancients and then hopped on the motorcycle. I said my goodbyes to Ayden's remains and peeled out of the parking garage.

Nineteen

The ride back to the mansion went quicker than I had expected. It was probably because I was thinking about what I was going to say to the others once I arrived home without Ayden. I wondered if Sabine could already sense that Ayden was no longer with us.

I couldn't stop the tears as I entered the house. The pain was almost too much for me to bear, but I had to tell the others. Sabine was in her office, as I had expected. I came into the doorway and she was already standing. She had to know.

I collapsed to the floor. "Sabine...I...am...so sorry..,I...couldn't save him..."

She ran to me and scooped me into her arms. "Shhh, Calista. Don't cry. I want to hear what happened. But first we must gather the others and give you some time to collect yourself."

She helped me stand and allowed me to lean against her. We walked slowly to the library. Sabine called out to the others as we made our way there. They were quick to respond. Once seated, I was able to compose myself. The tears had stopped but the pain in my heart was still strong.

I looked at each of the Ancients as I told the news of Ayden. "I'm very sorry to tell you all this but...Ayden is dead. A slayer attacked him as we were leaving the city. I couldn't save him." I bowed my head in shame.

Selene was the first to speak. She was furious. "What do you mean *he* was attacked? Were you not with him?"

"Selene." Sabine spoke in a firm voice.

"No, it's alright Sabine," I assured her. "I think I should explain." Now I gave my attention to Selene. "I was right here with him. And

I am telling you the truth when I say that there was nothing I could do for him. I tried, but he told me to go home and save myself. He knew that it was too late once the first arrow hit him." I tossed the silver tipped arrows on the floor in front of me.

Now it was Tristan's turn to ask questions. "I am a little confused though…why was only Ayden attacked if you were right there with him?"

"I knew this question would come." I bowed my head again. "I knew the slayer that killed Ayden…it was Trent Murdock. The one who had been following me while I was still human. He knew that I had come into contact with vampires and was determined to eliminate them. But what I don't understand is why he didn't know that I was a vampire. I think that is why he didn't attack me. He didn't know. He thought I was still human. But how could he not know? Weren't slayers trained to tell who was human and who was not?"

"That is rather interesting," Caelum said. "I am curious as to why he didn't know. You are correct that they are trained for that sort of thing."

The sadness came over me again and tears streamed down my face. "I'm so sorry that I couldn't bring back Ayden's remains for proper burial. I was scared that Trent would come back for me once he knew I was a vampire too. I had to get out of there."

Tristan walked over and put his arm around my shoulders. "It's alright, Calista. What matters right now is that you are safe. But now we must figure out what to do about Murdock. He has become an immediate threat to this household."

Selene was now looking out the window, deep in thought. But she had no trouble speaking her mind. "I will find him…and I will kill him myself."

Sabine stood up in alarm. "Selene! You know that in all the centuries that we have lived, there has never been a time when vampire hunted slayer. That's just pure suicide. We try to live our lives in peace. Slayers are only killed when they come to us and we must defend ourselves. I will not allow you to sacrifice yourself to those monsters. They would either kill you on sight or capture you for experimentation."

Selene didn't argue further. I could tell that she just didn't want to upset Sabine any more but there was no sign of her actually taking in Sabine's words. Selene had meant what she said about killing Trent. I had had those same thoughts myself when I watched him run from me. I would have done it right then and there had I not considered that I could have been led into a trap.

I didn't know what to do. I didn't have anything else to say but I wasn't sure that I wanted to stick around to hear Sabine talk more about how we had to lay low. My mind was on the same track as Selene's, but my heart was filled with pain. I just wanted to go to Ayden's room and think. I wanted to preserve the memory of him.

I stood to leave and everyone immediately looked at me. "Where are you going, Calista?" Caelum asked.

"I am going to Ayden's room…I need to be alone." I left the room without waiting for anyone else to speak.

Ayden's room looked depressing now that I knew he wasn't going to come back. I walked over to the bed and lay down on my back. The ceiling was covered with a beautiful mural depicting a scene from Greek mythology. It was the story of how Pegasus was born. As I stared at the ceiling, I began to think of all the things Ayden and I *didn't* get to do together. I still had a lot of training ahead of me, but Ayden wouldn't be there to take me through it. There were so many things in the future that I had thought of sharing with him and now I wouldn't be able to.

My training was one of the most important things that Ayden wanted me to accomplish. He wanted to make sure that I was strong enough to take care of myself, even though he would have spent eternity watching over me. That's when I decided that I would continue my training to fulfill Ayden's wishes. It meant a lot to him so it meant a lot to me. I would become the strong, independent woman that Ayden wanted me to be.

Every moment that I spent not training seemed to be a waste of time. The only time I took away from training was when I needed to feed. I didn't go into the city anymore though. It was too painful.

I asked Sabine if I could turn Ayden's room into my personal training room. I couldn't bring myself to use it as my own but I didn't want anyone else to use it. She, of course, agreed to my every request. I think she felt that anything to ease my pain would be the best thing for me. I didn't really care either way. They could have all abandoned me if they wanted to and I believed I would have been fine on my own.

The more time I spent alone, the more I could tell that the Ancients were worried about me. Nevertheless, I was getting stronger each day and getting a better handle on my powers. Reading others' thoughts was no longer a hassle. I could do it with ease. But my reach was still not able to penetrate the minds of the Ancients. They were far too advanced to allow an amateur like me to enter their valuable minds.

As each day passed, my thoughts were always with Ayden. I kept wishing I could go back to that night and save him. And as I continued to think about that night, Trent Murdock somehow entered my thoughts. He was Ayden's murderer. I wanted more than anything to go out and hunt for him myself, but I knew the others wouldn't allow it. Plus, I didn't want to go against any of Ayden's teachings. It would be far too disrespectful even though he was no longer there to watch over me. But the idea of it continually crossed my mind from time to time. I just couldn't help it. I wanted to avenge the death of my lost lover.

Interestingly enough, it was Selene who had the same idea as me. One night, she came to me while I was training and voiced her thoughts about hunting down Trent Murdock.

"I hope I'm not interrupting," Selene began as she busted into the room. "But I know what you have been thinking about lately and we need to talk about it."

I was certain she was going to advise against it. All the others had been doing it, why not her? "Look, I know it's a bad idea but I can't help but think about it. Why won't anyone take a stand to defend our kind?"

"I didn't come here to argue with you about it. I actually came here because I am in agreement."

I almost didn't know what to say. Was it possible that the one person I thought was always against me was actually willing to help? "Are you suggesting an alliance?" I asked, filled with intrigue. "Because I am pretty sure that you don't like me. Didn't you create me just to spite Ayden in the first place?"

I had hit a nerve with her. I could see her cringe as I had spoken those words. "Calista," she said, ready to bear her fangs at me, "that's not fair. I came here hoping to set aside those differences so that we could go after Murdock together. Two heads are better than one, don't you think?"

"Yes, I do. But Sabine will never allow it." I glanced toward the door, almost expecting Sabine to walk through the door to confirm my doubts.

"She may be the oldest of us," Selene began, "but I am still an Ancient as well. I think I have just as much to say as anyone else does. And I say that I am going after him with or without your help. If she has a problem with it, then I'll just leave. I won't put the rest of the household in jeopardy; she should know that. I just can't sit back and do nothing while that man continues to roam around and kill us off one by one."

That was all she had to say to get me on board. "I'm in. Let's get started tonight. Do we have the right equipment?"

"I have more than enough firearms in my quarters. We'll go get set up immediately. I want to find that bastard and watch him suffer…" Her voice trailed off and I could see the anger in her eyes.

As expected, Tristan tried to stop us as we were walking out the front doors. "You can't just run out and expect to find him! You're both putting yourselves in grave danger by doing this!" He stood in front of us, blocking the doorway.

Selene wouldn't have it. "Tristan, get out of my way. There's no stopping me. We are doing this whether you approve or not. I will not allow Ayden's soul to wander through the earth like this, without his death being avenged. Justice must be served, and we are the ones to do it."

She was being a little too aggressive about it so I tried to reason with Tristan as best I could. "Tristan, please. You know how much we loved Ayden, and I know you loved him too. This needs to be done. Think of all the other vampires this guy has killed. Others that may or may not have been close to you. Nevertheless, he is a murderer and something has to be done about it. I have never understood why no one has ever taken a stand against them. But now is the time. Please…" I looked deep into his eyes to try and find the answer I was looking for.

He did nothing, except lower his eyes and step to the side. I knew that he felt the same but was ashamed for it. Selene and I walked past him and didn't look back. I wasn't sure if I would see any of them again, but I couldn't worry about that now. It was time to find Ayden's killer…and destroy him.

Selene decided to take her car while I drove Ayden's motorcycle. She thought it would be a good idea to take separate vehicles incase we needed to split up at anytime. From listening to her, it seemed that she had been planning out the attack for a long time. I couldn't blame her.

Before we took off towards the city, we discussed where the best place to start searching would be. As we talked, Caelum came running out from the house.

"Hey! Wait! Don't leave yet," he called to us.

We both looked towards him, confused. "What's up Caelum?" Selene asked. "Come to try and stop us too? Tristan already tried that. Not going to work."

"I'm not here to stop you…" he said softly. He held out his hand. In it was a single sheet of paper.

I took it from him before Selene could. "What's this?" I asked, reading it over quickly.

"It's a list of possible hideouts that the slayers could be using. I did a little research and hacked into their database again. I may have gotten a few traces but they are not one hundred percent foolproof. But I thought it might be helpful for a starting place."

Selene was obviously shocked. "But Caelum…why are you helping us? You've always been one hundred percent behind Sabine and all the rules against this sort of thing. What made you change your mind?"

He looked at both of us with a fire in his eyes. "The slayers may have killed thousands of our kind. But this is the first time they have taken away someone that is very important to us all. A personal nerve has been hit and it's time to act against it."

Something came over me and I just couldn't resist. I gave Caelum a strong hug and a kiss on the cheek. "Thank you so much," I whispered in his ear.

He hugged me back and whispered. "You're welcome, Calista. You're part of the family now. Please be careful."

Selene and Caelum said their goodbyes and then we got ready to head into the city. Selene had looked over the list Caelum gave us and she knew where a couple of the places were. I recognized the names of a few other places as well. We chose one of the less crowded areas as our first search spot.

As we rode away from the house, I took a look back and saw Sabine standing in the window of her office. I couldn't tell if she was angry or upset, but she didn't send any messages of warning or wisdom. She just stood there and watched as we rode off into the night.

Twenty

The place Selene wanted to check first was an old abandoned warehouse. I was not surprised. It seemed like a complete movie cliché. Even so, it couldn't hurt to check. We had an entire list of other places to search if this one turned out to be a dud.

We parked quite a ways down the street. I thought we were going to go in through the basement but Selene said we would take to the roofs. Now, I had leapt up the four stories of our mansion to the roof before, but never had I jumped from one building to the next. Selene gave me assurance that I could do it. I tried to take her word but it was still hard, being my first time and all. But I had to do this for Ayden. I sucked it up and followed Selene up onto the roof. I watched her as she jumped with ease from one roof to the next. She was good enough to wait for me before going too far. I took a deep breath and with a running start, flung myself off the roof. I landed safely, on both feet, on the next roof over. Selene gave me a quick pat on the back and then jumped to the next building. We were only five more buildings away and then we would be at the warehouse.

It only took us about a minute to get to the roof of the warehouse. There were several skylights as well as a door leading to a stairway. Selene wanted to be the dangerous one and go through the skylight. I told her I would rather take the stairs.

"That's fine," she said as she looked for the latch on the window. "Just keep a look out. It's possible that they set up motion sensors or something. And keep quiet. If you make any noise to bring their attention, you're likely to get killed."

I waved her off and headed to the stairs. I checked the door for any wires or motion sensors. It was clean so I broke off the lock and slowly opened it. The stairway was dark, not even emergency lighting. My eyes adjusted to the darkness quickly and I started to make my way down the stairs.

The walls were cement, along with the stairs. At the first landing, I stopped to see if I could sense any human form. I picked up nothing and proceeded. I was still not able to sense anything until I reached the third floor. It wasn't very strong, which meant there were only one or two humans present. I pulled out the pistol that Selene had given me. I released the safety, cocked it and then prepared myself to open the door. I ran through my head what would happen if I found a slayer in the next room. Would I shoot immediately? Or would I hesitate? Should I aim to kill or aim just to wound so we could take him back to the house for interrogation? I guess I wouldn't really know what to do until I actually went into the room. So, I took a deep breath and slowly opened the door.

At first I didn't see anyone. The room was so spacious, I was sure that it was completely abandoned. But then I noticed a figure moving at the opposite end of the room. I could tell it was a man and not a woman because of the way the body moved. It was hard to tell if he had spotted me or not, but I took my chances and started to advance towards him. My first few steps were perfectly silent and I was now able to tell that he hadn't noticed me. As I got closer, I ducked behind the few support beams scattered throughout the room. At the very end of the room, the man was working at a table that was covered with four computers. There was no doubt that this was one of the slayers' hideouts, but I was a little suspicious that this guy was here alone. I thought that they would stay in groups in case there was a sneak attack such as one that was about to occur. And before I moved out from behind the pillar, I thought to myself, "What if this is a trap?" But it was too late; I was close enough for a clean shot. I came out from behind the pillar and aimed for the guy's heart. And just as I was about to pull the trigger, the man turned and faced me. My heart jumped into my throat when I saw his face. I almost fainted. His eyes widened once he fully saw me as well.

I lowered my gun slowly and whispered, "No…it can't be…" Tears were forming in my eyes.

He reached back for the table to steady himself. "…Calista? Is that really you?"

No! It's really him. The tears ran down my cheeks. How could it be? "It…it can't be you…Shane…" My first love. He was a slayer!

"Calista. It *is* you! What are you doing here?" He was so surprised to see me. He didn't even know what I was.

"Shane…" I said with tears still streaming down my face. I dropped the gun and began to back away from him. "This can't be true. You can't be…one of them…"

He wrinkled his brow. "What are you talking about? One of whom?"

I could have laughed at his ignorance. "Shane…don't you know what I am? Can't you sense it?" I couldn't stop backing away from him. I was in too much shock.

And once I said the words, I think he realized it. His small smile faded and he looked at me hard. "No…Calista…you can't be! It's just not possible!"

"I'm sorry Shane…" With that, I turned and ran from him. Ran as fast as I had ever run before. I could hear him calling after me as I ran all the way back up to the roof. I don't think he followed me though.

Selene was there waiting for me. She said she had searched the basement and the first two floors. There was nothing she could find. She wanted to move onto the next place on the list. But then she noticed the panic in my eyes.

"Calista. What's wrong? What did you find?"

"Selene…we need to go. I…I need to get back to the mansion. Now!" I no longer cared about finding Trent. I had to speak with the other Ancients.

"Calista! What are you talking about? We are going to find Murdock tonight!" I could tell she was irritated with me. Her quest to find and kill Trent Murdock was growing stronger by the minute.

"Selene, you can do what you want. I have to get out of here. But please be careful." I turned away from her to make my way back to our vehicles.

A second later Selene had me by the elbow. "You can't just leave now! Now that we are out on this mission. You committed, now we must finish it." I could hear the anger in her voice.

I pulled my arm away from her roughly. "No Selene! I can't finish this with you! Not now. I am leaving and you can't stop me."

Before she could move or say another word, I jumped off the roof to the next building. I didn't stop or look back until I was back at the motorcycle. I started up the bike and sped off towards the mansion. I kept on eye on my mirrors to make sure that I wasn't being followed but I couldn't get Shane's face out of my mind. I just couldn't believe it. He was the first man that I had ever loved and now he was my sworn enemy.

Once I got back to the house, I quickly parked the bike in the garage and sprinted into the house. I went straight for Sabine's office. She was seated behind her desk, as always. She could sense something was wrong the moment I stepped in the doorway.

"Calista! What's wrong my child?" She stood and came over to take me in her arms.

"Sabine," I said, melting into her, "the most awful thing has happened."

"Has anything happened to Selene?" She asked.

I pulled away from her so I could look at her. "Oh no! Selene is fine. She is still out there though. She almost didn't let me come home and she wasn't planning on giving up the search yet."

"Well, I will send out one of the boys to fetch her. I don't want her out on this silly quest any longer. We were not meant to hunt our predators, only our prey. And I would like for you to explain to me what happened to make you rush home so quickly."

"Of course. I'll tell you everything." I sat down in one of the chairs.

Sabine left the room for a short moment to have either Tristan or Caelum go out and find Selene. I told them where she was when I had left her, but Caelum still had a copy of the list he had given us in case she wasn't there. He said he would go out and look for her. That left Sabine and Tristan to stay with me and listen to what I had to say. I was scared to tell them but I knew I had to.

"Well, as you know, Selene and I left the house tonight because we were going out to search for Trent Murdock. He is the one who killed Ayden and we both wanted him dead. Please don't get mad at Caelum, Sabine, but he helped us by giving us a list of possible hideouts where we might find the slayers. So we took it and started right at the top of the list: an abandoned warehouse just off the Strip. Selene and I went separate ways but we were well armed. She went through the skylight but made her way to the basement first while I took the stairs and starting searching from the top down. When I got to the third floor, I could tell that someone was there. I cautiously went inside and found a single slayer there, working on about four different computers."

The mention of computers immediately caught Tristan's attention. "Did you see what he was doing? What kind of computers?" Sabine silenced him. "Later Tristan." She turned back to me. "I'm sorry Calista. Please continue."

I took a deep breath and continued to the hardest part of my story. "So, I moved closer to him, and right as I took aim, he turned around. The most shocking thing was that I knew him. His name is Shane. I was in love with him once when I was human. He was my first love actually. And because of that…I couldn't shoot him. I just turned and ran. And that's why I came back here in such a panic. I'm sorry Sabine." I looked down at the floor.

I was waiting for either one of them to scold me for not killing a slayer. But neither of them said a word for several moments. Then Sabine finally spoke. "Calista, please don't feel ashamed or any other feelings along those lines for not killing that slayer. I understand why you didn't do it. But I will advise you that you cannot under any circumstances try to make contact with him again. It's far too dangerous, to you and to the rest of the house. Perhaps we should look into moving again…"

"Are you sure, Sabine? We only just got here." Tristan sounded worried and upset.

"Yes Tristan, when it comes to the safety of those living in this house, I am positive. When Caelum returns, I want the two of you to start looking through the database for a new residence. I will speak with Selene about this crazy mission of hers. It will stop immediately. And we might as well start packing while we're here." She stood and left the room to go to her bedroom.

"I'm so sorry Tristan. I know that everyone doesn't like all this moving. It's all my fault. I should have never talked to that Trent person in the first place. I knew he was trouble the moment he spoke to me."

Tristan leaned forward and placed his hand on my shoulder. "Don't beat yourself up about it, Calista. We've all made mistakes when we were young like you. All you can do is learn from them. Try not to dwell on it. Why don't you go pack up your things and then get some rest. The sun rises in a few hours." He stood and left the room as well.

I sat there for a few moments, thinking about Shane and what Sabine had said. She said that I wasn't allowed to try and see him again. I understood why, but I couldn't help but think about possibly trying to. He was the only human I had ever loved; yet he was the one who had broken my heart. Not to mention the fact that he was a slayer.

I went to my room and packed up some of my training equipment. The movers could take out the rest of the stuff. Then I went to the next room over, which was where I had been keeping my personal things. I packed up everything and then headed downstairs to see if Caelum and Selene had returned yet.

They were arguing with each other in the library. Apparently Caelum had to physically put her in the car to bring her home. But that's the way Selene had always been: stubborn and always going against Sabine's rules.

Tristan had already broken the news about moving again. Selene was furious. Caelum was a little disappointed but he said he would help Tristan find a new residence right away. The two of them left me alone with Selene. I could feel the heat of her anger flowing out from her body.

"Why the hell did you leave me out there? I can't believe you abandoned me like that! I could have been ambushed as soon as you left."

Suddenly, I was angry with her. "Oh that's bullshit, Selene and you know it! I checked most of that damn building and there was *one* human there. One! And he was harmless. Just a computer geek. Not a threat to either of us."

"Oh, so now you're defending the slayers? The group of murderers who killed our Ayden. How could you?"

"*Our* Ayden, huh? I think there was only one person in his house that he truly loved, and that was me! You betrayed him, Selene! How can you love someone that has betrayed you?" The words had come out of my mouth without even thinking. I knew it was a tender spot but I punched at it anyways.

"Ayden loved me more than you could have dreamed! I was the one that took him into my arms when he was human. I made him what he was. He was completely devoted to me until you came along." She was right up in my face now.

I shoved her away from me. "Don't you dare say such things to me! He told me all about you and how you turned him without his consent, just like you did to me you selfish bitch! You did it just to spite him! Just because you knew that he didn't want this life for me. But you did it anyways and I hate you for it!"

She shoved me back. I took a swing at her and struck her right on her left cheek. She was quick to fight back. We continued to punch and kick each other until Tristan and Caelum came running in to separate us. They had heard us screaming at each other from across the house.

Sabine came running into the room as the boys pulled us away from each other. "What on earth is going on in here? What has caused this extreme hatred between the two of you? I don't understand it."

Selene screamed at Sabine. "She's a selfish, thieving whore, Sabine! Everything was fine until she came along. She stole Ayden away from me. I don't want her in this house anymore!"

Sabine stayed calm even with Selene screaming at her. "Selene, you know that I have no reason to banish Calista from this house. She has done nothing wrong. Bringing her here was a choice done completely by Ayden. It was you who turned her and for that, she may never forgive you. I have banished you once, Selene. I won't hesitate to do it again. You have no authority over who stays and who goes." She stared hard at Selene.

Selene shook Caelum off of her and straightened her clothing. "You want to banish me again? Go right ahead. I don't need you. I don't need any of you. I can take care of myself. Plus, I *am* going to find that Murdock and kill him. There's no stopping me. At least I'll be the one to put Ayden's soul to rest."

Sabine lowered her head in disappointment. "Selene, if that is the path you wish to choose, go right ahead. It's obvious that we can't stop you. But I will not be so gracious if you come back to us a second time."

"Ha! You wish that I'd come running back to you. I'm outta here." And with that, she left the room. It would most likely be the last time we would ever see her.

Sabine came over to me and cradled my face in her hands. "Calista, please don't feel that any of this is your fault. You had nothing to do with it. It's just some unfortunate events that have come our way, but we must accept them. If Selene wishes to lead a life of solitude, she is welcome to. In fact, anyone is welcome to do so. But most of us enjoy the company, so I implore you to stay with us."

I could only nod in acceptance. As much as I didn't want to be living out on my own just yet, the thought had crossed my mind several times ever since Ayden was taken from me. If I couldn't have him, then I really didn't want anyone.

I went down to the vault to gather the remainder of my belongings. As I tossed my last candle into a duffel bag, I glanced over at Ayden's coffin. I placed the bag on the floor and walked over to it. It looked so sad, so empty, without Ayden lying there. It had never looked that way when Ayden was still around, even if he wasn't in it. I took a quick walk around it, letting my fingers glide along the rim. I kept wishing that I could have gone back and gathered his remains, for proper burial. It just wasn't right letting him die out there in that parking garage like that.

Now what was I supposed to do about Shane? I couldn't just move without at least seeing him one last time. Even though seeing him was probably the greatest shock of my life, it was clear to me that my feelings for him were still there. They had come flooding back to me and left me yearning for more. I knew I had at least another night before we moved out of the house, so it was possible that I could sneak out and go find him again. He most likely wouldn't be at the warehouse since vampires had now found it, but he had to be close. Maybe I could try all the places that we used to go together. He was still human after all.

After I had all my things packed and piled up outside my room, I decided to call it an early night. I said goodnight to the others and went to the vault. Tomorrow night I would venture out on my own to find Shane. I would of course tell the others that I was going out to hunt. I just had to see Shane.

I didn't sleep well that night. Ayden's death had become a recurring nightmare for me. And my fight with Selene and seeing Shane just made things worse.

Twenty-One

*T*he *night began the same as it had the night Ayden died. Ayden and I rode into the city together to hunt. Everything occurred exactly the same as it had up until the point where we headed back to the parking garage. Something was different. Ayden could tell something was not right. He grabbed my hand and held it tight. The parking garage was thirty feet in front of us. And suddenly, Selene comes strolling out of the garage! We were surprised to see her. Ayden asked her what she was doing there. He thought she had already fed. She didn't speak a word to us. But she had the most evil looking grin on her face. It was the same smile I had seen when she had turned me. Ayden tried to shake it off as nothing but I asked him if we could walk around more. Maybe it wasn't safe to go into the garage just yet. He wouldn't listen. We walked into the garage and over to the motorcycle. Then I heard that awful noise: the noise of an arrow whizzing through the air. It struck Ayden and I looked all around to see where it had come from. Arrow after arrow continued to hit Ayden and I couldn't move to save him. I was frozen with fear and shock. The look in his eyes was terrible. It was as if he was condemning me for not trying to help him. But I tried to explain back to him through my eyes that I couldn't move. I just didn't know what to do. The final arrow hit his heart and turned him into ash. I stood there and watched, pain searing through my veins. And then the voice came. "Calista?" Only this time it wasn't Trent as it had been that night. It was Shane.*

I woke with a start, smacking my head into the lid of my coffin. It scared me to death to think that it was Shane who had killed my Ayden, although I knew it wasn't him. It was Trent. I saw Trent with my own eyes in that garage. Shane was not there, I hadn't seen him until Selene and I went to that warehouse.

The lid of my coffin slid open a few seconds after I had hit my head. It was Tristan. "Are you alright, Calista?"

I rubbed my forehead. "Yes, I'm fine. I just had a bad dream…hit my head."

"Be careful, dear. You could hurt yourself." He gave a small smile and held out his hand to help me up.

I took his hand and climbed out. "Thank you Tristan. I'm fine. Just a bad dream."

"We're leaving in about five or six hours. You should probably go feed before we leave. We have a long journey ahead of us."

Oh no! I didn't have the entire night as I had planned. But hopefully those five or six hours would be enough. "We're leaving tonight? That's really soon." I tried to hide my panic.

Tristan gave me a concerned look but then shook it off. "Yes, I know but Sabine is really concerned. She wants to get out of here as soon as possible."

"You said we have a long journey ahead of us…where are we going?" I had a bad feeling we were leaving the country.

"Ireland." Tristan said,

"Ireland!" I exclaimed. "Why on earth are we going there?"

"Is Ireland bad? We knew you weren't too thrilled about coming here to the States but I didn't know you had a problem with Ireland. Should we look for another location?" He seemed so concerned about my emotional stability.

"No…Ireland's fine…just so…far away."

He put his arm around my shoulders and started to lead me to the stairs. "Well, look at it this way, Calista. We are going back to Ayden's homeland. Think of it as our last respects to him. I think it will be good for you."

"Maybe," I murmured.

"Well, I saw upstairs that you're already packed up. So perhaps you should take this free time to go into the city and say goodbye. Make sure you feed. You'll need your strength for the trip." He patted my back and gave me a small shove up the stairs.

Sabine was in her office, as usual, packing up her things. I let her know that I was going into the city to hunt. She suggested that I go in with one of the boys but I told her it wasn't necessary. I'd be fine on my own. Plus, both the boys were busy packing; I didn't want to take them away from that. She was reluctant about it but she let me go nonetheless.

I hopped on the motorcycle and sped off towards the city. I figured I would get my feeding over with first so that way I would have more time and more strength for finding Shane. I chose a small, sleazy looking club on a lonely street corner. The people inside probably wouldn't even notice if I took care of some guy right in the middle of the room. However, I wasn't about to jeopardize my existence. I took on my usual routine and sat myself at one of the back tables. Lucky for me, a drunken man noticed me right away and came over to try and put his moves on me. I played along to let him think it was working. Within a few minutes of talking, I had him right where I wanted him. The opportunity was there, so I took it and drained the guy in one minute flat. It was ok to just leave him there at the table. Everyone would just think that he passed out from drinking too much. I wiped my mouth with the napkin on the table, dropped a few bucks next to it and then left the club. It was time to look for Shane.

Finding him was a lot easier than I thought it would be. He was hanging out at the casino I used to work at when we first met. I was a little hesitant about going in because I was sure that people there would recognize me. But I had to see if he would maybe talk with me. I wasn't sure that he would agree to it, now knowing what I was, but it was worth a shot.

I followed him around the casino for a few minutes. I did run into a few people that I had worked with before. They were so surprised to see me. They all thought I had run away to Europe, never to be seen again. I explained quickly how I had traveled to many different countries but I was just back in the States for a visit. Wanted to see how things were doing back in good old Vegas. Shane never left my radar, and if I lost him I was able to pick him up mentally.

He finally stopped at the lounge where I would go for drinks during my breaks. He sat by himself at one of the tables in the back corner. It was perfect. I would be able to get back there to talk to him without him getting away. Hopefully he wouldn't try causing too big of a scene when he saw me.

I strolled up to his table just as the waiter was leaving. I tried to play it cool. "Hi there, Shane. How are you?"

He nearly spilled his drink all over himself. "Calista! My god, what are you doing here?"

"What do you think I'm doing here? We need to talk." I slid into the seat next to him.

He looked a little bit scared. He swallowed hard. "Talk about what?"

I could now tell that he hadn't been with the slayers long. He was too jumpy and frightened of me. Plus, he hadn't been armed when I saw him back at the warehouse. He must just be a computer whiz, not a foot soldier. "Shane…I'm sure you know what I am after what happened last night…"

"You're damn right I know what you are!" he said, raising his voice. He leaned closer to me as he looked around the lounge and lowered his voice. "You do know that I am ordered to kill vampires on sight."

"Come on, Shane. Does this look like the type of place that you can just kill me without anyone noticing? Get that out of your head. I could snap your neck before you even pulled out a weapon. And by the way, I already know that you are unarmed. But that aside, what are you doing with these people, Shane? What made you become a slayer?"

He looked at the floor. "After you left…" his eyes lifted to look at me briefly, "I got into working with computers. It wasn't long before I was able to hack into just about any system and I became very knowledgeable about all types of computers and their programs. It was the slayers actually, who had come to me. They offered me a very well paying job working with their systems and tracking down vampires. I didn't really believe them at first but part of my induction was to go out with a field team and witness a killing."

I was disgusted. "Shane, that's just awful. You watch as innocent people are murdered by the people you work with and you get paid for helping them do it. It's all about the money, isn't it?"

"It hasn't always been about the money! Part of the reason I took the job was to get my mind off of you...."

"Why should that have mattered to you, Shane?" I asked angrily. "*You* were the one who cheated on me, remember?"

"Yes, I do remember. And I know that I can't take it back but every day that you have been gone...I wish that I could." He tried to reach across the table to touch my hand but I pulled it away. "I've missed you, Calista. I truly did love you, whether you believe it or not. I made a stupid mistake. One that I would never do again."

I leaned back in my chair and glared at him. "I'm not sure that I can believe you, Shane. How do I know that this isn't just some scheme that you're pulling to try and get me back just so you can hand me over to your supervisors so they can slaughter me?"

His mouth dropped open in shock. "Calista! How could you say something like that? You really think that I would try and kill the one girl that I have ever truly loved? Never!"

I was really having a hard time figuring out if he was telling the truth or not. But a part of me knew he was. We had loved each other, and I think that deep down we both still did. I tried scanning his mind for an answer but for some reason I couldn't penetrate his thoughts. "Shane...I want to believe you, but I have been instructed not to contact you again. I have already broken that order by being here right now, but I had to see you before we left. We are leaving tonight." I looked at my watch. "In four hours to be exact. But I just wanted to see you one last time."

He grabbed my hand and this time I didn't resist him. "What do you mean you're leaving? Where are you going?"

"Shane, I'm sorry. I can't tell you that. If you knew, you might tell the others and then my new family and I would all be killed. I can't put them in danger." I stood up. "I'm sorry...I have to go."

He stood and held onto my hand. "Please don't go, Calista. I don't want you to leave yet. Can't we talk for a little longer? You have a few hours. I miss you…" I don't think he had wanted those words to come out because he quickly blushed with embarrassment.

"Shane, I used to think that I didn't miss you, but traveling alone made me realize that I did. But now that I am…what I am…I can't possibly even consider staying in contact with you. It's just not plausible. Either your kind would kill me…or my kind might kill you…."

He bowed his head in disappointment and released my hand. "Can't you please tell me where you are going? Or at least give me a hint? A phone number? Anything? I want to see you again…well, at least talk to you again. Please?"

"I'm sorry Shane…I can't do that. But please know that I loved you even when I found you with that girl…perhaps I still do. But it's just not meant to be…we're literally from two different worlds now and nothing can change that. Goodbye Shane…Be happy."

And I left him there in the lounge thinking about what I said. I didn't look back though. If I had looked back, I probably would have stayed there with him and never gone to Ireland. It probably would have gotten me killed but I might not have cared so much.

Walking back to my bike, I started to feel a little guilty. Even though Ayden was no longer there, I felt like my feelings for Shane were pure betrayal to Ayden. But I had loved Shane far before I had fallen for Ayden. I hadn't even wanted to fall for Ayden. Either way, I couldn't let my feelings for Shane get too strong. I was still a vampire and he was still a human, a slayer. We were against each other whether we liked it or not.

I rode home to find the others already packing up the moving trucks. We were leaving a little earlier than expected. Sabine explained that we would take with us the essentials and the rest would be express shipped to Ireland. I grabbed the two duffels that had my important things in it and threw it in the back of the limo. The others had already tossed in their bags.

I then realized that Selene was nowhere around. "Where is Selene?" I asked.

The boys looked at each other and then at Sabine. "She's not coming with us," Sabine said. "She has decided to stay here and continue her ridiculous mission on killing that human. And based on her decision, I have told her that she will not be allowed back in our house ever again. I was too gracious the first time and it will not happen again. It will just be the four of us from now on."

"Oh," was all I could manage for a response. It was hard to think that I would never see her again, even though my hatred for her was still burning strong.

Sabine ushered us into the limo. It was time to head over to the airport. The movers could take care of the rest.

As the limo rolled down the driveway, I watched the house grow smaller and smaller. I was going to miss that house, mainly because it was the last place that Ayden and I had spent time together when he was still alive.

For the first time since I had been living with the Ancients, Sabine had arranged for us to take a private jet. It made me a little worried. Had she done this because of Shane? Perhaps she knew that he would try to track us if we took a public flight. I couldn't help but think it. Once we boarded the plane, Tristan sat next to me and put his arm around my shoulder. It was if he knew that I was feeling like everything was my fault and he wanted to show his support. I was thankful for the three of them. They had been so kind to me since day one and I wished there was some way I could show my gratitude.

Twenty-Two

When the plane arrived in Belfast International Airport it was early evening. Stepping out onto the runway, memories came rushing into my mind. We had flown into the same airport that I had chosen when I took on my search for Ayden. The last time I had been at this airport, I had been human.

Again, Tristan came over and put his arm around me. "Let's go Calista. The car is waiting to take us to the house. Grab your bags."

I nodded and picked up my bags. A limo was waiting for us not far from the airport gates. We piled our bags in the trunk and climbed into the car. Caelum said the ride shouldn't be long as long as traffic wasn't too heavy. Then he continued on and described the house to us as we rode along. It was apparently a lot different from the two we had recently been living in, but I wasn't really listening much. My mind was preoccupied with thoughts of Ayden and Shane.

The rest of our things were not at the house when we got there. It didn't matter much. The house itself didn't matter much to me either. I'd describe it but I honestly can't remember all that much of it. I grabbed my bags from the limo and walked into the house and straight to one of the bedrooms. I didn't even care if it wasn't supposed to be mine or not. I dropped the bags on the floor and plopped down on the bed. There was a mural on the ceiling of course, but I wasn't really seeing it. My mind was so deeply focused on Shane that I wasn't really seeing anything around me.

Who knows how long I was staring at the ceiling, deep in thought. But it certainly didn't take long for the others to get worried. All three of them came looking for me once they were settled in their rooms. Sabine, being the motherly type that she was, immediately suggested

197

that maybe I needed someone to talk to. Perhaps a therapist or something. She had the number of a vampire psychologist that she could easily contact. Apparently those were needed sometimes for the newbies. Caelum thought that that was pushing it a little too far. He felt that if I wanted someone like that to talk to, I would have to ask for it myself.

Tristan came over and sat next to me on the bed. "Are you hungry, Calista? Want to go out and get something to eat?"

I sat up and looked at him. "Yeah…I suppose I am a bit hungry. I guess I'll go out and get something quick. I may want some time to walk around and think about some things, if that's alright." I looked at the others for approval.

"Of course my dear," Sabine answered. "Whatever you need to do, please do it. We'll be here unpacking and such."

Tristan stood and almost grasped my arm as I started towards the door. "Do you want some company?"

His question startled me a little but I waved him off and kept walking. "No thanks, maybe some other time."

I made my way downstairs quickly, hoping that they wouldn't follow me. I needed some time alone. I grabbed my coat and went out to wander through the city. Most of it looked familiar from the last time I had been there. But it all brought back painful memories of Ayden. No matter, I decided to go check out the park where I had spent some time writing in my old journal.

The walk was pleasant. The air was warm and every now and then a cool breeze would come through. The moon was set high in the sky, but not quite full. Just a few more nights till full moon. The park wasn't as empty as I had been expecting but that wasn't necessarily a bad thing. One of the several people walking through the park would, unfortunately for them, become my meal for the night.

I quickly chose a young woman walking her dog. The dog was not of much use to me so I released it as I drank from the girl. She sank into my arms rather quickly. I sealed the wounds on her neck and laid her body down on a nearby bench. I was able to sneak away before anyone took notice.

The park was still occupied with couples here and there so I decided to stick around and just watch the people walk by. I found a small grassy area to relax. I lay down on my side, propping myself up on my elbow. The sky was mostly clear with the stars shining brightly.

I almost didn't realize how long I was lying there until I heard a familiar voice from behind me.

"Calista." I thought it was either Tristan or Caelum, worried about me yet again. But I was wrong.

I turned onto my other side so I could see who was calling me. "Shane!" I jumped to my feet. "What are you doing here? I just saw you nearly thirteen hours ago back in the States. How did you get here?"

He started towards me. "I took the earliest flight here. I had to see you. Once you left, I just couldn't stop thinking about you."

"But how did you know where I went?"

His face became red with shame. "I asked the movers. They told me where they were shipping all your stuff. I told them I was a relative. It's amazing what people will believe."

I was actually rather happy to see him, but my happiness quickly faded. "Shane...do you realize what could happen to you if the Ancients found out that you were here?"

"Ancients?" he asked with a confused look on his face.

"I'm sorry...they are the people I live with. That's the title I have always known them by. But they are just like me...only older and stronger. They would certainly kill you if they knew you were here."

"I don't care," he said as he came close and grabbed hold of my hands. "Like I said, I had to see you again. The entire time after you left, you were the only thing on my mind. I've been doing a lot of thinking ever since I left Las Vegas."

I wasn't sure what to do. Part of me wanted to let him go, for his own safety. But the other part of me just wanted to hold him tight. That latter part of me took over completely. I gently squeezed his hands. "What do you mean you've been doing a lot of thinking? Thinking about what? Wait! What about the other slayers? How were you able to come here without them knowing? Are they tracking you?"

"Calista, calm down! Everything's fine. I promise we are not being traced. I was actually able to get a vacation from the team. They were happy to give it to me since I have been working just about nonstop ever since they recruited me."

His words were sincere, but I was still skeptical. "I don't know, Shane. I wouldn't underestimate the people that you work for. They are capable of so many things. Maybe we should try going somewhere not so out in the open."

"That's fine, we can go anywhere you want." He smiled. That boyish smile…oh how I had missed it.

"Well, there's this little café just up the road from here. It's pretty quiet, not a lot of people there. Should we go there?"

"That sounds just fine."

We started walking towards the park exit. Surprisingly, Shane took hold of my hand as we walked. I was feeling a little bit confused by how natural my hand felt within his.

We had just about reached the edge of the park when I sensed someone was following us. "Wait." I stopped, pulling Shane back with me.

"What, what is it?" He could tell something was wrong.

I started searching our surroundings. "Someone's here…"

He looked around too and saw a few other people nearby. "Of course there are other people here. It's a public park." He couldn't hold back his smile.

"No, that's not what I mean. Someone is following us."

He let go of my hand and started to scan the park in a panic. "What? Are you sure? But there's no way they could have followed me here. I'm on vacation."

I turned and held him by the shoulders. "Shane, don't you think they did that just so they could watch you? They probably knew that you had spoken with me. They must have known you would come to me. It was a trick just so you would lead them right to me."

He shook my hands off and backed away from me. "No, it can't be. They wouldn't do that. They're like a family to me. They just wouldn't do something like that."

I was about to speak when another voice entered the conversation. "Unfortunately for you, we *do* do things like that."

I turned to see whom the voice belonged to. It was none other than Trent Murdock. "Trent!"

He jumped down from the rock he was standing on and strolled over to us. "Yes Calista, it's me, you're good friend Trent Murdock. How've ya been?"

"You bastard." I started to advance towards him. "I should kill you right now."

Shane grabbed my arm. "Don't Calista. Please."

I looked at him with anger in my eyes and pulled my arm away roughly. "How could you possibly tell me 'no'? Don't you know what I am? Don't you know what he does? He kills people like me for a living. He killed my one true friend and the only man I have ever loved since *you*." I pointed at Shane. Rage was coursing through my veins but I restrained myself from wringing Trent's neck.

"Oh come on now, Calista. Why such hatred in those beautiful eyes of yours? I was just doing my job." The ridiculous grin on his face never faded.

I started to move towards him again. "You asshole!"

"Now now, Calista. Calm down. Look, I thought I was protecting you, ok? I didn't know you were...a vampire at the time. Why can't you just drop it? You're lucky I haven't killed you yet."

"I'm lucky?" I shouted at him. "Please Trent. You think you're this wonderful slayer, but you're just a human. Just a mere human who can be more easily killed than I."

Shane stepped in front of me. "Please Calista, don't do this."

"Shane...please step aside. I don't want to hurt you..." He didn't budge.

"Oh come on, Shane. You think you can stop her? She'd snap you in half without breaking a sweat. And you, Calista. You really think you can just kill me right here and now? In the middle of a public park?" Trent was starting to circle us.

"Watch me," I said with confidence.

"Calista, I beg you. Please...don't." Shane was starting to look desperate.

"Shane, you better move out of my way right now." I couldn't control the rage building inside me.

"Just let her try, Shane. I want to see what she's got. I could make things even more interesting if you'd like." The smile on his face grew larger. "You want to know something, Calista? We knew about you and Shane the whole time. We knew that you two had been involved when you were still human. That's why we recruited him. So that he would hopefully lead us right to you. And he did."

That was the last straw. I pushed Shane out of my way and lunged at Trent. "I'll kill you, you bastard!"

I tackled Trent to the ground. He tried to pull out a weapon from his pant leg, but I pinned his hand to the ground. I pinned down his other hand and sat on his chest.

"Look who's the one in trouble now, Trent. No one is going to help you. I'm going to strangle you and watch you suffer, just like the way you made Ayden suffer." He tried to wiggle his way out of my grip, but I was far too strong for him.

Shane ran over and tried to pull me off Trent. "Calista, don't do this! Please let him go. Maybe we can talk things out?"

Trent started laughing. "I don't think that's a plausible idea. She's not much of a talker. Always a fighter. Aren't you, Calista?"

I pushed down on his arms and chest. He winced in pain. "Maybe I just don't like talking to *you*, Trent. Ever think of that?"

"And why is that, Calista? I thought I was a nice guy to you."

"Yeah, a bit too nice. More like a stalker. It freaked me out and I was starting to get the idea that you were using me to get through to the vampires who had contacted me."

He smiled yet again. "You *are* as smart as you look. That's exactly what I was doing. But I got a little too carried away because a crush developed. We're taught not to get close to any outsiders, but I don't think you realize how gorgeous you are."

His flattery was starting to make me more angry than relaxed. "Give it up, Trent. Your time is up. You're finished."

Shane put his hand on my shoulder. "Calista…I really think you should let him go…people are starting to stare…."

I looked up. He was right. A few people had stopped to see what was going on since I had Trent pinned to the ground. I was reluctant to let him go. "Trent...you lucked out this time. But next time, you won't be so lucky. I can promise you that." I released him and stood up.

He stood up and nonchalantly brushed himself off. "Oh how nice of you, Calista. Letting me go like this. Wouldn't want to bring any attention to 'your kind,' right?" He just knew how to push those buttons that make you angry.

I had nothing else to say to him. I stood there, arms crossed, waiting for him to leave. Even with the few people watching us, I wanted nothing more than to wring his neck. He didn't move for a few moments and then turned his back and walked away from us. Shane came over to me and put his arm around my waist.

"I'm sorry you had to witness that, Shane. I know that you both belong to the same organization. But I couldn't just let him get away with what he did."

Shane lowered his head. I tried reading his thoughts. He was feeling a little jealous that I had fallen in love with someone else after him. "It's alright," he said, "I just didn't want anyone to die in the middle of this park like that, you know?"

I turned so that we were face to face. "Look Shane, I know that hearing me being in love with someone else hurt you. And I am sorry for that. I didn't mean for it to happen, it just did. I didn't think that I could love anyone else after you, but it happened. But that doesn't mean that I ever fell out of love with you. You know that, right?"

A look of surprise filled his face. "How could you possibly still love me after what I did to you? I'm lucky that you are even talking to me right now."

I motioned for us to start walking. "Shane, love like what we had doesn't happen every day. And when you love someone as deeply as I loved you, it doesn't just go away. It's something that, well I think, lasts a lifetime."

He grabbed my hand and squeezed it gently. "I completely agree with you. I never stopped loving you either, Calista. I made a stupid mistake and I have regretted it ever since you left."

I suddenly stopped and faced him. "Shane...there's no possible way we could ever pick up where we left off. You're human...a slayer...and I'm...."

"I know...a vampire," he finished. I could practically feel his heart breaking.

I started walking again. "Shane, it's just not possible. Either one of us would be killed before we could even find a place to hide. And even if we did get away, what's to stop them from tracking us down over and over again? The other slayers would hunt us down and probably kill us both. And the Ancients would never allow it. They've already forbidden me from seeing you and may even kill you on sight. It's just...not possible."

Sadness filled his eyes. He turned away from me and continued walking. "Please Calista...I can't bear to lose you again."

I didn't know what to say to him. More than anything, I wanted to stay with him. But I knew how complicated things would become if I made that decision. I think he knew it too, but I could feel the strength of love in his heart. How does that saying go? Love conquers all. I wasn't sure if I truly believed it or not but I was beginning to feel like we would find out soon enough.

I caught up with Shane and grabbed onto his hand. "I hope you know what you're getting yourself into." I told him. "I sure hope *I* know what I am getting into...maybe I should talk to the Ancients...."

He stopped and pulled me to a stop as well. "Wait. What do you mean go talk to the Ancients? You mean you're going to tell them about me? Are you sure that's a good idea? What if they order you to kill me?" He was more nervous than I was.

I placed my hand on his shoulder and gave him the best smile of assurance that I could muster. "Don't worry about it, Shane. I'll take care of everything. I think it'd be best to handle this now instead of later. The longer we wait, the more dangerous things will become. Trent already knows that we are here together...he practically planned it. He'll surely be sending in a team very soon...and because of that...I think you should come with me."

"What? Are you so sure that's a good idea? I don't know, Calista…" He rubbed the back of his head. "I just don't know if I should go with you…they could kill me right then and there."

I frowned. "I would never allow it! Sabine is all about the rules and she would certainly give me a chance to explain before any action was taken. She gave me a chance when I was human; she has to give you a chance too. Because she trusted Ayden and his judgments, now it's my turn to be trusted."

We walked the rest of the way through the park and made our way to my car. I drove quickly back to the mansion. I was anxious to speak with the Ancients. This problem needed to be dealt with immediately. As we drove, I told Shane to let me do the talking. As long as he stayed close to me, everything would be fine. The Ancients were civilized people. Talking was the best way to deal with them.

Twenty-Three

When we pulled up to the house, I heard Shane suck in a deep breath. He was ridiculously nervous, but he was also amazed by the size of the house. I guess the slayers didn't live as lavishly as we did.

I parked the car in the garage and got out. Shane followed. I could sense that everyone was present except for Selene. I was somewhat relieved and then I remembered that she hadn't even come to Ireland with us. She was still in Las Vegas. It was better that way though.

Sabine was, of course, in her office. I asked Shane to wait in the hall so I could speak with Sabine alone first. He agreed and stood just outside the doorway.

Sabine was writing when I entered the room. She didn't even look up as she spoke to me. "It's not necessary to leave the young man in the hall, my dear. You may bring him in."

Man, she always knew everything before I could even open my mouth. "Oh…well, I wanted to talk to you alone first."

"That's fine," she said, setting her pen down on the desk. She looked at me, finally and folded her hands together in her lap. "What is it you'd like to talk about, Calista? A lot has been going on with you ever since…Ayden's departure."

I sat down in the chair directly across from her. "Yes I know, Sabine. And I am not really sure what I can say about it all. Should I apologize? I'm not really sure. But I should probably apologize for bringing him here." I stuck out my thumb in the direction of the hallway. "I didn't really know what else to do. I fear that we're both in danger and I felt this was the safest place for us to go."

Sabine leaned back in her chair. "I trust you took the usual precautions before bringing him into this house?"

"Oh yes! Of course! You must know that I would never put this house into any sort of danger. Ayden taught me well on that account." Both of us lowered our heads in mourning at the mention of his name.

"Well, I think there is no sense in leaving the young man out in the hall any longer. Please, bring him in. I will call for Tristan and Caelum." She closed her eyes and folded her hands in front of her. I was able to pick up her call to the boys as it travel throughout the house.

I got up and went out into the hall to grab Shane while she finished summoning the boys. I grabbed his hand and pulled him into the room. He didn't speak a word, as I had asked him not to. But I could see the wonder and admiration in his eyes once he saw Sabine. As I have said before, Sabine is quite stunning. Especially when dressed in her favorite medieval style gowns. I put my hand on Shane's shoulder and gently pushed him into the chair next to mine.

Several moments later, Tristan and Caelum came into the room. Tristan squinted his eyes at Shane as he walked by. Surprisingly I caught a short thought from him. *"Who is this human?"* It must have slipped out without him knowing. Caelum paid no attention to Shane whatsoever. He took his usual position next to Sabine and crossed his arms over his chest.

Sabine thanked them for joining us and then spoke to me. "Well Calista. It's time you told us what is going on."

"Yes…well…first, let me introduce you to Shane." I held out my hand to my left. Shane immediately grabbed it. I could tell the Ancients were confused and surprised by his action but I ignored it and continued talking. "Shane is…well…he's my first love. I fell in love with him a long time ago when I was still human. And I still love him, I always have. But there are a few complications, which is why I brought him here."

"And what might those complications be?" Tristan asked with a scowl on his face. I couldn't figure out what was making him act so strangely. I'd never seen him act this way before.

"Well, first would be the fact that he is…."

"Human." Caelum finished my sentence.

"Yes…" I replied, lowering my head. "But here is where things get *really* complicated…"

"What could be more complicated than the fact that he is a human?" Tristan exclaimed. "Just him being here is bad enough."

"Now wait a second!" I stood up in anger. "You can't do that! None of you acted this way when Ayden brought me into this house and I was still a human. Selene was the only one who gave her disapproval and now you are sounding just like her. What has caused you to act like this?"

Sabine held out her arms, asking for silence. "Sit down Calista. There's no need to get upset. But Tristan, she is right. We gave Ayden the chance to speak for her. Let us give her a chance to speak for this young man."

I slowly sat down, sending confused glances towards Tristan. "Thank you Sabine…well…like I said, here is where things get even more complicated…Shane is…a slayer."

Gasps came from all three of them. Sabine's eyes widened, I thought she was going to start yelling. Tristan looked like he was ready to leap across the desk and strangle Shane. Caelum was staring at me with disgust.

Sabine and the others started arguing amongst each other. Sabine wanted me to explain more but Tristan and Caelum were convinced that this whole thing was a trap and that we would surely be attacked.

Shane couldn't take it anymore. He whistled loudly to get their attention. "I'm sorry to stop all your conversations but I think you should give at least Calista a chance to explain…or maybe even me."

The right corner of Sabine's mouth turned up just the slightest bit. I could already tell that she was already starting to like him. She had made that same small gesture when I had tested my boundaries and spoke with them for the first time. "Alright then young man. Go ahead. We're listening."

Shane looked to me for approval. I nodded, urging him to speak. "Well, as of right now, I may not even be a slayer anymore. While Calista and I were in the park, we ran into Trent Murdock. So now that he has seen me with her, he'll surely tell the organization and I'll be kicked out. Doesn't really matter that much to me anyways. All I did was computer work. But nevertheless, he's probably setting up a team to send over to Ireland, if there isn't already a hidden group somewhere."

I could tell both the boys were intrigued the moment Shane said he did computer work for the slayers. They had both been hacking into that system for so long; they probably thought they could use him to gain even more access.

Shane suddenly stood and approached Sabine's desk. "The thing is...I am in love with Calista. I always have been ever since the first day we met. I am sure she told you that I cheated on her...but it was the biggest mistake I have ever made in my entire life. I don't even know why I did it. I honestly don't even remember how it had happened. All I remember is Calista finding us together and her throwing her engagement ring at me. That was the last time I saw her until the night at the warehouse. I want to be with her. I know that may seem stupid right now considering that we are two completely different species, but I don't care what it takes. I want to be with her and I will do anything to stay by her side."

Sabine sat there for a moment, not saying anything. I think she was trying to absorb all that Shane had just poured out to her. But after a few moments, she finally spoke. "Calista. Shane. The boys and I will need a few moments alone to talk this over. Would you please wait either in the hall or in your room, Calista?"

"Of course. Please, take your time." I wanted to do anything that I could to persuade them to let Shane stay with us but I didn't want to cross any lines. It was one hundred percent their decision and so we left them to it.

I brought Shane into my room, even though it was cluttered with exercise equipment and weaponry. He didn't seem to mind although he looked a little surprised to see several guns lying around the room. I assured him that I hadn't put them into use...yet.

We both sat down on the small couch near the window. Shane placed his hand over mine. "What do you think they'll decide?"

"I'm not sure. All I can do is hope that they'll decide in our favor. There are several options that they could choose...let's just hope that it's not the worst one…" I couldn't bear the thought of them wanting to get rid of Shane. "But things could run in our favor. This is pretty much the same situation as when Ayden brought me here while I was still human. All we can do is sit here and wait to see what they decide."

The two of us sat in silence for the rest of the time we waited. I suppose neither of us really knew what to say to each other. My mind was preoccupied with wondering about what the Ancients would decide.

A half hour had passed before we were called back into Sabine's office. Tristan and Caelum both looked unhappy but I wasn't sure what to make of it. We wouldn't know until Sabine told us what they had talked about.

Once Shane and I were seated, Sabine finally spoke. "Well, we have talked things over. As much as Tristan and Caelum feel that Shane should be destroyed…"

I didn't even let her finish. I stood up in a rage. "No! I won't allow it! If he dies, I die too!" Shane jumped up and grabbed me by the shoulders.

Sabine held up her hand to silence me. "Now, now Calista. You didn't let me finish. Please be seated." Shane gently pulled me back into my chair and then sat down himself. "As I was saying, as much as they would both like for that to be the answer to this dilemma, I have said no to it. Shane has made a good argument and he is right…he is most likely not a part of the slayer organization anymore. However, you are both right about there most likely being a team sent in after you. And because of that, I cannot allow you to stay within the mansion any longer."

I bowed my head in sadness. I was overjoyed that they were going to let Shane live, but now we were being expelled from the mansion. Sabine and the others were sending us out on our own. We were to fend for ourselves.

"Now, we shall arrange for you to stay in one of the vampire homes, wherever it is you'd like to go. I hope you weren't expecting us to just throw you out with nowhere to go. Caelum shall search the database for you and find a suitable home for the two of you." Caelum stood and gestured for Shane to follow him. Shane stood and looked at me with worry. I shook my head and gave him a reassuring smile. The two of them left the room. "And Calista, I would like to speak with you some more in private." With that said, Tristan stood and left the room as well.

"Sabine, I am terribly sorry about this. I never meant for any of this to happen. Maybe it was a mistake to have Ayden bring me to you in the first place. I was the one that asked him to do it. I...."

Sabine stopped me. "Please dear. It's all in the past now and you can't change that. You have to just accept what has happened and move on. And now you must worry about protecting yourself and the one you love."

"Yes, I know that. But what can I do? How do I know we'll be safe wherever we go? And how can this work: human and vampire together? There's so much more I wish you could teach me..." I looked at the floor.

"My child, you're very strong now. And even though there *is* more for you to learn, you are more than capable of learning it on your own. Just because I am asking you to leave doesn't mean that we will not help you when you may need it. Please know that we are still here for you. We are still family."

"Thank you Sabine." I looked up at her with tears in my eyes.

She stood and came around the desk to sit next to me. "There is one more thing that I must speak with you about before you leave."

"What is it?" I was rather curious.

Sabine grasped both of my hands and looked deep into my eyes. It felt like she was trying to look into my soul. "Your young man is a human. You are a vampire. Living in this way will be most difficult to cope with. You may become frustrated with it at times and so shall he. There will come a time within the near future where you will want to turn him. Or...he may in fact ask you to do it."

I gasped at her words. "Sabine! I don't think I could ever do that to him! I care about him. I don't want this for him."

Sabine smiled. "Oh, how you sound so much like Ayden when you say that. He said the same thing about you, remember? But that time will come. And I advise that you do not give in to the temptation unless Shane truly wants it. Selene made you against your own will and because of that, you will always have a bit of hatred inside you. If you do the same to him, he may never forgive you. But with his consent, the love between you may grow stronger." I looked out towards the hallway. I wanted to go to him. Sabine turned my face to look at her again. "Please listen to this advice that I give you. It is very important. Do you understand it?"

I nodded. Just her mentioning Shane becoming a vampire scared me a little. I knew that I wouldn't be able to bring myself to turn him. After being turned by Selene, the thought often frightened me. That night sometimes still haunted my dreams.

Sabine and I walked together through the house one last time. She helped me gather my things and she also arranged for a limo to take us to the airport. We found Shane and Caelum in Caelum's office. They were searching the database for available houses. Shane thought that we should go to Peru. I told him that I didn't really care where we went; as long as I was with him I was happy. He smiled, walked over and hugged me. Then he hugged Sabine! It startled her but after a few seconds she gave into it. He whispered his thanks to her and then released her. He quickly thanked Caelum for his help and told him that if he ever wanted information about the slayers' systems, not to hesitate to get in touch with him. Caelum shook his hand in thanks. He seemed to be in much better spirits than before. Perhaps Shane's kindness was getting through to him.

We were all packed up and ready to go when I realized that I hadn't said goodbye to Tristan yet. The limo was waiting for us out front. "Wait! Where's Tristan? I didn't get a chance to say goodbye yet."

"I think he may be in his room," Caelum said.

"Thanks, I'm going to go find him quick." I turned to Shane and kissed his cheek gently. "Wait here, I'll be right back."

I ran upstairs to Tristan's room. There he was, standing at the window. I walked into the room and took a seat on one of the plush chairs.

"Hi Tristan. I came to say goodbye."

"You're leaving with that human, are you?" he said without turning around. There was a touch of disdain in his voice.

"His name is Shane, Tristan. And yes, I am leaving with him. I love him."

"What about your love for Ayden? Or your love for your family? *This* family. Is that not enough to make you stay and send that human away from here?"

I stood and started to walk towards him. "Tristan. What has gotten into you? I have never seen you like this before. It's almost as if you're..." I covered my mouth as I realized what it was. Tristan was jealous. But how could this be? Things were never like this when Ayden and I were together. What made this so different?

"As if I'm what, Calista?" he said, turning to face me. "Jealous? Yes, you read my thoughts correctly. I am jealous. I have watched you every day ever since you came into this house. And you won over everyone's love. There's something about you that just enchants everyone you touch. But who was the one that received your love in return? It was Ayden. And now a lowly human."

"Tristan! How could you say that? I knew and loved Shane way before I even met Ayden. And I met Ayden before I met any of you. I don't understand what has brought all this on. But there's nothing that can be done about it now. I am going...I just came to say goodbye. I hope that you'll be able to speak with me again someday. Grudges aren't supposed to last forever...and we have all the time in the world. I wish you happiness Tristan...goodbye." I turned and left the room. I didn't even care if he had anything else to say to me. I said what I needed to say. Plus, it wouldn't have changed my mind even if he did.

We said our final goodbyes to Sabine and Caelum. Everything was in the limo, ready to go. Shane and I slid into the car. I turned and watched out the back window as the limo pulled away. I felt an overwhelming sadness as the house became smaller and smaller. I was going to miss everyone...even Tristan.

Twenty-Four

The ride to the airport was long enough to allow me to think about the last things Sabine had said to me. What if the time came when I *did* want Shane by my side for all eternity? Would I be able to go through with it? I wasn't really sure. And I couldn't be sure if he even wanted it. I decided that I wouldn't worry about it for the time being. We both had more important things to worry about.

Shane and I were the first to board the plane. I dragged him to the very back of the plane. He said that there was a possibility that we may land in Peru right before the sun set. I got extremely worried and considered getting off the plane.

Shane held onto my hand and squeezed tightly. "Don't worry Calista. I'll keep you safe, I promise. I won't let the sun hurt you. If it hasn't completely gone down before we get off the plane, we'll keep you covered in a dark blanket inside the building." He put his other arm around me and rubbed my shoulder.

His words were soothing but I was still a bit concerned. I wouldn't let go of his hand the entire flight.

Lucky for me, the plane landed in Peru shortly after sunset. I was so relieved. I had never encountered any problems with the sun before and I hopefully never would have to in the future. Shane grabbed our carryon bags and followed me off the plane. We didn't check any bags because Sabine insisted on her sending them over via express mail. I hadn't argued with her.

Not surprisingly, there was a limo waiting for us outside. Sabine, as usual, had been a sweetheart and made sure we were taken care of. Shane tossed our bags in the trunk and then got in the car with me.

We took off moments later. Our new home was several hours from the airport. Shane took the time as an opportunity to sleep. I sat there and watched him, wondering what he was dreaming about. And then my conversation with Sabine came back to me again. What would it be like to have Shane as my immortal companion? The beautiful and sexy body that he now possessed could be contained forever. The more I watched him, the more I wanted him. Perhaps I could persuade him to take me in one of the beds as a housewarming gift. The thought was tantalizing.

Shane awoke as the limo rolled to a stop in front of the house. I opened the door and stepped out onto the gravel driveway. Shane was quick to follow and once he saw the size of it, his jaw dropped open in amazement.

The house wasn't nearly as large as the one we had left behind in Ireland, but it was still huge. The usual large white columns held up the front. Two beautifully carved mahogany doors held the entrance.

I playfully gave Shane a push and said, "Stop gawking already! Let's go inside. I want to check the place out before I have to…" I winced a little thinking about what I had meant to say. I felt bad speaking that way in front of a human.

"It's ok Calista. I understand. Let's go inside." He grabbed our bags and headed towards the front doors. I thanked the limo driver, handed him a fifty-dollar bill and jogged up to the house. Shane patiently waited as I unlocked the doors. I got them open and we stepped into the foyer. More jaw dropping came from Shane as he ooh-ed and aah-ed over the ceiling murals and spaciousness of the place.

"I sure hope you'll get used to this fast. You look absolutely silly with that look on your face," I joked.

"Oh come on, Calista. You're telling me that you didn't act the same way when you first stepped into one of these vampire mansions?"

He had a point. "Yeah, I suppose I did…sorry."

"It's alright. Let's check out the rest of this place."

I was in agreement, but I was more focused on him. He started off towards the stairs, probably to take our things up to the bedrooms. Every movement of his body was driving me wild. I was anxious to get him into bed.

Shane led the way upstairs. I couldn't take my eyes off him. How was it that I couldn't remember him ever being this irresistible?

We stopped at the first bedroom we came to. It was just as beautifully decorated as the rooms at the other houses. I would have been surprised if it wasn't. The whole vampire nation sure knew how to live luxuriously.

Shane dropped our bags on the floor next to the closet. I walked over to the bed and sat down. My eyes were still glued to Shane. I leaned back on the bed thinking about what it would be like to have him inside me. We had slept together a few times before, when I was still human, but now I was a vampire. The feelings of pleasure, I had found out with Ayden, were extremely heightened.

Shane leaned himself against the closet doors and looked at me. "What is it, Calista? Why are you looking at me like that?"

A smile crept across my face. "I'm just remembering what it was like back when we were together. If I remember correctly, our sex was pretty good, wasn't it?"

His face quickly became red. "Yeah…it was." I knew he was thinking about it too. He was just being shy about it.

"What are you being so shy about, Shane?" I stood and walked towards him. "There's nothing to be shy or ashamed of. There's no one here but the two of us. We have this entire house to ourselves."

I was waiting for him to answer but he said nothing. I was about to speak again but he didn't give me a chance. Before I could even open my mouth, Shane grabbed my arms, pulled me to him and kissed me roughly. At first I was surprised but I soon gave into his passionate kiss. I wrapped my arms around his neck and kissed him back.

He started kissing me all over my face and neck. Each time his lips touched my neck, a chill ran through me. It made me wish he were a vampire so that he could bite me as we made love. Ayden had done it and it was the most wonderful thing I had ever felt in my life.

Shane started running his hands all over my body. I couldn't take it anymore. I went straight for his belt and unbuckled it as quickly as I could. Not ten seconds later, his pants were on the floor and he was working on mine. I helped him out to make things go quicker. While I stripped down, he pulled off his shirt. Once I was fully undressed, he pulled my tightly against his body and pressed my body against the closet door.

I held onto him tightly and whispered into his ear, "Take me now, Shane. I want you inside me."

That was enough for him. He lifted my left leg with his right arm and entered me. I let out a soft moan as he plunged in. My moan must have turned him on because it made him thrust a little harder. I didn't mind it at all. Sometimes I actually like it a bit rough. This happened to be one of those times. The passion between us was so strong that I wanted nothing more than for him to dominate me. I pulled him against me as he continued to thrust. Harder and harder he pounded me against the closet door. I could feel the pleasure rising. My moaning became louder, which in turn made Shane enter me harder and faster. I was seconds away from orgasm and I could tell he was almost there too. He got in a few more thrusts before we both came. I let out one last, loud cry of pleasure. Shane and I looked into each other's eyes as we climaxed. I had wanted to bite him during those last few seconds but I didn't want to scare him. And at the same time, I was again wishing that he could have bitten me to make the sex all the more enjoyable. But it was still fabulous nonetheless.

Out of breath, we made our way across the room and collapsed on the bed. Shane was asleep within seconds. It was actually perfect, that way I could go out and hunt without him worrying or arguing with me about it. I kissed his forehead and got dressed. I took one last look at Shane before heading out the door. He looked so innocent when he slept. I began to wonder how long it would take before I couldn't handle him being human any longer.

I got through with my feeding as fast as I could. I didn't want to leave Shane alone in the house for too long. He needed my protection but I think on some level I needed his as well. A girl always wants to have the security of a man who will do anything to keep her safe.

Shane was still sleeping when I got home. I kissed his cheek and covered him with a light blanket before unpacking our things. Thankfully I was able to be quiet enough not to wake him. He stirred only once when I accidentally allowed the closet door to slam shut.

After I had placed all our clothes in the closet and drawers, I decided to check out the rest of the house on my own. I wanted to see if all the necessary supplies were here just as they were in the other houses. The vault was the first place I went to. There were four coffins located in the vault. It would be a bit lonely down there by myself but I was sure I could handle it. I just hoped that Shane wouldn't ever go down there. It wasn't really something he needed to see as a human. If he saw that I slept in a coffin each day surrounded by concrete walls, I was sure he would have an emotional breakdown.

The usual stash of wine bottles was located in a separate room within the vault. There was enough blood there to last me several years. If Shane and I ever had to hideout in the vault, I knew I would be able to survive without ever harming him. But I knew he would need other nutrients so I made a mental note to get some regular food down there.

The library was the next place I checked out. It was filled to the brim with books. As I scanned over the titles, I noticed that most of them were the exact same ones as in the other houses. There were shelves and shelves of different books, which must have been books that the previous residents were personally interested in. The other books, however, must have been protocol for each vampire mansion. They were books about vampires but also books containing information about our enemies. I pulled a book entitled *The Way of the Slayer* off the shelf. I thumbed through the pages, reading snippets of several pages. The book told all about the honorary code that the slayers had to abide by when they joined the organization. It also gave a lot of information about the habits and tactics the slayers used in their pursuit to eliminate our kind. I was rather surprised that neither Ayden nor Sabine had ever given me this book to read. It would probably be something good for me to read soon. Especially with basically the entire slayer organization after us.

I sat down to start reading through the book when I heard a large bang come from the kitchen. I dropped the book and ran to the kitchen. Happily I only found Shane messing around in there, wearing a blanket around his waist.

"You're awake," I said as I strolled into the room. "Did you sleep well?"

"Yes, thank you. I was hungry so I thought I would see what was in the kitchen. Unfortunately, there's not much here. Would you mind if I ran out to the store quick to buy something? Then in the morning…" He stopped and embarrassment filled his cheeks.

"What's the matter? Of course you can go out to get something." I walked over and caressed his cheek. "Why the long face?"

He lifted his head and looked into my eyes. "I'm sorry, Calista. It's just when I started to talk about going out in the morning, I realized that you wouldn't be able to go with me…you'll be asleep."

"Oh…" I said, dropping my hand from his face. "Right…"

"I'm so sorry honey. I knew this would be difficult for the both of us. But I would understand if you were upset. What do you want me to do to make things easier?"

I held my finger up to his lips to quiet him. "Please…don't even mention it. It's not even an option." He tried to protest but I kept my hand steady. "Shane…I just…can't."

He gently pushed my hand away. "Alright…perhaps we'll talk more later. But right now I am going to go out and find something to eat. Would you like to come with?"

I glanced at the clock on the wall: midnight. "Sure thing. I've still got a couple more hours until sunrise. I'd rather you not go out alone anyways."

Shane kissed my lips long and soft, then ran upstairs to put something on. I waited patiently in the foyer. Five minutes later we were out the door and headed to the downtown marketplace.

Luckily we found a twenty-four hour store so Shane would be held over until morning. He bought a few things and we were on our way back to the house. We were sure everything was going fine until we pulled up to the iron gates of the mansion. There was a small black car sitting right outside the gates. Shane's body became rigid, but I placed my hand on his knee to let him know things were all right. I wasn't completely certain about that but I didn't want anyone to panic just yet.

I rolled the car up next to the black one. I motioned for Shane to wait in the car. He started to protest but I waved him off. I climbed out of the car and waited for the mysterious person to get out as well.

I was expecting either Trent or some other slayer to step out of that vehicle. But much to my surprise, when the door opened it was Selene who appeared.

"Selene! What on earth are you doing here? And how did you find me? I thought you were staying back in Vegas." I was almost relieved to see her.

She held up a hand for silence. "Don't get your hopes up just yet, sweetheart. I come bearing some rather upsetting news, along with a warning."

A frown came across my face. "What are you talking about?"

She glanced into my car behind me, checking out what I was protecting. "Could we possibly take this inside? I think both of us would rather not be out here in a few more hours once the sun starts to rise, am I right?"

I followed her eyes over to Shane and then nodded. "Yes, let's go inside. I believe there is much we both must talk about."

She gave a quick nod and climbed back in her car. I got into my car and pressed the button to open the gates.

"Who is that?" Shane asked.

"She's one of the Ancients," I explained without taking my eyes off Selene's car. "She says she has come with bad news and a warning. We both must speak with her. I'm sure it has something to do with the slayers."

"Are you sure this is safe?" He was so cute when he got worried.

"Yes, I know her...she's the one who made me."

I pulled the car into the garage. Shane and I both got out. He headed inside first while I went out front to show Selene in. She had already parked and was waiting at the front doors.

"Nice place," she said, leaning up against one of the columns. "Sabine gave you this place, didn't she?"

I unlocked the door and led her inside. "Well, if you must know, yes. Just because I wasn't welcome in the house anymore doesn't mean that she had to be cold hearted."

"Unwelcome in the house, huh? Well, now you know how I felt."

It was a low blow but I did understand her meaning. "Yes, perhaps. Only I didn't do anything nearly as bad as you and I wasn't banished…just asked to leave."

"Ouch. Calista's learning how to dish it out." She laughed.

I made sure the front doors were locked and then had her follow me into the library. Shane was quick to follow. He sat down at the farthest end of the long table. I sat next to him and Selene took a seat at the opposite end.

"So what is it that you want to talk about, Selene?" I asked, folding my hands on the table.

"Who's this guy?" She asked, completely ignoring my question.

"That's not what I asked, but if you must know…his name is Shane. I knew him when I was a human."

She leaned far forward. "Ah, I see! He's the reason that you got kicked out of the mansion back in Ireland, huh?" She looked him over with her dark eyes. "Sweet deal I guess."

"Enough of these games, Selene. What is it that you came here to tell me?" She was starting to get on my nerves already.

"Well, I guess now is as good a time as any to tell you…" She stood and walked over to one of the windows. "I bring you grave news from Ireland…"

"Great," I said, leaning back in my chair and propping my feet up on the table. "What rules did Sabine say I have broken now?"

"Calista…Sabine is…dead."

"What!" I nearly fell over in my chair. I jumped up and ran over to her. "What do you mean? How did such a thing happen? Are Tristan and Caelum alright?"

Selene still wouldn't look at me. "I went there to ask for some help. Sabine has always welcomed me back whenever I had been sent

221

away. But this time, I went to the house and it had been completely obliterated. There was barely anything left. The place had been set on fire. Somehow, it got down into the vault and incinerated all three of them. It must have been started during the daytime, otherwise they would have been able to escape."

Tears had formed in my eyes. But nothing could hold back the anger that was building up in my gut. "Slayers did this," I growled.

She finally turned to face me. "I believe you're right. And that's partially the other reason I have come. The slayers are on their way here."

This time is was Shane who freaked out. "What!" he exclaimed, jumping from his chair. "What do you mean they're on their way here?"

"Exactly what I just said, idiot! They're coming *here*."

"Hey! Don't talk to him like that!" I snarled at her.

"Whatever! I thought I would come here to maybe help you out, but you obviously don't want it. I'll leave the two of you to your demise then." She shoved her way passed me and headed for the door.

"Wait," Shane called after her, "how do you think you could help us?" Oh, bless his sweet heart.

Selene stopped in the doorway. "Well, if you really want, I can stay and tell you what your options are."

Shane put his arm around my waist. "Please, tell us. I'll do anything to protect her."

Selene turned and showed us a mischievous grin. "Well well. Looks like you have an admirer, huh Calista? Think this human's going to keep you safe? Hope you're right."

I glared at her hard. "Leave him alone and just tell us what you had planned, Selene. I have every right to kick you out of here. This is *my* house now."

"Yeah yeah yeah." She waved her hand at me as she walked passed. She sat down again. Shane and I made our way back to our seats as well. "Well, I figure you can do a few things. But what you actually do in the end is all up to you."

"Alright, out with it already!" I gave her another hard stare.

"You better watch those looks, missy. Sometimes that's what gets you into trouble." She leaned back in her chair and crossed her arms. "Well, first option: you can run for your lives. But honestly, if you run now you'll be running forever. They may even catch you eventually. So that wouldn't be my first pick. Next option: you can stick around here until they show up. You can fight them off or even try to reason with them, but we all know that reasoning is not one of Calista's best qualities."

The more she talked, the more she was starting to sound just like Trent. I was starting to get a really bad feeling deep in the pit of my stomach. Maybe Selene wasn't here with the best intentions.

"And your last option is to either give yourselves up to them or put yourselves out of your misery. Because I can tell you that if you give yourselves up to them, it won't be pretty." That smug look returned to her face. Something was up.

I stood and tried not to let on that I knew something was going on with her. "Those don't really sound like the best of options, Selene. I don't think you put a whole lot of thought into those." I tossed a look for help in Shane's direction as I walked around Selene's chair. He immediately understood and stood up as well.

"What are you talking about? Of course I put plenty of thought into those options. They were the best ones I could think of for the two of you. There's really nothing else you can really do except choose one." I tried to read if she was suspicious of me yet but her mind was blocked. Even if she was, she didn't budge from her seat.

Shane calmly walked over to the window and looked outside. He gave a small wave to let me know there was no sign of an invasion yet. Perhaps she was bluffing. It was hard to tell, especially without being able to read her thoughts.

Before I could even ask her another question, Shane had grabbed one of the heavier books off the shelf and clocked Selene right across the back of her head with it. She fell to the floor, unconscious.

"Oh…wow Shane. Um, good job. I wasn't really expecting that but at least we have her now. We should get her down into the vault and bind her before the sun rises. I really think that she may have been bluffing about the whole slayer attack thing. Help me bring her downstairs."

He nodded and grabbed her feet while I grabbed her hands. We easily carried her down the stairwell and into the vault. I quickly ran back upstairs to find some rope. There was plenty in the garage. I brought it back downstairs and we tied her hands and feet separately, then tied them together as well. I wanted to make sure she wasn't going to get away. Once she was secure, we picked her up and placed her in one of the empty coffins. I pulled the lid shut and then placed a few cinder blocks on top, just in case.

I sat on the lid and looked around. "Oh crap!" I gasped and threw my hand over my mouth.

"What? What is it?" Shane asked, coming to my side.

I put my arm around his shoulder. "I am so sorry Shane…I really didn't want you to see this place. It's just something I didn't feel you would *want* to see."

He took my face in his hands. "Calista, it's really ok. I understand. Just because you aren't human like me doesn't mean that I think any differently of you. I still love you just as I did before, because you are Calista. You're the same girl in here," he pointed to my heart, "that I fell in love with. Don't ever forget that."

I pulled him to me and hugged him tight. "I love you, Shane." I looked down at my watch and saw that it was only a half hour until sunrise. "Oh man, I better get to sleep. Sun's almost up. Will you be alright till dark?"

He pulled away from me. "Absolutely. I can take care of myself. Plus, the house seems pretty secure. But I will double-check all the locks and the security system after you go to sleep. I promise I will be fine."

I hugged him again and kissed him gently. I gave him a small push towards the stairs and walked over to my own coffin. He stood at the foot of the stairs watching me, but I gave him a hard look so he'd go upstairs. He took the hint and left. I climbed into the coffin and pulled the lid shut. The sun was nearly up so it wasn't long before I fell into a deep slumber.

Twenty-Five

It hadn't felt like I had slept that long when I was woken up by sounds of screaming and images of bodies writhing in fire slicing through my mind. I threw the lid off my coffin and sat up, holding my head. Shane was running down the stairs within minutes of hearing my coffin lid crash on the opposite wall.

He came rushing over to my side and held me in his arms. "What is it Calista? What's wrong?"

"The screaming…the fire…where is it coming from?" I held my head tighter as if it would help squeeze out all the madness.

He looked around the room. I wasn't sure what he was looking for but it felt like nothing would make the images go away. I soon began to realize that the writhing bodies were those of Sabine, Tristan and Caelum. And it was Sabine's screams that pierced my ears.

Shane ran over to Selene's coffin and pushed off the cinder blocks. He pulled off the lid as quickly as he could and dragged Selene out of the coffin. He held her with one hand and pointed at me with the other.

"Make it stop!" he screamed at her.

She merely smiled at him and then the chaos in my head was gone. I collapsed over the side of my coffin, my head and arms falling to the cement floor. Shane dropped Selene and rushed over to me. He lifted me out of the coffin and laid me down in his arms.

"What happened to her?" he asked Selene. I could hear the anger in his tone. Selene didn't answer him. She just lay there smiling, even though she could barely move. He gently rested my head on the floor and walked over to her again. "Maybe you didn't hear me." He grabbed her by the throat and lifted her so she could see me. "*What* happened to her?"

Selene wiggled in his grip but he wouldn't release her. "Alright!" she choked out. "Just let me go and I'll tell you."

He let go of her neck and she fell to the floor. "Talk."

"Sorry about that, Calista." She chuckled. "Just thought you'd like to see your old friends one last time. Too bad they had to die such a terrible death."

I picked myself up off the floor and glared at her. "I'll kill you…you did it to them, didn't you?" I walked over and placed the heel of my foot on her windpipe. "Don't lie! I know it was you! I was suspicious ever since you showed up here."

She coughed and writhed under my foot. "Aren't you going to let me explain?"

I let off a little bit of pressure. "Go ahead. Explain."

Shane looked around. "Shouldn't we bring her upstairs or something? This place is creeping me out."

I looked at him and then at her. My foot came up and tapped her chin. "You should thank him."

Shane and I grabbed the ends of her and brought her back upstairs. This time we settled into the lounge. We propped her up in the most uncomfortable chair in the room. I sprawled myself out on the comfy sofa just to spite her. Shane took a seat on the floor next to me. He just wanted to stay close to me incase anything were to happen.

"Alright Selene. Start talking."

She cleared her throat. "Well, if you insist. I lied about the slayers. They aren't coming here. But they will be at some point. You can count on that. Just a few more hints and they'll certainly figure out where you are."

I sat up on the couch. "Hints? What hints? Who's been giving them hints?"

She laughed. "Who do you think, you stupid bitch?"

"But why?" Shane asked. "Why would you want to oust your own kind?"

Another laugh escaped her lips. "Ha! Why money of course, you imbecile. Why else do you think I would? Just because they think I'm pretty and I want to be nice? Fuck that."

"Well, now that I know you've been dropping hints to the slayers, you know that I can't let you leave here," I said in a dull tone.

"And you're going to keep me imprisoned here and actually be able to deal with me? I could easily send some more of those horrible images your way if you'd like. Crazy is a fun way to be these days."

Shane stood up and blocked my body from Selene's sight. "Just go ahead and try it. I'll take you out if you even so much as look at her the wrong way!"

Selene laughed so hard she nearly lost her balance. "Take me out? Calista, where do you find these guys? First him and then Ayden? I admit, I was the one who originally found Ayden, but he hadn't turned into a softhearted sap until you showed up. But this guy, man he certainly is wrapped around your little finger, isn't he?"

I placed my hand on Shane's shoulder to steady him. He covered my hand with his and took a seat next to me. "That's enough, Selene. Just keep talking and you'll stay alive. I have half a mind to kill you myself but if Shane wants to, I'll allow it."

"You'll allow it?" She laughed in my face again. "You sure have that leash of his tight."

Shane couldn't stand it anymore. His rage boiled over the top and he firmly walked over and slapped her hard across the face.

"Shane!" I yelled, standing to stop him from doing anything further if need be.

He looked back over his shoulder at me. "I'm sorry, love. I couldn't help it." He turned and came back to sit on the couch.

I continued to stand and looked down at him. "There was no need for that. Would you please just sit here and let me handle this?"

He nodded and bowed his head in shame. The sadness in his face broke my heart. I would have dropped to my knees and kissed him right then and there, but I didn't want to do that in front of Selene, in case she took it as a sign of weakness. He'd be fine sitting it out for a few minutes.

I waltzed over to Selene's side and crouched beside her. "Well, what will it be, Selene? Some more abuse? Death? Or maybe life? It's your decision. Depending on what you say determines your fate."

She shook her head as if it would help toss away the pain in her face. "What is it that you want to know?" she asked, squinting from the pain. Her cheek was already turning red. Shane had hit her pretty hard, but she could handle it. She *was* a vampire after all.

I knelt down and leaned in close to her. "You need to tell me all that you know about the slayers. And how you came to be connected with them. If you tell me what you know, perhaps I'll let you go."

She looked straight into my eyes. "Done."

"Alright," I said, walking back to the couch and seating myself next to Shane. "Start talking."

Selene tried to shift her body in the already uncomfortable chair. "Well, it all started about three years ago. I met up with that Murdock fellow in an alleyway one night. We fought it out but neither could kill the other. He was good. Quick on his feet. Then we got to talking. He offered me something that I couldn't refuse."

"And what was that offer?" Shane interrupted.

Selene gave him a quick glare but then continued. "He told me that if I gave him valuable information about the vampire species, that he would give me full immunity from the slayers and I'd live in very comfortable surroundings for as long as I'd like. I couldn't pass it up."

I raised one eyebrow. "But Selene…that sounds kind of like a foolish deal. You were already living in a very comfortable setting with Sabine and the others. What could he have given you that was so much better?"

"You didn't let me finish," she said with a smile. "He was also willing to build me a small army. And then I would be able to have full control over certain territories throughout the world. I'd be able to build my own empire."

"So you gave up information and your own kinds' lives for riches and power? How much more typical could you be?" Shane said, rolling his eyes in disgust.

"You humans. So typical with your emotions. Calista here seems to forget that I feel no emotion for such things. I am one hundred percent cold hearted. Ask Ayden, he knew the moment I turned him. Oh wait, that's right. I gave Murdock orders to kill the two of you. I am rather disappointed that he only completed fifty percent of his task."

This time it was I who jumped towards Selene and hit her hard. "You bitch!" I screamed at her as I hit her twice more.

Shane ran to my side and held my arms away from Selene. "Come on Calista. You wanted to hear what she had to say. Plus, if I'm not allowed to hit her then neither are you."

I didn't resist his hold. "You're right, hon. I'm sorry." He let go of my arms and we sat down yet again on the couch. "One more outburst like that, Selene, and I promise I won't have second thoughts at all about placing a stake through your heart."

"Well, the sun will be rising soon. Why not just stick her outside and let the sun take its toll?" Shane suggested.

Selene tried to straighten herself in her chair again. "You can torture me all you want. You can even kill me. But it won't save you from the death that will soon find you."

I stood and walked over so that I was standing directly in front of her. "I've heard enough. You have killed all the people that were close to me. Sabine and the others…they brought me in as one of their own. They became my family. And you took them all away. Now, I'm going to take away all that you care about."

"And what might that be?" she asked with a smug smile on her face.

I leaned far forward so that my lips were almost touching her ear. "Your life."

Her body tensed as I spoke the words. For the first time ever since I had known her, Selene actually showed me fear. Her body trembled and tears began to form in the corners of her eyes. Seemed that she truly believed I would never kill my maker.

"Let's lay her out in the back yard. We'll gag her first, of course. And then leave her there for the sun to take care of. After a few minutes in the sun, she'll be a pile of ash and no one will ever think anything of it." I grabbed her bound wrists and started to drag her towards the back of the house.

Shane was quick to his feet and grabbed Selene's legs. We carried her together out the back doors and dropped her body hard onto the cement patio. Shane ran to the kitchen and found some duct tape. He ripped off a few pieces and placed them over her mouth. She tried to scream and struggled hard to escape from her restraints but it was no use. I had made sure to tie the rope tight enough so as to cut off the circulation to her appendages.

Shane and I left her there, wiggling around on the patio floor. I asked Shane to stay and make sure that she didn't escape or somehow get rescued. He agreed and kissed my cheek. I held his face in my hands and studied his face. If only I could bring myself to make him as I was. Our lips met in a gentle embrace and then I was downstairs and in my coffin moments before the sun rose. As I lay there, waiting for the deep sleep to take over my body, I listened to the agonizing screams escaping Selene's mind. And as much as it should have panged my heart, I couldn't help but smile as my maker was burnt to a cinder under the scorching sun.

When I finally awoke the next night, Shane was patiently waiting for me at the foot of the stairs.

"Oh, it's so nice to see your gorgeous face first thing in the evening," I said to him while stretching. But then I noticed that he wasn't smiling. "Is something wrong?"

"Selene is dead, just like you wanted. I put her ashes in a bucket out back. Wasn't really sure what you wanted to do with them." His eyes wouldn't rise to meet mine. It seemed as if they were stuck in place, glued to a certain spot on the floor.

I walked over to him and sat down on the stair beside him. "What's with the face, honey?" I asked, putting my arm around his shoulder.

He shrugged off my arm but continued to look at the floor. "I guess I am just still trying to understand why you felt the need to do that to her. It was an awful way to die."

Instead of keeping my cool, I stood up with force. I was actually rather disgusted by what he had said. "What? And you would have rather set her free to send the slayers after us? You would rather have her tied up in this house driving me mad with her sick visions? I don't understand. You were ready to kill her yourself when we were talking in the lounge. Would you have rather shoved a stake in her chest?" I stormed past him up the stairs.

He jumped up and followed me. "Calista! That's not fair. You can't just turn it around and have it be all about you. So yeah, I was ready to kill her. She deserved it. I just wasn't prepared for it."

I stopped at the top of the stairs. "I'm sorry, Shane…that's my fault. I should have at least talked to you first." I lowered my head.

He ran up the stairs and put his arms around my waist. "It's ok Calista. I just wish you would try talking to me before making such rash decisions. We are both a part of each other's lives now and I think that we need to be able to communicate. I know that you have been used to being independent for the past six years but sometimes you need to let someone in to help."

I ran my fingertips across his hands and arms and leaned gently back against his chest. "I'm so sorry Shane! You're right. I am too rash sometimes. It's just the way that I've become accustomed to ever since I left Vegas."

He let me go and turned me around to face him. "I understand that. But I just want us to be able to do things together instead of separately. Separate is what makes us argue."

"You're right my darling." I hugged him tight. "Come, let's at least go give her a proper burial. I owe her that much. She was, after all, the one who made me."

Shane nodded in agreement and we walked together to the back yard. The bucket was sitting on the patio, just as Shane had said. I couldn't bear to pull off the lid to see what it looked like inside. It frightened me to think that I could possibly, one day, look like the gray dust settled on the bottom of the tin bucket.

Shane took the bucket from me once he saw the concern on my face. "Where do you think we should bury her? Or do you think she would have preferred to have her ashes scattered?"

"No, I think burial would be better. There really wasn't any place that Selene felt was her own. She was a wanderer, like me. We should probably just bury her down by the river."

Shane grabbed a shovel from the garage and we got into my car. The drive down to the river was short but silent. For some reason, Shane and I couldn't find anything to say to one another. And surprisingly, his mind was completely void of all thoughts. I wasn't able to pick up anything at all.

231

Shane offered to dig the hole. I guess he figured that I would want a few last moments with Selene's remains. As usual, he was right. I needed some time to apologize to her, even though she deserved her fiery fate. I also took the time to silently say a few words to hopefully put her soul at peace now that she was on the other side. I prayed to the Great Goddess to take Selene's soul into her realm and forgive her for all that she had done wrong. At some level, I think I was praying for my own soul. Once my own time came, I would have to hope and pray that the Great Goddess would take my soul and give it peace as well.

I placed the bucket into the ground and said my last goodbyes to Selene. Shane said a few small words asking for her to forgive us both for what we felt we had to do. He was a good man. I knew that his future in the afterlife would only be filled with peace and happiness.

Once in the car, Shane couldn't help but bring up the subject of the slayers. "Do you think she really sent a team after us?"

"Unfortunately, I do," I answered.

"So what should we do about it? Perhaps I could reason with them. I did used to be a slayer, remember?"

"Yes, I remember. But if I recall correctly, you never physically slew a vampire. You were their computer bitch."

He laughed at my phrasing. I was happy that he took it lightheartedly. Normally something like that would have upset him. "Well, yeah I guess I was their 'computer bitch.' But I know a lot of valuable information that they wouldn't want to go public. Maybe we could bargain with them? My silence for sparing our lives?"

My eyes drifted to him, filled with love. He had the body of a man but the heart of an innocent child. "Honey, I know you think that may work but these days, people like that just don't talk anymore. Physical force is their way of dealing with things. You saw the way that Trent and I duked it out at the park. Not a whole lot of reasoning was going on there, just our desire to kill each other."

"Yeah, I know…" he replied, looking out the window and letting out a big sigh.

I pulled the car into the driveway, parked and then rested my hand on his knee. "Baby, what happened to the outgoing and aggressive Shane that I met back in Vegas? It's almost as if our personalities have been switched around."

"A lot has gone on since those days, Calista."

"I know…" I rubbed his knee. "Hey Shane, what do ya say we stay in tonight? I won't go out hunting tonight. There's plenty of reserves in the vault. I'll go have some of that and then we can do whatever you want."

When he turned to look at me, he had a huge grin on his face. "Whatever I want?" he asked, winking at me.

I smiled back at him. I knew exactly what he was thinking. "Baby, you can have me all night long."

A huge smile spread across his face. He lifted me up and carried me upstairs to the bedroom. We made love four times that night. It felt so amazing. I actually came close to biting him once, but I contained myself. It just wasn't right that way. Even though the bite always made the pleasure that much more enjoyable, I couldn't bring myself to do that to him. I was too in love with him.

After the fourth time we were both utterly exhausted. But my hunger suddenly revealed itself. I needed to feed. It had been suppressed by the pleasure during our lovemaking. I kissed Shane's forehead and left him to rest while I went down to the vault for provisions.

I drank an entire bottle of blood before heading back upstairs. I hadn't realized my hunger was that strong. Might have even been part of the reason I wanted to bite Shane earlier. The thought of it was horrible. I shook my head as if to throw it from my mind. I left the empty bottle in the kitchen and went back to the bedroom.

When I got there, Shane was already fast asleep. I could certainly understand why; the sex had been so good yet so tiring that it crashed his system. I was getting ready to fall into my deep sleep as well. It was already four in the morning, so the sun would be rising within the next couple hours. Unfortunately, the bedroom wasn't dark enough for me to sleep there with Shane. I made a mental note to redecorate the room so that I would be able to spend some mornings with Shane. I wanted more than anything to be able to fall asleep in his arms. But this time it just wasn't possible. I found some paper and a pen and wrote him a quick note:

> *Good Morning My Darling,*
> *I am so sorry that I had to leave you alone in bed. It made me sad to leave your side. But it's nearing dawn as I write this and I must get down to the vault before sunrise. I hope you understand. But I do hope that we can fix up this room and make it dark enough so that I may be able to sleep next to you. Perhaps you could get a head start in the afternoon.*
> *I have left you plenty of money on the bedside table so that you may go shopping for whatever you'd like. Also, make sure to remind me tomorrow night to show you were the safe is. That way, if I am not around you can get money if you need it. There is money in the safe but Sabine also provided us with a joint bank account. I believe there are some checks in the safe and I'll have to give you the account number.*
> *I hope you slept well and dreamt the sweetest of dreams. I'll miss you until the sun goes down. But please feel free to do whatever you'd like.*
> *I Love You,*
> *Calista*

I left the note and a few hundred-dollar bills on the night stand. I took one last good look at my slumbering angel and kissed his cheek. He stirred slightly but then was still again. I whispered, "I love you" to him and then went down into the vault.

The morning before, I had left the vault door open in case Shane had wanted to venture down there. I had been completely against it when we first moved in but then I realized that I couldn't completely keep him away from every aspect of my vampire lifestyle. It was usually discouraged to leave the vault open, rendering us vampires vulnerable while we slept. But this was now Shane's and my home and we could make the rules. Even though it was probably dangerous to leave the vault open with slayers trying to track us, I did it anyways. I was hoping that Shane would come into the vault come sunset and wait for me to rise like he had the night before.

I lay down in my coffin and pulled the lid shut over me. I was sleepy from the sex, the blood and the sun being nearly up but my mind couldn't help itself. It got to working fast, thinking about everything that had happened and all that may happen in the future. Selene could have been telling the truth about leading the slayers to our mansion. But then again, wouldn't they have attacked already? And my heart still ached for the loss of Ayden and the Ancients. They had become my family. I never thought that I would have to be on my own without their guidance and love. I had no idea how long I continued to think on all those things. It must have been a long time because I was forcibly pushed into sleep by the rising sun.

Twenty-Six

The next night, when I woke, my mind picked up right where it had left off. I thought again about the Ancients and how much I missed them. Ever since I had left the mansion, I often wished I could go to Sabine for advice.

Another aspect that pained me was my final conversation with Tristan. I just couldn't imagine him having those types of feelings for me. He had seen the way that I was with Ayden. Ayden and I were so into each other; I didn't give Caelum or Tristan nearly the amount of attention I had given to Ayden. But perhaps that was the reason why Tristan was so jealous. He had seen how happy Ayden and I were together and he wished he could have the same thing. But I would never really know. Tristan was gone forever and I would never be able to speak with him again. It hurt me to recall our final words to each other. If only we had parted on better terms.

I didn't even realize I had been lying in my coffin for hours until Shane pulled off the lid.

"Calista, what are you doing in there? Have you been asleep this whole time? I was getting worried."

I sat up and looked around the room for a clock. "What time is it? How long have I been in here? I didn't even realize…I was just thinking about a lot of things."

He caressed my cheek and helped me get up. "It's alright, it happens. I was just worried, that's all."

I smiled and kissed his cheek. "My gorgeous worrier. What am I going to do with you? You worry about me far too much."

"Ah, but I have every reason to," he said with a smirk. "We both know that you can be quite stubborn sometimes and will do whatever the hell you want. Plus sometimes your decisions are a bit rash, but I still love you anyways."

"Oh, why thank you." My reply was full of sarcasm but he took it well.

"I got your note," Shane said, quickly changing the subject. "I already went out to the markets and bought tons of dark, heavy fabric to drape over the windows. And I bought some black lights for the lamps so that it won't be so bright in there."

"I hope you know that artificial light doesn't bother us my dear. Just the sun."

"Yes, yes, I know! But I just thought it would set the mood better and go along with the whole 'dark' theme we're going to have going on in our bedroom, you know?"

I couldn't hold back the smile that appeared. "You are just too damn cute, baby."

He laughed. "I think you're the cute one, babe. And you're also so irresistible! It's so hard for me to look at you and not want to ravish you."

I was a little shocked to hear those words coming from Shane. He had never talked like that before. But it was turning me on. "Well! Since when did you become a nymphomaniac?" I teased.

"Ever since I first laid eyes on you," he said in a sexy voice as he walked over to me. There was so much desire in his eyes, I thought he was going to rip off my clothes and take me right then and there.

I wrapped my arms around his neck and pulled him close. "Well, what can we do to satisfy your craving?" I asked with a smile.

He answered by kissing my lips long and hard. I hugged him just a little tighter. It felt like I wouldn't be truly satisfied until I pulled the whole of him straight into my body. Things were getting pretty heated when my hunger popped into the picture. I had to stop him before we went any further. With my hunger already present, who knows what would happen if we started to make love and I lost my inhibitions.

"Shane darling," I said, gently pulling away from him. "I really need to feed before we go any further."

The look on his face was heart wrenching. "Oh…ok…"

"Sweetheart, please don't do that. It hurts me to see that look on your face. But I am saying this because it's best for both of us. If we start going at it while I am already hungry, then who knows what I might do. Once my inhibitions are lost, I could bite you…and I don't want that for you. It's not something you should experience."

"But what if I want you to bite me?" he asked.

I was in total shock. I didn't think he had even thought of the possibility of becoming a vampire. As much as I wanted him to be by my side, the thought of turning him still haunted my conscience. "Shane…"

He came up and grasped my hands tightly. "Baby, why not? Why shy away from the idea? Don't you want us to be together? Think of it! You and me, always together. Forever!"

I gently pulled my hands from his and turned my back to him. "It's not that I don't want us to be together. I just…"

"What? What is it? You just what?"

"I just can't bring myself to do that to you. I don't think I would be able to take away your life and give you a new one. I guess I just don't feel like that power should be mine. It's too much and I don't want to hurt you, even if it will result in you becoming an immortal."

There were no more words that could be spoken between us. We both had our minds set and were too stubborn to budge or compromise. Until the time that I was ready to make him a vampire, if that time ever occurred, he would just have to accept being a human and me being a vampire.

Shane took hold of my shoulders and turned me so I was facing him. Just as he leaned in to kiss me, the doorbell rang. We both looked towards the upstairs in alarm. "Who do you think it is?" Shane asked me.

"I don't know…but it worries me. Who could possibly know that we were here? And there's no way a solicitor would have gotten past the front gates." I walked passed him and started up the stairs.

"Baby! What are you doing?" Shane cried out.

I stopped and gave him a weird look. "I'm going to go see who's at the door. That's usually what you do when someone rings your doorbell."

"Are you sure that's a good idea? What if it's the slayers? They could slaughter you the second you open the door!"

I let out a sigh and came back down the stairs and planted a kiss on his soft lips. "Why is it that you get so cute when you're worried?" I caressed his cheek. "Don't worry my love. I'll be fine."

I turned and started up the stairs again. The doorbell rang a second time. As I ascended, I tried to send my mind outside to figure out who was there. As far as I could tell, there was no immediate threat waiting behind that door. Shane was just worrying too much as he always did.

At the front door, I checked the peepholes in each of the doors. What I saw sent me beyond shock. I flung open the door.

"It can't be…" The words escaped from my lips like a gentle breeze through an empty room.

There before me stood the last person I expected to see ever again. It was Tristan.

"What's the matter, Calista? Not happy to see me?" He leaned his lean body up against the doorframe.

"Tristan!" Came a voice from behind me. Shane had followed me upstairs to ensure that I remained safe.

"Yes, it's me: Tristan. Why are you so surprised to see me?" His look of happiness changed into a look of confusion.

I didn't know what to do or say. I felt faint. My body involuntarily tilted and I reached for the door to steady myself. Shane ran up behind me to help keep me standing. "This…this can't be…" Was I seeing a ghost? I couldn't be…Shane saw him too. Tristan stepped inside the doorway and closed the door behind him. "Shane, why don't we take her into the lounge or something and let her sit down. Then perhaps we can talk and you can explain what is going on."

Shane nodded. He pulled my left arm around his neck and wrapped his other arm around my waist, leading me into the lounge. Tristan followed us in and then stepped ahead to arrange the pillows on the sofa so that I could be more comfortable. Shane carefully sat me down on the couch and rested my head against the pillows. He then lifted my legs onto the couch and seated himself in the chair next to me. Tristan remained standing, awaiting my explanation of why I was so shocked.

"Tristan…" I spoke so softly; I didn't think they would be able to hear me. But neither of them asked me to speak up. "Are you really here?"

"Yes," he laughed, "I am. Why would I not be?"

"Because…you're supposed to be dead."

"Dead? Well, of course I'm dead. I'm a vampire, am I not?"

I tried to sit up but Shane rested his hand on my shoulder to keep me lying down. "No, that's not what I meant. I meant *dead* dead."

"Wait, you mean like stake-through-the-heart, decapitation, burnt to a crisp dead?" He threw his arms open wide. "Why on earth would you think that?"

This time Shane jumped into the conversation. "Because Selene came here and told us that you were dead. All of you."

"What! That's absurd! Sabine, Caelum and I are all perfectly fine! I can promise you that no one has been killed off. Why would Selene say such a thing?" Tristan was starting to get agitated.

"She had sided with the slayers. She's been helping them. Giving them hints as to where we're all located. I'm actually surprised that she didn't outright say where everyone was. But we all know that she would prefer to play around with them first and let them figure it out on their own. But I was sure you were all dead…when she was here…she threw images into my head…images of you all…burning in a huge fire…the mansion burnt to the ground…" Even the mention of those horrifying images was making me feel queasy.

Tristan started to pace in front of me. "Where is Selene now? We'll get to the bottom of this. We'll take her back to the Ireland mansion and Sabine will know what to do."

"Well…there's a problem with that plan…" Shane said. I shot him a disapproving look.

Tristan stopped pacing and looked between the two of us. "What do you mean? What sort of problem? What's going on?"

This time I sat up and didn't let Shane hold me down. "Tristan, I'm sorry…see what happened was, she came in here being all nice and everything. But then the next minute she springs it on us that you were all killed in a horrible fire at the Ireland mansion, started by slayers during the day. And I was one hundred percent certain she was telling the truth when she planted those images in my head. I was in such a rage and wanted vengeance for your deaths…so…we bound her up and stuck her outside for the sun to take its toll on her…" I looked at the floor in shame.

Tristan knelt down in front of me and placed his hands over mine. I could see out of the corner of my eye that the gesture had made Shane extremely uncomfortable. Tristan was getting a little too close to crossing an unspoken line between men and their women. I tried to shrug it off and listen to what Tristan had to say.

"Calista, please don't blame yourself or feel guilty about what you did. Selene tricked you into thinking we were dead and that rage and pain from losing someone you care about is only natural. Your reaction was actually rather natural for a vampire."

A single tear rolled down my cheek as I thought about the painful death I had bestowed upon my maker. "We buried her ashes down by the river. We can dig them up and bring them back to Ireland if you think Sabine would prefer a better burial."

He patted my knee. "No, don't even think about that. At least you had the respect to give her a proper burial. There's no need to disturb her remains now."

Shane had had enough of Tristan touching me. He flopped down on the couch next to me and wrapped his arm around my shoulders, pulling me close. "So what do you think we should do?"

Tristan sensed the lack of comfort that Shane was feeling and backed away. "Well, how would you feel about going back to Ireland for a few days to speak with Sabine? I think that you should tell her yourself about all that has happened since you've been here. And I think it would be good to let her know about the information you now possess about the slayers."

"Yes, I think that's a good idea." Shane answered for the both of us. He rubbed my shoulder and stood up. "Let's go pack our bags, we can leave tonight."

I nodded and stood as well. I glanced at Tristan before exiting the room. His face was full of contentment. It confused me greatly. This was different from the Tristan that I spoke to when I was last at the Ireland mansion. The last time we spoke, he was full of jealousy and anger. But now he seemed to be filled with nothing more than pure contentment. I wondered what brought about this change in him.

"We can talk about that at another time." He had read my thoughts without my detection. I definitely had to work on that power a lot more.

Shane quickly packed a weekend bag for the two of us and we hopped into Tristan's limo. Shane and I sat on one side, his arm protectively around my shoulders. Tristan sat on the other. I could tell there was a tension between them. Change of heart or not, Tristan still had some jealousy lingering inside him.

As much as I was relieved that my new kin were still alive, there was still something inside that just didn't feel right to me. I couldn't quite put my finger on it but I had a feeling I was soon going to find out what that feeling was all about. Sabine would know what to do. Once at the mansion, I would request some time alone with her so I could let her know what was going on in my head and obtain her advice. I also thought that perhaps I should talk some more with her about our last conversation. There had been some new developments since then and I desperately need her advice on the matter.

Twenty-Seven

Tristan had taken a private jet over to visit us. The same plane was waiting to take us to Ireland as we pulled into the airport runway. Shane had a look of fascination in his eyes. The slayers must not treat their employees to such great luxuries as we are privileged to.

We sat in the same fashion on the plane as we had in the limo. Shane wouldn't let me go for a second. It was obvious that he didn't trust Tristan when it came to me. I tried to not let it bother me. Things like that were trivial compared to our current situation. There were much more important things to worry about than feuding, jealous boys.

The ride was quick and painless. No one said a word the entire flight. It was probably better that way. I had a feeling that anything said between the two of them would be misunderstood and turn into a major fight. And although I would have protected Shane lest something like that had happened, I knew he was no match for Tristan. In most battles between human and vampire, the vampire always triumphed.

A limo picked us up and drove us to the mansion. As we pulled up to the front gates, a sigh of relief escaped my lips as I saw that the mansion was still standing beautifully. It was only more proof that Selene was a liar and a traitor. I wondered if Sabine would be relieved or saddened to hear about Selene's death.

Caelum and Sabine were waiting for us in the lobby. I immediately ran to them and crashed into Sabine's fragile looking, but sturdy body. I hugged her tightly, tears coming to my eyes.

"I'm so glad you're alive," I whispered.

Sabine gently pulled me away from her and looked down into my eyes. "Why, of course we're alive, Calista."

Tristan set down our bags and folded his hands in front of him. "Sabine. Caelum. I think we should all proceed into the study so that Calista can explain what has happened in her absence from us."

Everyone nodded and we followed Tristan into the study. As usual, Caelum and Tristan took their places next to Sabine while Shane and I sat opposite them. This time Shane kept his hands to himself instead of holding onto me, most likely in a respectful gesture to Sabine.

"Now my dear," Sabine began, "tell us what has troubled you since you left for Peru."

I looked from her to Shane and then back to the Ancients again. "Well, a lot has happened in the short time I've been gone. I am rather relived that Tristan came to check on us because otherwise I wouldn't have known what to do…I'm in need of your guidance."

"Well," she said looking from Caelum to Tristan, "we shall do our best to help with this situation. Please continue."

I took a deep breath and let it out slowly. "Ok. While Shane and I were in the house in Peru, everything was going great until just a couple nights ago. Shane and I were returning home from shopping and Selene was waiting at the front gates in a dark car. I wasn't going to be rude and turn her away, so I invited her in to see what she wanted. One of the first things she told me was that the three of you were dead. Killed in a fire in this house, started by the slayers by daylight."

Caelum was shocked to hear this news but Sabine remained a blank canvas. No emotion whatsoever came to fill her face.

Since no one said anything, I continued. "Well, Shane was able to knock her unconscious and we tied her up. Then we interrogated her for a bit. She spilled the beans. Told me that she had been dropping hints to the slayers about where we all lived. She had made a deal with them for a lot money and power in exchange for giving up our whereabouts. And in the midst of her telling me these things and sending me horrendous images of you all burning in flames, I lost my control in a fit of rage and left her out in the sunlight to die…" I bowed my head and stared at the floor. I was afraid to look up and see expressions of anger, disappointment and shock.

Finally, after several minutes of silence, Sabine spoke. "Calista, please don't feel guilty or ashamed about what you did. You had every right and to be honest…she deserved it. She was a liar and apparently a Benedict Arnold as well. And now that we know this information, we must prepare ourselves for any type of attack or ambush. Did she say anything about when such attacks may occur?"

I was still feeling too horrible to look up, even to speak. Shane noticed and spoke in my place. "Well, she did tell us that she had sent a team of slayers to attack us in Peru but nothing ever happened. She may have been bluffing. She also explained that she was only dropping them hints. She wanted to play with them and make them figure it all out for themselves."

"Well, at least we have some time to make a plan," Caelum said. "Maybe some part of her was trying to give us a fair chance to defend ourselves."

"I doubt it," Sabine stated in a deep tone. "When it comes to money and power, most other emotions fall away and you are left with nothing but greed. Greed overpowered Selene's mind and led her to nothing but a swift and painful death."

"The thing is, we have no idea if the slayers are really going to come after Calista and Shane or not." Tristan offered his input. "How are we going to know what kind of plan to implement?"

"Well, since the slayers never showed or made any attempt to infiltrate the Peru mansion while the two of them were there, then perhaps Selene *was* bluffing. But they may show up sometime within the near future if Selene truly has been dropping them hints. But for the time being, I think they will still be safe at the house. They will just need to stay on guard and build up the security at bit more." Sabine seemed ready to protect us all by any means necessary but she also seemed skeptical about the whole thing.

Caelum stood and looked at Tristan. "Why don't we head up to my office and start looking through the systems? Maybe we can find out if the slayers are planning any attacks and then go from there." Tristan nodded and followed him out of the room.

I looked up at Sabine but she spoke my exact thoughts before I could even open my mouth. "Perhaps we should have a few moments alone. There are things I need to speak with you about." She must have known that I didn't want Shane to become worried or know about what I needed to tell her.

Shane merely nodded at her words, kissed my forehead and left the room. He was probably going to go hang out in the library, or maybe go help the guys out with the slayers' database. He had said that he would give them any information they wanted..

Sabine came over to sit beside me and placed her hand on my shoulder. "I know that you didn't want to speak in front of him, nor have him be suspicious. Now do tell me what it is *you* wish to speak with *me* about."

Tears welled in my eyes but then burned away. "He asked me."

A wave of confusion passed over her. It kind of surprised me. I was certain she would know what I was talking about. "Who asked you what?"

I wrinkled my brow but quickly shook it away. "Shane. He asked me to turn him."

"My dear, you knew this would happen sooner or later."

"Yes, I know! I just didn't think it would be this soon. We've only been alone together for a few days!" I shifted uncomfortably in my chair.

"Well, at least tell me how you feel about his asking you," she said, leaning back in her chair.

"I feel a lot of different things. There are times when I would love to have him by my side for eternity. I love him. But then Ayden enters my mind and I feel guilty. Guilty for moving so quickly from one love to the other. But there is also a strong feeling within me that says I just cannot do that to him. I can't take away his human life. I just…can't."

A smile invaded her serious lips. "Your human soul is still so strong within you. You worry too much about the consequences of things and how others will feel about your actions. As much as we are all saddened by the loss of Ayden, you cannot worry about him. He has left this world and unfortunately no longer has a say. What you do with your life is entirely up to you. And you may live it with whomever and however you wish. There is no reason to feel guilt for loving Shane."

"But what should I do?" I asked with so many questions still lingering in my eyes. "Should I turn him? He says he wants it and I know you said not to without his consent. But I don't know if I can bring myself to do it. My gut tells me no. But when he and I are...together...I almost can't stop myself." My cheeks became pink with slight embarrassment of mentioning Shane's and my bedroom endeavors.

Sabine straightened herself and thought for a moment. "Well, I can offer you some choices and I hope that you do not become offended by it. Here are your options: You can allow either me or one of the boys to turn Shane as long as he consents to it. That way, the burden of taking his human life will be lifted from your shoulders. However, should you choose this option, the two of you may not have as a strong as a connection as would be if you turned him yourself. You had a very strong connection with Selene but there was much more hatred for her because she took you against your will. However, a consensual turning will create an extremely strong, eternal bond between the two of you and you will be inseparable. So, the choice is really up to the two of you. Perhaps you should discuss it with him."

I nodded. "Yes...I did already speak with him some back in Peru but I basically told him flat out that I wouldn't do it. But being able to have such a strong bond with him would mean the world to me...to both of us."

Sabine nodded in agreement. "Then the two of you need some time to talk. Feel free to take that time here while I check with Caelum and Tristan to see how they are progressing." She stood and silently swept herself out of the room.

A few moments later, Shane entered the room. Sabine must have sent him in. He circled the room, like a cat looking for the best place to settle down. Finally, he grabbed a chair and dragged it across the room so that he would be sitting directly in front of me.

"Hi..." he said softly, lowering his body into the stiff wooden chair.

"Shane...please don't act all sad like that with me. I know that you haven't been happy with me ever since I said that I wouldn't change you. But right now we need to have a heart to heart about that…I just spoke with Sabine and she felt that we should definitely talk about it. I need to know how you feel and I definitely need to let you know how I am feeling about it. Ok?"

His eyes brightened just the slightest bit as he nodded. "Of course, Calista."

"Alright," I said, leaning back in my chair, feeling a little more relaxed. "Why don't you start?"

"Oh man, well, ok…" He was obviously caught off guard, not expecting to have to speak first. "Well, you know that I love you, Calista. I would do anything for you and do anything to keep you safe. I know that you're going to say you're capable of taking care of yourself but I *want* to take care of you. I feel like it's my duty. And because we are so different and I'm quite sure that you turning back into a human is not an option, I figure that me becoming a vampire is the only way that I can stay with you." I sat up straight, about to interject but he stopped me and continued. "I don't want to stay human and grow old without you. I don't want to die while you still live on without me. I don't want you to have to bear another loss by having me die a natural human death. It's just not fair to either of us. I don't want this human life anymore. All I want is you."

His words had come straight from the heart and I felt it beating within my own. He truly wanted this. How could I say no to him? He was my love, wasn't he? How could I possibly deny him that right to be whatever he wanted to be? I was torn between the two distinct feelings of wanting and not wanting to turn him. "Shane…I know you love me. And I love you! And before you say anything else, please allow me to say all I have to say." He gave me a nod of approval. "First, I should let you know that Sabine and I spoke about this before we left for Peru. She warned me that someday I would probably feel the urge to turn you. But she warned me not to do it without your consent. Because if I did that, you would only feel a bitter hatred for me. That's why I felt so much malice towards Selene. She had made me against my will and I could never forgive her for it. But now that I am what I am, I must accept it and live my life as a vampire."

He moved to speak but I prevented him from doing so. "Come on, Shane. You agreed to let me say all that I had to say." Another nod. "Thank you. So, those nights at the mansion, I panicked. I was so torn. I had wanted to turn you, mainly while we were having sex…it's because the senses are heightened so much that inhibitions are lost and the bite always increases the pleasure ten-fold. I wanted you to feel that same pleasure. But I restrained myself because you had not yet consented. And then when you asked me, my mind flew into intense stress mode. Like I said, I wanted it but at the same time I just couldn't bring myself to do it. I didn't want to be the one that took away your human life. It was yours and you deserved to live it, unlike me."

Once I bowed my head, he knew that I had said all I needed to say. He took the opportunity and poured his heart out. "Calista, I want this more than anything. And it's because it means that I'll be able to be with you forever. That's the only thing I want in the whole world: to be with you."

Tears formed in my eyes but I pushed them back. "Well, then I suppose I should tell you what Sabine and I just discussed."

"I guess it has to do with all this, huh?"

"Yes, she asked to speak with me alone because she'd read my mind that I desperately needed to talk with her about this. She knew I didn't really want you to get worried for wanting to speak with her alone. I thought it would upset you." I thought about raising my gaze but I was still trying to hold back the tears.

Shane dropped onto the floor and knelt in front of me. "Baby, you can do whatever you want and talk to whomever you want about whatever you want! I just want to be a part of your life." He grasped my hands, the warmth of love flowing through them and into mine. "What is it that you two talked about?"

"Well, she informed me that we have two choices in the process of your turning if you so choose it. First is that either herself or Caelum or Tristan can turn you if I don't feel up to the task. But she told me that if I do not make you myself, our connection will not be as strong. Only with you being turned by me would the connection between us be its strongest. But I really think that the decision is yours."

This time he took my face in his hands and lifted my eyes to meet his. "Baby, you know now that I want this more than anything. I want to be your lover, your protector…even your husband…if you'll have me. Please do this. And I want it to be *you*. I want that strong connection that will follow us through the centuries."

A smile crept across my face. He was already starting to sound like a wise vampire. "As you wish, Shane. But I want to speak with Sabine and have her talk me through it. I have never turned anyone before and I don't want to harm you in any way during the process. I want it done right."

It's almost too difficult for me to describe the joy that filled his eyes and his heart. He hugged me so tightly and so long that it felt like we were sitting there for ages. It wasn't until Caelum entered the room that we realized how long we had been there.

"Is everything all right in here? I'm not interrupting, am I?" Caelum said in his usual gentlemanly manner.

"Oh no! Not at all!" Shane stated with such excitement. "We actually have some wonderful news!"

Caelum looked to me for an answer. I wasn't sure if I should be the one to give it to him or not but I spoke up nonetheless. "Well, Caelum. Shane and I have been talking. I badly want to make him a part of this family. I want him by my side. Not as a human, but as one of us. And he has consented to it."

His expression did not change but I could tell he was not completely enthused about it. "I see…" he said, his eyes wandering away from mine.

"What's the matter?" I asked.

"Well, are you sure this is a wise idea?" he said with such authority.

"Why is it a problem? We both want it and Shane has consented, just like Sabine said he must if I ever wanted to turn him. Sabine has approved! You have to as well. I don't want Shane entering this family unwelcome!" I pouted and wrapped my arms around Shane's neck.

"My apologies," Caelum said dryly. "As long as Sabine has given her approval, then I accept."

"Alright then." I wasn't completely satisfied but I was willing to accept his answer. I could tell he still wasn't happy about the decision. And he might have even been a little angry that Sabine had even agreed to such a thing.

The three of us left the room and headed up to Sabine's office. It was time to tell her the final verdict. Shane definitely wanted to be turned and I was going to be the one to do it. But I was certainly going to need her guidance in order to do it.

Sabine was sitting behind her desk, writing frantically. When we entered the room, she looked up with a smile. "Hello! Please take a seat. I assume all went well?"

I looked at Caelum. He calmly sat beside Sabine but was unemotional. My eyes shifted to the left and I was surprised to see that Tristan was not there. I looked all around to find that he was not even in the room. "Sabine, where is Tristan? Why isn't he here?"

Sabine's happy demeanor faded. "He was in much need of sustenance, my dear. I sent him out to feed. The traveling wore him down."

Caelum left out a loud huff and rolled his eyes. "You're such a bad liar, Sabine. They can see right through that." He turned his attention to me. "The truth is Calista, that Tristan did not want to be present for this atrocious event."

Before anyone could let out another word, Sabine's hand flew from her lap and landed squarely across Caelum's cheek. A gasp escaped my mouth. Shane's entire body stiffened at the sound of Sabine's hand striking Caelum's face. And for the first time since I had known him, I saw true shock fill Caelum's face.

Sabine herself actually seemed surprised by her own actions. She shook her entire body as if it would help her gain composure. "I'm sorry…but Caelum, that statement was completely uncalled for. Tristan is in fact out hunting but Caelum is still a little correct. Tristan did not want to stick around whilst Shane was turned. And I think we all know as to why that is so there should be no reason to discuss it. The matter at hand is what needs to be conversed."

Shane suddenly stood and moved himself to the very front of Sabine's desk. "May I say something please?"

"Well of course you may, but there's no need to stand. We are all familiar here. You may be seated." Sabine gracefully directed her hand towards his chair.

Shane sat back down but on the very edge of his seat. "Well, I know that neither Caelum nor Tristan are very fond of me. And I think I know why. Part of it is because I am human, but not only that, I used to belong to the slayers' organization. And second I believe is because of Calista. They both seem very protective of her and Tristan particularly seems to have a deep affection for her. I can't blame him. But I assure you that I want this. I want to be able to stay by Calista's side and live a long life with her. I love her. And I would love to become a part of this family. You have been so kind to me, even when she told you that I was a slayer. Being accepted into your household means a lot and I hope that you'll give me the chance to be a part of it all."

A gorgeous smile appeared on Sabine's face. "That was lovely, Shane. Are you sure you didn't rehearse that?" She winked at him and practically giggled like a schoolgirl.

Her smile made him blush but he quickly regained his composure. "I swear it wasn't rehearsed. I meant every word of it. And I was hoping that things would not start out with extreme tension between myself and Tristan and Caelum. I never intended to barge in or step on anyone's feet. I love Calista and I want to be with her. That's it."

Sabine leaned forward slightly and formed a steeple with her hands. "Well, it is clear what the decision is and what the following action shall be. And I do know that Calista will need our help going through the process. We intend to be as supportive as she needs us to be." She shot a hard glance in Caelum's direction. "Does anyone have any questions?"

"I would sure hope that you expect several questions from me," I chimed in quickly. "This is a whole new thing for me and I have no idea what I am supposed to do. The only thing I can remember from my own turning was that Selene bled me until I felt like I was going to die and then offered me an open wound to drink from. And it was from that vampire blood that I became what I am. But how will I know when to stop drinking from him? How will I know when he has taken enough of my own blood? How do we even know that I am strong enough to turn him? What if my own blood isn't powerful enough?"

"Whoa honey!" Sabine cried, waving her hands in front of her to try and calm my nerves. "So many questions at once. And yes, I did expect as much. But try to breathe in between sentences." She laughed. "But to answer your questions, drinking from him will be no different than if you were drinking from a victim. You know how to stop before the heart stops. It's just like that. And as far as Shane taking blood from you, well, he'll most likely pass out before he can take too much. You shouldn't be weakened much from it."

It was now Shane who had so many questions. "Well, I have a few things going on in my head…will it hurt when she drinks from me? And what's to stop me from *not* drinking from her? Blood, as far as I know, tastes awful, but that's because I am human. And when you say 'pass out,' am I going to feel anything? Will it hurt? What happens to my human soul?"

Again Sabine threw up her hands in a plea for silence. "Shane darling, calm down. Everything will be all right. The only pain you will feel will be a slight prick when Calista first bites. After that, you will feel only drowsiness and a swooning sensation. The outward flow of blood drains you of all energy. I promise, you will not feel any pain except for that initial sting of her fangs. And the reason you pass out is because so much blood has been lost and then quickly regained in your body. Your body shuts everything down in order to recuperate. Once you awaken, you'll feel like a whole new man."

Shane was starting to look like he felt better about it but something still bothered him. "That all sounds fine…but…what about…my soul?"

A small laugh left Sabine's lips as she smiled at him. "What a wonderful innocent you have found, Calista. He is simply adorable. But to try and answer your question, I don't really think I have really a solid answer for you. I have never seen a soul leave a person's body once they have become vampire. However, who's to say we have souls to begin with? But if one believes in that sort of thing, then maybe we do. I don't know. But I also don't know what happens to it once you have turned. It's certainly not my decision so I can't really tell you. I suppose that whatever happens to your soul happens because that's what you want to happen. So, if you believe it stays with you, then I am sure it does. I may have an inkling that our souls stay with us, or at least a part of it does. Calista is a prime example. She is constantly concerned with consequences of one's actions and how other people are feeling about things. She cares more about other people than she does herself. I believe that that is a strong quality of a human soul. And it has remained with her in her passing over."

"What about your own soul?" The question was a bold one, but Shane had no problem stepping up when he felt like it.

"Well, it's hard to say. Sometimes I feel like a small part of it still lingers. But at most times, I feel that it has faded away over time. Emotions have become less and less of a concern as the years go by."

Shane thought on it for a few moments. Perhaps he was trying to decide if he really wanted to go through with it or not. I couldn't tell. His mind was hard to penetrate. Finally he looked at Sabine. "Let's do this."

Sabine stood and we followed suit. "Let's adjourn to the vault. I think that would be the best place. No windows and well protected."

Twenty-Eight

Sabine led the way. Shane and I followed closely behind her, him clinging tightly to my waist. Caelum came as well, but he was lagging behind. From our previous conversation, we all knew that he was not pleased about what was about to happen. Tristan was even more displeased, hence the lack of his physical presence. Even though I was disappointed that Tristan would act in such a way after his pleasant attitude back in Peru, I did my best to push it all aside. It was time to finally have Shane by my side forever. We would be eternal lovers and companions. I would do anything in my power to protect him and I knew he would do the same for me.

Seeing the vault again was exhilarating yet sorrowful. My coffin had been untouched since my departure. It was still wonderfully decorated; it made me remember the night when I had asked Ayden if I was allowed to do so. He was rather happy to see me take pride in the somewhat mundane place in which we all slept.

Sabine led us to a far corner of the vault. There was no furniture of any kind, nor any of the wine racks which held the bottles of blood.

Shane and I stood before her and awaited her instructions. Caelum held back and sat on the lid of his own coffin. "I thought it would be best to tell you what we shall do once the process is complete. When Shane becomes unconscious, we shall carry his body and place it in one of the empty coffins so that he may rest and complete his turning. And once he awakens, I suggest on having him drink from the reserves instead of hunt right away." She turned her full attention to me. "Teaching him the ways of feeding will be your responsibility."

"Alright, that sounds reasonable enough." I accepted.

"So now what happens?" Shane asked so innocently.

"Now it is time to begin," Sabine responded. "Calista, it's now all up to you. You must drink from him and then allow him to drink from you. But remember what I said, drink no differently than you would from any other human. Stop before the heart stops."

Shane and I slowly turned until we were facing each other. Now was the hard part: taking away the human life of my loving partner. I took in a deep breath and then took a step forward towards Shane. He didn't back away, although I wasn't sure why I was even expecting him to do so. He actually took a step towards me. And when he did, he grasped my hands and looked into my eyes. Just from his look alone I could tell that he was letting me know that he trusted me.

I took one last look at Sabine and she gave me a reassuring nod to proceed. I took Shane into my arms as gently as I could and leaned into his neck. I hesitated for just a moment before setting my fangs into his throat. His body tensed in my arms at first but then quickly relaxed. I closed my eyes and focused on the beating of his heart. Once it began to slow, I eased up on my draw. Finally, I heard his heart slow down to a crawl and I withdrew.

The look in his eyes was dreamy. It eased my heart to know that he was not in any pain. He was starting to fade though. Sabine pressed gently on my shoulder to let me know I had to offer him my blood now or else he would slip away. Shane was unable to stand on his own, and to my surprise Caelum had walked over to help. He supported Shane quite easily. I brought my wrist to my mouth and slid one fang about a half inch across my wrist. The dark red blood began to flow from the wound. I brought it to Shane's mouth before a single drop could hit the floor.

At first the blood just flowed into his mouth and down his throat. He was so weak. But after a few moments, the vampire blood began to work its magic. Shane had locked his mouth against my wrist and was gently sucking on it. His strength was building. He was, however, still unable to support his own weight.

The more Shane drew from me, the weaker I began to feel. I

wasn't sure how long I would be able to last before I lost all energy. But I remembered Sabine telling us that he would pass out long before I would come into any danger of losing too much blood.

The moment the thought had finished passing through my mind, Shane's eyes rolled back into his head and he fell against Caelum. He had had his fill and would now sleep while the vampire blood took over his body and turned it completely. Sabine came to me and lifted my wrist. She looked at it for a moment and then slowly wiped her thumb across the open wound. I was amazed to see that the wound was fully healed! I never knew that Sabine had possessed such power. Normally I would have had to clean the blood away and then place a few droplets from my tongue to seal the wound. But Sabine was able to do this with the mere touch of her hand! I made a mental note to ask her about that later.

Caelum had already placed Shane in a coffin when I turned to help him. I went over to make sure Shane was comfortable. He looked the same as he had before he had drunk from me, only a little bit pale. But that was to be expected. I placed a kiss on his forehead and allowed Caelum to shut the lid.

I placed my hand on Caelum's arm. "Could you please not close it all the way? I don't want him to wake in the darkness and panic. At least if it is partially open, he won't have a panic attack. And I will stay down here and wait for him to wake up."

"That sounds like a good idea. I remember we did not place you in a coffin while you turned. We actually had you up in one of the bedrooms." She wrinkled her nose. "Why, what on earth are we putting him in a coffin for if we didn't do that with you? Goodness gracious! Caelum, get him out of there immediately and take him up to one of the spare bedrooms. I know that Calista's room no longer has a bed due to the equipment, so any of the open bedrooms will be just fine."

Caelum only nodded and slid back the lid. He easily lifted Shane and carried him up the stairs.

I went to follow but was stopped by Sabine's voice. "Well, what did you think my child?"

I turned to face her. "It was actually not as bad as I had thought it would be. I guess the process just had a stigma on it because of Selene. The way she had turned me was so violent and malicious that it frightened me to actually do it to someone else."

Sabine came to me and placed her arm around my shoulder. "Yes dear, but when the turning is performed with love and care, it is simple and void of all pain."

Sabine and I walked together up the stairs and to the room where Shane was resting. I sat beside him on the bed and Sabine stood in the doorway. Caelum had already left the room.

"Please feel free to call on me if he needs anything. And if you need anything as well. I would suggest grabbing a few bottles from the vault for when he wakes up. As well as for yourself, you haven't fed since you left Peru."

"Ok, that sounds like a good idea. Thank you Sabine. Thank you for everything."

"Anything for the loved one of our sweet Ayden. Always for family." She flashed a smile and left.

Caelum had only placed Shane on the bed without covering him. I pulled off his shirt, though it was a lot tougher since he was unconscious. I then pulled back the covers and laid his legs beneath the sheets. I watched the rise and fall of his beautifully smooth chest to make sure his breathing was steady. I also checked his pulse. It was a little fast but his body was probably still in the process of turning. Normally there wouldn't be a pulse. I gently kissed his forehead, both cheeks and then his lips before exiting the room. I was only leaving to retrieve a few bottles from the vault reserves as Sabine had suggested. I didn't want to leave Shane alone in the house while I went out hunting, so I thought it best to stay with him for the first night and enjoy the endless supply of blood from the vault.

I made my way down to the vault to grab a couple of bottles. Four should be plenty for the rest of the night. There would probably be an extra bottle or two for the following night as well. Shane would want more when he woke the next night. I remember that I had.

As I was taking the bottles off the rack, I could sense that someone was standing nearby. I turned, with four bottles in my arms and saw Tristan standing at the foot of the stairs. He was leaning against the wall with his arms crossed against his chest.

"Why'd you do it, Calista?"

"Nice to see you too. Why'd I do what?"

"You know what I'm talking about."

"Well, obviously I don't since I asked you." I started to walk towards the stairs.

Tristan stepped out in front of the stairs, blocking my way. "He's not worthy to be one of us."

I gave him a hard look of disgust. "I don't think that's for you to decide. I can't believe you would say something like that." I tried to walk past him but he shifted to remain in front of me.

"Just because Sabine approved doesn't mean that it's ok. She may be the oldest of us here but she isn't supreme ruler or anything. We make decisions as a group."

"Well, looks like she left you guys out of this one. Tough shit. Deal with it. Shane is plenty worthy of being a vampire. He belongs with me. And if you don't like it, too bad. Shane and I aren't staying long anyways. We're going back to Peru as soon as he's ready." I roughly pushed my way past him and up the stairs.

He followed. "Why did you go to a human for love and protection? Why did you never even consider Caelum or me? We could take much better care of you than him."

I stopped halfway up the steps and faced him. "I don't get it, Tristan. You were perfectly fine when I was with Ayden. There was no jealousy or tension between anyone. But the minute he was out of the picture and Shane entered, you got crazy about it. And what happened back in Peru when you told me that you were changed? You seemed happy and things weren't really all that awkward. You're on a rollercoaster and I don't want to stay on the ride anymore." I turned and walked up the rest of the stairs. I didn't wait for anything else from him and I didn't care if he followed me. I just wanted to go be with Shane.

Shane was still resting peacefully when I got to the room. I quietly placed the four bottles on the bedside table and lay down in bed next to him. My kiss to his lips woke him.

He slowly opened his eyes. There was a dreamy but loving look in them. "Evening sunshine," I said with a smile.

He smiled back. "Hi there gorgeous. What time is it?"

I glanced at the clock across the room. "Almost one."

He sat up in alarm. "In the afternoon! What are you doing up here? You could be fried by the sun any minute!"

I placed my hand on his chest. "Calm down sweetie. You're obviously still stuck on a human bio-clock. It's nearly one in the morning. We'll have to go down to the vault in a few hours before the sun rises."

"The vault?" He sat up fully and looked around the room. I could tell he was seeing things in a different light now. His change was certainly complete. But I think his mind was having trouble accepting it. He seemed to be confused on whether or not he was still human. I had been the same way. It takes a few minutes to realize the change.

"Yes sweets, the vault. You know, the place in the basement where we have to sleep during the day so that the sun doesn't touch us?"

He looked at me with some confusion in his eyes. "We? Wait...am I...?" His words drifted away. I think the realization was finally setting in.

I scooted in closer to him and held him by the shoulders. "Yes honey, you are. You are a vampire now. Don't you remember what happened earlier? Do you remember anything? Please talk to me. And don't panic, please don't panic. You wanted this. Don't you remember?"

He sat still for a moment and thought about what I had said. "Oh yeah! I do remember. We had talked about it for a couple days. I wanted to be with you and you said no. But then when you thought about it and talked with Sabine, you said OK. I'm just glad that we can be together now." He smiled big.

"Oh! I'm so glad you remember! I thought you'd forgotten. If you had, I'm sure you would have panicked and blamed me for turning you without you wanting it. Oh thank god!" I pulled him to me and hugged him tight. He hugged back and I could feel his incredible strength. His embrace was almost a little too tight on my ribs.

"Oh! I'm sorry baby. Did I hurt you? I didn't realize…"

"No, it's alright, I'm alright. You just don't know your own strength yet. It'll come to you though. You just need to learn. But don't you worry, I'll teach you everything you need to know."

He cocked his head to the side, like a puppy would when you try to teach it something. " Will the others help you with teaching me things? Why wouldn't they want to help you?"

I held out my hand and caressed his face. "No sweetie, it's not that they won't help. It's just that I don't think Caelum or Tristan will *want* to help in teaching you. They helped Ayden teach me but I think they had their own reasons for doing so. Sabine was a huge help to me as well. I'm sure she would help but the boys most likely won't."

He took my hand and kissed my palm. "I still don't understand why they wouldn't want to help you."

I shifted my weight on the bed. "See, here's the thing. I just spoke with Tristan downstairs actually. And…well I guess the way to put it is…he doesn't like you. He doesn't think you're worthy enough to be a vampire and he doesn't think you're worthy enough to be with me. He said that either Caelum or himself could take much better care of me. But I don't like either of them *that way*. I am in love with *you*. They are more like a family to me, brothers. But he doesn't seem to understand that."

Shane was staring at the far wall. He was definitely upset that Tristan thought those things about him and about me. It was obviously starting to piss him off. "Perhaps I should talk to him. Let him know what the deal is."

"No, no, no! Please don't do that. I don't want either of you getting more pissed off and then start a male ego battle. I think it's best to just ignore it. We won't be staying long anyways honey. We're going right back to Peru as soon as you're ready."

"I'm ready now!" he said, holding his arms out wide. "Let's get dressed, pack and then get the hell out of here."

"You know we can't leave now. By the time we get there it'll be far too close to sunrise and neither of us has fed yet. And I think Sabine is going to want to talk with us both before we leave anyways."

"Speaking of feeding…" Shane said, touching his stomach. "I'm feeling hungry. But the thought of regular food is not making me feel good at all. What is up with that?"

I couldn't help but laugh. "I hope this doesn't come as much of a surprise to you but you need to have blood in order to satisfy that hunger."

"Oh yeah…I almost forgot about that part…" He looked sad for a moment but then looked back at me with a tiny bit of happiness. "Well, you better hand me one of those bottles already because I'm starving!"

I laughed again and grabbed one of the bottles for him. He popped the cork with no problem and downed the entire bottle without taking a breath. I watched his gorgeous throat as he guzzled down the blood. His neck looked so sensuous. I wanted to sink my teeth into it and give him the best pleasure of his life.

I shook my head to break the enchantment. There was plenty of time for that stuff later. We had an eternity together now. Once Shane was finished, he ran his tongue around the rim of the bottle and then tossed it toward the end of the bed.

"Are you still hungry? Do you want another one?"

"No thanks, babe. I think I'm all set for now. But you should feed. You're looking a little pale."

"Oh yeah! I'm a bit hungry. Thanks for reminding me. I was so worried about your change and making sure that you were all set first that I completely forgot about myself! But that's the way it should be, don't you think? My darling man comes before me." I smiled at him.

He pulled me close to him and kissed my forehead. "Actually, I think my darling girl should come first. In more ways than one." He lifted my face to his and winked. I giggled as he pulled my face toward him until our lips met. "We can take care of that later. Why don't you pop open one of those bottles for yourself and then we can chat or do whatever it is you feel like doing."

I nodded and sat up again to open a new bottle. The blood tasted great. Sabine always made sure to have the best in her house. I made another mental note to talk with Sabine about stocking the Peru mansion. It was already stocked well but I wanted to know how to restock in case the reserves ever got too low.

I sucked out the rest of the blood, down to the very last drop. It would be a shame to waste such a delicious treat. I tossed my empty bottle next to the one Shane had left at the end of the bed.

"What do you say we go see Sabine? I'm sure she'll want to talk and see the newly transformed you."

"Ok," he said climbing out of bed and grabbing his shirt I had so clumsily taken off earlier. "What do you think she'll want to talk with us about? Did she talk with you after you were made?"

"Hmm…no, not really. It was mainly Ayden who had prepared me for the vampire life but I think that was because he was much older than I am. Since I am still considered a newbie, Sabine will want to make sure you know everything. I'm still kind of learning as I go."

"Ok, whatever needs to be done, let's do it. The sooner we get things done here, the sooner we can leave and be alone. I don't like sticking around here knowing that the other guys don't want me here." He pulled the shirt over his head and then smoothed it over his chest and stomach.

I walked over to him and put my arms around the back of his neck. "I know you don't really like them either. We'll be out of here first thing tomorrow evening, I promise. Ok?" I planted a kiss on his soft cheek.

He held my face in his hands and kissed my lips and then tickled them with the tip of his tongue. "Alright my love. Let's go see what Sabine would like to say and then maybe head to bed? I am starting to get tired already."

"Yeah, Ayden and Sabine said that that happens for a while once you're a newborn. But once we get older we can start staying up closer to sunrise and having more time together. Same thing will happen with waking up as well. You'll probably sleep a bit late tomorrow but don't worry about it. I am sure I will as well, I've still been doing it."

Shane threaded his arm around my waist and we left the room to go to Sabine's office. Luckily we didn't run into either of the guys on our way there. Not only was it uncomfortable for Shane to have to endure their glaring, but it was also uncomfortable for me to feel that tension between them. It's rather unpleasant to belong to a family where people don't get along with each other.

Twenty-Nine

Shane and I appeared in the doorway and I lightly tapped on the open door to let Sabine know we were there.

She was standing at the bookcase with her back to us, browsing through the many volumes on the shelves. "There was no need for that knock, Calista. You should know that by now." Her tone was instructing yet playful.

"I know, sorry about that. It's just a habit. I'll have to remember to not knock only for you." I teased back.

She found the book she was looking for and turned towards us. Her gorgeous blue velvet dress was flowing perfectly in sync with her body movement. "What can I do for the both of you?" she asked with a smile.

Shane politely gestured for me to take a seat before him. "Well, I thought that you would probably want to speak with Shane and me before we went to bed. We plan on leaving first thing tomorrow night."

A look of surprise came over Sabine as she sat at her desk. "Why on earth would you leave so soon? We haven't even begun Shane's training."

I looked to Shane for help but instead of coming up with a quick lie, he went straight for the truth. "The thing is, Sabine…neither of us really feel all that comfortable here. Now, I really don't want you to bring hell to either of the guys but I know they don't like me and Calista just hates feeling that tension. So we thought it best to head back to Peru and she can train me there. If there are any problems, I can promise that Calista will call on you for assistance."

I looked over at him. He was just too cute. Everything about him melted my heart. I knew that I would never regret making him a vampire.

265

Sabine now looked at me for confirmation of Shane's words. "Calista, is this really true? I can't imagine that things between you and the boys would be that dramatic to force you away."

"Sabine, I love you all like a family but it just isn't fair for Shane to be feeling such animosity from the others. I know that you like him, but Caelum and Tristan obviously do not. And I have continually gotten odd looks from both of them. I have even spoken to Tristan and didn't care much for his words. I just think it would be better for everyone if we went back to the Peru mansion."

Sabine pushed the book aside and folded her hands firmly on the desktop. "I will certainly have to have a talk with those boys. It's extremely impolite to treat our newest member like this! I just won't have it!"

I held out my hand to stop her from continuing her thoughts. "Please Sabine. There's no need to speak with them. I don't think it'll do any good. And even if they were kinder to Shane, it wouldn't be genuine. And there's something else…I don't think they feel like they're a part of a 'team' anymore. They feel that you are running this place and that they don't have a say in anything." Sabine looked absolutely appalled so I had to keep going to try and help subside her anger. "This isn't something I have heard directly from them, it's just something that I am speculating from the way they have both been acting. Tristan had even said that just because you approved of Shane's turning didn't mean that it was OK. Decisions were usually made as a collective group."

Her look of anger faded and a look of shame took its place. "Perhaps you are right, my dear. There hasn't been much done around here with everyone's complete approval. I have been doing most of the decision-making. That's my fault. I will make sure to speak with them on that and consult with them on everything from now on. That is, after all, the reason why we are the *Council* of the Ancients."

"I think they would appreciate that," I replied.

"Well now!" She slapped her hands on the table. "What is it that you feel we should talk about before the night is over?"

I straightened in my chair and took hold of Shane's hand. "Well, as I said, we are leaving first thing tomorrow. But I would like to see what it is that I should teach Shane. I know the basics that Ayden had taught me, but is there more? Also, if there is any advice that you would like to give Shane, it would be a big help, I think."

Sabine leaned back in her chair. "Well, let's see. Where to start? There is much to learn. But you are right, definitely start with the basics. The basics usually cover a lot of ground but not everything. And there is quite a bit that you must learn as you go. It can't really be taught verbally or physically, you just have to learn by doing." Shane nodded. He was hanging on her every word. I could tell she was very enchanting to him, especially through his new vampire eyes. "But the most important thing you must teach him, Calista, is about the slayers. I know that he probably knows much about them considering he once was one, but it still must be engraved in his mind. The slayers are not to be trusted. They are our sworn enemy and we must protect ourselves and each other from all attempts of assassination and entrapment."

I heard every word that Sabine was saying but the sun was rising within a few and it was starting to catch up to me. I let a yawn slip out and tried to hide it. But Sabine noticed it. "I'm sorry Sabine, sleep is catching up to me I think."

"No need to apologize my dear." She glanced at the large grandfather clock next to the bookcase. "Ah, the sun is close at hand. You have every right to be yawning! You two should get down to the vault. It's late. Go on now, shoo!"

We both stood and Shane waited for me to lead the way. "I promise we'll say goodbye before we leave tomorrow."

"I know you will," she answered with a smile. "Now go on to bed."

I thanked her for our quick talk and then grabbed Shane's hand to lead him downstairs. There were several empty coffins downstairs that Shane could choose from. I would allow him to sleep where he wanted. If he felt uncomfortable sleeping in any of the other coffins, I would certainly give him mine for the day.

I was hoping that we would have the vault to ourselves just until we got to sleep but unfortunately Caelum was already there rummaging around for something in a corner of boxes. Caelum looked up as we entered the room and his gaze lingered for just a moment. It made Shane grip my hand even tighter, though I didn't mind.

I pulled Shane over to my coffin. "Well, this is where I sleep, if you couldn't tell." I laughed softly as he looked over my area.

"I think the Egyptian décor gives it away, honey." He chuckled and kissed my cheek.

I smiled at him and then looked around at the other coffins. "Sabine, Caelum and Tristan all sleep beside each other at that end. Myself, Ayden and Selene would have slept here . There is one more empty coffin. So, I guess your choices are Ayden's, Selene's or the empty one. But if you aren't comfortable with any of those, I can sleep in one of them and you can have mine. It's up to you."

"I don't mind sleeping in Ayden's, as long as it's ok with you. I don't want to overstep any boundaries or anything. I just want to be right here next to you." He placed his arms on my waist and pulled me to him.

"Too bad there's not enough room in my coffin for both of us," I said with a wink. "But yeah, sleeping there is fine. There's no problem. We were going to put you there earlier when you were going through your change but I didn't want you to wake up inside a coffin and panic."

"Well, I am glad you brought me upstairs because I *definitely* would have panicked waking up in there!" He leaned towards Ayden's coffin and took a look inside. "You really sleep in here? Good thing I'm not claustrophobic."

"Yes, we do sleep in these. It's part of the deal. Are you uncomfortable with it?"

"No no. It's fine. But remember what I said about changing around our bedroom back at the mansion?"

"What? About the dark heavy curtains and stuff?"

"Yeah."

"Yeah, I remember. What about it?"

"Well, I was hoping that we could still do it. You know, completely sun proof the entire room. That way we can sleep next to each other every night. The thought of sleeping in a coffin and being separated from you every night is not sitting well with me." He hugged me tightly.

"Aww honey! Would you rather us try and sleep somewhere else? Is this going to be too uncomfortable for you?"

"Oh no baby! It's fine; I am just going to miss holding you. But I think I can handle one night. Don't you worry." He kissed my cheek again.

"Alright sweetie. Sleep well and I will see you in the evening." I glanced over in Caelum's direction. He had been watching us but quickly looked away to make it seem like he was busy doing something else. I brought my gaze back over to Shane. "I love you." I leaned in and kissed him softly on the lips.

"I love you too. Sweet dreams." He kissed me back and then climbed into his coffin. I watched as he pulled the lid over his head and then climbed into my own.

I lay inside my coffin filled with happiness. It was so nice to finally have Shane with me. We were as one. But I wasn't prepared for my happiness to be overtaken by the treacherous dreams that came to me.

I awoke in my bedroom in the Peru mansion. There was a warmth on the sheets next to me. Shane had recently been lying there. I sat up and looked around the room. Things seemed normal yet there was something strange lingering in the air. I couldn't quite figure it out, but I felt something was wrong. I climbed out of bed, put on a robe and ventured downstairs to see if I could find Shane.

The first places I checked were the most obvious spots he would be. First the library, then the lounge, then the vault, but he was nowhere to be found. I tried calling out his name, but my cries came out in a whisper. Panic started to course through my veins. What if something had happened to him? Had slayers come during the day and stolen him away from me? My quickening heart made my feet take flight throughout the house. Everywhere I looked, Shane just wasn't there. The tears were starting to collect in my eyes.

The one place I had yet to check was outside. But what would he be doing out there? And that's when I heard the awful sound of crackling fire. I rushed out into the dark night to find Shane bound and gagged to a large wooden pole. There were several burning torches surrounding him, stuck deep into the ground. My body's immediate response was to rescue him. This was indeed the working of the slayers. I rushed towards him but was stopped by an invisible force. It knocked the breath clear out of my lungs. I sat up, stunned by the mysterious blow. There before me stood Selene. But it couldn't be! She was dead! I had heard her screams; Shane said he had witnessed the event himself.

Selene stood in front of Shane's rigid body holding her out her hands. She was holding me back with this strange invisible force. I tried throwing curses at her but my mouth only released silence. With one hand still holding me back, Selene used her free hand to remove a torch from the ground. I watched in horror as she tossed it over to Tristan. The look on his face...I had never seen a look so evil as the one on his face.

It seemed like the next few moments happened in slow motion. Tristan turned and smiled at Shane. Shane struggled against the chains that held him against the stake. Then I noticed the dark puddle beneath Shane's feet. It was gasoline; I could smell it. I watched in horror as Tristan tossed the burning torch into the puddle. The ground burst into flames. The roaring fire quickly engulfed Shane's body. I couldn't move; I couldn't speak. I was completely helpless and unable to save my love. Selene's power held me hard to the ground and I was forced to watch Shane writhe, as he was burnt alive. Tristan stood and watched with pride.

I tried to sit up quickly. My head hit the lid of my coffin hard. It must have woken Shane, for he came running to my coffin seconds after my head made contact with the lid. He slid the lid back and looked at me with worried eyes.

"Calista! Are you all right? What happened?" Then he saw the tears that had stained my cheeks. "Oh my god, Calista. What's wrong?"

I wiped at my face, not only trying to remove the tears but to push away the remnants of the nightmare. "I'm ok. I just had a bad dream and tried to sit up too quickly without removing the lid first. I'm fine, I promise." I rubbed the spot where I had made contact with the coffin.

Shane reached down and lifted me from the coffin. "A nightmare? Are you sure it wasn't more visions or something? I hope that Tristan or Caelum are not trying to torture you like Selene did."

"Come on now, Shane! Why would they do something like that? Neither of them is as coldhearted as Selene. It was just a bad dream. Happens all the time."

"All the time? That's not very healthy, Calista."

"I didn't mean it like that. I meant that it happens to everyone. Don't you have nightmares every now and then?" I playfully pushed at his shoulder.

"Calista," he said taking my face in his hands. "I'm really worried about you and this whole nightmare thing. Don't you think that you should at least mention it to Sabine before we leave tonight?"

I patted his hands and started walking towards the stairwell. I was trying to play it off like it was nothing even though the recurrent nightmares had begun to rattle my nerves. "Nah, I don't think so. I don't want to bother her with such trivial things. Besides, I don't really think it's all that big a deal."

"Damn it, Calista! Will you stop being so stubborn for one minute! This is not just some trivial thing. There is something going on with you that you're in denial about. You need to deal with it now or it's going to become much worse later on down the road."

His anger surprised me a little. I hadn't realized how much my joking around wasn't being accepted. "I'm sorry Shane." I bit down on my lower lip. "I didn't know that you felt so strongly about this. If you really want me to say something to Sabine, then I will."

"Thank you," he said as he walked towards me with his arms wide open. "That's all I needed."

I fell into his embrace and let him hold me for a bit. I loved the feeling that came over me when I was in his arms. "Well, if I am going to talk with her about it, I think I should do it now. Because I know you want to get out of here ASAP and I am anxious to leave as well."

He reluctantly released me. I took hold of his hand to let him know that I wasn't going anywhere without him. We walked hand-in-hand up the stairs to Sabine's office. To both our surprise, Sabine wasn't in her office when we got there. I let my senses take a quick scan of the house. Two other persons were present; I was hoping one of them was Sabine.

I asked Shane if he wouldn't mind packing up our stuff while I searched the house for Sabine. He quietly agreed and took off toward our bedroom. I directed myself towards the library. It was always the best place to check first if someone wasn't where you had originally expected him or her to be.

Thirty

Of course, the library was not empty, but the person there was not whom I was looking for. Tristan was seated in the back corner of the room, feet propped up on a small table reading a book. I tried to catch a glance at the title. It looked like some sort of horror novel.

"Hey there, Tristan. Whatcha reading?" He didn't answer my question; merely held up the book so I could read the cover on my own. I didn't bother with it. "Hey, do you happen to know where Sabine might be?" I asked with as much aggravation in my voice as I could avoid.

Again no answer; just a shake of his head. His silence was starting to annoy me. However, I didn't want to create any more tension than there already was. I gritted my teeth and tried to ask him again.

"Well, do you at least know if she is in the house?" I questioned him again. And yet again, I received no answer. Another shake of his head was all I got out of him. But the final answer of silence had tested my patience and I had failed miserably. "For crying out loud, Tristan! Will you just answer me already? I am sick of this whole cold-shoulder and evil glares crap. Shane and I are leaving as soon as I finish speaking with Sabine and then you can stop being an asshole. But right now I need to know where Sabine is. It's extremely important that I speak with her before I leave."

Tristan casually closed the book and placed it on the table. "All you had to do was say 'please'."

Was he purposely trying to piss me off? Because it was working marvelously. "God! Please! Ok? This is ridiculous. Please tell me where Sabine is. It's absolutely imperative that I talk to her now!"

"Alright, alright!" he exclaimed, taking his feet off the table. "She went out hunting. She should be back momentarily. I'm sure if you wait for her in her office, she wouldn't mind."

"Thank you! Was that really so hard?" I asked; the question was loaded with sarcasm.

"Everything has to be hard when it comes to you," he shot back.

I sneered in his direction. "Are you naturally antagonistic or are you just purposely trying to piss me off?"

"What does it matter to you? You can take my actions any way you'd like."

I'd had enough; I wasn't going to sit there and take his piercing words any longer. "Whatever Tristan! You can sit there and say all the hurtful things you want, it won't change anything. Man! I can't wait till Sabine gets back so Shane and I can get out of here." With that said, I turned my back on him and stomped out of the room.

Shane was waiting for me in the foyer. Our duffels were already packed and waiting by the door.

"Everything alright?" he asked. He must have detected the annoyance I was feeling.

"Yeah, everything's fine. Sabine isn't here. She's out hunting but should be back soon. We can wait for her in her office." I pecked him quickly on the lips and then stomped over to the stairs.

"Are you sure you're alright? You seem a little…aggravated."

"Oh yeah, just peachy!" I sarcastically replied. "I just had a lovely chat with our friend, Tristan. He is acting so childish. He kept saying things to purposely piss me off. I had to storm out of there just so I didn't have to listen to him anymore."

"Well, at least you did that instead of picking a fight with him. I'm not sure I am strong enough to contain you," he said with a playful tone.

I turned to face him and let go a big smile. "Yeah, I don't think you could have handled it, babe. I might be a little too rough for you." I gently poked his chest.

He wrapped an arm around my waist and pulled me to him. "Eh, I like it rough."

"Is that so?" I leaned back a little when he came in for a kiss.

Now both arms were around me and he moved his hands down to my ass, squeezing it almost a little too hard. "Well, if I remember correctly, you like it rough too." The smile on his face just kept growing and growing.

I played along and pushed against his chest. "Yeah? So what if I do? What ya gonna do about it?

"You'll just have to find out later when we get home," he replied with a wink.

He leaned in to kiss me but the sound of the front door opening stopped him. It was Sabine, finally returning home.

"Now, now," she said with a smile, "don't let me stop you from such cute displays of affection." A childish giggle escaped from her womanly figure.

"Ah, Sabine! We were waiting for you." Shane pulled away from me as he spoke. "We're getting ready to leave but Calista has something she needs to talk with you about first." He looked over at me and I rolled my eyes at him. I was hoping he wouldn't have mentioned it. But when it came to his woman, every worry he could possibly come up with had to be resolved immediately.

"Yes?" she replied, looking from Shane to me and then back to him again. "What is it that needs to be discussed? A lesson plan for our newborn?"

"No, nothing like that." I stepped forward. "I have been having nightmares more and more often lately and Shane is just convinced that something is wrong. So, he wanted me to talk to you about it." Shane tossed me a hard glare for placing the blame on him but I didn't care.

"Nightmares you say?" She pulled open the door to the over spacious coat closet. She searched for an empty hanger and having found one, placed her coat upon it and closed the door. "Well, let's go into my office, then. Both of you." Sabine scurried past us to the stairs.

As we followed her, a message from Shane slipped past my mind's defenses. *Way to place the blame on me, babe. I may be concerned but I know you are as well. Or at least you should be.*

You can think what you want, my love. I still think this is not as big a deal as you're making it out to be. But I guess we can just wait and see what Sabine has to say about it.

"Yes, I'll let you know what I think once you tell me about these dreams of yours," Sabine commented. She had obviously caught wind of Shane's and my, what we thought was, private conversation.

As we entered Sabine's office, I was stopped dead in my tracks. Shane came crashing in behind me. He brushed himself off and gently pushed me to one side so he could see what I was gawking at.

Sabine's office had been completely changed around. The bookshelves were on the opposite side of the room but it seemed that the books there were either new or just in a different order from what I remembered. Her desk was no longer made of the dark mahogany wood that I had admired. It was now a beautiful forest green marble with streaks of white entwined throughout. The remaining furniture was upholstered in matching green leather. Her office now looked more modern and rather cozy.

"Well, what do you think?" Sabine asked spreading her hands out wide.

"Wow, I love it. It looks great. When did you have this place redecorated?" I asked her as I sat down in one of the comfy leather chairs.

She laughed loudly. "You think I had some silly humans come in here and decorate this place during the day? Of course not! I had ordered everything several weeks ago and it finally arrived earlier this evening. I took care of organizing everything myself."

Shane looked rather surprised at this. I'm sure it was because of her misleading figure. Her body looked too delicate and frail to be able to move heavy furniture on her own, especially a marble desk!

She noticed the amazement on his face. "What? You think just because I am female that I can't handle all this myself? Come now young, Shane! You should at least know by now the incredible strength that this vampire blood gives the body!"

"I'm sorry." He bowed his head. His cheeks flushed with embarrassment. "I didn't mean for it to seem that way."

"No worries," she replied. "Now, let's get on with this nightmare business. I know you are both anxious to leave here, though I will miss you once you depart."

"Well, like I said, Shane seems to think that these dreams are a huge deal indicating that something is terribly wrong. Something perhaps wrong with me but I think it's all nonsense. Everyone has bad dreams now and then."

"Yes, but not as often as you have been having them!" Shane shot at me.

I turned until I was facing him and placed my hands on my hips. "And just how exactly do you know how often I have been having them? That one last night could have very well been my first one!"

"I'm not stupid, Calista. And you should have figured it out by now that I got it from your own damn mind. You think about them just about as often as you think about me, which is apparently a lot."

My mouth dropped open in shock. How could he? My own lover prying into the secrets of my mind. "Shane! How could you do that to me? My mind is private and not for your viewing pleasure like a damned television! If I wanted you to know, I would have told you!" I was furious.

"You can't just keep all that stuff bottled up inside! Damn it Calista! You need to open up and let somebody in. It's ridiculous the way you feel the need to be independent from everyone all the time." His own anger was starting to get to the point of uncontrollable. It seemed he had known about this for a while and it all just boiled inside of him till he couldn't hold it in anymore.

By this time, Sabine had had enough of our shouting at each other. She finally stepped in to put a stop to it. "That is ENOUGH! You two are quarreling like five-year-olds. We need to focus on the main point of discussion. Please Calista, will you tell me what these dreams have been about?"

"To be honest…these *have* been going on for quite some time. They had actually started when I first met Ayden and received your letter." I could see Shane staring at me out of the corner of my eye. I brushed it off and waited for what Sabine had to say.

"Oh, I see. And what has happened in these dreams? Are they recurring? I mean is it that same exact dream over and over again?"

"No, each one has been different, but never happy in any sense of the word. The first was a few nights soon after I had met Ayden. I was in the pyramid I had visited when first arriving in Egypt. And the walls began to seep blood and it filled the corridor until it swallowed me up. The next was right after I had received your…second letter I believe…I dreamt that Ayden and I were on the balcony of my hotel room. You were there but you had no face since I didn't know what you looked like yet. You had instructed Ayden to push me off the balcony…and he did. I woke before I hit the ground." Bringing back the memories of these dreams was almost painful.

Sabine's face became one filled with concern but she urged me to continue. "Please go on. What about the others?"

"I have had a dream concerning Ayden's death…" The tears began to form but I would not allow them to be released in front of Shane. "It was the same as the night when he had actually…been taken from us. Only this time Selene was there. She had come out of the parking garage before we entered and the look on her face was of pure evil. Then, the arrows pierced Ayden and I was helpless to save him. And this time, instead of it being Trent who emerged from the shadows…it was Shane…" I couldn't hold them back anymore. The tears freely rolled down my ruddy cheeks.

Shane reached over to hold my hand. I allowed it. Sabine honored my need for a few moments to get control of myself.

Once I gained my composure, I continued on. "The final dream that occurred just hours ago involved Shane as well. We were back in Peru and I had awoke to find Shane nowhere within the house. Then I ran outside and found him chained to a large stake in the ground. Selene was there and she was keeping me from saving him by using some powerful invisible force. She never spoke a word; she only pulled a torch from the ground and tossed it to Tristan. And from there, Tristan dropped the torch into the puddle of gasoline that was surrounding Shane's body. I was forced to sit there and watch him burn…."

I couldn't speak of it anymore. It was too horrible. The tears continued to flow. Shane squeezed my hand. I wanted him to hold me but I think I needed to hear what Sabine had to say.

Sabine pondered for a moment, increasing the agony of waiting for her analysis. Finally, she spoke: "Calista, my darling girl. I can assure you that you have nothing to worry about with these nightmares. They are nothing more than your mind playing tricks on you."

Her words should have comforted me but instead I was surprised. Shane was as well. "What do you mean 'nothing'? They *have* to be something! How could nothing be wrong when I continue to have these horrible dreams? I don't understand."

She leaned forward and half-smiled. "Calista, as I said, it is nothing more than your subconscious playing tricks on you. I believe that there is some part of you, perhaps that you are unaware of, that fears the dangers that could come with certain events you have encountered. For instance, when you first met Ayden and received our letters, there was the threat that you wouldn't be able to stay in contact with Ayden. And your subconscious took that small threat and turned it into something much bigger than it really was. Your dream made you think that the verbal threat could be turned into a dangerous physical one."

I was still not satisfied with her explanation. "But what about the dream concerning Shane...burning at the stake. What if that means that something terrible is going to happen to him?"

Sabine let out a laugh but I didn't think she meant to. "I can assure you that that is not the case. The one concerning Shane is merely another fear you have deep inside you. You are scared that someone is going to take him away from you. And this is because of the deep love you share. The only reason that Selene and Tristan were the evildoers in the dream is because you shared a deep malice with Selene and because Tristan is jealous of your relationship with Shane. Because of these facts, your mind led you to believe that they would be capable of taking their feelings to the extreme and killing the one you love."

Shane let out a sigh of relief. He had been so worried that my dreams were indications of disaster ahead. I felt a little better but there was still something bothering me. "But Sabine, what if the dreams continue? How can I make them stop?"

"It's all really a matter of controlling your thoughts and feelings. You need to overtake the part of you that contains this fear and clear it out. There should be no reason for you to fear anything at all. You are a powerful vampire, an immortal. Practically nothing can stop you now. I think the part of you that is holding you back is that human soul that still lingers."

"Ah yes…we had talked about this before…." I recalled from a previous conversation.

"Yes, we did." She now looked from me to Shane. "And I am actually rather surprised that dear Shane has not yet had similar nightmares. His remnant of human soul is nearly as strong, if not stronger than your own."

I looked to Shane for confirmation that there have been no such dreams. "Honey, you haven't had any have you? If you had, you would have told me, right?"

He bit his lower lip. "I'm sorry Calista." His eyes went straight to the floor in pure shame and embarrassment.

"You have had them!" I exclaimed, jumping from my chair. "I can't believe this! After all the shit you gave me for trying to brush off the dreams, you have been having your own! And I told you that they were nothing, and Sabine has confirmed it."

His eyes never left the white carpet. "Look, I know that they are now nothing but I didn't think that when I first learned you were having them too."

"That's not what matters right now! What matters is that you were having nightmares as well and you didn't say anything and then you made me talk with Sabine about it when I didn't want to." I was becoming furious.

Sabine saw the anger in me rising. "Now Calista, please calm down. There's no need to shout about this. Please sit and we can talk about this calmly and rationally."

I turned to her and folded my arms across my chest. "I'm sorry Sabine but that is not going to work for this situation. He kept this from me and made a huge deal about it on my end." I faced him again even though he refused to look me in the eye. "Why would you keep this from me? Honesty is supposed to be a key part of a relationship."

"It's not like that, Calista!" He quickly brought his sorrowful eyes to mine. "This was a matter of pride and masculinity!"

My arms dropped to my sides and my jaw practically hit the floor. "Pride and masculinity? Like that's supposed to make it OK?"

Sabine stepped in. "He was afraid that you would judge him and think him less of a man if he admitted to having childish nightmares that frightened him."

I knew that she had taken this directly from his thoughts. I understood then. My anger subsided enough for me to feel sympathy for him. I knelt down on both knees in front of him and placed my hands atop his. "Shane, my darling, my love. Please know that I would never think any differently of you because of something like that. I love you so much and it's because of the person you are, not because of silly dreams that go on in your head. Nothing will ever change the way I feel about you, I can promise you that."

He finally looked me directly in the eyes. "I love you so much, Calista. There are just times when I'm afraid that something will cause you to change and not love me anymore. Or that I'm going to lose you. And I don't think I would be able to handle losing you a second time…."

I held his face in my hands and kissed him hard. "I love you so damn much it's sickening."

He gave a small laugh. At least he was loosening up a little bit. I hated seeing the hurt in his eyes.

Sabine stood and walked around her desk to embrace the both of us. "Well, I am glad to hear that we have that settled. You know, perhaps it is not just your minds playing with your fears. It's quite possible that it may be something that comes along with the change in your blood. However, that would not explain Calista's pre-vampire dreams." She furrowed her brow with a bit of confusion.

"But why would changing into a vampire give you nightmares? That just doesn't make a whole lot of sense." Shane was always trying to go for logic instead of "what-if" scenarios.

Sabine shrugged. "Who knows? I could be wrong. God knows I have been before. I may be wise from my years but that doesn't mean I know everything. A single being can't know *everything*, you know?"

I let out a loud sigh. "Well, glad that's all settled. Now I think that Shane and I should be going. I'd like to get back to Peru before it gets too close to sunrise over there. We'll both be hungry when we land."

"You're leaving so soon? I wish you would stay longer my dears. There is much to teach young Shane and we truly have missed you." Sad was the only word for Sabine's tone of voice.

I was about to explain why it was best for us to leave but Shane beat me to it. "I really think it would be better if we left now. As much as we'd love to stay, it's just not a good idea. Both Tristan and Caelum are agitated by our presence and we don't want to cause any more trouble. But I greatly appreciate the offer and all you've done." He gracefully plucked Sabine's hand from her waist and kissed the back of it.

"Yes Sabine, we really do appreciate it, but Shane is right. I think we should go and just leave it at that. But we'll be in touch."

I grabbed Shane's hand and started to lead him from the room. "Wait!" Sabine called after us. "Aren't you going to say goodbye to the boys?"

A shiver ran down my spine. It felt like someone had hit me with ice water. I was really hoping that she wouldn't have mentioned it. "Do you really think that's a good idea, Sabine? After all that you've seen from them?"

Shane touched my shoulder. "Honey, why don't *you* at least say goodbye to them. It's me that they're not fond of. Go ahead, I'll wait in the car." He kissed my cheek.

"That's not a bad idea. I am sure they would bitch and moan about it all night if I didn't at least tell them we were leaving. I'll make it quick, ok?" I kissed him back.

"Take your time, babe." He gently patted my butt and walked out to gather our things.

"What a thinker," Sabine stated soon after Shane had disappeared from the room.

"Huh? What?" I had been in a slight daze watching him leave the room I almost forgot what I was supposed to do. It was infinitely harder these days to keep my eyes off his scrumptious body.

"Shane. He's quite a thinker. Very smart and rather compassionate. It's not a surprise that you snagged such a handsome, smart guy."

"Oh, oh yes. Thanks. Yeah, he is pretty smart considering he was a computer whiz for the slayers. And he's extremely handsome. I love everything about him!"

Sabine rested her hand on my left shoulder. "Yes my dear. I can tell just by the look in your eyes."

I turned around and hugged her for what seemed like a long time. I was thankful for everything she had ever done for me. And for some reason, as we stood there in a warm embrace, I had a bad feeling that I was never to see her again. I pushed the thought to the back of my mind as quickly as I could. I didn't want to think about it but I also didn't want Sabine to pick up on it.

We finally released one another and said our goodbyes. I left the room to find Tristan and Caelum before heading for the car. For the first time since I had become a part of the vampire family, I found Tristan in his office tapping away on his computer. However, I was a little disappointed that his eyes did not waiver from the screen when I entered the room, even after our argument in the library earlier.

"Hi Tristan. I am sorry to bother you but I just wanted to let you know that Shane and I are leaving now. I know that you could care less about Shane but I wanted to say goodbye to you myself instead of Sabine telling you."

His eyes still would not lift from the screen. "Ok."

I couldn't believe he was going to start this up again! "Ok? That's it? That's all I get from you? Fuck, Tristan! These childish games of yours are just stupid and rather ridiculous! It's not funny and it's not making anything any better. Why don't you just accept it already? You are my family and I love you but that's it. End of story! I am so tired of trying so hard to make you happy and get you to be nice to Shane. And also be nice to me again! This was my last attempt and you lost it. So here's goodbye, I probably won't ever talk to you or see you again so I hope you're happy." With that said, I stomped out the door. I didn't look back to see if he followed. And if he had, I wouldn't have cared. I would have just shoved him away from me so I wouldn't have to hear anymore of his bullshit.

I was beginning to wonder if it was even worth trying to say goodbye to Caelum as well. But I knew he would throw a fit if I didn't. I stormed into his office without knocking. He was working away at his computer, just like Tristan was.

"Alright Caelum. Here's the deal: Shane and I are leaving now. I came by to say goodbye to you. I don't know if you care or not and frankly, I don't really care. But I wanted to say goodbye. So, goodbye. Hope you and Tristan can pull your heads out of your asses someday and learn to stop acting like children."

His jaw dropped to the floor. He certainly wasn't expecting that at all but Tristan had pushed me over the edge twice already. I didn't bother waiting for a reply, however. My exit was a replica of that from when I had left Tristan's office. And again, I didn't care if he followed.

I saw no sign of Tristan as I strode through the foyer and out the front door. And there was also no attempt to stop me made from Caelum's end either. I was surprised, yet at the same time, not. They were both acting like brats and I was sick and tired of it. I was actually quite proud of myself for putting my foot down. It wasn't really much different from how I used to be. If I had something to say, I'd say it and no one would dare argue back. I had never let people push me around. Things had changed for me personality-wise, along with my blood but I didn't want to lose what was left of my soul. I made sure to grasp on to that last bit of firmness I had left in me.

Shane was leaning up against the side of the limo with his arms crossed against his chest. He immediately straightened when he saw me fling open the front door and come stomping out.

"What's up?" he asked.

"Nothing. Let's go." I walked right past him, opened the door myself and slide across the seat.

He didn't question me further. He knew I wasn't in a state of mind to be chit-chatting. The car ride to the airport was filled with silence. The plane ride wasn't much better. But I could feel Shane's uneasiness with each minute that passed. He was anxious to know what happened but kept his mouth shut for the sake of not starting an argument.

Thirty-One

We arrived at our home in Peru about four hours before sunrise. Plenty of time to go out and find someone to eat. I didn't even want to unpack when we walked into the house. I was anxious to get out and feed.

Shane dropped our bags in the foyer and looked at me with a worried expression. "Honey, don't you think it would be better to wait a little bit before we went out hunting?"

I scrunched my face in antipathy. "What on earth are you talking about? The longer we wait, the closer the sun gets. I want to go out *now*." The pent up aggression slipped out into my voice.

"I'm sorry hun, I don't mean to make you more upset but I just think it would be best if you settled down before hunting. If you hunted in this state, you could easily maim someone. And I don't think you want any vicious deaths like that on your hands tonight. We really don't want the cops on our asses. Maybe it would just be better if we ate in tonight. What do you think?"

For once, I was warming to his suggestion. Normally I would be completely against it because I always did what *I* wanted to do. But now that I had finally let someone into my heart, I was learning that everything was all about compromising. And sometimes it was also about giving in to what the other person wanted. Shane, my darling love, was now asking something of me. He wanted me to calm down and spend a quiet evening with him. Not only was he looking out for the safety of any human that I may have chosen as my meal, but he was looking out for my own safety as well. He didn't want me to lose my temper and then have something horrible become of it. I loved him for it.

I took a deep breath. "Alright sweetie. That actually sounds like a good idea. A quiet night in tonight." I walked up to him and hugged him tight. "Plus, you're right. I need to calm down."

He hugged me back and kissed my cheek. "I'm sorry honey. I just didn't want you to go crazy or anything and then have something bad happen to you."

"No, I'm the one who's sorry. I shouldn't have snarled at you earlier. It's just that things with Tristan and Caelum went sour back at the mansion and it really pissed me off."

"So I noticed," he said playfully. "What happened…if you don't mind me asking?"

I let out a sigh and went to pick up my bag to bring it upstairs. "Well, I can tell you while we unpack. Let's go upstairs."

He nodded and picked up his own bag and followed me up the stairs to our bedroom. Dropping my bag on the bed, I remembered what Shane had suggested about changing our bedroom around. Just thinking about it really made me want to do it. Being able to spend every moment of sleep next to my true love would be absolute heaven.

"Hey gorgeous!" I called to him out in the hallway.

Shane popped his head in the doorway and then entered the room. "Yeah? What is it?"

"Not to get totally off topic but I was just thinking about what you had said about changing this room around. You know, the heavy curtains, totally blackening it out?"

"Yeah…what about it?" He seemed worried that I had decided I hated the idea.

I pulled him to me and kissed him hard. "Let's do it! I want to blacken this entire room. Make it one hundred percent sun proof! We could heavily drape the windows, even tint the glass. But I also want heavy heavy drapes all around the bed. A large canopy of dark reds and blacks. Wouldn't that be amazing?"

"It sure sounds like heaven to me, babe. Sexy." He smiled and kissed me.

"Excellent. I want to get things started first thing tomorrow night. As soon as we wake, I want to get to the nearest store and we can pick everything out together. And then we can put everything up right after we get home. Sound good?"

"Absolutely baby. Now, not to totally change the subject, but do you want to tell me what happened back at the mansion?" He flew right into the question without giving me any warning. I was prepared but at the same time I really didn't want to get into it.

I gently pulled away from him and started to unpack my bag. "Do we really have to talk about that right now?"

"I don't understand why you are avoiding the subject. All I want to know is what happened between you and the guys when you told them we were leaving. Obviously things went over badly since you stormed out of that house like an angry bull. You wouldn't speak a single word on the ride over here. And on our way upstairs you said you'd tell me while we unpacked. What's the deal?" I could hear the frustration in his voice.

"I'm sorry honey…it's just a touchy subject." I continued to unpack.

He sat down on the bed but made sure that I was facing him. "Why exactly though, is it such a touchy subject? You've been a part of this so-called family for what? A year? Maybe a little more than a year? It's not like you've been with them for a lifetime, but you sure act like it. You seem to be so protective of them. Why?"

"Look, they are my family no matter how long or short of a time I have been with them. You're a part of this family too now. And yes, perhaps I am protective. But it's just the way people act when it comes to people they are close to."

"I understand, because I've seen the way you've acted when you seem to think that the guys are a threat to me. But I guess I just don't really understand what your relationship is like with those guys. And maybe even how it was before I came into the picture…" His voice trailed off.

I stopped in the middle of folding a pair of jeans. "Oh sweetheart!" I sat down beside him and wrapped my arms around his shoulders. "You're not implying that I maybe had something going on with one of them or currently have feelings for them, are you?"

"Maybe I am. The thought has crossed my mind more than once ever since I've been with you. It's just by the way you act with them. And I've seen the way they look at you."

"What? What are you talking about? What way do they look at me?" I turned on the bed so that I was completely facing him.

"You know, they give you that look. That look when a guy sees something that he wants but can't have. A temptation, an angel, something so precious that they feel they must have it."

"Oh come on! Please! You're out of your mind. They never look at me like that!" I stood up and started pacing in front of him.

"Oh I'm out of my mind? Come on! You can't tell me that you don't see it. It happens every time you're in the same room with them."

I stopped, placing my hands on my hips. "No, I don't see it. I'm sorry. There's no reason for them to look at me that way anyways. They know how I felt about Ayden when I was with him. I was with *him* before I was with you, not Tristan or Caelum. I never even thought about getting involved with either of them. They're Ancients and I was just a measly human wanting the enchantment of being immortal and living among them. And now they both know how I feel about you. I have told them countless times, so they should have moved on from it."

Shane stood and came to me. He grabbed me by the shoulders, forcing me to look at him. "That doesn't matter. Just because you say something to them doesn't mean they are going to listen. Guys are like that. Plus, I don't think you realize what a knockout you are."

I couldn't stop the redness from flushing my cheeks. "What are you talking about? I'm nothing to look at."

"Are you insane? Look at you!" He dragged me over to the nearest mirror. "You are absolutely gorgeous! I think you are the most beautiful woman I have ever seen." He slid his hands down my arms and lovingly wrapped his arms around my waist. He nuzzled his mouth up against my neck. For a brief moment I was hoping he'd nick me, just a little. I longed for the passion we had several nights before. "I love you so much, baby. I'm just scared that some day, someone is going to come along and steal you away from me. You're so incredibly beautiful. You could have had any man you wanted but for some reason you chose me."

I turned around and hugged him tight. "I love you so much too, sweetheart. And I want you to know that you have nothing to worry about. I don't understand why you would ever think that I would leave you. I love you and *only* you. I would never leave you no matter what the situation might be. You really need to know that."

"I hear it, baby, and I believe you but for some reason it doesn't bring me much comfort. I guess it's something that comes with having a drop-dead gorgeous girlfriend. It's just an insecurity that I'm going to have to get over."

I pulled back and left a quick peck on his cheek. "Well, we'll just have to work on that then. I'll help you, honey. Whatever I can do to get you to trust me, I'll do it."

"Babe, it's not that I don't trust you. It's not that at all. I *do* trust you. I trust you with every ounce of my being. I told you, it's just that I am scared some guy will come and sweep you off your feet. Steal you away. It's something strange inside me that needs to be resolved. But I promise I'll work on it, sweetie."

"Ok honey. Well, we'll just take things one step at a time. For the time being, let's finish getting unpacked and then go downstairs to get a bottle or two. I'm a bit hungry."

"Yeah, me too. Sounds like a good idea." He snatched up his bag and dumped its contents on the bed.

I slinked up behind him and gently tickled his waist, making him squirm. "Darling…any chance we might be able to get a little something-something in before the sun rises?"

He glanced at the clock and grabbed my hands. "Hmm…it's possible. Depends on how much time we take feeding. We only have a few more hours."

I gently dragged my fingertips up and down his thighs. "Oh, I can assure you that we will have plenty of time to at least get in a quickie. I said I was *a little* hungry, not starving. I have been badly wanting that hot body of yours ever since we left Ireland."

Shane suddenly turned, grabbing my ass with both hands and pulling my body tightly against his. "You know, I'm thinking maybe we should skip out on dinner for now."

"What? What do you mean?"

"We could go down into the vault, strip down, have amazingly awesome sex and then, if we still have time of course, feed and then go to bed. If it's too close to sunrise, at least we'll be down in the vault already where the sun can't reach us. And we'll be near the blood supply once we wake so we won't have to go too far to regain our energy."

"Oooh baby! I love when you start thinking like that!" I kissed him hard. "That sounds like a fabulous idea. Let's hurry and get downstairs. I want to get you naked as soon as possible." I pulled at his shirt.

"Wow baby. And you thought *I* was the sex fiend!" He laughed.

"I can't help it honey. You're just so sexy! And the sex is always so amazing. How could I not want you all the time?" My lips instinctively moved to his for a long embrace.

We didn't waste any more time. Instead of finishing unpacking like we had originally planned, we left everything all over the bed. We were much more interested in each other's bodies than anything else.

As we made our way downstairs, we both did a quick check to make sure all the doors and windows were locked tight. We couldn't have any random burglars or slayers invading our home while we were vulnerable.

We entered the vault and double-checked that the door was securely shut and locked. As in all the other mansions, the vault was impossible for humans to penetrate. It didn't relieve us of our cautiousness, however. It was better to be safe than sorry.

I had started to descend the stairs but Shane caught my arm and pulled me to him. We hadn't even made it halfway down and we were already stripping each other of our clothes. Once completely naked, Shane lifted me off my feet and carried me the rest of the way down. I wrapped my legs around his waist.

He didn't bother bringing me to the nearest coffin. Instead, we did it right next to the stairwell, standing up. It was as passionate and erotic as all the other times we had made love to each other. When he finally bit into my shoulder to heighten the pleasure, I almost begged him to suck me dry. The feeling was so powerful that I wanted it to take over every ounce of my body. I was willing to give in to it completely. Shane finished off the bite several seconds later and sealed it with a quick drop of blood from his tongue. He kissed the wound after it had healed.

I got to kissing him all over his face, neck and shoulders after the deed was done. I was surprisingly ready to go yet again. But I figured he would need a few more minutes to recuperate so I slowed my kissing to a gentle whisper.

We had sex twice more during those early hours of the morning before the sun came up. By the time we were finished the third time, we were both so exhausted that we could barely move. I wanted to just lie there on the cool concrete floor and sleep for ages and ages. Shane obviously had more energy left than I did because he rose up off the floor and carried me to my coffin. Kissing my forehead, he quietly slid the lid closed over my head. The moment it was shut, so were my eyes and it was time for a much needed deep sleep.

Thirty-Two

It was seven fifteen when I woke to the sound of gunshots. I could tell right away that the sound was from a shotgun and not a simple automatic pistol. An alarm immediately went off in my head: Shane! I flipped the lid off my coffin. It flew across the room and shattered against the far wall.

"Whoa!" Shane yelled to me. "What's wrong with you?"

"Oh thank god!" I screamed and ran to him.

"Are you alright? What the hell is going on?"

"Did you hear the shots?" I slightly trembled against the firmness of his chest but quickly gained composure.

He moved his head around as if he was sniffing the air for a particular scent. "Yeah, I heard it. Shotgun. Double barrel. More than one though. Possibly three."

I pulled away from him and gave him a look of confusion. "Since when do you know so much about guns?" I asked.

He playfully pushed my nose. "Since I used to be a slayer, silly."

"Oh yeah." I relaxed my body. "Well, what should we do? Stay here? Or should we try and seek help from the others?"

Shane looked from one side of the room to the other. "Well, I am not sure exactly where you are suggesting that we escape out of here. But the possibility of a bullet penetrating the vault is slim to none."

"But why should bullets matter? They can't really kill us as long as we aren't hit in the head or heart."

"You forget, my dear. Slayers use silver bullets. Even if you're hit in a non-crucial spot, you could still easily be killed." He rubbed my shoulders. A look of fear came over him. His mind slipped and sent me a quick flash of his thoughts. He was worried about me being killed.

"Baby, please don't think like that. Whenever people think bad things, it always seems to come true." I caressed his face.

"Not always honey. You're too superstitious."

"Well, it does in the movies!" I stamped my foot. I must have looked like a four-year-old at the start of a tantrum.

"Well, my love, this is not the movies. And do we really need to be having this conversation right now while there is gunfire going on upstairs in our house?"

"You're right. I'm sorry. But we better think up something fast."

"Why don't we just call out to Sabine with our minds? She'd be able to hear us, right?" Quick on his feet but not thoroughly thought through.

"Nope. Can't do it. We're not strong enough to send out a telepathic call that far." One idea down and apparently no more to go.

"Well, that's really all I have for the moment…got any ideas?"

"No! We better think up something fast though! They are tearing the place apart up there! Our beautiful home." The water was starting to form behind my eyes. It would soon surface and I wouldn't be able to control the rage.

"Are we even sure that there are slayers up there? What if it's just a bunch of South American drug dealers looting a rich house? We could take 'em."

"Oh come on, are you really going to buy that theory? It has to be slayers. Druggies wouldn't ransack our home. We have plenty of security and they would know it and not be able to bypass it. Slayers are trained to override sophisticated systems and hack into computers."

"Baby, I have a strong feeling that those humans up there are *not* slayers. I know that this vault is pretty much impenetrable but I can still send up my sensors and I just have this strong feeling about it. Will you please trust my instinct? *We can take them!*" He gripped my shoulders and stared into my eyes. I felt like he was trying to burn his last sentence into my skull so that I would fully understand. "If they were really slayers, I am positive that they wouldn't be making so much noise to alert us. I know this. I used to be one, remember?"

"I know. It's not that I don't trust you. I would just feel better if we were one hundred percent sure. For some reason I can't get a lock on any of their minds. Perhaps they know how to block telepathic intrusion? Or maybe the walls are far too thick and I'm not strong enough yet to go that far..." I was starting to go off on a tangent and he knew it.

"Honey? You're rambling. Can we please get to the situation at hand? I think we should just storm up there and take them. I don't think there are more than three of them and you know we could easily take on five at a time. Probably even more since there are two of us." He looked deep into my eyes again.

I hesitated, but only for a split second. "Alright honey. Let's do it your way. I really hope that I won't have to say 'I told you so' later on."

He smiled and kissed my cheek. "You won't. Is there anything down here we could use for weapons?" He began searching in all the nooks and crannies of the vault.

"The only thing I can think of off the top of my head is the blood bottles but it would be sad to see some of those go. But then again, we have a fresh meal waiting upstairs. We better hurry up there before they take what they want and leave." I licked my lips in anticipation.

"That's the spirit baby! We'll just take two a piece. Even if we only injure them we can still take them unarmed." He grabbed two bottles and tossed them to me.

"I wonder if they even know this room is down here," I whispered to myself.

Shane grabbed two bottles for himself but turned when he heard me speak. Even a whisper is audible to a vampire. "What did you say?"

"I was just wondering if the humans upstairs even know that this room is down here. I mean, if they aren't slayers then they probably don't know, right? Don't the slayers know we have vaults? If there were slayers upstairs they would have immediately tried to get in here instead of trashing the house." I spun the bottle around in my palm.

"Yeah...you're right. Slayers do know about the vaults. We were all told during training that there was a vault in every vampire house. It was built to keep them safe and away from the sun. We're probably just going to be dealing with a couple of looters but it's better to be safe than sorry." He gripped the bottles tightly and headed for the stairs.

I followed his lead, but I was suddenly not sure of myself. I wanted to believe that Shane was right and it was just a couple of drug runners robbing us. But there was a small feeling of doubt in my mind. What if there were really slayers upstairs? They could be setting a trap for us. The ransacking of the house could just be a way to draw us out into the open and then they'd move in for the kill.

I did my best to shake away the doubt. I trusted in Shane and his judgment. If he was certain that the thieves above us were not slayers, then that would have to be good enough for me. I would follow him upstairs and help take care of the situation.

We had reached the top of the stairs; for some reason we tiptoed the entire way up. Shane must not have realized that the walls surrounding the secret room were practically sound proof. No matter, it was time to move into action.

Shane spun around both bottles so that he was able to firmly grip them by the necks. "You ready, baby?"

I made the same change with my bottles and nodded. "Let's get this door open. I'm starving."

We used both our minds and our physical strength to push the door open as quietly and as slowly as possible without alerting our prey. One step at a time we emerged from the opening; like a pair of lions sneaking upon the helpless gazelles grazing in the prairies. It was then that we were finally able to fully scan the house and find our soon to be meals. One was in the lounge, rummaging through drawers hoping to find something of value. Another was upstairs, most likely running from bedroom to bedroom. The only truly valuable things up there were vases and possibly a few paintings. The third and final party member was in the kitchen interestingly enough. Looks like our thieves were also hungry.

Shane made eye contact with me and quickly relayed a message. *Let's split up. I'll take the kitchen, you get the lounge and then we'll both take the guy upstairs.*

I nodded but quickly sent back a reply. *Make sure to kill him quietly. If he screams, he'll alert the guy upstairs and then we may lose him.*

The corner of his mouth went up in a half grin. *Of course! You forget that I was once a trained professional member of the slayers' organization. Killing silently is always the objective.*

I didn't forget. Just reminding you in case you felt like trying doing something crazy like pull a Rambo. I stuck out my tongue at him.

He returned the gesture and then turned in the direction of the kitchen. I headed in the opposite direction. Shane took off quickly but thankfully he was quiet about it. I started walking in the direction of the lounge. I picked up the pace just the slightest bit so to hopefully catch the guy before he left the room. I didn't want to get into a bad situation by having to chase the guy around the house. Wasn't really my style. The smooth and simple trap in an isolated area seemed best.

I crept up to the doorway of the lounge. Luckily, he was still there throwing objects all over the place. Why is it that looters always feel the need to trash a house when they're looking for treasure? Why can't they just find what they need quickly and quietly without ravaging the place?

The door was open but not far enough for him to see me standing just outside the doorway. I ducked behind the door and peered at him through the crack where the hinges joined door to frame. Papers, books, pillows and broken pieces of vase were all over the floor. He had emptied every drawer in the desk and was now attempting to knock every single book off the shelf. At least it wasn't the library. He'd have a hell of a time doing that chore. I took a brief moment to penetrate his mind to see what was going on in that drugged up head of his. The book project was an attempt to find a hidden safe or room where priceless trinkets may be concealed. Sadly for him, he was not going to find such a thing. First of all because there was no safe or secret room hidden behind that bookshelf. And second, because he wasn't going to be living anymore in about another five minutes.

Even though I had told Shane to make the kill as quick and silent as possible, I for some reason felt the need to play with this one.

Messing with the mind of a human turned out to be rather enjoyable the first time I did it. I admit it sucked whenever someone tricked me or fooled with my thoughts when I was a human, but now that I could do it with such ease, it was one simple pleasure I would allow myself every now and then.

I gently placed the bottles on the floor in the open doorway. I wanted them to be accessible even after I entered the room. Next, I unbuttoned a couple buttons on my shirt and pushed up my bra a little further so that cleavage was showing. For some reason, which I still to this day cannot understand, cleavage always diverts the attention of men.

I rapped gently on the door and slowly pushed it open. The thief turned around in great alarm, throwing more books all over the floor.

"Hey there stud," I said in a sexy voice, leaning up against the doorframe. "What ya doing in here?"

His eyes were wide with suspicion but within a few seconds his eyesight drifted to the bulge of my shirt. "Who are you?" he demanded.

I leaned over, bending at the waist instead of the knees and picked up one of the bottles on the floor next to me. "Sadly for you, I'm the owner of this house. And also sadly for you, turns out I'm your worst nightmare."

"Sadly for me, huh? Ha! What you think you're gonna do missy? That wine's not good for much except drinking. So unless you're gonna share it with me, I suggest you get yourself out of here before you get into some trouble. My boys in the other parts of the house won't be as nice to you as me."

I leaned over and picked up the second bottle. "Oh I don't think you want any of this darling. It's not of your taste."

A grin formed from his thin lips and he advanced towards me. "How would you know what my taste is? Why don't you let me be the judge of that?" He continued to move closer.

As I entered the room, I kicked the door shut but I don't think he really noticed. "Well, I would except you don't really know what's inside these. That's where the problem is."

"Of course I know what's in those, you silly girl. It's wine. And since it's so dark, it has to be red." His advancement was unfaltering. I wasn't looking forward to having him be so close to me but I was just getting to my favorite part of the game.

Now I was the one to advance towards him. He took notice and stopped in his tracks. "No no baby. There's no wine in these bottles."

His grin faded and turned into confusion. "Not wine? Well then what the hell's in 'em?"

I was only a few feet away. I leaned in close shifting the bottles in my hands so that they were held by the necks again. "Blood," I whispered.

His body tensed as soon as I spoke the word. He knew what was coming but that didn't help him at all. My left hand came up so quick that I don't think he even saw it. The bottle smashed up against his temple and shattered; blood exploded out of the glass and flew in all directions. Before he could cry out in pain, I brought up my right hand to the opposite side of his head. The bottle made full contact but didn't break. Instead he was knocked to the ground unconscious. I was pleased that the second bottle was saved. It was a shame to waste it.

I was even more fortunate that the second blow had rendered him unconscious. An easy first meal for the night. I placed the unharmed bottle on a nearby table and then knelt down beside the limp body. He was on his stomach so I turned him over onto his back. I then lifted his upper body towards me so I could get a better angle at his neck.

The neck was not smooth but it was nevertheless clean. I pulled away the shirt collar and sank my teeth into the tough flesh. The flow of blood was warm and sensuous inside my mouth. It rushed down my throat in large waves. It only took me a total of two minutes to fully drain him. I didn't bother letting him live. He was a criminal and would be his whole life if I had left him alive. Nothing would change that.

I stood and stared at the body on the floor of the lounge. His limbs were still soft and limp but would soon become rigid once death sank in. I didn't bother disposing of the body. Shane and I could always take care of that later. What mattered now was getting rid of the remaining intruders in our home.

Shane was still on the main floor. I shot out a quick message to let him know one man was down. Within seconds he sent back a message letting me know the kitchen man was finished as well. It was time to go upstairs and find our dessert. We met up in the foyer, stopping at the foot of the stairs. Shane and I both took the effort of mentally scanning the upstairs area to check if the thief had sensed any danger yet. Lucky for us, he was completely oblivious to the fact that his comrades had just been turned into medical cadavers.

Shane nodded at me and started to climb the stairs. I fell in behind, locking in my step with his. Silence was key. The second that Shane's bare foot touched the landing; the sound of a helicopter filled our heads. It was almost as if an alarm had been tripped. And from listening for only a few seconds had let us know that it was headed in the direction of our home. Although we could hear it, our human friend could not. It was too far away for human ears. Nevertheless, it alerted the both of us that someone was headed our way and we better do something about it fast.

Shane! My thoughts shot into his mind. *Take out the human. I'll prepare the house and get an SOS to Sabine and the others. When you're finished with him, get the equipment.*

There was no need for a response; he knew exactly what to do. I raced down the stairs towards the lounge. It was the closest phone that I could think of. As much as Sabine wasn't fond of the telephone, this was an emergency.

I pressed the speed dial button and waited for the inevitable ringing. After waiting for what seemed to far too long for the normal ringing of a phone, Caelum answered.

"Revere residence. How may I help you?"

"Revere? That's your last name?" In all the time I had known them, their last name had never been revealed to me.

"Calista? Is that you? What's going on? Is everything alright?"

"Yes Caelum, it's me. We've got trouble. I'm calling because it was the quickest way I could get a hold of you. I'm not strong enough yet to send telepathic messages overseas. There's a helicopter headed this way. Something's gonna happen, something big. We need help."

"Calista, it's simple. Get out of the damned house! There's nothing more to it. Don't try and be the heroine this time. Just get Shane and get the hell out of there!" I could hear him hold his hand over the mouthpiece and whisper to someone in the room that it was I on the other line. It had to have been Tristan because Sabine probably would have snatched the phone right out of his hand.

"But where are we supposed to go if we just high-tail it out of here? I know it's still early but is there any way we'd be able to catch a flight in time to come to you?"

His breath caught in his throat. "Calista, do you even realize what you just said to me? Come here? Are you mad? You'd lead them right to us. You need to get out and *hide*! Hide wherever you can for at least a day or two. That way they'll lose your trail and *then* you can come to us. Otherwise, forget it. It's too risky."

A growl formed in my throat. "God damn it, Caelum! Why do you have to make things more difficult than they already are? The only reason I'm not going to argue with you about it is because we don't have time. I'll contact you again once we're sure the coast is clear." I didn't bother waiting for a response. The phone hit its cradle with a loud thud.

Seconds later, Shane rushed into the room. He must have mistaken the odd sound, created by my slamming down the phone, for something else. "Are you alright in here? What happened?"

"I'm fine. Just a little angry. Caelum wasn't much help. He said we just need to get out of here ASAP and hide. But under no circumstances are we to go directly to the Ireland mansion. He said it would lead the slayers right to them and we'd basically all be slaughtered."

"I hate to admit it, but he does have a point, baby. So let's not stick around here any longer and get out! I don't want to be here when the slayers bust in." He leaned his head towards the doorway.

"Alright alright! We shouldn't take anything with us; it would only waste time. So let's just go." I grabbed his hand and pulled him towards the nearest exit.

He saw I was headed for the front door and pulled us both to a stop. "No baby! Back door! Front door is too obvious." We changed direction and headed for the back.

The helicopter was close but not yet overhead as we ran out the back of the house. The woods right behind the house were thick enough to conceal us for a short time. It would suffice until we were able to find a road to hail a cab or something.

The road was a lot farther away then we had anticipated. We had been weaving in and out of trees for nearly ten minutes and still nothing even resembling a road.

I slowed myself down to a jog. The helicopter was still audible but I could tell it was now stationary. "Honey, something's up. Where is the damn road? We should have found one by now."

"Babe, we are in South America for crying out loud. We *chose* to live here with our home in an isolated area. That's where the other vampires had originally built it. Don't you remember? There's probably not a road for another couple of miles or so. Who knows, it might even be further than that. We just have to keep going until we find one. Stopping now would be pointless and not helpful to our escape at all."

"I know, it's just that being out in the open like this is starting to make me nervous. They're going to come after us once they find that we're not in that house. I just want to be safe in a building somewhere…somewhere where there are lots of people. Slayers won't attack in crowds, right?" I grabbed his hand in hopes that it would make me feel a little better.

"I know how you feel, sweetie. We'll be somewhere safe soon. I promise. But let's keep moving so we get there quicker." He gave my hand a squeeze and then pulled me along with him.

Thirty-Three

I think it was another ten or fifteen minutes before we finally came to a road. A sigh of relief broke free from my lungs as my feet touched pavement. It was then that I realized I was barefoot. Looking down I saw Shane was as well. We had never put shoes or socks on back at the house before taking care of the thieves. And we were in such a hurry to evade the slayers that it had never even crossed my mind.

"Shane...we're barefoot! No one is going to give us a lift to a hotel or something! Barefoot with perfectly fine clothes looks too strange." I was in a panic.

Shane grabbed my shoulders and held me firmly. "Baby, will you get a grip on yourself? We're going to be fine. Someone is sure to pick us up. If not, we'll make our way into the city on foot and buy some shoes. I have some cash in my pocket."

Not even seconds later, headlights were seen rounding the bend. "Quick, lift me up!" The command was firm but not made in anger.

"What? What on earth do you mean 'lift you up'?"

"Lift me up! If we look stranded, this person may just give us a lift. Sympathy for others is one human character that is easily manipulated. Just do it."

No matter his confusion, Shane did as I ordered. He quickly cradled me in his arms and I clung to him, creating a look of catatonia. Shane held me to his chest, slowly making his way towards the center of the road. Our bodies came into view of the headlights and the car slowed. It finally came to a stop about fifteen feet away from us. Shane carried me over to the passenger side window.

"Oh please sir, could you please help us?" Shane leaned forward to make eye contact with the driver.

"My goodness! Is she all right? What happened?" He looked genuinely concerned: exactly what I was hoping for.

"Please sir...our house..." He looked back towards the woods where we had emerged. "Our house was robbed...the thieves...they came in while we were asleep...my wife...my wife, she was attacked."

"Don't speak another word! I'll take you to a hospital right away!" The driver started to open his door.

"No! A hospital isn't necessary. She just needs to rest, as do I. I was able to fend them off so to get us both to safety. She is merely saddened by the horrible tragedy that has befallen us. A hotel in the city would suffice. We can call the police from there." A smile almost surfaced but I was able to hold it back. Shane was playing this guy all too well.

"Of course! Please get in. Lay her in the back if you'd like. There's plenty of room and a blanket." The driver got out of the car and came around to open the back door.

Shane kissed my forehead as he slid me across the back seat. He slid in next to me, resting my head in his lap. The driver grabbed the blanket from the floor and handed it to Shane. "We really appreciate this, sir. If there is any way that I can repay you."

The driver held up his hand in protest. "Absolutely not! In fact, I won't accept anything at all. I'll do anything to help those who need it." He gently closed the back door and hurried around to the front again.

Shane lovingly ran his fingers through my hair as we rode towards the city lights. *You were right, you sly girl.*

I looked up into his big beautiful eyes. *Of course I was right, gorgeous. I'm always right.* I gave him a quick wink to show I was playing.

Thankfully the ride into the city was long enough to give us a head start over the slayers, but it wasn't long enough to make us less anxious. Shane had asked the driver to just drop us at the first hotel he came to but the driver insisted upon us staying in a quality hotel. Although we had enough cash on us to pay for a night's stay, the driver also insisted on paying for our room on his credit card. As much as Shane didn't want to take advantage of the man's hospitality, there was just no way around it. The guy was too insistent, almost pushy.

The man paid for the room and then said his goodbyes. He was almost adamant about seeing us to our room but Shane quickly protested. I continued to play my catatonic role until we were in the elevator, away from prying eyes.

"Man, I was expecting some poor shmoe with a little compassion but not *that* much! I almost thought you were going to have to kick him back in his car." I leaned against Shane's chest. Our room was on the fifth floor, not as high as I usually liked but the concierge had said all higher floors were booked solid. The fifth floor was the highest floor he could get us on. Oh well.

Shane kissed my forehead. "Yeah, I know honey. But like I said earlier, you were right. Human emotions can easily manipulated. It's actually sad to think that we used to be like that."

"I wasn't..." My voice trailed off. I was thinking about how I had been as a human *after* I had caught Shane with another woman.

"What?" Shane asked, pulling away so he could see my face.

"Nothing. Just thinking out loud."

"Yeah, I figured that much. Would you please repeat that?" He obviously wasn't going to let this one slide.

"I just said that I wasn't like that..."

"What do you mean? You were so loving and carefree when we were together. You were Miss Independent but you loved everyone around you."

The memories were flooding back but mixed emotions were coming with them. "Yeah, I know...but I wasn't talking about that time...I was talking about *after*...."

Shane pulled farther away from me and leaned up against the elevator wall. The doors opened ten seconds later. I walked out into the hallway. Shane almost didn't follow but then caught the door as it began to close. "Please explain," he said, stepping out into the hall.

"Can I explain in the room please? I don't want to stand out here and have everyone hear us arguing." I started walking down the hall in front of him. He followed reluctantly.

"Yeah, I suppose. But you better keep your word and explain the moment we step into that room."

I took my time walking to the room. Shane knew I was stalling so he walked quickly ahead of me and slipped the key card into that slot. He opened the door and waited for me to go inside first. I did and flicked on the lights. The room was a typical hotel room. Not too lavish but still elegant enough. A large king-sized bed sat against one wall in the middle of the room, a couch to the left of it and a desk to the right. The TV was resting on a dresser directly across from the bed. A mini fridge sat in the far corner of the room, closest to the window. The bathroom was immediately to one's right when entering the room.

Shane followed me in and closed the door behind him. He walked past me to the bed and sat down. "Alright Calista, sit down and start explaining."

I pulled up a chair from the desk and sat across from him. "Shane...I really don't see why you are making such a big deal out of this. It's really not what you think it is. All of this anger from manipulating a single human?"

"You know that's not why I am angry. Don't stray from the subject. You said that you weren't emotionally like that man when you were human. Calista, I know for a fact that's a lie. When you and I were together, you were more than passionate. How could you say you weren't?"

"I wasn't referring to when we were together, Shane. I was talking about how I was *after* all that."

He looked down in shame because he now knew exactly what I was referring to. "Oh..." was all he could say in response.

I inched the chair closer to him. "Shane, you have to understand how I was feeling. After I found you with...you know...I had an emotional break down. All feeling of love and everything that goes with it completely left me. I didn't care about anyone or anything. I barely cared enough about myself."

"Calista…" Shane got off the bed and knelt in front of me. "You should never not care about yourself. You are the most important person that you need to care about. Your own self always comes first, you know that."

"But not when I was with you. When I was with you, you were my whole world. Anything about me came second…you were what came first for me. And once my world had been shattered…I left. I had to get out of there. So that was why I spent those five or so years traveling the world. I wanted to see distant places and forget about you. Well, let me tell you…it didn't work."

"Yeah…I kind of found my way back into your life, huh?" He clasped my hands.

"Yeah, and not in a way I had expected. I thought about going back to Vegas a couple of times but I made myself avoid it. I didn't want to go to Vegas and find that you were still with her." I looked at him, catching his eyes before he could turn away.

He straightened up on his knees and pulled me to him. "Calista, I hope you know that you have always been the only girl that I love. Nothing will ever change that." He kissed my cheek and pulled away so he could look at me. "It's hard to tell if you're crazy or if I am the luckiest guy on the planet."

I wrinkled my nose at him. "Why do you say that?"

"Either you're crazy for taking me back after what happened…or I am the luckiest guy because you came back to me. I am the happiest I can ever be because I have the most perfect woman by my side."

"Oh Shane! I am anything *but* perfect!" I stood up.

He stood with me. "No Calista. You *are* perfect. You need to realize how incredibly beautiful and wonderful you are. I *know* you are. Don't let anyone, even yourself, tell you different." He pulled me to him again and held me for a long time.

I hugged him back but then pulled away quickly. "I'm sorry to cut short our Kodak moment but we need to focus on our ridiculous situation right now."

"You're right. Perhaps you should try calling Caelum again?"

"You think I should? I can't decide if he is going to get mad at me for calling again or be relieved to hear that we're still alive."

Shane rubbed my shoulders gently and gestured towards the phone. "Let's hope it's the latter. Go call him. And see if you could maybe talk to Sabine. Caelum seems way too high strung for drastic situations like this."

"I agree. Alright, I'll try." I picked up the phone and pressed the button for the front desk. "Hi, I need to make a call outside the country."

The desk clerk quickly patched me through to an outside line and I dialed the number for the Ireland mansion. Unfortunately, it was Tristan who answered this time.

"Revere residence."

"Tristan! It's Calista."

"Calista! Where are you?"

"We're at a hotel just a little ways into the city. We were able to catch a ride from a guy on the road near the house. He insisted on paying for our hotel room, which now that I think about it was absolutely brilliant. Now we won't have to worry about the slayers trying to trace us through credit card purchases."

"I agree, fortunate for you. However, you have no way of knowing if this line is sterile. You should have gone to a pay phone." I could hear the disappointment in his voice.

"May I please speak with Sabine? I want to know what she thinks about all this." I was more concerned with speaking to her because I knew she would be the most rational one out of the three.

"Calista this is Sabine." She had grabbed the phone from Tristan. "Are you two alright? Where are you?"

"Hi Sabine, yes we're fine. We're just inside the city at a hotel. Caelum had told us to lay low until we were sure it was safe enough to come to you."

"His instructions were correct. I would have told you to do the same. But as much...I want you two home as soon as possible. Don't make a move until dark tomorrow. You'll need to make certain arrangements so that no one disturbs you during daylight hours. Are you sure you'll be safe enough during the day?"

"Yes, I think we can manage. We'll arrange things around in here to make sure the sunlight stays out.. I'll have Shane inform the front desk that we are not to be disturbed for any reason at all during the day. We can just say we have jetlag or something and need to rest all day." The lie would probably work.

"Good, it sounds like you have things under control for the time being. But please be careful. I want you to call me again once you rise tomorrow night and let me know that you're alright. We'll let you know if we find out any information on the slayers."

"Absolutely Sabine. I'll call you first thing tomorrow. Goodnight." I hung up the phone and looked at Shane. He knew what to do since he already heard everything I had said to Sabine.

He stood up and headed towards the door. "I'll run downstairs and make arrangements with the desk clerk. I'm going to put the 'Do Not Disturb' sign no the door. Don't leave this room until I get back."

I nodded and watched him leave. I felt somewhat safe knowing we were far enough away from the slayers but at the same time, I was feeling weary. Perhaps it was because Shane had left me alone and I no longer felt one-hundred-percent at ease without him there with me. At least he would only be gone a few minutes. I got to draping the large bed comforter across the window so as to block out all possible light. It worked out quite nicely. Shane returned a few minutes after I was finished.

"This seems like it's going to work OK but I still think we should lie underneath the bed. How did things go downstairs?" I plopped down on the bed and curled my legs under my body.

"Everything's all set," he said taking the chair I had sat in earlier. "I explained that we had been traveling for days on end and the jet lag was really hitting us hard. So we would need complete isolation for the entire day. He was very friendly and agreed to everything I said."

"OK good. The other thing I didn't think about was having reserves…I didn't grab any bottles on the way out."

"There was no time," Shane replied flatly.

"Shane, will you please talk to me? Is what I said earlier still bothering you?" I inched towards the edge of the bed, not sure if he wanted me to come to him or not.

"A little. But not as much. I am more concerned for our safety. Are you sure that we'll be OK here? I really think we should have gone straight to Sabine's but I understand how they feel about that. We probably would have put them in serious danger if we had gone there."

I got up and walked over to him, lowering myself gently into his lap. "Gorgeous, we are going to be OK. I promise. We just need to hide out here for the day and then we can go to Sabine's. We'll make sure that there's nothing suspicious here at the hotel and then we can head out. Piece of cake." I wrapped my arms around his broad shoulders.

"Easier said than done, my love." He kissed my cheek.

"We'll find out tomorrow night. Let's get some sleep." I kissed his lips with the beautiful force of love behind it. He accepted and returned the passion.

Shane stood up lifting me up with him. He was carrying me to bed as he had done several times before. But this time, I could tell there was more to it than just his usual love and affection. This time he carried me a little more tightly, wanting to protect me with every ounce of his being. I welcomed it with open arms.

Thirty-Four

The next night came sooner than either of us had anticipated. But we were both relieved to wake and find that our room had not been disturbed as requested. Shane and I crawled out from beneath the bed and stretched. I walked out into the middle of the room and started stretching out all the kinks gained from sleeping on an extremely firm floor. My back cracked several times as I twisted my body. I could see Shane grimace at the sound as he walked over to the window.

Shane tried to ignore my strange acrobatics and gingerly removed the comforter from the window. He took a peek out the curtains but refused to open them. He wanted to make sure that we were safe before taking any action.

"Everything looks pretty normal outside. I can't see the likes of anyone who may be watching us. I can't sense anything either. As far as I can tell, the coast is clear." His words were there but there was no confidence behind them.

"Do you think we should make a run for Ireland?" I was anxious to get out of there.

"I think you should call Sabine first. You told her you would."

"You're right." I walked over to the phone and again asked the clerk to connect me to an outside line.

Thankfully, Sabine was quick to answer the phone herself. "Calista, is that you?"

"Yes, it's me. We're fine. Still at the hotel. Shane took a quick surveillance and says the coast is clear. Should we start making our way to you?" Just the thought of staying in that hotel room for another moment was making it seem like the walls were closing in on me.

"I want you to get here as soon as you can. I have already arranged for your flight. Private jet of course. It's not at the main airport though. The boys thought it to be too risky. We arranged for the plane to pick you up in a small airport just near the coast. Can you make it there?" Sabine's voice sounded frail. It was obvious she was far more frightened for our lives than we were.

"Yeah, we can make. Will it be waiting? I want to get out of here ASAP."

"Yes dear. The plane should already be there. Please hurry, my darlings. I grow more worried each second you are away from the safety of this house."

"I know, Sabine. We'll be there soon. Take care." She whispered a short goodbye and hung up the phone. I looked to Shane. "I'm sure you heard all that."

He raised his eyebrows. "Are you accusing me of eavesdropping?"

"It's kind of hard not to, what with the enhanced hearing and all. But I'm not accusing. Just asking to make sure you know what the plan is." I practically threw myself in his arms. He received me with the gentleness of a down pillow.

"I have been feeling the same way you have: I want to get out of here now. So let's get going." He kissed my forehead, grabbed the room key and pulled me out the door.

The desk clerk was sad to hear that we were checking out so soon. Shane tried to be nice about it but the clerk insisted on trying to make us stay just one more night. I finally had to butt in and explain that we were in a hurry to leave because we just received terrible news from home: a death in the family. The clerk was immediately sympathetic and called us a taxicab. We thanked him and waited for the cab in the lobby.

Against all hopes, the taxi took far too long to arrive at the hotel than it should have. The driver apologized multiple times once Shane started to give him a hard time. I placed my hand on Shane's arm to let him know it was all right. He apologized to the driver and instructed him to take us to the small airfield that Sabine had mentioned over the phone. The driver explained quickly how he knew exactly where it was and he would get us there very fast if it would please us. I squeezed Shane's hand and told the driver it would please us very much. And so the driver took off at high speed to make sure to satisfy his fair.

The plane was waiting on the runway as expected. Shane paid the driver, leaving a generous tip. I took a quick survey of the surrounding area before heading towards the plane. If there was an ambush waiting, I'd sniff it out before anyone even flinched.

Shane could sense my wariness and took hold of my elbow. "Is everything OK? Do you sense something?" He looked around us with frantic eyes.

My mind scanned the area a second time, just to be sure: nothing. "No, there's nothing here. Just the plane as Sabine had arranged. I just wanted to make sure there wasn't going to be an ambush or something. Although I have no idea how the slayers would have ever figured out we were going to come here. But it seems we're safe for the time being."

Shane now grasped onto my hand as we walked towards the small jet. "What do you mean 'for the time being'? You don't sound so sure."

"I just have this bad feeling that we're not done dealing with the slayers. I think we'll be seeing them again...soon..." A frown was the only expression to go with my gut feeling.

I pulled Shane onto the plane. We quickly passed the stewards before they could dish out their greetings. After taking our seats, however, one steward came toward us to try his luck.

"Good evening, Ms. Logan. Madame Revere told us you would be flying with us this evening. Is there anything I can get either of you before we're airborne?"

"No thanks." Shane spoke up for the both of us. "We're just tired and need some rest."

"No problem, sir. There are pillows and blankets in the compartments just above your heads. Make yourselves comfortable."

"Just a moment," I said, placing my hand on the steward's forearm. "How long is the flight expected to be?"

"No more than five hours. The skies are clear tonight with no stops planned. Please, enjoy your flight." He turned and walked back toward the front of the plane to let the captain know we were ready for takeoff.

Shane grabbed one of the aforementioned blankets and we curled up beneath it. He held me close the entire trip until the plane landed safely at the airport in Ireland. I quietly thanked the stewards as we exited the plane. Much to my surprise there was a limo waiting for us on the runway. Earlier I hadn't been sure as to whether or not Sabine would send a car. I thought perhaps not since we were trying to be cautious so as not to be followed. But it looked like she had decided otherwise. And the thing that shocked me the most was that Tristan had stepped out of the car to greet us.

"Tristan? What on earth are you doing here?"

"Well, good to see you too," Tristan replied with a sarcastic smile.

"I'm sorry. I didn't mean it that way; I'm just surprised to see you here. Even if Caelum were here, I'd still be surprised. I didn't think Sabine would allow, let alone send, someone to come get us. Aren't you all worried about getting followed and all that other stuff?"

"No need to worry. We made sure to take all necessary precautions before I headed out here. You really think I would be here if there was anything suspicious going on?" He leaned back against the vehicle, crossing his arms across his chest.

"I suppose…I just still have this bad feeling that something's up. Something bad." I gripped Shane's arm tightly. He did his best to console me without words.

"Will you two just get in the car already so we can go home? Sabine is anxiously awaiting your arrival." Tristan stepped to the right of the door and held out his arm, gesturing for us to enter first.

I climbed into the black stretch limo and Shane slid in after me. Tristan followed, taking the seat across from us. As he shifted himself in the soft leather, he gave Shane a quick look over. Shane took notice and made his own evaluations in return. It was clear the tension between them was still present. But in light of the circumstances, there was nothing I could really do to create ease for either of them. It was something they would have to get over on their own.

No words were spoken during the journey to the Ireland mansion. Tristan felt it was best for Sabine to speak with us directly and as a group. All we could do was wait until we arrived at the house, then a plan would have to be put into place.

The car pulled up to the mansion nearly thirty minutes after we had left the runway. The driver came around and opened the door for us. Shane slid out first, then Tristan and me. I took a moment to look at the house before entering. It brought back memories even though we hadn't been away from it for that long. Shane gently tugged my hand, pulling me out of my short reverie. I wrapped my arm around his waist and we walked together up to the large front doors.

Sabine opened the door before we had even reached the top step. "Darlings! I'm so glad you've arrived safely." She pulled me to her and hugged me tightly. I returned the kind gesture. She then did the same to Shane, who accepted her with a friendly smile. "Please do come inside. We have much to talk about."

Sabine led the way into the house with Tristan trailing behind us. We went straight to her office: our usual meeting place when it comes to serious matters. Caelum was already there waiting. He stood as we entered the room and shook Shane's hand. He gave me a quick kiss on the cheek and expressed how glad he was that we were safe.

Sabine took a seat behind her desk. Caelum and Tristan took their usual spots beside her. Shane waited for me to sit first and then finally sat down as well.

"Well now, it seems we have a major problem on our hands. I'd like to hear how it all started, if you wouldn't mind." Sabine leaned forward, clasping her hands in front of her on the desk.

I looked from Sabine to Shane and back again. "Well, honestly we're not really sure how it all started. We woke up last night to some thieves ransacking the house. We took care of them quickly but that's when we heard the helicopter heading towards the house."

"Strange that they would use a helicopter," Caelum interjected. "Such a noisy contraption. Easily detectable by vampires."

"Yes, we thought the same. Nevertheless we knew we had to do something. That's why I called you. It may not have been the best decision but it was necessary. I apologize for that."

"No need, my dear," Sabine said. "At least you are here safe and sound now. That's what matters. Please continue."

"Well, we ran from the house as you had told us to. We finally found a road and a human gave us a ride to a hotel. We kind of manipulated him a little bit, which is why he drove us right up to the hotel front doors and insisted on paying for the room."

"That turned out to work to our advantage. The man paying for the room was perfect because the slayers wouldn't be able to try and trace us through the registration or credit card purchases," Shane added.

I placed my hand on his. "As you know, from there we called you again and spent the day in the hotel room. We were sheltered well enough and made arrangements with the front desk so as not to be disturbed for any reason whatsoever. And now we are here." I looked at each of them looking for a solution or advice of some kind.

Several minutes passed before anyone spoke. "I would like to express my thoughts on the matter, as long as that's alright with everyone." Caelum looked at each face in the room.

Sabine was the only one to speak; everyone else just nodded. "Yes, I think that everyone would like to hear all opinions on this matter."

"Honestly, I think that the looters back at your mansion in Peru were sent there as a diversion in order to draw you out into the open. The slayers know they can't penetrate the vault; their best chance at capture or kill is by having you out in an open area. They knew you'd come out to get rid of some random people invading your home. However, what baffles me is the fact that they began their approach using a helicopter. Slayers do not commonly use such vehicles because they know the noise makes them too easily noticed by us."

"Which makes you wonder if they used it on purpose…?" Tristan chimed in.

Sabine, along with everyone else, immediately gave Tristan full attention. "What do you mean by that?" Sabine asked.

"Well, I'm just saying that since it's unheard of to use loud vehicles or equipment like that, then why would they suddenly use it now unless they were hoping to get a certain reaction out of it? By using the helicopter, they probably knew Shane and Calista would run. They probably even assumed that they would come running to us. So it's quite possible that they could have run into a trap and now we are *all* included in their overall plan." Tristan looked around the room.

"You know, he's got a point there," said Caelum. "We just may be in for a huge ambush..."

"Oh god...what have I done?" I whispered.

Shane gripped my hand. "What? What did you say?"

I leaned over to whisper in his ear while the others continued talking about the possible entrapment. "What have I done, Shane? I've endangered all the people I care about. I have to leave...I can't allow anything to happen to them...or you."

"No!" Shane practically shouted at me. His voice came as an alarm to the others, causing them to stop their conversation.

"What's going on?" Sabine asked.

I was too ashamed to answer so Shane took the liberty of answering for me. "Calista just told me that she feels the need to leave because she has endangered us all."

"What? That's absurd!" Sabine cried, quickly rising from her chair. "I will not allow you to leave this house and put yourself out as a direct target. If there *is* any danger, we will all deal with it together."

"I just feel awful, Sabine. Why didn't I see the trap before it was too late?" I bowed my head.

"It's not your fault, sweetheart. People make mistakes all the time. It's natural." As much as they should have been, her words were not comforting.

"But we're not...people! We're vampires. Aren't we supposed to do anything and everything without mistake or flaw?" Humans were the ones that made mistakes...not vampires. I didn't want to be the cause of several deaths because of a "mistake."

Sabine came around the desk, took hold of my shoulders and gently lifted me from my chair. "Vampires *are* people, my dear. Just a different kind of people. Mistakes are made in this world no matter what species one might belong to. It's unavoidable. So please don't beat yourself up about this. It could have been any one of us." She pulled me in for a soft hug.

I hugged her back, trying my best not to cry. "I just wish bad things wouldn't happen to the people I care about, wherever I go. First Ayden and now this...."

She pulled back and held my shoulders tight, forcing me to look into her eyes. "Listen to me. Ayden's death was not your fault! You did all you could. It's in the past and you need to let it go. The only thoughts of Ayden that should be drifting through anyone's mind are the happy ones." She released me and I sank back into the chair.

"So what do you propose we should do about the slayers, Sabine?" Caelum asked.

"Perhaps we should ask the former slayer," Sabine suggested. All eyes turned to Shane.

"Who? Me? I don't know how much help I can be for this. I only worked on the computers. I was never actually in the field."

"Nevertheless, you have a lot of information that could be useful to us and our survival. You must know how they plan their attacks and what their strategies are." Sabine's eyes filled with hope.

Shane looked to me for guidance but I couldn't help him. "Well?" Tristan asked. "Do you or don't you?"

"Yes, I do know that stuff. It was always documented on the computers."

"Excellent! Then let's hear it!" Tristan exclaimed.

"Well, I'm not really sure where to begin...there's so much...do we have enough time?" Shane was becoming flustered from the pressure.

"Of course we have enough time! Even if those bastards showed up right this minute, we'd still have time!" The heat in Tristan's eyes was growing more intense with each second that passed.

"Alright alright!" Shane cried out. "Can you just let me relax for a second? This is all coming at me fast. I need a minute to think."

"Of course," Sabine said. "Why don't we crack open a few bottles from the reserves downstairs? I would advise not going out to hunt tonight...as a safety measure."

Everyone agreed and we all made our way down to the vault. Each of us grabbed two bottles apiece and headed up to the kitchen.

Shane was a little shaky and nearly dropped one of his bottles but was able to compose himself by the time we reached the kitchen.

Caelum pulled out several wine glasses and passed them around the table. The bottles were uncorked and the glasses filled to the brim. The first sip was heaven as the delicious liquid drizzled down my throat. I was glad there were special heaters for the reserve to keep the blood warm. Cold blood tastes awful and it doesn't really do much for the body anyways.

Sabine quickly finished her first glass and refilled it. "Shane, whenever you're ready."

Shane gulped down his first glass. I actually half-expected him to chug straight from the bottle but he didn't. "Well," he began, "the slayers tend to work in a pattern when it comes to carrying out their attacks. They will use one of two tactics: entrapment or full-on attack."

"Could you explain each of those tactics, please?" The request came from Shane's left: Caelum.

"Um, sure...the entrapment usually involves some strategists who come up with a way to draw out the vampire where they are most vulnerable. Each case is usually different because each vampire has a different weakness. All vampires are kept under surveillance at first. It's best to figure out each one's habits and quirks so that the best strategy can be planned for that vampire."

I lowered my glass to the table. Shane's explanation was making my stomach churn.

"But how on earth are they able to keep an eye on us without us detecting them?" Tristan asked.

Shane cleared his throat and continued. "No bugs have ever been planted inside a vampire home. It's too difficult with the security and they'd be found too easily once nightfall hits. It's mainly been video and audio surveillance from a distance. Distance cameras and radio signals. There has been personal surveillance as well by team members but it doesn't usually last too long. We have learned quickly to sense when we've been detected."

"This is intriguing but true. Over the centuries the physical presence of the slayers has diminished because they were detected before they could gather enough information," Sabine commented.

"Yes," Shane agreed, "and now with such advanced technology, it's easier to keep watch on anyone and anything without being picked up on vampire radar so quickly."

Tristan shifted his position. He was becoming impatient. "Yeah, yeah. We know all this! Get back to the entrapment tactic."

Shane sent a glare in Tristan's direction and then continued. "So, an entrapment plan is what may be going on in our situation. It's a way to carry out an attack or kill without causing too much noise. Entrapments are meant to be quiet ways to capture or kill vampires."

"Ok," Caelum said, leaning back in his chair, "that all makes sense and could definitely apply to our situation. But what about the full-on attacks?"

"Well, full-on attacks are exactly what it sounds like. No strategic planning. No trickery used to draw out the target. Plain and simple: the target is identified and the team just goes straight in for the kill."

"That doesn't really sound like what we have going on here," Sabine stated. "If it was, they would have done it already since all of us are here together."

She had a point. "True, but I think the big question is: what should we do?" I wanted more than anything to take the aim off of them but there was no way Sabine was going to let me out of her sight.

To everyone's surprise, it was Shane who spoke up in response to my question. "Well, I think we have two choices. We could run and hide but if we do, we'd be running for centuries to come. The slayers won't stop until they have accomplished their goal."

"Which is what, exactly?" Tristan questioned.

"To hunt and destroy the vampire race," Shane stated without hesitation. That phrase must have been drilled into their heads during training. "On the other hand, we could stay and fight. Slayers hunt and kill in teams but the team is usually no more than ten men. Honestly, with there being five of us, we'd have a good chance at survival."

Caelum looked at Sabine. "Sabine, the final decision is really yours but I vote for fighting. From what Shane has told us, I believe we could win this battle. It may not be winning the war but at least it gives us a head start at making a stand."

Tristan now took his turn voicing his opinion but it was more on the hostile side. However, I wasn't as surprised about it as I should have been. "Can we really trust that what Shane has told us is the truth? What if he really has no idea how the slayers do anything and is just making it all up? I mean, he said so himself that he wasn't ever in the field. Just a computer nerd."

Sabine was the one who had always been defending Shane ever since he crossed over, but now it was my turn. "Now wait just a minute!" I shouted, jumping from my chair. "There is no reason for you to doubt a single word he has said. Why would he lie to us? If he truly didn't know, then he would have said so. You're just saying that because you're stubborn and jealous." I glared at him hard.

My words must have startled him because he couldn't come up with a rebuttal. He stood there wide-eyed with his mouth hanging open. The shock passed quickly and turned into contempt. But it was enough to shut him up and leave Shane alone.

Sabine let the dust settle and then started discussing our options. "I do believe that what Shane has told us is the truth. And I think that his options for us are the only viable ones we have right now. So, it all comes down to what everyone thinks is our best option. I'd like everyone's input please."

"I say fight," Shane spoke up immediately. "We can't keep running forever."

"I agree with Shane," I said softly.

"We already know that Caelum agrees with them as well so it's down to you and me, Tristan. What is your choice?"

Tristan was hesitant. His mind was racing and as I listened closely, I could hear his heart pounding in his chest. A single bead of sweat trickled down his temple but he quickly wiped it away. After a few moments of silence, he came up with an answer. "I suppose I have no choice but to fight with all of you. If I didn't, that would be abandonment and I can't leave behind those that I love. If you all think we've got a chance, then let's do it."

Sabine nodded in agreement. "Then it's settled. We will stay and fight. Caelum, what's our status on weaponry? Do we need to acquire more artillery?"

Caelum leaned over the table onto his elbows. "Well, we do have some equipment here. Especially in Calista's old room. We haven't touched anything since she left. There are also some supplies in the holding box down in the vault. So basically we have quite a bit but I think we may want to gather a bit more ammo just in case."

Tristan now became interested in planning out a strategy. "Sounds good. Which storage facilities are nearby so we can gather more? I think the closest ones would be the best to get them from. We don't want to have to stray too far from the house."

Caelum straightened himself and looked at the ceiling. "Well, it looks like our best bet is probably the facility about twenty miles down the road. That's the closest one I can think of. I suggest having two of us retrieve what supplies we need and have the others stay here to prepare. What do you think, Sabine?"

"I think that sounds like a feasible plan so far. Caelum, why don't you take Shane with you to get the extra supplies? I want Calista to stay here with me and Tristan as well so he can try and strengthen the security system for the house." Sabine stood and headed for the door.

"Ok. Shane, let's go. There's a pickup truck in the garage. We'll take that." Caelum stood and exited the room.

Shane took my hands and kissed my cheek. "Don't worry, baby. I'll be back soon. Help out the others and we'll be back in no time. Love you."

"I love you too. Please be careful." I planted a strong kiss on his lips before he left to follow Caelum.

Tristan got up without saying a word and went straight to his office. He already knew what he was supposed to do so there was no need to discuss things further with him. I rose from my chair and followed Sabine out the door. We decided to start in my old room. All the workout equipment and weapons were still there, just the way I had left them.

"Calista, there is a cart just down the hall in the second guest room. Would you mind grabbing it so we can load it up with all this? We can use the dumb waiter to get it all downstairs." Sabine started emptying the first box of guns onto the small sofa.

"Sure thing. But don't you think we should leave some weapons up here as well? I think it would be more beneficial if we were fighting from different height levels instead of just one. We may have a better advantage that way."

"Smart girl!" Sabine said as she faced me. "Still get the cart though. We'll need quite a bit of this downstairs. And on your way back, would you do me a favor and check on Tristan to see how he's coming along with the security?"

I nodded and left the room. The cart was where she had said it would be. It was pushed up against the wall next to one of the windows. I grabbed it and began to wheel it down the hall. I made sure to make the quick stop at Tristan's office on my way back to my room. He was furiously typing away at his computer.

I popped my head in the doorway. "Hey Tristan. Sabine wanted me to come by and see how things were going."

"Jeez! What does she think I am? A speed demon? I've barely started. But things will be fine. Just tell her that, ok?" he said without lifting his eyes from the computer screen.

"Ok Tristan. No problem." I left the room without saying anything more. I didn't want to get him any more aggravated than he already was.

I pushed the cart into the room just as Sabine was finishing emptying one of the boxes. She had somehow emptied two other large boxes while I was gone! I still sometimes forgot that her slim figure had more strength that ten body builders.

She looked up at me and smiled as she placed the last gun from the box onto the floor. "How is Tristan?"

"He's fine. He seemed a little aggravated though. Told me to tell you that he has barely started but everything will be fine."

"Of course," she replied. "I wouldn't worry. I just wanted to make sure there were no problems for him. If there were, I'm sure he'd let us know."

"Yeah, he would…so how much of this is going downstairs?" I asked, changing the subject. The topic of Tristan wasn't exactly what I wanted to have on my mind while we were awaiting an attack.

"Let's move about half of it, ok? The boys will return soon with some more equipment and I think that will be plenty for the bottom floor. Oh wait!" she exclaimed, placing her hand on her forehead. "I completely forgot about the vault. There are weapons down there as well. So, only load one third of this onto the cart and we'll leave the rest up here." She lifted up several guns and gently placed them on the cart.

"Ok, sounds good. I was thinking that maybe we should spread the guns out into different rooms so that we can spread out up here. If we're all clumped together in one room, it would be easier for the slayers to corner us. Attacking individuals is a lot harder than attacking a group."

"Good point my dear," Sabine said. "I'll do that while you take the cart downstairs. Either use the dumb waiter or feel free to test your strength." She gave me a wink.

Interestingly enough, I chose to carry the weapon-filled cart down the staircase. It was a lot easier than I had anticipated. Mostly because I was still learning my own strength and trying to heighten it to its full potential. I left the cart in the foyer at the bottom of the stairs and proceeded to the vault. I figured I could just bring the entire box upstairs.

The box was hidden quite well in the back corner adjacent to the reserve closet. It was painted the same color as the cement walls, which would make it easy for any human to miss. Luckily it wasn't bolted down so I didn't have to rip the thing out of the wall.

When I brought the ammo box into the foyer, Sabine was sorting out the guns from the cart I had left. "Oh goodness! You didn't have to bring the entire thing up here!"

I placed the box on the floor, not all that surprised that I wasn't breathing very hard from the effort. "It's no big deal. I figured we would need everything we've got. It's better to be over prepared than under."

"Good point again my dear." She gathered a few guns and started heading towards the lounge. "Oh, by the way, Shane and Caelum are back. They're unloading the truck in the garage. Feel free to go help them out if you'd like." She disappeared into the east wing of the house.

I ran to the garage to help out the boys. I was more excited to see that Shane had made it back safely than to help them unpack the truck. Nevertheless I helped them out to make things go quicker.

"How did things go, guys? Everything ok?" I asked, pulling a rather large machine gun from the truck bed.

"Yeah, everything was alright but the slayers are definitely on their way here," Caelum said as he pulled out a rocket launcher.

"What?" I cried out and nearly dropped the machine gun on my feet. "How do you know? Have you told Sabine?"

"Yeah, I told her. She said we should just keep prepping as fast as we can. We probably have about another hour till they get here. Lucky for us, they aren't going to be attacking too close to sunrise." Caelum continued to unload the vehicle, seemingly unfazed by the fact that a heavily armed team was on their way to try and obliterate us.

"But how do you know?" I practically screeched at him.

"We heard the SUV's they're driving and they were communicating via walkie-talkie," Shane replied. "Like Caelum said, we've got about an hour before they get here."

"Well, let's get finished with this stuff and then see how Tristan is getting along with the security system." Caelum pulled the last box off the truck and slammed the tailgate shut.

We placed all the weapons in the foyer. Shane and Caelum took off to check on Tristan while Sabine and I finished dispersing the guns and ammo among the rooms of the first floor. The three boys returned within minutes to explain the security situation.

Tristan stood before Sabine to give her a full report on the security system. He looked like an army soldier standing at attention, awaiting instruction. "Sabine, everything is all set. The perimeter has motion sensors located fifty yards out. Anything crosses them; an alarm will go off in the house. It doesn't sound the same as the actual house alarm so you'll be able to tell the difference. The house alarm has been upgraded to super sensitive mode, so I would advise not opening any doors."

"Um, just one question," I chimed in. "What about the windows? Will they go off if we open them because I was figuring we should open them in order to shoot out of from above."

Tristan turned to face me. "Yes, they are, which means I'll have to turn that feature off so we can open whichever windows we want first. After, I'll make sure to turn it back on, but only activate the closed windows. I assume no one plans on leaving their post once the window is open."

Thirty-Five

I t was agreed that no one would leave his or her post unless it was absolutely necessary. The next step was deciding who would take which posts and where. Sabine preferred being on the second floor, having a better view of the battlefield. I had the same feelings but explained that I would go wherever I was needed. It was finally decided that three of us would stay on the main level and the other two up on the second floor. The main floor was a more likely area to be penetrated than the second story.

Sabine and I would take the second floor while the boys stayed downstairs. Only one of them would take a stationary post while the other two would move around. That way all entrances would be doubly secure, not allowing for any fluke break-ins.

I set up shop in my old room. Tristan had briefly shut off the window alarms so I could open up the windows. Sabine had done the same in her chosen station. She took the middle room facing the backside of the house. My room was located relatively in the middle of the house facing the front side. Now the front and back ends of the house were covered. We weren't sure how the boys had set things up downstairs but we knew they would be fine on their own.

All of us were now able to hear the approaching vehicles. As they closed the gap between us, I began to scan the vehicles to see if I could get a head count. I figured knowing how many we were dealing with ahead of time would make it easier for us to keep track of them while fighting.

There were only two vehicles, each containing four men. Shane had been right about the number of men in the team. Less than ten would certainly make it easier on us. It made me wonder if they had even anticipated how many vampires they would actually be encountering. Unless of course, they had egos the size of hot air balloons and were sure they could take out an entire army of vampires if need be.

The trunks were well equipped with guns and ammo. Each man had a radio attached to his belt and a gun to his hip. Each was determined to take out a vampire within the first ten minutes of battle. Their thoughts were quite amusing.

Waiting the final twenty minutes before the slayers arrived at the mansion was pure agony. I just wanted to kill them all and get it over with. But I could only sit and wait, hoping that all of us would make it out alive.

Caelum wasted no time when the first SUV pulled up the driveway at high speed, which had already set off the perimeter sensors. He quickly blew it up with a rocket launcher causing a massive explosion of fire and metal parts. The car was blown into the air and came crashing down onto the pavement. I think it was safe to assume that all passengers had been terminated by the explosion.

The second SUV had lagged behind, trying to stay out of our line of fire. Suddenly I heard gunfire coming from across the hall. Sabine had opened fire onto a target in the backyard. I wasn't supposed to leave my post so I sent her a silent message to see what was going on.

Sabine! Is everything all right? What's going on back there?

There are more of them! she screamed back between spits of gunfire. *They were hiding back here the whole time! There are more than we had anticipated. The ones out front must have been sent as a diversion.*

Do you think we can take 'em? My question was filled with worry.

I'm not sure but I've got help from Tristan right now. Keep an eye on the front for the second SUV. And any other assholes that decided to hide out in the bushes all evening!

My eyes returned to the front of the house. The second SUV had finally driven up to the front of the house but unfortunately Caelum had only brought back one rocket launcher. And just as Sabine had mentioned, several men jumped out from behind bushes and trees as the SUV came bounding up the asphalt. Who knows how long they had been hiding there! I thought we would have detected them long before now. Apparently they somehow made it onto the grounds before Tristan had set up the perimeter sensors.

A couple of the men on foot spotted me up in my perch in the window and opened fire. I ducked below the sill as frame and brick siding were riddled with bullets. Luckily the thick walls were strong enough to stop the bullets from passing through.

I took a moment while bullets were exploding above my head to take a quick scan of the house. There was still plenty of gunfire coming from Sabine's post. She was also yelling obscenities at the slayers below. Comical, but not something I had time to linger on. The boys downstairs were yelling commands at each other and running around checking doors and windows while shooting like crazy.

Suddenly the house alarm sounded. One of the slayers had gotten passed someone's aim and entered the house through a door or window. The bullets above me had finally stopped and I popped my head up to evaluate the situation. A slayer was standing below, keeping his aim on my window. Once my head was in sight, he began to fire again.

Guys! I've got no shot up here. A guy is focused on my window. You've either got to take him out or I move!

I don't see him! Caelum yelled back. *I've got the front post but I don't see a stationary. Where is he?*

He's right below me, towards the middle of the house! How can you not see him?

Wait! I see him. He's history. A single gunshot pierced the air and the slayer below me dropped to the ground. *Alright Calista, you're clear!*

Thanks Caelum!

I lifted myself back up to the window opening and started to open fire on the slayers scattered around the front yard. I hit two as they were advancing on the house but I only managed to wound them, no kills. I think one of the boys ended up finishing them off though.

I was beginning to feel confident about our situation but then things started to get bad. From somewhere beyond the house perimeter, flaming arrows were being shot into the windows of the second floor. One came in through my open window and plunged into an armchair. It quickly caught fire and began to spread through the room. I picked up as many guns as I could carry and hurried out into the hall, slamming the door shut behind me.

Sabine was out in the hall, her door closed as well. "They're using fire now."

"I know," I said as I dropped my armload onto the floor. "My room caught fire as well." "We need to go downstairs and help the boys then. The slayers won't enter the second floor since it's now aflame. Let's hurry!" Sabine grabbed only a couple guns so as not to overwhelm herself and raced towards the stairway.

I stuffed two pistols into the back of my pants, grabbed two Uzis and ran after her. The first floor was complete chaos. Bullets were flying in from all directions. Caelum had opened the front door and was just maiming anyone who stepped within his eyesight. Shane and Tristan were running around elsewhere within the house gunning down every slayer they ran into.

I called out to Shane as I ran through the house. I just wanted to be with him. He was my safety net and I was starting to fall. There was too much violence, too much chaos. I was having trouble handling it. Don't get me wrong, I killed each and every slayer that stepped in my path as I searched the rooms for Shane, but there was no pleasure in it for me. This was all about survival and I was a wild animal backed into a corner, ready to defend myself at any costs.

I finally found Shane near the kitchen. He was covered in blood. My first thought was one of panic. I thought he was injured. A quick scan of his body and mind proved otherwise. Then of course, my animal instincts kicked in and he just looked so irresistible. I wanted to drag him to the nearest bed and ravish him. But then I pushed the thought aside and ran to his arms for protection.

"Shane! I'm so glad I found you! We need to get out of here. It's just too much! We'll never kill them all!" I trembled in his arms.

"We have to, Calista. This is the only way we'll be able to live freely." He held me tight.

I looked up and saw Shane was staring down the hallway. His eyes were wide with awe and anger. I turned to see what he was staring at. It was Sabine…and she was sprinting down the hallway towards us. Her hair disheveled, her dress was ripped in several places. I could see the tears streaming down her face. Shane pulled me to one side against a wall, out of the line of any possible fire. He started towards Sabine but then noticed that there were three slayers running behind her, guns aimed at her back.

Shane screamed at the top of his lungs. "NOOOOOOOOOOO!" He began to run towards her, hoping to pull her out of the way before the slayers could get a shot at her.

But then it was too late. The guns went off and we were sure Sabine was done for. Suddenly, out of nowhere, Tristan jumped in behind Sabine grabbing her waist and tackled her to the floor. The bullets barely missed but the slayers were still after her.

I couldn't just stand there and do nothing. I pulled out the Uzis and shot every single bullet inside those guns at the three slayers down the hall. A few bullets went astray, but the rest hit their intended targets. The three men fell to the floor.

We ran over to Sabine and Tristan to make sure they were ok. Shane kept an eye out for all of us to make sure we didn't receive any surprise attacks. There were only a few more slayers roaming about and Caelum seemed to be taking care of them.

Shane helped Sabine stand. She was all right, just a few scrapes and bruises but nothing serious. The wounds would heal themselves within the next couple of minutes. Apparently the slayers had gotten a hold of her and even tried to torture her to get the rest of us but she was able to fight her way to freedom.

Tristan, on the other hand, was not as fortunate as she had been. He was lying on the floor not really moving. I was checking his pulse when I noticed blood on the floor to his left. His pulse was slow but steady. However, the blood pool on the floor was growing larger bit by bit. I leaned over and saw a large hole in his left side.

"Oh god!" I screamed. "Tristan's been hit! We have to get him out of here!"

Sabine began to panic thinking that Tristan was going to die. Shane gently pushed her up against a wall so she could hold onto it for support and then came to where Tristan lay motionless. "We should get him down to the vault. We'll be safe there. He's been shot but not in too vital of an area. But the bullet is silver. It will eventually kill him if we don't get it out."

"But what about Caelum?" I asked. The tears had already found their way to my cheeks at the sight of Tristan's motionless body.

"He can take care of himself. We need to get Tristan to safety and fast. That bullet needs to come out *now*!" With that said, Shane lifted Tristan into his arms and headed towards the vault. "Calista, I need you to be the lookout. Shoot anything that moves in our direction. Sabine, follow behind me but watch your back."

I did as Shane had asked but I knew I wasn't going to accompany them down into the vault. I couldn't just leave Caelum there all by himself. He needed my help and I was going to be there until every last slayer was dead.

Two slayers noticed our movement towards the vault but I quickly shot them down. No one else bothered us after that. Caelum must have been laying down one heck of a diversion. Sabine and I helped open the door and then made sure that Shane got inside safely. Sabine went next. I was supposed to follow, but instead I pushed the door as hard as I could so it would close. It closed more slowly than I would have liked. Sabine noticed and tried to stop me.

"No Calista! You must come inside! Caelum can take care of himself. Tristan needs us!" She pushed back against the door, her strength obviously much stronger than mine.

"No Sabine, I can't! Caelum needs help. I'm not going to leave him out here to die. Tristan needs *you* and Shane…not me. Shane knows what he's doing. He'll have to understand. You will too. I can't leave Caelum like this. You'll be safe. I'm going to be up here until every last slayer is taken down." I looked hard into her eyes, trying to make her understand.

There was no use arguing and she knew it. Reluctantly, she released her pressure on the door and allowed me to close it. Once the door was firmly in place, I turned and ran towards the front of the house. It was the last place I'd seen Caelum and could only hope he was still there.

Lucky for me, he was almost in the same exact spot where I'd seen him before. This time he wasn't using the giant machine gun that sat only ten feet to his left. It had run out of ammo and he resorted to the small automatics that he had clipped to his belt. I took a quick count and saw there were only five slayers left. A decent number against two vampires but still beatable.

Caelum saw me running towards him out of the corner of his eye. "Hey! Good to see someone's still fighting around here. Where are the others? Are they alright?"

I placed a bullet in the head of one of the slayers in the front doorway as I ran towards him. "Yeah, everyone's safe. Tristan's been shot though."

"What?" Caelum's concentration broke and nearly cost him his life. A bullet whizzed past his face, barely missing him.

"Shane took him! He's taking out the bullet. He has to or it will kill him." Caelum refocused and shot down two slayers, one right after the other. Now only two left. "He took a bullet while saving Sabine. I promise they're safe. Tristan is in good hands." I fired at the remaining slayers but missed.

"Well let's finish these two off and go help him! I want to see them with my own eyes." He fired the last four bullets from his gun, dropped it and slid across the floor to pick up a new one.

One of the slayers saw it as his chance to take him out but Caelum was too quick. He grabbed the gun, spun around and shot the slayer in the thigh. The shot caused the slayer to fall to the ground and I finished him off with a shot to the neck. One slayer down and one more to go.

Caelum glanced over at me and I knew exactly what he was thinking. We could easily charge the guy and take him out with one little bullet to the head. Caelum stood and began to walk towards the lone slayer. I followed suit and watched the slayer's eyes widen as he realized what was about to happen. He tried to turn and run but Caelum put a bullet in his back before he took one step away from the door.

I took in a huge breath of relief and looked at our surroundings. The house was a wreck and there was blood everywhere, but we had won. We finally beat the people who had been hunting our kind for centuries. Sure, we didn't kill the entire population of slayers but this was a dent in the system. The slayers would now know that we were taking a stand against them.

Caelum looked over at me with a big smile on his face. "We did it. We actually did it!"

I smiled back. "Yeah we did."

Caelum approached me to give me a warm embrace but then something moved in my peripheral vision. "Caelum look out!" I screamed.

The next thing I knew, Caelum was lying on the floor. Somehow, we had miscounted and there was one slayer left. He had shot a bullet into Caelum's chest, who was now lying in a pool of his own blood. I could see that he was going to start fading to ash within a few seconds.

I ran to his body, holding his head in my hands. He looked up at me with his big beautiful eyes. He couldn't speak, the blood was flooding his lungs and escaping through his mouth. His skin was beginning to darken to the color of ash. He was fading fast.

With tears streaming down my face, I looked up to see who the killer was. I nearly screamed when I watched him walk through the doorway. It was Trent Murdock.

"I'll kill you, you son of a bitch!" I screamed at him as I rested Caelum's head on the floor. Seconds later his body completely turned to ash. A breeze swept through the hall and carried it away.

"Oh will you? I don't think so. You couldn't bring yourself to do it. I befriended you on that plane and now you just can't kill me." His smug smile was only creating more rage inside of me.

"You're crazy to think that I wouldn't kill you just because of that. You're no friend of mine. I HATE YOU! First you killed the man that

I loved and now you kill one of my closest friends. He was family! I'll make you suffer like no one has ever suffered before!" I lunged forward and grabbed him by the throat.

He struggled against my grip and tried to reach for a weapon. I grabbed his hand and twisted until I heard his wrist snap. He screamed in pain. I squeezed his neck just a little harder but I didn't want to kill him just yet. For the lives he had taken, he deserved to suffer before death found him.

I then noticed that he had his trusty bow and arrows strapped to his back. I smiled at the sight of the sharp, sleek objects protruding from the carrying case. My gaze moved back to his terrified face and watched as his eyes widened with fear at the sight of my evil smile.

I tore the case off his back and threw the bow to the ground. I dragged Trent over to the nearest wall, still holding firmly to his neck. He continued to claw and squirm under my grip but it was no use.

I pulled his body up against the wall and looked into his eyes. "I hope you are prepared for the pain I am about to put you through. There's nothing you deserve more than a torturous death. Sorry, but there'll be no swift death for you, Trent."

I slowly pulled one of the silver arrows from the case, making sure not to touch the silver tip. The tip of the arrow shined in the light. I held it near Trent's face just so I could further see the terror in his eyes. He continued to squirm around helplessly. I watched closely the movement of his hands, looking for the opportune moment. Finally, that moment came and I plunged the arrow into the palm of his hand. The arrow went straight through his hand and into the wall, pinning his hand where it was. He screamed and screamed as the pain rushed through his hand and up into his arm. I then grabbed his other hand and pinned it up against the wall. Grabbing another arrow from the sheath, I could barely hear his ragged voice as he begged me not to do it. I ignored his pleas and plunged the second arrow into his other hand. More screams erupted from his gaping mouth.

I stepped back to look at the man pinned to the wall. His arms were spread apart as if he were on a crucifix. I have to admit, I was pleased with my work.

Trent continued to scream in agony. It seemed as if his lungs had a never-ending supply of air. It was the screaming that caused the others to emerge from the vault.

"Calista! What the hell are you doing?" Shane ran to me and pulled me away from Trent.

I struggled against his hold but he was surprisingly stronger than I was. "Let me go Shane! He has to pay for what he did!" I began to cry.

"What's happened here?" Sabine questioned. Her eyes suddenly became sad. "Where's Caelum?"

"He killed Caelum! That son of a bitch right there! He did it!" I screamed through the tears. "He put a bullet in Caelum's chest and I had to watch him die right in front of me. Just like I had to watch Ayden die. And *he* was the one that killed Ayden!" I tried to lunge at him but Shane kept me at bay.

Shane was so worried about keeping me away from Trent that he didn't even notice Sabine pick up a knife that was lying on the floor. She took one long look at it and gripped it hard. Her next move was so swift; I don't think Trent even saw her move. She lunged at Trent and slipped the knife into his ribs. Trent's screams died to a gurgle. The knife had punctured his lungs, which were now filling up with blood.

Shane finally let me go once he saw what Sabine had done. I fell to the ground because I was struggling so hard to get away that when Shane let me go, all of my efforts were released and gravity took its course. Shane picked me up off the floor but he couldn't take his eyes off Sabine and the dead body tacked to the wall.

Sabine was standing erect in front of the bloody corpse. And only a few words escaped her lips. "I pray the gods take mercy on your soul. For you will be sent to the depths of hell for what you've done."

I walked up behind her and wrapped my arms around her shoulders. She stiffened at first but then accepted my embrace. Shane came up behind us and did the same. We held each other for what seemed an eternity.

Finally, I think we all snapped back into reality. "Oh my god! Tristan! Is he ok?" I asked with worried eyes.

"Yes, he's fine. Very weak but he'll pull through. The accelerated healing process will help a lot. The bullet wasn't too deep so it was easy to extract. He did lose quite a lot of blood but we were able to get him to swallow some from one of the bottles downstairs. He's asleep now in his coffin. He should recover within the next few days." Shane was confident with his evaluation.

"Oh thank goodness!" I exclaimed falling into his arms. I hugged him for a few moments and then turned to Sabine. "So…what are we going to do now?"

Sabine faced me and surprisingly a smile came to her face. "We're going to continue living, my dear. The slayers can't stop us now. Not after what we've done tonight. But first we need to clean this place up. And then, once Tristan is fully recovered, we're going to pay a visit to some friends of ours…"

"Friends?" I was skeptical on her meaning of friends.

"Yes my dear, friends. Vampires to be precise. We're going to create a legion and wage war against the slayers until every last one of them is slaughtered."

This was a side of Sabine neither of us had ever seen or even expected for that matter. "Are you sure you want to do that?" Shane asked.

"Absolutely," she replied with a twinkle in her eye. "It's already begun. Tonight was the start of the great war between vampire and slayer. Now there's no turning back."

We spent the few remaining hours of the night cleaning up the house as best we could. Sabine said she'd have to have a cleaning and repair crew come in during the next couple days to fix everything else. We didn't argue with her.

Several days later, Tristan was fully recovered. However, he was heartbroken to hear that Caelum had been killed soon after we thought we'd won. I did my best to explain to him that it was Trent who had killed him but I think some part of him blamed me. I can still feel it every time he looks at me.

Epilogue

It's been six years since that dreadful night at the mansion in Ireland. Shane refuses to speak of it but continues to provide his undying love for me. Tristan and Sabine are living in their own place somewhere deep in the mountains of Russia but keep in touch as best they can.

Shane and I have taken up a beautiful mansion in the south of France. We are inseparable and have decided that we don't want to take any part in Sabine's "great war." I've had my share of violence and death and it was something that I don't think I could ever deal with again.

Though I continue living the life of a vampire, nothing could ever take me away from Shane. He is the love of my life. I know I said that about Ayden, and it was for the most part true. Ayden was the one to bring me into this new world and show me that it was OK to love again. Nothing could diminish my love for him. But it's just not as strong as my love for Shane.

When this all started, I had said that my heart had been broken, so much that it couldn't be mended. But it turns out that I was wrong. It's quite possible to pick yourself up after so much pain and heartache. But I never thought it would be a vampire who would show me how to love again.

Now I know you're probably hoping that I'm not going to end this with some sappy advice about life and love. There's really no moral to this story. It's just a tale that needed to be told, nothing more. But every human should know: no matter where you go and what you do, I'll always be there…lurking in the shadows. And if you should cross my path, I can promise you that your flesh will become mine…because the thirst always wins.

www.ingramcontent.com/pod-product-compliance
Lightning Source LLC
Chambersburg PA
CBHW070535260626
47161CB00002B/401